"_____ ook."

"Susa_____ nation of

"S_____ ways
keeping _____ arren's
book_____ out

TAMING RAFE

SUSAN MAY WARREN

TAMING RAFE

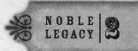

NOBLE LEGACY 2

Tyndale House Publishers, Inc., Carol Stream, Illinois

Visit Tyndale's exciting Web site at www.tyndale.com

Visit Susan May Warren's Web site at www.susanmaywarren.com

TYNDALE and Tyndale's quill logo are registered trademarks of Tyndale House Publishers, Inc.

Taming Rafe

Copyright © 2007 by Susan May Warren. All rights reserved.

Cover photograph of man copyright © by IT Stock Free/Jupiter Images. All rights reserved.

Designed by Jessie McGrath

Edited by Lorie Popp

Unless otherwise indicated, all Scripture quotations are taken from the *Holy Bible*, New Living Translation, copyright © 1996, 2004. Used by permission of Tyndale House Publishers, Inc., Carol Stream, Illinois 60188. All rights reserved.

Scripture quotations marked NIV are taken from the HOLY BIBLE, NEW INTERNATIONAL VERSION®. NIV®. Copyright © 1973, 1978, 1984 by International Bible Society. Used by permission of Zondervan. All rights reserved.

Library of Congress Cataloging-in-Publication Data

Warren, Susan, date.
    Taming Rafe / Susan May Warren.
       p. cm. -- (Noble legacy ; 2)
    ISBN-13: 978-1-4143-1018-3 (pbk.)
    ISBN-10: 1-4143-1018-8 (pbk.)
    1. Rodeo performers–Fiction. 2. Children of the rich–Fiction. 3. New York (N.Y.)–Fiction. 4. Montana–Fiction. I. Title.
    PS3623.A865T36 2007
    813'.6–dc22   2007025923

Printed in the United States of America

13 12 11 10 09 08
 7   6   5   4   3

For Your glory, Lord

⁓ACKNOWLEDGMENTS⁓

"Contend, O Lord, with those who contend with me; fight against those who fight against me" (Psalm 35:1, NIV). This was the verse that my mind fed on during the season of writing *Taming Rafe*. I struggled with this story on many levels—wanting to get the bull-riding scenes right, wanting to make the story different from the typical "rich girl meets wild boy." As I struggled, God was my contender against the voices of doubt inside me that said this book wouldn't happen. I so richly saw Him provide resources and encouragement, wisdom and words, especially through the following people:

Allan and Jan Lloyd, Montana ranchers. Thank you for letting me see your life and showing me the balm of Gilead tree. The memories of that week continue to fill my spirit with sweetness.

Pam Meyer and Ed Crowder, PBR enthusiasts. Thank you for looking over my bull-riding scenes for craziness and helping me get it as close as possible. Any mistakes are mine alone.

Michele Nickolay, Sharron McCann, and Jane Howard, my writing buddies who took my whining and helped me craft my fledgling story. You have no idea how much I need our monthly therapy sessions.

Christine Lynxwiler and Rachel Hauck, fellow authors and brainstorming buddies who spent hours hashing out the intricacies of this plot over and over and over and over. . . . Thank you for your patience and perseverance!

Aven Grace, songwriter extraordinaire. Thank you for taking a kernel of an idea and helping make "For All You're Worth" come to life. Your friendship is a blessing to me.

Randy King, the next great country singer. Thank you for singing Jonas's song.

Karen Watson and Stephanie Broene, who labored with me on plot and characterization. I appreciate your wisdom!

Lorie Popp, who once again smoothed out all the rough edges. Your talents are a blessing to me.

Keri Tryba, stone-skipping pal and fashionista. You make everyone feel like they are the only one in the room. Thank you for giving me Cari.

Travis Thrasher, who can always make me laugh and keeps it real. Thank you for helping me research New York. It was the highlight of my year.

Gillian Brown, my right hand. Thank you for keeping it all running and for talking me down from my own waaz moments.

David, Sarah, Peter, and Noah, who remind me what's important.

Andrew Warren, my hero who, through his love, shows me how good God is to me.

*Work hard to show the results of your salvation, obeying
God with deep reverence and fear. For God is working in you,
giving you the desire and the power to do what pleases him.*

PHILIPPIANS 2:12B-13

≈ PROLOGUE ≈

Rafe Noble, two-time world champion bull rider and current king of the gold buckle, had never met a bull that he feared. Oh, sure, he knew well the tension before a ride that buzzed his nerves and slicked his hand inside his taped-tight leather glove. But normally he shook it off the second he wound the bull rope, sticky with rosin, around the animal's chest and wedged it into his grip. Then the adrenaline, the heat, took over.

And for eight long, harrowing seconds, it was just man against beast.

In Rafe's world, man usually won.

However, as Rafe straddled the champion bull known as PeeWee—which had to be some sort of joke because the bull was the biggest, orneriest creature Rafe had ever ridden—coldness rushed through him. Something foreign and overwhelming ignited a tremble from deep within his bones.

For the first time since he was thirteen, he felt . . . terror.

Maybe it was just the residual agony of watching one of his fellow bull riders being carried out on a stretcher only minutes earlier. Maybe it was the roar of the crowd hammering at the raging headache he'd nursed most of the day. It could be the fact that he rode in pain, that he'd had to tape his hand and wear his knee brace, and the sports medicine doctor had reminded him that one more fracture to his neck would land him in a wheelchair permanently.

Or perhaps it was just the eerie feeling that hung in the air, along with the smells of animal sweat and popcorn and leather and dirt, a surreal sense that tragedy lurked right outside the arena of spectators.

Whatever the reason, as Rafe worked his rope around his hand, through his pinkie, then pounded his fist with his other hand to lock it in place, he couldn't shake the bone-deep feeling that tonight someone would die.

Even the bullfighters, the men who distracted the bull as the riders scrambled to safety, seemed jumpy. Manuel Rodriguez caught Rafe's gaze. Dressed in a blue and red vest, black cowboy hat, long shorts, and cleats, Manuel had agility that kept him ahead of horns and made the crowd gasp. He'd saved Rafe's hide on more than a few occasions.

Manuel nodded, and despite the distance between them, the roar of the crowd, the voice of the announcer, and the advice from fellow riders as Rafe settled into his riding position, he could hear Manuel's mouthed words—*"Get 'er done."*

Rafe returned the slightest nod and refrained from searching for Manuel's eight-year-old son, Manny, and pretty wife, Lucia, in the audience. Rafe had arranged their tickets and trip up from Mexico to see Manuel perform under the big lights of the GetRowdy Bull Riding World Championship in Las Vegas.

"You're my favorite bull rider," little Manny had said as he handed Rafe his hat to sign at the pre-event celebrity showcase.

Behind Manny, a leggy blonde with a black T-shirt emblazoned with the GetRowdy Bull Riding logo gave Rafe a loaded smile.

Rafe winked at her and turned his attention back to Manny. "Are you going to be a bullfighter like your daddy when you get big?" he asked, signing the brim.

"Oh no. I wanna be just like you," Manny had said, his hero-worshiping gaze fixed on Rafe, who chuckled and plopped the hat back on Manny's head.

"Our next bull rider, two-time world champion and overall leader going into the short round . . ."

The announcer brought Rafe's attention back to the snorting animal he straddled. Clearly, his mind wasn't in the game tonight. Which probably gave credence to the voice inside. He scooted up tight against his bull rope, blew out several short breaths, and banged his protective vest with his free hand. His biceps tightened against the rolled-up sleeve of his shirt, and he pulled up his fringed black and red chaps at the knees before he set his legs astride the bull, ready to dig in with his spurs.

And right then, the fear rushed him, poured through every cell. Right behind it, words or perhaps an impression.

Don't ride.

What was wrong with him? Nerves, maybe. After all, his title hung on this ride.

"All the way from eastern Montana, riding the champion bull PeeWee . . . ," the announcer droned on.

Some men prayed before they got on a bull. Rafe had known plenty of cowboys to shoot up prayers afterward, while stretched out on the ground as a furious animal tried to trample their brains. But not Rafe. He hadn't prayed since . . . well, God had stopped listening to him years ago. Rafe wouldn't waste his breath.

Instead, Rafe reached deep, past the fear to the grit he'd been born with, and wrapped his free hand around the smooth top rail of the metal chute.

His sister, Stefanie, never understood why he rode. Couldn't grasp the fact that sometimes it just needed to be him against animal. That when he rode the bull for those full eight seconds, he felt, just for a fraction of time, like the king of the world. Invincible.

He'd never even tried to explain it to Nick. His big brother wouldn't have a clue what it might be like to always feel . . . less.

Don't ride.

The voice crept up his spine as the bull shifted beneath him. He took a deep breath, focused on the ride.

This is for you, Mom.

"Go." Rafe nodded.

The chute opened, and the bull lunged into the arena. Everything inside Rafe went silent. Heat seared his wrist, his arms, his legs. PeeWee writhed in fury as he landed on his forelegs.

Rafe fought for balance while the bull rocked him forward. He barely missed cracking his nose on bone, being speared. The animal bucked again, and Rafe stiffened his arm and realigned his spur position, hooking with his left spur, trying to pull himself back into position and dig himself out of a fall.

PeeWee snorted, throwing back his head.

Rafe's grip jarred, but he kept his seat. *C'mon, bull, fight me.*

He not only needed an eight-second ride but PeeWee needed to fight him hard to up his points and keep Rafe ahead of a feisty rider from Brazil on the leaderboard. The bull stretched out into the air, landing with a jerk that rattled Rafe's teeth.

The roar of the crowd filled his ears.

PeeWee's hindquarters changed direction. Rafe knew the bull had won.

Rafe grabbed with his spurs, fought to make the eight-second whistle. His bicep spasmed.

The bull bucked again. And then Rafe was off. Only not quite.

Hung up by the bull rope, the cowbell thrashing on the opposite side, Rafe flopped like a rag doll as he fought to free his hand.

The bull flipped him.

The crowd went eerily silent.

Manuel blurred past Rafe as the bull took him round and round. His shoulder burned, the muscle ripping deep inside, maybe his rotator cuff or his shoulder dislocating. Hopefully he wouldn't hit his head or snap a c-bone in his neck. He lunged again at his rope. *Please.*

Manuel snared it. Rafe fell free. He landed in the dirt, dazed, and threw his arms over his head. The bull's hooves exploded the dirt beside him.

Get up! But his wind had been snuffed out. Darkness edged his sight.

"Rafe!" He heard Manuel's voice, felt hands grabbing his vest.

Rafe looked up, past Manuel's dark expression. Everything turned black and white.

Don't ride.

Rafe saw the bull's hooves crashing down over him and knew fear had spoken the truth.

Tonight someone would die.

❧

The heat slithered through Katherine Breckenridge's pores, devouring her energy and consuming the last remnants of hope that little Eva would live to see another sunrise. The child lay in a hospital bed, her breath so slight that her chest barely moved, and she'd long ago stopped sweating. Her black hair fanned over the pillow, and she looked painfully innocent and oddly at peace.

An itchy line of sweat trickled down Katherine's temple and dripped into the collar of her cotton short-sleeve shirt. It stung the burn she'd received this afternoon as she'd toured the village. Now, as dusk entered the grimy, poorly screened windows of the clinic, she longed for the touch of the wind off the Sierra Madre Mountains to the northwest, the smells of pine and oak that seemed to overtake her, even revive her as she drove into the hills earlier this morning. Something to lift the oppressive odor of death that hovered in the room.

A metal fan buzzed in the far corner, and flies landed now and again on the cotton bedsheets, turned gray and thin from decades of use. Fifteen children, all in various stages of cancer, lay motionless in their beds—if that's what they could be called. A mattress no thicker than one of Angelina's tortillas could hardly be classified as a bed.

Across from Eva's emaciated body, Katherine's housekeeper—which seemed such an inadequate label for the woman who'd practically raised her—Angelina Rivera held Eva's motionless hand to her own forehead, her lips moving in silent prayers, as if infusing life into the little girl.

Angelina had spent hours in the night lighting a candle, praying in the chapel for the lives of the children under the care of this Mercy Doctors hospital. Just as she'd prayed for years for Katherine.

The prayers of a righteous woman availeth much.

"Katherine, can you change Carlos's bed?" This from Sister Marguerite—Angelina's sister and one of the nuns who lived in the clinic, bathing and feeding children. Strong and steadfast like her sister, Marguerite didn't bother with manners and couldn't care less that Katherine came from wealth, that she had originally traveled to Mexico for a two-day fund-raising, publicity-gathering event. Apparently she'd earned points with the nun when Katherine elected to stay with Angelina after the fund-raiser was over.

Not that she had been any great help. No, she fit in here, in a scorching and smelly Guadalajara clinic about as well as she did in Manhattan.

How she ached to be like Marguerite and Angelina. The sisters held the children as they writhed in pain and wept as the little ones slipped into eternity. Angelina had accompanied Katherine's mother, Felicia, numerous times to this Mercy Doctors clinic—the only one that the Breckenridge Foundation supported. But Katherine had never guessed that Angelina got her nursing skills from tending to the needs of these dying children. If it hadn't been for her mother leaving the Breckenridge Foundation in Katherine's not-so-capable hands, Katherine would probably still be attending NYU, getting another useless degree.

Katherine hadn't cried, but for a week now, her chest had ached, and right in the center, it burned.

She took a fresh, folded stack of bed linens and found Carlos—fourteen yet emaciated to the size of an eight-year-old—curled in the far bed. He didn't look at her as she untucked his feet. "It's okay," she said in Spanish. But how okay was it when a grown boy soiled his sheets?

Katherine rolled the bedsheet under him, tucked the clean sheet into one side, then rolled him onto it. New beds. One more thing on her list of requests from donors. She'd list them right after medicines.

She removed the soiled sheet, then tucked in the clean linen. "There you go," she said, covering him with a thin top sheet.

A single tear ran over his nose.

There went the burning again, deep and now so consuming it took her breath.

If only I'd come sooner. The words speared her, turning and chewing at the tender flesh of hope. She'd known the clinic was in jeopardy. Since her mother's death by car crash high in these very mountains three years ago, the organization had been on a slow slide toward extinction. Katherine simply didn't have her mother's knack for fund-raising with the upper crust. But this firsthand, painful face-to-face with the needs of the hospital felt like a punch right to her sternum. It put suffering faces to her failures.

Katherine threw the soiled sheets in the hamper and went to find Sister Marguerite, who'd disappeared into her tiny office to fill out reports.

"Yes?" the nun asked without looking up.

Katherine leaned against the door and sighed. "How is he?"

Marguerite met her eyes. "Carlos?"

Katherine nodded. Something about the boy, the way he suffered in silence, even refused to acknowledge the suffering, the cancer eating away at him . . . His pain, even more than Eva's, felt like Katherine's own.

Marguerite shook her head, then went back to writing.

"What about his parents? Shouldn't they be here?"

Marguerite put down her pen. "Carlos has no one. He showed up on our doorstep, already too far gone for us to help him."

Which meant that Carlos was a street child. Alone and fending for himself. Katherine closed her eyes. *Lord, it's too much. Too . . .*

If only she'd found a way to urge donors to dig deeper into their pockets, or if she'd managed their finances better . . . if only . . .

It had probably been these very *if only*s, the ones that burrowed deep and ate away hope, that had compelled her mother to pour out her life for the children in this part of the world. Their sunken, dark eyes haunted Felicia Breckenridge and drove her forward on the fund-raising path, an ambassador of goodwill, hoping to touch one more life. If anything, this trip to the other side of reality had given Katherine enough perspective to understand why her mother had spent so much time away from her as a child.

Katherine felt grimy and knew dirt streaked her face, layering her skin. Back home, her friends shelled out five hundred dollars an hour to bathe in such mud. But Katherine, like her mother, preferred to use her bank account for purposes that ministered to the soul rather than the body. If her wealth couldn't be used to help these children, then what good was it?

Still, it seemed that no amount of cash could heal Eva, resurrect her from the sagging hospital bed to play with her one-legged Barbie dolls and draw colorful pictures for supporters. Nor would it give Carlos a family, a home, a future.

Katherine shuffled down to the laundry room, where Marguerite had fixed cots for her and Angelina. She sat on the end of the cot, fatigue washing over her.

Just one life. That's all she wanted. To somehow make a difference in just one life.

Lying down and drawing her legs up, she closed her eyes. Five minutes, and then she'd . . .

"Katherine?" Angelina's voice pulled her from the tug of slumber.

Katherine woke with a shot, blinking into the darkness. Night had invaded the room, along with moaning from down the hall. Her dark hair lay plastered to her neck, having fallen out of its ponytail. "I fell asleep. I'm sorry. I—"

"Come." Angelina held out her hand, and as Katherine had done numerous times when she was a child, she took it and followed Angelina down the hall.

In the shadowy embrace of night, Carlos lay in his bed, his breathing labored, every rise and fall of his chest accompanied by a wheeze and moan. Marguerite stood at the foot of his bed, her hand on his leg, her head bowed, her mouth moving.

Carlos's dark eyes locked on Katherine's. His mouth moved, but through his parched lips, no sound emerged.

Katherine looked at Angelina, who gave her a sad smile, squeezed her hand.

Katherine crouched next to Carlos, her face close to his. She pushed his hair off his forehead. Pain filled her throat, her chest, and she bit it back for his sake.

Carlos swallowed and reached out to touch her hand. "Senorita," he said so quietly it seemed more of a breath, "gracias."

Thank you? Katherine stared stupidly at him, feeling brittle. For what? She'd done nothing to really help him; change a sheet, hold a hand—what were those things? Placebos.

It wasn't enough. Not *nearly* enough. She pressed her forehead to his hand, feeling tears begin to bubble out of the pain in her chest. "No, Carlos, it's I who must thank—"

Angelina pressed her hand on Katherine's shoulder. "He's gone."

Katherine looked into Carlos's sightless eyes.

Angelina ran her hand over his face and closed his eyes.

Katherine sat motionless, tears dripping off her chin, a hot rage swelling through her. *Lord, please, for Eva, for Carlos . . . somehow, help me be . . . do . . . enough.*

☙ CHAPTER 1

KATHERINE RUSSELL BRECKENRIDGE's ability to choose the right pair of shoes to wear with her seafoam green ball gown certainly wouldn't stop world hunger or cause peace in the Middle East, but tonight it might raise enough money to give a child like Eva a fighting chance for life.

At least—*please, Lord*—she hoped so.

Wrapped in a bathrobe, Katherine sat on her dressing stool in the walk-in closet of her penthouse suite and bemoaned her lack of fashion sense. Her supermodel mother, Felicia, would have instinctively known which shoes to pick.

"Should I wear the metallic snake slingbacks, the black peep-toe pumps, or the leopard thong sandals?" Katherine asked her assistant, Cari, on speakerphone.

"Wear the silver open-toe slingbacks. They're gorgeous with that dress," Cari said.

"How about my pink horsey slippers? They're kind of cute."

Silence at the other end told her the answer.

"I was just kidding," Katherine said as she swept up her yoga pants and the T-shirt she'd napped in and dumped them in the hamper.

"Sure you were," Cari said in an I-know-you tone.

Katherine sighed in defeat. Get her in a pair of heels and she suddenly felt like a bull in Tiffany's. Why couldn't fund-raising come easy to her—as it had for her mother? "It would have helped if my mother left me her fashion sense to go along with the Breckenridge Foundation charity events."

Outside, the sun had half settled just beyond the Manhattan skyline, lighting the windows of surrounding buildings platinum. It flowed into her adjacent bedroom, turning the Turkish rugs to a brilliant turquoise. Katherine hadn't had the desire to redecorate. Everything in the master bedroom, from the gold-tasseled bed linens to the silver-plated mirrors to the antique silver vases holding the daily supply of yellow roses, still bore her mother's flair, her style.

Katherine didn't have the foggiest idea how she might improve on that.

"She *did* leave you her fashion sense, Katherine. The only problem is, her legacy comes in a size two. And it doesn't match your own, uh, style."

Katherine didn't need to glance in the mirror to confirm that she'd inherited her *father's* style. Her preference for jeans and cowboy boots. If only he'd also given her his charisma, his never-say-die spirit that had made him a champion bull rider. But she possessed neither her father's courage nor her mother's glamour. Felicia Breckenridge and Bobby Russell had been America's beloved poster couple.

So why hadn't their daughter inherited their magic? Magic she so desperately needed if she hoped to pull the Breckenridge Foundation away from the abyss of bankruptcy.

She just hoped that her grandfather and his wolfish board of directors would stay in their corners until she got through this little soiree and out into the financial clear.

"You'll be beautiful," Cari said, and her voice softened. "Put on your best Katherine Breckenridge smile, shake everyone's hand, and I promise that the five-course dinner you put together will have the donations pouring in. The board will see your efforts, forgive you for a few bad investments, and everything will be fine."

"A few bad investments?" According to Katherine's last balance sheets, her accounts had lost over five hundred thousand dollars in three months. And if Grandfather Breckenridge turned down her request to underwrite her donation to the Mercy Doctors clinic for another quarter, children like Eva might not live to see next year. "Now who's living in a fairy tale?"

"Maybe you and your life-is-but-a-dream mentality are rubbing off on me. I'm even willing to consider that a handsome prince might ride into the lobby of the Breckenridge and whisk me away to my castle, complete with my private entrance to Tiffany's and an unlimited expense account. But barring that, I believe you have a winning night planned. The weather is even cooperating. The heat wave will drive everyone inside to the air-conditioned ballroom of the Breckenridge Hotel, and they'll pay just to stay indoors." Cari's voice contained a smile. "And it won't hurt that you get to sit next to Lincoln Cash all night. I wonder what other celebrities are going to show."

At the mention of the actor's name, Katherine glanced at the issue of *America, Now!* in her trash bin. Sadly, it hadn't contained even a word of the press release she'd sent out about tonight's event. Although she'd also invited a passel of other actors and celebrities, she banked on a confirmed appearance by Lincoln Cash to lure the press. "I don't care if I sit by him—I just want him and his gang of photographers."

"Oh, please, there isn't a woman alive who wouldn't stand on a bed of coals to sit next to Lincoln Cash."

"He's not my type, which only adds to the fact that my mother and I were nothing alike. I prefer a well-barbered, silk-suited man to a whiskered, rough-edged scoundrel who considers a wink the invitation to dinner or more. Besides, I have Bradley."

Cari sighed. "Right."

"Bradley is stable. And patient. Everything a woman could want."

"If you're a houseplant."

"Stop."

"Okay, but only if you put down the black pumps."

"How do you do that?" With a look of longing, Katherine slid the pumps back into their drawer.

"Ten years of boarding school with you."

Katherine held up the green dress and the silver sandals and fleetingly wondered if she'd even fit into any of her outfits after last week's taste test with the catering company. Even if she'd only picked at the outrageously extravagant dishes, she still felt slightly traitorous after spending the last two weeks visiting the Guadalajara clinic. Again. But seeing Eva's smiling face—miraculously pink with health—gave Katherine the incentive to nail down every detail of tonight's annual event. "I just thought it would be easier."

"Easier to fill your mother's shoes?"

Katherine lifted a shoulder, staring into the mirror, trying for the thousandth time to see even a hint of Felicia's famous blue eyes in her own hazel ones.

"Or easier to realize that you're not her?"

"Thanks. I appreciate that show of support." Katherine laid the dress on her bed, dropped the sandals to the floor.

"So you're not your mother. You have your own style; you just don't know what it is yet. And when you get your rhythm, you'll be the wow she was."

"In the meantime, my grandfather is going to convince the board to write off the Breckenridge Foundation as a loss and swallow the entire charity into the maw of Walter Breckenridge Enterprises. I will have successfully driven my late mother's life work into the ground in the span of three years. I think that might be some kind of record."

"Tonight is going to be a success. By the way, the director of social services called again. She said something about an appointment at the Seventh Avenue children's shelter. Last time you did that, you wanted to adopt three children."

"I wasn't serious. Just . . . moved."

"I'm not saying homeless kids don't tug at my heartstrings, honey, but you gotta stop trying to adopt every charity case you meet."

A knock came at her door. "Katherine?"

Katherine said a quick good-bye to Cari and disconnected the call. "Come in, Angelina." Her voice sounded fatigued, even to herself, despite the forty-minute nap she'd just caught.

Angelina strode past her into the bedroom. "You're not ready yet? Senor Lymon is on his way up."

Oh, perfect. Bradley hated being late.

The early evening sun poured through the French doors at the far end of her dressing room, yet heat shimmered in the twilight and reflected off the windows of Trump Tower across the street. From the balcony off her bedroom, Central Park, with its lakes and cool breezes, beckoned like a favorite novel, someplace to lose herself.

Maybe Cari was right. Tonight would be perfect. She had plotted every detail. All the same, it would be nice if the Almighty could send her a memo or something to assure her that she was on the right track. *Lord, please make this night successful.*

It seemed that ever since Katherine had returned from her first trip to Mexico six months ago, she'd had disaster touch every part of her life, from her seemingly bad accounting to her strained relationship with her grandfather to her health. It just wasn't natural to be so tired all the time, regardless of how many herbal remedies Angelina concocted, how many vitamins Cari made her swallow, and how many doctors Bradley made her visit. And now, another of her weekly migraines edged in on her.

Angelina led her to the dressing table in her bathroom and made her sit as she helped her style her hair. As usual, Angelina hummed from her repertoire of hymns, songs that Katherine still equated with warm, solid arms and unconditional comfort.

Angelina was the closest thing Katherine had to a real mother. The kind who'd known of her secret nest in the closet, with her horse posters, her Flicka books. The kind who woke her from her nightmares and fed her hot chocolate for breakfast. The kind who had prayed her through her teenage confusion and helped her find her own spiritual footing, beyond her Catholic boarding school. If it weren't for Angelina, Katherine might have turned out just like her grandfather, someone resembling the ice sculpture down in the ballroom. Sometimes she wondered why he even raised her. Maybe because her mother had been so busy—

"Katherine?"

She held her bathrobe at the neck. "Come in."

The bedroom door opened. "Hey there, beautiful." Bradley poked his head into the room. Concern filled his brown eyes. "Are you feeling okay?"

She managed a nod. "I'll be out in a moment. Make yourself at home."

"I have a quick meeting to attend. I'll meet you downstairs." Bradley gave a slight frown, then glanced at Angelina. "Do your best work, Senora. I have a special evening planned." He winked at Katherine and closed the door behind him.

Angelina's eyes shone, evidence she'd fallen under Bradley's spell. With his highlighted blond hair that he wore in a slightly mussed style and his lean, gym-toned physique, Bradley exuded a charm that made Katherine forget everything but the silly smile on her face and the way he put his hand on the small of her back.

A special evening. Funny, she had waited for such a special evening all her life, but now she only felt a crimp in her stomach.

It had to be nerves. Just because Grandfather Breckenridge had introduced them didn't mean that successful attorney Bradley Lymon wasn't the man of her dreams. Katherine should stop trying to figure out why Bradley wanted her in his life, give up trying to make a difference in the world, and let herself relax.

She sat up straight on the velvet stool and stared into the tall, silver-plated mirror as Angelina put her hair up, letting the wisps curl down over her ears.

"Your mama would have been so proud," Angelina said, bringing her face close to Katherine's.

Katherine smiled, patting Angelina's hand. "Gracias." But she knew the truth. Angelina saw the girl she'd raised, the Breckenridge princess. However, next to Katherine's willowy blonde mother, Katherine had been . . . well, more like a buffalo.

Maybe she resembled her father, Bobby, the man who'd died riding bulls when Katherine was a child. She had a faded color photograph of them together. Katherine was five and wearing red cowboy boots and a grin. Another photo displayed Bobby's wide smile, the way he lazily hung his hand from his giant gold championship buckle, the gleam in his dark brown eyes.

Felicia never, not even once, spoke of the man who'd died in her arms. And she'd refused to let Katherine speak of him either. Even her father's obituary had been sketchy. "Complications from a bull-riding fall" could mean anything in her curious mind.

And the fact that his death happened months after said fall raised even more questions.

Someday, Katherine vowed, she'd have answers.

Katherine put on a pair of teardrop diamond earrings, a recent present from Bradley, then added a matching necklace—last Christmas's gift, an extravagant gesture two weeks into their courtship. She slipped on the ball gown, and it pinched at the waist as she zipped it up. Thankfully, the tasting spree hadn't left its ravages.

"It's time," Angelina said as she hung up Katherine's robe.

Katherine dug out her most recent migraine prescription, quickly swallowed two capsules, and massaged her temples.

If people didn't look too closely, they'd never notice the extra makeup covering the circles under her eyes or the way her smile didn't quite dazzle. She grabbed her clutch, hoping that she could remember State Representative George Brennan's newest wife's name.

As Katherine let herself out of her suite and into the elevator, she felt the effects of the painkiller start to hit, the bludgeoning in her brain subside. With it came a surreal calm, the sense that she wasn't really connected to this moment but was somewhere else. Maybe on Grandfather's yacht, smelling the briny surf. Or better yet, that place in her childhood dreams where she found herself more and more lately—lost in Montana, riding horseback, the wind at her back, the smell of wildflowers beckoning her to freedom.

But that serene life was about as likely to happen as a longhorn steer charging through the lobby of the Breckenridge Hotel and taking a bath in the center fountain.

The picture made her smile.

Please, Lord, make this night successful. For Eva. For kids like Carlos.

The elevator doors opened, and she inclined her head to the applause that greeted her from her assembled guests in the lobby. Bradley stepped forward and took her hand, and she grasped it, grateful. Possibly even happy. *Definitely* happy. Bradley looked resplendent in his tuxedo as he tucked her hand in the crook of his arm.

Yes, tonight had the makings of the perfect evening.

<hr />

John Kincaid stared at the blinking light of his answering machine and knew that in two weeks life as he knew it would end. He pushed Play. The voice detailed the time and place everything would change, and a cold sweat trickled down his spine.

He'd always anticipated this day. Especially with the string of good fortune he'd experienced over the past few years. However, with the good came the compromises, the secrets.

John sat down in his leather chair and drummed his fingers on the glass-topped desk, staring at the picture of his father, the late John Senior.

"You'll always be a rancher, Son. Get that through your head."

But John refused to end up like his father.

He smiled and slowly lowered the picture facedown. Then he opened the desk drawer and pulled out a small velvet box. Opening it, he stared a long time at the simple brilliant-cut solitaire diamond in a white gold setting. He'd had it for years, just tucked away in the drawer, waiting for the right words. For a man whose life re-volved around words, the task seemed idiotically impossible. *Will you marry me?* Simple enough, but the first and only time he'd asked, Lolly had shaken her head and run off crying.

If that didn't scream a big no, he didn't know what did. Since then, she hadn't breathed a clue as to why. Being a Montana man, a rancher, and patient at heart, John didn't push. Obviously, he'd have to find a different set of words if he hoped for a yes.

John took out the ring and slipped it over his pinkie, holding it in the light and imagining what it might look like on Lolly's long, elegant ring finger. He closed his eyes and let her image fill his thoughts—her playful smile, the way her dishwater blonde hair spilled over her shoulders, the twinkle in her hazel eyes. For all Lolly's charm and flirtation, she still seemed a mystery to him. As if her life had started the day she arrived in Phillips, a twenty-year-old wanderer.

He'd watched her that day from his pickup in the feed store parking lot, the wind catching her hair, dust kicking up around her blue jeans, her hands in her back pockets as she stared at the vacant lot on the corner. Right then, something happened inside his chest. Not a lightning bolt zinging him with love at first sight but a soft and breathtaking peace that someday, if he bided his time, she'd be his wife.

Maybe this time when he asked, she'd say yes. *Please, God.*

John swallowed back the rush of too many emotions and closed the box. It felt small and soft in his work-worn hand. Sort of like his dreams.

But the blinking light on the machine told him that some dreams came true. And when they did, nothing would ever be the same again.

❧

Sitting in his pickup, staring at himself—all twenty feet of glowing hot neon in the center of Times Square—Rafe Noble realized what a fake he'd become. The image shone for thirty seconds, then flipped to an advertisement of *America, Now!* magazine, on which Rafe's face graced this month's cover.

They'd airbrushed the growl right off of him, made him look downright tame. But Rafe knew the truth. Inside that GQ image of a man who wrangled two-thousand-pound beasts for a living was a rough-edged, broken cowboy just trying to keep up with his press. He'd been living for the last six months on the notion that if he rode hard enough, played fast enough, even risked enough, he could drown out the howl inside and fool everyone into thinking he was fine.

Even himself.

But no matter how many women, bulls, cars, or even occasional shots of Jack Daniels filled his life, he could still hear Manuel Rodriguez's low moan of pain as he lay dying in the dirt.

Manuel hadn't even lasted long enough for the other bullfighters to corral PeeWee, the killer bull, and send the medics out with a stretcher. By the time they took him away, Manuel's blood covered Rafe's hands, his chaps, his soul.

He knew he'd never, ever be fine again.

Rafe ran a hand through his dark, unruly hair and stared at himself in the rearview mirror. He needed a shave. And if the guy behind him didn't lay off his horn, he might just get out and–

The light changed, and he surged forward into traffic on Forty-second Street. Heat slithered into the cab of his 1984 Ford pickup, the air conditioner barely able to stay ahead of the furnace outside. It was the heat wave of the century in New York City, and he'd agreed to appear at some hoity-toity charity event.

How he hated this town and the smells of grilling beef from the gyro stands, cigarette smoke, trash fermenting in the piles of black bags on the sidewalk, bus exhaust fouling the air. He hated the sounds of brakes squealing, cabbies arguing for space, the cheeps of pigeons fighting for crumbs. The few times he'd been here, he cut his trip short, needing open spaces like the rest of the city needed air-conditioning.

He cut a left at the next light, then slammed on his brakes before he plowed over a couple of fast-walking suits arguing into their BlackBerries.

Rafe took a deep breath and wrapped his hands around the steering wheel. The truck still smelled of hay and dust, despite the fact that it hadn't been on Manuel's farm since Rafe had traded it for his late-model Silverado with Manuel's widow, Lucia. She needed something dependable. He'd spent a month there after the funeral, helping Manny Jr. cope with his father's death. At least

Manuel had lived long enough to see his son's leukemia go into remission. Trading the truck felt like the least Rafe could do, especially if he hoped to purge from his mind the haunted look in Manny Jr.'s eyes.

"I know that you'll be the man I taught you to be. A Noble man."

Rafe felt so far from his mother's prophecies that it made the hollow place inside him throb. He found solace only in the fact that she hadn't lived to be disappointed.

Fatigue put a rasp into his voice, betraying the way he'd spent the better half of the night remembering the premonition he'd had the night Manuel had died. He should have forfeited his ride, but he'd wanted the prize—again—the proof that he was the best. Apparently, it was something he'd never prove to anyone, not his sister and brother and especially not himself.

The light changed, and he drove past Radio City Music Hall, hoping he was headed in the right direction. But he'd rather be dragged behind a herd of rampaging Angus before he'd ask for directions.

For a month or so after Manuel's death, he'd entertained the idea of going home, of pitching in at the ranch and investing in the life that the rest of his family loved. But a trip home to his brother's wedding fixed that. One look at Nick's beautiful life—his wife, Piper, who obviously adored him, not to mention his dreams to resurrect and rebuild the Silver Buckle—and Rafe knew he could never return. Especially now that Nick had claimed his throne.

It was quite possible Rafe had never belonged in the kingdom, anyway.

But Rafe didn't belong in the bull-riding arena anymore either. Deep in his gut, he knew that he'd killed Manuel. No, not directly perhaps, but he'd endorsed Manuel's abilities to GetRowdy, encouraged him to be a bullfighter, and practically pushed him under PeeWee's hooves. Rafe had been trying to be a friend, but in the end, he killed the best one he'd ever had. Right in front of his son's eyes.

The grief pushed Rafe out of bed every night, made him stare at the bright lights of whatever city he happened to be touring and wish that he'd been awake enough to wrestle Manuel out of the way.

He slammed his brakes, stifling a blue word as a taxi driver cut him off. He'd never been the swearing type, but a lot had changed in six months.

He'd also never been the whiskey type, but this morning he'd tossed an empty pint in the trash. Then he'd tried to ease his headache with four aspirin and a beer. Only that hadn't helped in the least. Despite an entire pot of coffee and another beer, he felt soggy and cranky at best. Some hero.

Spotting an opening in traffic, Rafe cut into the clear lane. He'd never driven in Manhattan before, and the traffic irked him. Not to mention the double takes by other drivers at the two long horns attached to the front of his truck's hood. So he was from out of town. He—or at least Manuel—had worked hard for this truck. And he'd like to see any one of these people go head-to-head with a one-ton killer.

He barely missed a red light and sped through to honks and the screech of tires. He looked up at the sign and cut a right on Fifty-seventh Street. The next light was yellow—or *pink*, the reckless inner voice taunted. As he came up to it and the traffic cleared the intersection, something inside Rafe snapped.

Maybe it was the concoction of beer and coffee playing with his courage, maybe the aspirin deadening the pain. Maybe it was Nick's return to the Silver Buckle to take over the family ranch. Probably it was little Manny, staring at him in the rearview mirror as Rafe had driven off in his daddy's truck.

But *something* grabbed ahold of Rafe. With a growl he punched the gas to the floor and hung a left. This late in the day, pedestrians clogged the street corners, but prudence kept them from streaming out into the crosswalk. He heard screams, but he didn't stop. Couldn't stop.

Even when he'd turned the wrong way on the one-way Fifth Avenue.

Rafe stifled another blue word and dodged a cabbie, who switched lanes for him. Another car plowed into a hot dog vendor on the side of the street. Horns chased him as he searched for escape.

Then he saw two grade-schoolers crossing the street, laughing as they ate ice cream cones. They were coming right toward him.

Rafe slammed his brakes, turning the wheel left. A trash can rocketed into the air as he blasted through a plaza, scattering pigeons, loungers. He bumped toward a green canopied entryway of a tall building. Bellboys leaped for safety.

Rafe aimed for the brakes but missed. The pickup hurtled through the side glass door, and glass waterfalled over his truck. Rafe threw an arm over his head, ducking, as the truck bounced through the lobby. He cranked the wheel, then slammed his brakes.

The truck careened down the stairs that circled a two-tiered fountain.

Adrenaline, hot and too familiar, rushed his veins. In that moment, he knew he'd escaped it. The pain. The grief. The howl inside.

The truck dead-ended at the fountain, toppling the sculptured tiers, the cherubs with their pitchers of water, and scattering the pennies cast in hope.

As pain exploded in his knee, his shoulder, his head, something new filled the vacuum left behind.

Despair.

CHAPTER 2

LOLLY STUART'S MOTHER had taught her two things in life. One, a perfect pie crust includes a half teaspoon of vinegar. And two, never trust a man wearing a suit on any day but Sunday.

Which was why, when John Kincaid walked through the door of her diner, decked out in a sleek, black two-piece Brooks Brothers suit, a white shirt open at the neck, and a pair of shiny black boots, Lolly knew she couldn't trust him as far as she could throw him.

And John was a big man. Not easily thrown.

She flashed back to Piper Sullivan and local ranch owner Nick Noble's wedding, when she'd been John's date. For a moment, she'd wondered what it might be like to be the bride to this handsome man. But she'd told him no once, and he'd never asked again.

Still, Big John Kincaid, owner of the Big K Ranch, cleaned up well.

John nodded at her, giving her that smile that always filled her with longing, and slid onto a stool at the counter.

She said nothing as she set a piece of key lime pie down in front of Egger Dugan, then refilled his coffee and handed a menu to Libby Pike at the end of the row.

Libby had her nose buried in a book. "I'll take a burger and an order of o-rings," she said, ignoring the menu.

Lolly tipped her head down to look at the book and made a face. "Don't tell me you read that trash. Everywhere I look in town, people are reading a B. J. King romance."

Libby turned the page. "It's not trash. It's fascinating—set in the 1930s during the dust bowl years—"

"Spare me the details, really." Lolly took out a glass and poured Libby water.

"*Unshackled* is a really great book," Libby continued, unfazed. "I'm nearly finished, and I can't put it down. I think this is B. J.'s best one yet. It's about this cowboy who's a singer, and he's been in love with this rancher lady for years and years, and she doesn't know it, yet he's loyal to her anyway—"

"Oh, sure, *that's* real life." Lolly shook her head, a little surprised at her jaded tone.

She caught John's strange expression as she turned away. He'd been acting odd lately. He still came around every night, just as he had for the past twenty years, helping her clean after hours, walking her home to her trailer behind the railroad dining car she'd turned into a diner so long ago. Two nights ago he'd asked her if she'd ever thought of living someplace else, maybe farther west. His words had jarred her.

"Of course not," she'd answered, probably too abruptly, because he stayed silent a long time after that, his arm around her as they sat in her old metal glider and stared at the stars. Perhaps once upon a time she'd dreamed . . . but that didn't matter anymore, did it? Her life was in this little town of Phillips and in keeping a promise to herself.

Lolly turned to John, set a cup and saucer down in front of him, and poured him coffee. "You going to a funeral? You're sure dressed up nice."

He gave a slight smile and sipped the coffee. "Got a meeting in Sheridan this afternoon."

For a second, it felt like they might be an old married couple, so familiar were his hands on the cup, the wide cut of his shoulders. His brown eyes filled with a gentleness that she'd come to cherish. Those eyes had been what caught her that day when she stood staring at the vacant lot she hoped to make into her future.

Lolly had happened upon Phillips a broken woman, holding on to life with just a promise and a wad of cash in her pocket. She'd seen John watching her from the parking lot of a feed store. He got out of his truck, crossed Main Street, and asked in that low, delicious Western drawl, "Ma'am, is there anything I can do to assist you?"

She wasn't sure how to answer him. Especially when she looked into that handsome, square-jawed face shaded by a white, flat-topped Stetson and saw a smile that curved sweetly up on one side. She'd wanted to like him, oh, so very much. But she'd trusted a man once, and she wouldn't let herself make that mistake again. So she'd thanked him politely and sent him on his way.

But John had returned over and over, until seeing him sitting at her counter for morning coffee seemed as natural as watching the sunrise. He was a strong man, so much like her big brother had been, over six feet tall, with a frame used to hard work on the range. But he didn't have her brother's wildness, his bravado, and most of the time that filled her with relief. Over the years their friendship had healed her jagged wounds.

All but one. The one that hadn't allowed her to say yes to John's only proposal years ago. The wound that would always keep her from really finding freedom and a life with this man or any other.

John looked away from her and ran the handle of the cup between his thumb and forefinger. "See, I was thinking that, well, maybe you could come with me—"

"I have the diner—"

"Cody can run it." He looked up at her, and her world tilted a little. Something in his expression—need? vulnerability?—scared her, like it had the night over a year ago when fellow rancher Cole St. John had nearly died. For the first time, she'd realized she might lose John, like she'd lost Bobby, and then . . .

Well, she'd have no one, would she?

She swallowed back the taste of grief and glanced at Cody, working at the grill. "He's still pretty green."

"He's been here for a year. I think he can handle it."

"No, John." Lolly reached over and opened the donut case, took out a nut-sprinkled bismarck, put it on a plate, and slid it toward him. "I'll be here when you get back."

His smiled faded. He nodded, and life righted itself.

See, this was why John, in all the important ways, was the perfect man for her. He didn't push and was content to leave things as the status quo between them. Simple. Safe.

Even though sometimes she wondered what it might be like to be John's wife, to have more between them—something the town had believed for years and she had never corrected, despite John's attempts—Lolly knew she could never accept his proposal. She should be thankful he never asked again.

"Stop by when you get back," she said softly, needing to affirm that they were okay.

"Yep," he said but didn't look at her. Then, taking his bismarck, he strolled out. Something about the hitch of his shoulders, the sigh in his step made her mother's words echo in her thoughts.

Lolly refilled Egger's coffee, her attention on the television and a news flash from the station in Billings. She set down the coffeepot as Rafe Noble's handsome face flashed on the screen, followed by what looked like a gaping hole in the entrance of a multistar hotel in New York City. Lolly turned up the volume.

". . . the notable GetRowdy Professional Bull Riding champion was taken to Mount Sinai and listed in serious condition. Among the injured were hotel heiress Katherine Breckenridge and four others who had gathered at the Breckenridge Hotel for a fund-raiser. More news at noon."

Lolly turned the volume down, hearing only the thumping of her heart, feeling the world begin to tilt once more. But this time, she wasn't sure if it might ever be righted again.

❦

"I look like a drowned rat!" Worse, deep inside, Katherine felt like one.

She folded up the paper, her front-page color picture turned to the inside, and tossed it onto her bed, where it fell near a pile of books, her scrapbook, her Bible, and three other newspapers, all capturing the same beautiful image of her just after she'd been sprayed with the wall of water that the driver sent crashing over the edge of the shattered fountain. One photographer even managed to get that oh-so-lovely shot of her strapped to a gurney, pale and barely conscious, after nearly fainting into a heap of seafoam taffeta.

She *hadn't* fainted. She'd been a little weak from hunger and heat . . . and shock. What was that thing he'd been driving, anyway? Part truck, part bull?

The pictures of the event confirmed the damage she'd seen only briefly. The entire lobby had been ruined—glass columns and windows shattered, the carpet and the furniture destroyed by water. Thankfully, no one had been seriously hurt—just one attack of angina and three ladies who'd sprained their ankles. But even twenty-four hours later, the threat of lawsuits made Katherine want to put the pillow over her head.

"What is wrong with me that everything I touch turns out a chaotic mess?"

"I hardly think it's your fault Rafe Noble drove his pickup through the front door of the hotel." Cari plopped down on the end of the bed, flipping off her sandals and smoothing out her black skirt. "It's just too bad it didn't happen about four hours into the night—you could have had headlines *and* donations."

Katherine rubbed her temples. "How is he?"

"Noble? Gorgeous, and if you want confirmation on that, I dug this out of your trash." She tossed a magazine on Katherine's lap.

The guy she'd seen last night bore little resemblance to the one on the cover of *America, Now!* complete with danger in his brown eyes, a slight smirk over his whiskered face, and dark hair curling out from under his black cowboy hat. The editors hadn't had to Photoshop in those muscled arms or wide chest, barely hidden by his black protective vest. He had *trouble* written on every inch of him, and he'd brought it right to her doorstep, or rather, *through* her doorstep.

Katherine tossed the magazine to the floor. "Please. So he cleans up well. If you forgot, he *eviscerated* my event. I can't believe this is happening."

"Speaking of, the board wants to meet with you. Half your donors walked."

"Of course they did! Because who's going to support an organization so far under they have to use spelunking equipment to find their way out?" She rubbed her eyes, hoping to dispel her headache. "He lives near my uncle, you know."

"What? Who?" Cari got up, poured a glass of water.

"Rafe Noble. His family has a ranch near my uncle Breckenridge. Uncle Richard sent me a box of my mother's things right after the funeral. One of the pictures was wrapped in the *Phillips Journal*, and Rafe Noble had made front page for donating a bunch of money to something."

"Maybe he's stalking you."

"Yeah, that's it. He's been after me for years, just waiting to crash his truck into my fund-raiser. It's a textbook scenario."

"The guy in the paper doesn't sound like the guy who decimated your event." Cari handed Katherine the water.

"*Eviscerated.*" She took a sip. "And people change."

Cari raised a perfectly groomed eyebrow, folding her hands over her chest. "Maybe not so much. He did fall at your feet."

"Not in repentance. He was hurt." The memory of Rafe Noble—and she had recognized him immediately, thanks to his Kong-size image in Times Square—falling out of his truck, windshield glass in his forehead, holding his knee as he writhed on the ground flashed through her mind. If she never saw a man in pain again it would be too soon. Still, the way Noble had looked churned up all those feelings she experienced at the Seventh Street shelter—pity, fear, and helplessness.

Then she'd gotten a whiff of him, which was probably what had made her woozy and sent her to the hospital. The drunken sot had destroyed not only her event but century-old architecture. So what that the police report came back clean—she'd asked Bradley to check—she knew what she'd smelled. And what Noble had cost her.

"I'm trying not to desire his suffering."

"Well, suffering he is. According to the papers, he's holed up in his hospital room, not taking visitors," Cari said. "The lawsuits are pouring in, and he has a few charges tallying up. His press agent issued a formal apology, but it hasn't done much to calm the lynch party outside the hospital, some of whom want to string up the Breckenridge Foundation beside him."

"That's just beautiful. Did we get any pledges at *all*?"

"I don't know yet. Maybe you should put the covers over your head, because the board has decided to audit our accounts. You've been cordially invited to a meeting this afternoon to hand over our books."

Katherine closed her eyes, feeling the faintest brush of pain in the back of her skull. Not now. The last thing she needed was another migraine. "That's probably a good thing." She hoped they could figure out where she went wrong. Why she couldn't seem to find the black hole where a half million charitable dollars had vanished thanks to the recent plunge of the stock market. "Sometimes it seems that the harder I try, the more overwhelming life becomes."

"Join the human race, honey." Cari picked the magazine off the floor, studied it for a moment, then tossed it back onto the bed. "The guy's cute, though. And all this press won't hurt his marketability. A couple months and a few donations and everyone will say this is our fault for having a hotel in his traffic pattern. It's all about spin." She gathered up the newspapers. "My take is that you need to escape for a few days."

"I'm not running, if that's what you're suggesting. I didn't do anything wrong."

"No, I mean . . . go on vacation. Get away from the pressure for a while. The Breckenridge chain has a hotel in the Bahamas, right? Get some sun."

"It's June in New York, Cari. I have sun galore."

"Isn't there a Breckenridge hotel in Paris? When's the last time you were in Paris?"

"I don't like Paris."

"Who doesn't like the city of romance?"

"I have romance: Bradley."

Katherine watched as Cari tried to find words. Apparently she came up blank because a simple "Oh" emerged.

"Don't start."

"Did I say anything?"

"I . . . love him. You know, Bradley couldn't be a better match for me if I picked him out myself. So what if my grandfather introduced us? Besides, Bradley has every reason to be overprotective—can you imagine losing your wife only a month after your wedding? He's just . . . wounded."

"And I know your soft spot for wounded souls, Florence."

"He'll make a good husband."

"I only want you to be happy. Maybe find true love."

"What makes you think I haven't?"

Cari's eyes lit up. "Wait—I know! Doesn't the Breckenridge San Francisco have that spa addition? I'm calling to make you a reservation right now. You'll come back a new woman, I promise. Maybe one who wants to live life on the wild side." She held up a finger and dug into her purse for her cell. "Let me take care of it."

"I don't do wild—!"

"That's your problem." Cari got up and disappeared out the door.

Two weeks at a spa. Aside from the fact that Katherine could use a decent massage, the idea seemed like a colossal waste of time and money, especially when she was trying to *raise* money.

Still, she could use a dose of rest . . . and peace.

No, what she could use was about five hundred thousand dollars.

She glanced at the magazine on the bed.

And she might know just where to get it.

❦

"You've really done it now, Rafe."

The voice brought Rafe out of the place of shadowy quiet into the harsh realities of a sterile hospital room. Sunlight slanted in through the venetian blinds, striping his white cotton blanket. Blocking Rafe's perfectly good view of the Manhattan skyline was his clearly miffed brother, Nick. He stood with his arms folded over his black T-shirt and wore a white Stetson just like the hero everyone called him. But if Rafe was hoping for sympathy for his injuries, he'd have to find it in some other Noble because Nick's dark eyes could chill him to the bone.

"Good to see you too, Nick." Despite his neck brace, Rafe tried to look the other way, only to find assailant numero dos in his beautiful twin sister, Stefanie. Her black hair tumbled down her back, her eyes sharp, as she tucked her hands into her jeans and shook her head. "Hiya, Sis."

He thought he saw a glistening of tears and knew he was right when she gritted her teeth and turned away. "I suppose I should just be glad you're alive."

That was nice. Rafe gazed at the ceiling, since it seemed to be the only safe place, and sighed. "I didn't ask you to come out. I don't—"

"Need help?" Nick cut in. "Well, let's see. Aside from the barrage of telephone calls and reporters camped outside the hospital, you've been charged with reckless driving, you have a manager who says he's suing you for breach of contract claiming that you jeopardized your marketability, which is true because you've been dropped by your sponsors, and I've counted four lawsuits for damages from the hotel and property. You've shattered your knee, dislocated your shoulder, barely missed losing an eye, and have a hairline crack in your third cervical vertebra. One lower and you'd be in a wheelchair. Your doc says he's amazed you aren't bedridden with a tube down your throat. You may as well kiss your career good-bye because you might not be able to walk again, let alone get on a bull."

Nick shook his head. If Rafe didn't know his hardheaded brother better, he would have thought he saw a flash of sympathy on his face.

Nick sighed. "You might consider letting us help you, just a little."

Itchiness crawled over Rafe, a familiar residue of the painkiller they'd doped him up on after surgery. He clenched his jaw against the frustration boiling out of his chest. The IV pinched as he brought his hand to his face, covering his eyes. How had he gone from a guy who invested his life in learning how to handle a bull to a reckless jerk who destroyed people's lives?

"Was anyone hurt?" he asked softly.

Stefanie sat on his bed, put her hand on his leg. "A few sprained ankles. Someone fainted. But no serious injuries."

Oh, thank You, God. But the words, easily uttered so many times when he'd gotten off a bull or even stayed on for the full eight seconds, seemed insolent now. God had to be shaking His head, as disappointed as Rafe's mother would be.

For a second, Rafe wondered if it might have been better if he'd just gone flying right through that windshield. At least then Manny and Lucia, his beneficiaries, would get the life insurance.

"I think you're the worst off." Stefanie gave him a small, reassuring smile. They'd always read each other's thoughts, and even now he saw more concern than chastisement in her expression.

Nick, however, wasn't finished. "Thankfully, you were under the legal limit for sobriety, so be grateful they only charged you with reckless driving. But seriously, Rafe, what were you thinking?"

He *hadn't* been thinking. Just going on gut instinct, something he'd been doing pretty much all his life. That same instinct had him longing to launch himself at Nick, needing to put his anger *somewhere.* But pinned down by his IV and the awkward arm sling, he could only put bite into his tone.

"I was thinking that it would be great to deep-six my career, alienate my fans, and declare bankruptcy. Oh, and the added bonus is that if I so much as breathe near a bull again, I could land in a wheelchair for life." He realized how bitter he sounded. "You haven't a clue what it might be like to be me."

Nick looked out the window, disgust in his voice. "Yeah, it's so difficult to be admired by women around the world and to buy your house with your checkbook. You had it rough, didn't you? We all feel *so* sorry for you."

Rafe stared at him, a thousand memories stinging him. He lowered his voice. "It's easy for you, isn't it, Nick? You have the perfect life—beautiful wife, the ranch, everyone thinks you're a such a *great* guy—"

Nick rounded on him, his mouth open. "Where have *you* been for the last ten years? Apparently not in touch with reality because who was the one who gave Dad a heart attack? Who was the one who disappointed him, broke his heart? Yeah, my life is great now, but believe me when I say it came with a price."

Rafe gave an incredulous huff. That was the problem. No, Rafe had never disappointed Bishop Noble . . . because his father hadn't invested enough hope in his youngest son to register disappointment when he left home at eighteen to ride the rodeo circuit.

Nick didn't have the *slightest* inkling what it meant to pay a price for your dreams.

"Go home, Nick. Go back to the Silver Buckle and your perfect life." Rafe didn't even have enough energy to glare at his know-it-all brother. He turned to Stefanie. "Thanks for coming to see me."

"We didn't just come to see you," Stefanie said. "We're taking you home. You need to rest and get better. And the ranch could use you. We have a new crop of calves, and the Buckle has a great chance of getting back in the black if we can sell them fat and healthy in the fall."

"Unless you missed something, I'm in a leg cast, my arm is in a sling, and I can't move my head." Rafe had no intention of returning to the Silver Buckle. Not now, not ever.

Only, what could he do? He swallowed back a wave of panic. He was a bull rider. At best he could teach others to ride. At worst, well . . . he'd tried his hand at announcing, and it came out in half-finished sentences and a lot of dead air. And maybe Nick was right–after this fiasco, he could kiss his sponsorships good-bye.

"You need rest, Rafe, and time to figure out your future." Stefanie took his hand, compassion in her touch. "Let us take you home and help you find your footing."

In her dark eyes he saw understanding, that unspoken way they had of communicating and the uncanny feeling that she could see inside his soul. She gave the slightest of nods, as if she knew that the healing he needed wasn't in his bones but deeper.

Nick apparently couldn't stop himself from adding, "You can't afford anything else. You're going to be broke by the time this is done–"

"Nick, go easy–," Stefanie began.

"After all he's been given, he just throws it away." Nick closed his mouth, a muscle pulling in his jaw, as if holding back a torrent of words.

Right then, Rafe felt about nine-years-old, watching his big brother shake his head in disappointment as Rafe failed yet again to lasso the dummy steer head in the yard.

Rafe looked away from the two of them, listening to the sounds of frustration thumping in his chest.

The phone ringing cut through the silence.

Stefanie picked it up. "Hello?" She listened, eyeing Rafe. "Uh, yeah, I guess so. . . ." She extended the phone to him. "It's a woman.

Says that she got your number from your manager, who told her to call you."

Rafe stared at the phone. "It's probably a fan," he whispered in Nick's direction as he took the receiver. "Hello?"

"Rafe Noble?" The voice on the other end had a New York accent.

"Yep."

"My name is Katherine Breckenridge. Do you know who I am?"

Rafe tossed the name around in his head. "Uh, I don't suppose you're related to the, ah, hotel?"

"I am, Mr. Noble. In fact, I am the president of the Breckenridge Foundation, organizer of the event you totaled last night."

President? How had this woman gotten his number—hit his manager over the head with something? "What do you want?"

"I want . . . I want amends, Mr. Noble. I want integrity. I want . . ." She cleared her throat, apparently not quite sure what she wanted.

"How can I help you, sweet thing?" Even though everything inside Rafe curdled at the good-old-boy disrespect he put in his tone, Nick was watching, wasn't he?

"I'm the furthest thing from your sweet thing, cowboy." He would have guessed a spark in her eyes accompanied those words.

"Spit it out." Rafe's arm had begun to ache again, and he just wanted to close his eyes, go back to yesterday or a year ago when he had been at the top of the standings, nothing in his way to victory. To respect. "What do you want?" he repeated.

"I want . . . five hundred thousand dollars. Which will only get you started on the damages, but it'll be enough to recover what you cost me last night—"

"What?" He didn't really know the Breckenridge family, had

only agreed to attend the event for his sponsor's sake, but seriously, was she out of her mind?

"Let me spell it out for you. You eviscerated my event and left me hanging out for my grandfather to pick my organization apart, all before I raised even a nickel for Mercy Doctors." She caught her breath, and for a second, he thought she might be crying. But she rebounded with both barrels. "So, you owe me. And I need your help. Five. Hundred. Thousand. Dollars. I'll take a cashier's check."

Rafe winced. Behind her bold words and the anger that sizzled, he could still hear the faintest threads of desperation.

He knew all about desperation, which was why he softened his voice when he said, "I . . . don't have that. And I'm pretty sure this is called extortion, so unless you want my next call to be to the cops, don't ever call me again. I can't help you." Only, for a second, he hated being the bad guy and wished—really wished—he could help.

But a guy as bankrupt as he, in too many ways to count, couldn't even help himself, let alone anyone else.

Rafe leaned over the bed rail and hung up the phone.

Silence hung in the room. Yet in it, Rafe heard the truth. Despite the trophies, the gold buckle prizes, the fans, the fame, and the riches, he would never measure up to the Noble men of the Silver Buckle.

CHAPTER 3

"I DON'T THINK this day could get any worse." Katherine toed off her sandals, cradling the phone against her shoulder.

"Just tell me what happened." Cari was on the other end.

"Where do I start? The part where instead of throwing the phone against the wall after talking to Rafe Noble, I rip his smug magazine cover into tiny shreds? Or the fact that after I tried to call back to apologize, the jerk nixed my call? Or maybe he checked out of the hospital, with no forwarding address. Hiding, of course." From responsibility. From *her*.

What had come over her? She'd never talked that rudely to anyone in all her life.

"I spent part of the afternoon arguing with my insurance agent and issuing a press release about the damage to the hotel. Then I joined the board for two hours of recriminations. I've inherited six stone-faced men who apparently think I have the brains of a goldfish."

"I take it your grandfather's not extending your loan?"

Never had Katherine imagined the dressing-down or the ultimatum delivered by her grandfather over speakerphone via his office in London. "Raise half a million dollars by next quarter or dissolve the Breckenridge Foundation."

"Ouch," Cari said. "Three months to dig up a small fortune?"

If Katherine were thirty, she'd tap into her inheritance. But Walter Breckenridge had an iron grip on her trust fund, and Katherine wouldn't see a dime more than her monthly allowance for five more years—or until she married, whichever came first. Apparently her grandfather still belonged to the Neanderthal Club.

"Even better, Bradley and I went to The Water Club for lunch, and he not only ordered salmon for both of us but told me again how I was in way over my head."

"Again, I know you think he's perfect, but—"

"I'm not in the mood to defend him, so stop. He's a good man. Just overly concerned about me traveling and spending every waking minute worried about where I'm going to scrape up money. And . . . he told me that he wants us to think about our relationship. I think he's going to ask me to marry him."

"What?"

"It wasn't a proposal, but knowing Bradley, he wants violins and an Italian restaurant and red roses. And photographers."

Cari said nothing.

Katherine sat on the bed, putting on her running shoes. "Safe isn't a negative trait, regardless of what you think."

"Honey—"

"I don't want to fight about it." Katherine stood, walked to the window, and stared at Central Park. "My focus has to be on getting that money."

Rafe Noble might run, but he couldn't hide. Not from her.

She didn't care what he threatened—he hadn't heard the last of Katherine Breckenridge.

However, at this moment, she had no idea how to talk Rafe into seeing beyond himself and his current tragedies. Yes, she could agree she'd been impulsive on the phone with Noble. What would she say to someone who called and asked—no, *demanded*—five hundred thousand dollars? Then again, she hadn't crashed her pickup into any large, historic buildings. He had the money; she knew it. And probably wouldn't even miss it—okay, maybe a little, but she certainly missed both the foyer of her grandfather's hotel and a positive balance in the Breckenridge Foundation investment account. Even so, perhaps she should approach him with her request from a kinder, gentler angle.

"We'll think of something, Katherine. Don't worry," Cari said, as if reading her mind.

"Thanks, Cari." Katherine hung up, tossed her phone on the bed, and let herself out of the apartment. She took the back stairs of the hotel down all nine flights.

The hot air hit her like a sauna as she stood on the corner, waiting for the light to turn, barely hearing the city traffic or the rush of water from the fountain in the plaza. The light changed, and she crossed into Central Park. The stress began to slough off her as she watched ducks paddling in the pond, as the breeze cut through the heat radiating from the paved path toward Hallett Nature Sanctuary.

She passed Wollman Rink and the Chess and Checkers House and headed for the ancient carousel. An old Karen Carpenter tune met her before she topped the hill, and the stress further uncoiled inside her.

She needed just one ride to sort out her current dilemmas.

The smells of cotton candy, popcorn, and aging wood greeted

her as she bought her ticket to the carousel. Only one child joined her, and he waved to his mother, who stood just outside the ringed circle. Katherine chose her favorite horse—the black one with the wild tail, red saddle, and prancing feet. She had been Wild Kat on that horse. Cari was right—she *did* have a wild side. After all, she'd lit out on Rafe's trail, her guns blazing. Except she hadn't exactly rounded up that outlaw, had she?

The carousel started, and as she floated up and down, she hung on to the pole and remembered her childhood daydream. Hornet— her horse—galloped through the fields, her father's laughter min- gling with the wind in her ears. Not the father in her mother's autographed eight-by-ten glossy professional photos but the father in the cheesy photo strip taken at a photo booth. He was laughing, half kissing her mother, and she was smiling into the camera, her eyes shining, looking so deliriously happy in his arms.

Had Katherine ever looked like that when Bradley held her? Surely, yes.

The ride slowed, and Katherine tried her old silly trick, imagining that if she closed her eyes and wished hard enough, the first person she'd see when she opened them would be her father smiling at her, waiting to collect her from the ride.

Seeing only the darkened, shadowed carousel building, she forced a harsh laugh at the way she backed herself into these mo- ments of pain.

She would never ride a real horse. Never live out West. Never know her father. Only the picture of them—him crouching behind her, one hand on a lasso in her hand, the other on her shoulder, their smiles matching as she posed in a turquoise cowgirl outfit, a pair of red boots, and a red hat—made her believe that she had in any way been connected to the rough-and-tough cowboy who had won her mother's heart.

"Another ride, miss?" the attendant asked as she dismounted.

"No, thanks." Katherine walked up the path, out toward Fifth Avenue, looking for a cold drink. She bought a Bomb Pop from a vendor. Next to him, another sidewalk salesman sold stacks of books. She picked up the new B. J. King novel. The cover featured a silhouette of a man in the distance, watching a woman who stared out at a harsh background of prairie land. "*Unshackled*," she read aloud as she paid the vendor for the book. She knew all about shackles. . . .

"*Go on vacation.*" Cari had probably already booked her ticket for the San Francisco spa. Yet the last thing Katherine needed at the moment was a group of attendants fawning over her, especially while her grandfather's leeches gobbled up her books, sucking her organization dry.

I don't know what to do, Lord.

Katherine sat on a bench, staring at the sky feathered with cirri. She had been a Christian for so long—thanks to those early days when Angelina had dragged her to church—that praying felt as natural as taking a breath. She'd begun her dialogue with God in boarding school when the loneliness pressed through her pores, consuming her breath. Even then, it had been spaces with sunshine and blue sky that had called to her, a window to the divine.

I let my mouth run off with my brain. I should never have spoken to Noble that way. I don't know what to do next, how to get through to him. Or even if he can even help . . .

An in-line skater whipped by, scaring the little mutt leashed to the woman sitting next to her, and he barked, jumping up on Katherine, knocking her book from her lap.

"Sorry," the woman said.

Katherine nodded, smiled at her, and picked up the book. She traced the cover of the B. J. King book. *Unshackled.*

She stared at the woman on the cover, her posture containing such an aura of desperation, it shook Katherine.

Except . . . what if . . . ?

Nothing would pry her from New York. Nothing but . . . a business trip. No, a *rescue* mission. To rescue her organization. Children like Eva . . .

Maybe . . .

Returning to the hotel, Katherine took the elevator up, aware that she looked like she'd just run a marathon, sweat darkening her blue tank top, glistening on her forehead. Despite her fatigue, she felt something alive inside her. Hope, maybe. She'd forgotten the feeling.

She closed herself in her room. Taking the framed photo of her and her father from the bureau, she freed it. The scrawled handwriting on the back had faded, but she could still read: *To Kat, with love from Aunt Laura.*

Aunt Laura. Mysterious Aunt Laura, whose name had once made her mother cry. Who had written below her name, *Phillips, Montana*, where Katherine's uncle Richard Breckenridge, the family rancher, still lived and ran his herd of prize-winning bulls.

Phillips, where Rafe Noble's family lived and ran a dude ranch, according to last fall's edition of *Montana Monthly*. She'd bet anything that he would head home to family for healing and hiding from the media instead of his ranch in Texas.

Maybe if she just got close to Rafe, helped him see the children who needed his help, he'd reconsider. However, she could lay bets that he'd run her off the ranch the second he recognized her name. What had he said—call the cops?

Unless she approached him on his terms—in a cowboy hat and a pair of jeans. Katherine stood at the mirror finger-combing her hair out of the ponytail, imagining herself with a cowboy hat. She didn't have to be the snooty society princess he expected.

Maybe she'd disarm him just long enough to make him hear her out. To rally to her cause. Wasn't that what fund-raisers did?

She'd give herself two weeks—the duration of her stay in San Francisco. Possibly she'd even be able to tap into the cowgirl inside, who had her father's brain and bravado to stand up to an arrogant bull rider and make him see that, contrary to his belief, he could help her.

And that maybe, in fact, deep inside, he wanted to.

John sat on the front steps of his ranch house, cradling a steaming cup of coffee as he briefed his foreman. "Check the fences on the southern end of Butter's table. This winter I caught a bull on Silver Buckle land, and I think he must have gotten through near the southeastern corner."

Crockett, a thin man with graying whiskers and a ponytail under his straw hat, had been with John for three years after he'd stumbled into Phillips, down on his luck. John had hauled him out of the Buffalo Saloon a time or two, but the taste of trust, the smell of hard work, and the feel of a paycheck in his pocket had kept Crockett away from the bottle and turned him into a dependable hand. The fact that he stayed on made him valuable.

"What about the water tank in the heifers' field?" Crockett

chewed on a toothpick, then used it to pick at his teeth. "The windmill's still not workin'."

"I'll use the water truck and fill the tank manually." John didn't add that he had no intention of spending hundreds of dollars fixing the windmill that ran the tank. He'd let the next owners do that.

The *next* owners. As soon as he signed the papers in Sheridan to put the ranch on the market, he would feel as if a thousand-pound bull had climbed off his chest.

And with the crew from Tumbleweed Productions due to arrive later next week, the price would skyrocket. He hadn't yet figured out how to explain Lincoln Cash's presence on the Big K Ranch. But how could John turn down the production company's request to shoot location shots at the Big K?

He took a sip of coffee, his enthusiasm fading at the memory of Lolly's mocking of B. J. King's newest book. *Unshackled* had been John's biggest seller yet. Probably because it had been written from the raw and painful places inside his own heart. He intimately knew what it felt like to pine for a woman who didn't return his love.

The best books were the ones that cost the author a piece of his soul. That much he had learned years ago when he wrote the story of a man trying to stand up to his abusive father. It had been the first time he'd confronted the pain inside, and it had probably taught him everything he needed to finally write the book of his heart, *Unshackled.* But the Book of the Year Award he'd won for his first novel had been worth the pain of remembering the past, and for the first time, John had glimpsed freedom.

If only John Senior had seen it. But then again, John might never have had the courage to write it had the old man been around to read over his shoulder.

John only regretted that he'd never told the people he loved the most—namely, the good folks of Phillips and most particularly Lolly Stuart—about his success.

But he wasn't stupid. Big, tough cowboys didn't write love stories. They loved their horses, their trucks, and then their women. He would have been laughed clear out of the county. Lolly certainly hadn't made him feel anything but silly when she rolled her eyes at his kind of books, calling them romantic rags.

She might feel differently now. Not only had his book been optioned for a movie and put into production, but Lincoln Cash agreed to play the part of Jonas.

Which meant the time had come to finally say good-bye to this life.

John loathed herding cattle; fixing fences, trucks, and tractors; mending saddles; making ends meet—or *not* meet as the case had been for the past ten years. Without his book income, the Kincaid ranch would have folded the year John Senior died. Perhaps he would have been more thankful for the forty thousand acres and thousand head of cattle if his father hadn't also left him with thousands of dollars of gambling debts.

"Anything else, sir?" Crockett asked as he pulled out a tin of chewing tobacco. He wedged a pinch into his mouth and talked around the bulge. "The truck's running rough. I'm thinking it needs a new fuel pump."

"Leave the truck," John said. He'd ordered a new car—a black BMW Z4 convertible. Yes, he had this dream of driving up to Lolly's Diner and seeing the expression on her face when she saw his wheels. He'd definitely turned into a teenager.

A *desperate* teenager, especially two days ago when he'd

spontaneously asked Lolly to accompany him to Sheridan. He kept thinking that when he signed his intent to sell the ranch, then took her out for dinner and gave her flowers and a ring and got down on one knee, she'd see that he hadn't given up on them.

But she'd squashed those hopes, and he'd had to face the raw truth. Lolly didn't want his name, his life. He wasn't so stupid as to get kicked in the teeth again.

John took a sip of coffee, letting the bite soothe him. Maybe it would be better all around if he just left without saying good-bye.

Only what if . . . what if he went in right when Lolly was closing shop and slipped Cody the cook a crisp Benjamin Franklin to clean up the place. He'd wait while Lolly changed, then take her out to the divide, where his land met the Breckenridge place, where the stars seemed to fall into the horizon, where he'd told her he loved her the first time. And there, he'd get down on one knee . . .

"Did you hear about that Noble kid?" Crockett's question brought John back to now and his cooling cup of coffee. "His brother's bringing him back to the ranch. Guess he made a real mess of that fancy hotel there in New York."

John nodded. He remembered Rafe from way back, when he was a gangly kid with big ears trying to stay on a steer. He especially remembered the day he'd been fooling around with his daddy's truck while waiting for Nick to pick up supplies at the hardware store and driven into the plate glass of the Buffalo Saloon. John had watched from Lolly's as Nick dragged his kid brother out by the scruff of his neck, kicking and screaming all the way home.

Yeah, that Rafe had a wild streak, something that branded him as trouble. John hadn't rightly kept up with his shenanigans, but he'd heard he'd become a big-time bull rider. Probably trying to find the one thing tougher, wilder than himself.

Perhaps in a way, all of them were trying to find something bigger than themselves.

John had found it in Lolly—or his love for Lolly—worked out on the pages of his Westerns. But unless he found a way to tell Lolly the truth before Lincoln Cash showed up, the pages of his books were where his feelings were likely to stay. She wasn't the type to let this oversight—his author status—go with so much as a shrug.

Then again, he couldn't exactly label her Miss Tell-It-All, could he? She kept her past locked up tighter than a bank on a Sunday. He'd stumbled onto her secrets purely by accident. Although he'd never breathed a word, never gone probing where he wasn't invited, he knew her wounds still pained her; he saw the shadows of hurt range occasionally through her gaze. Yes, Lolly had secrets. And he hoped the fact that he'd helped protect those secrets counted for something when he came clean about his pen name.

John grimaced, thinking again of her laughter at the B. J. King book. Would she laugh when she discovered that his "romantic rags" had purchased them a new life?

He threw the now cold coffee out on the ground and placed the empty cup on the stoop. "I'll get to that water truck," he said to Crockett, who spat on the ground and followed him to work.

No, he wouldn't miss this life at all.

ᘓᕔᕮᕲᕩ

"The Mercy Doctors grant proposal this year is requesting funds to open three more traveling clinics—"

"I know, Cari. I read their new budget proposal. I'd sell a kidney on eBay if it would help keep even one clinic open. Which is why we need to get the Breckenridge Foundation back in the black." Katherine adjusted the cell phone headpiece as she hightailed it west. She felt a small smile, despite the panic in Cari's voice.

"I don't know where we're going to dig up the money. But I'll go over our donor sheets, see if we forgot to contact anyone."

"Did you go over our short list?" Katherine hoped that the Rafe Noble she'd read about in the newspaper so many years ago still had a soft spot for the hurting. In fact, she had poured all her plans into that idea.

"I have a call in to a couple of other foundations that might be willing to cut us a one-time check. But we're down to the dregs."

"I'm not giving up. Not yet."

"I can't believe you're *driving* in San Francisco. Who drives any-more? What's wrong with going first-class?"

It wasn't exactly *how* she was traveling but *where* that Cari should be asking. She'd be shocked to know that in the last three days, Katherine had planned her flight to Nowhere, South Dakota, where she rented a car and started driving to Montana. She'd read an in-terview a year ago about how Rafe had rented out his ranch while he went on tour this year. Please, *please* let her hunch be right and let him be in Phillips.

She didn't want anyone talking her out of her insanity. Thankfully, Angelina didn't seem to think it insane when she caught Katherine packing. Not only did the woman swear to secrecy, but she gave Katherine a sort of divine blessing with her "May God's grace and peace go with you."

Please, God, let this trip be fruitful. Katherine harbored a crazy mix of fear and hope as she'd landed in Rapid City, rented a Jeep Liberty, and picked up an atlas.

As if to add visual credence to her jumbled emotions, the landscape in this stretch of Montana was at once harsh and beautiful, jagged rock pushing through lush carpets of field grass that rolled over hill and beyond, dotted with purple and white flowers, and bordered by miles upon miles of fencing. A perfect big blue sky told her that she had pointed her Jeep in the right direction coming out of the airport.

Maybe this wasn't insanity after all. Her ever-present headache had nearly subsided, and for the first time in months, she suspected she was thinking clearly.

She *would* talk Rafe Noble into helping her, even if she had to hog-tie herself to his truck until he said yes. She wasn't leaving Montana without a check written out to Mercy Doctors. Or, if he wouldn't give her the money, a thumbs-up to the plan she'd concocted to raise the cash. Even she had to admit her plan had facets of brilliance.

"I like to drive," she finally answered Cari. "What is the latest on our insurance claims?"

Katherine passed a car piled with luggage and two children with headphones staring out the passenger windows. She waved at them and they waved back. Her heart gave a small tug. Bradley didn't want children—they would stand in the way of his political aspirations. But deep inside, Katherine wanted at least one. A little girl, with long braids, who would wear red cowboy boots.

"Your grandfather's insurance company is suing the Breckenridge Foundation *and* Noble for the damages, but his people are saying he isn't at fault—"

"He drove the wrong way—"

"They called it reckless driving, and his insurance only covers it so far. They're claiming it was an honest mistake. Our insurance company will go after them, but we might have to eat the damages."

"It'll wipe us out. We don't have coverage for this kind of thing." She kicked the AC on high, seeing heat ripple against the highway. "Besides, it *wasn't* an honest mistake." An ace that she planned on using, should Noble put up a fuss.

"Despite what you smelled, Katherine, according to the police reports, he wasn't legally drunk."

Katherine had done her research on Rafe Noble over the past three days, and everything she read screamed trouble. Worse, he'd managed to slide out of said trouble with his slick charm and boyish smile every single time.

That only fueled her anger. She'd show Noble exactly what he'd cost her . . . and how to atone for his crimes.

"Besides," Cari continued, "Noble is MIA. His agent isn't answering questions, and I can't nail down a forwarding address. He has a place in Texas, but the number is disconnected."

"I just wish that guys like him didn't get away with their stupid behavior. Anyone else would be handcuffed to their hospital bed."

"Listen, Katherine, Bradley isn't going to let him walk away from this. You can bet that by the time he's done, Rafe Noble will have paid through the teeth."

Get in line.

She wasn't sure why, but that only made Katherine feel worse. Maybe it was because she wanted Noble to *want* to help, not to have to force him. But that might be expecting a bit too much, even for her. . . .

"I'm glad you're getting away," Cari said, cutting through her thoughts. "Forget about New York. Do some shopping; buy a new outfit. This will all be sorted out when you get home."

"I hope so." Katherine switched lanes to fly past a semi. "Thanks, Cari. I'll be in touch." She clicked off, then pushed the Play button on her CD player.

A collection of books on CDs had caught her attention at the last place she gassed up, and she couldn't believe that they'd had the B. J. King Western–the one she'd shoved into her suitcase. It seemed like providence, a sign from God or something to help her find the courage to face Noble, so she'd purchased it.

She didn't expect to feel a kinship with the heroine, a widow with an infant, left on her own in the middle of Wyoming.

WYOMING, 1933

Mary Sutton stood at the edge of the grave, her feet in the dry, lifeless soil, the hot sun sending a trickle of sweat down her back, and knew that she'd never be whole again. The baby fussed in her arms, and Mary readjusted Rosie's bonnet, pulling it low so the dirt couldn't find her eyes. Even so, it caked her little mouth and nose, just as it dusted Mary's skin, her dark pleated skirt, the once-white blouse. She felt soiled all the time.

Or maybe that feeling came from deep inside her soul.

"'Bout ready, Mrs. Sutton?"

Mary turned and squinted at Matthias Thatcher, the man she'd agreed to marry, to raise Charlie's daughter. Her stomach turned. Matthias was fifty, with a paunch that told her exactly what she'd spend her time doing, and he owned the land where

Charlie had run their tiny head of cattle. Matthias wasted no time telling her that he owned her, too. He didn't own her soul. But they had to eat, so . . .

"I'm ready, sir."

He didn't hold out his hand to help her into his Ford Model A. Charlie had dreamed of owning a car, and when Matthias drove out to the fields—usually to harass her poor husband—Charlie had stopped his work to watch the dark machine motor toward him. If Matthias's whiskey-induced diatribe affected Charlie, he didn't show his irritation as he let his gaze wander over the sleek machine.

It felt traitorous to ride in it now, away from their two-room shanty to Matthias's big two-story house. Just like every rancher in Wyoming, Matthias hadn't had a decent crop of calves for years, and his herd had dwindled to a handful of bony cows unable to reproduce. But he made his money in his vast land holdings, in squeezing the small rancher of every drop of profit and working him until he crumpled into the soil at the age of thirty-one.

Leaving behind a child, a wife, and nothing else.

Mary swallowed back a wave of grief and soothed the baby. At least Charlie had seen his daughter before his heart gave out. She'd given him that much.

They pulled up to the unpainted house. It sat in a dip between two weather-beaten, grassless hills. The effects of the last dust storm had piled dirt against the barn and porch. Dirty curtains flapped from the open windows, and a pot of dead geraniums told her that Mrs. Thatcher—God rest her soul—had been a woman of hope.

Matthias's bulk jiggled the car as he got out. "Preacher's inside. Hurry up."

Mary thought he might grab her case from the jump seat, but he marched into the house without so much as a glance backward.

She had no time for tears. Rosie needed a home. She needed work. Mary eased open the door. Weakness rushed through her, a ripple of despair that had the ability to crumple her. She couldn't do this. A tear squeezed out, and she wiped it against Rosie's head, brushing her lips against her daughter's skin.

"Mary!" Thatcher stood on the porch, the preacher behind him.

She saw anger in his eyes and stiffened. *Please, Lord, help me.*

"Can I get your case for you, ma'am?" The voice beside her, a soft drawl, seemed calm against her racing heart.

She looked up, way up, into the blue, shadowed eyes of one of Thatcher's hands. He tugged on his work-worn cowboy hat with a gloved hand. Wearing a dark blue, long-sleeve shirt pushed up at the forearms and a pair of faded brown canvas work pants, he looked about twenty-two, just a couple of years older than her.

He lowered his voice. "You okay, ma'am? It's awfully hot out here."

She managed the slightest nod.

"It's going to be all right," he added.

Mary closed her eyes, suddenly angry that he might have the slightest inkling of what it felt like to bury a husband and marry another in one day. "Go away," she whispered.

But he didn't move, was still standing there when she opened her eyes. In his expression she saw a compassion that found all the bleeding places inside her.

"I'm not going anywhere," he said quietly. "I promise."

Perhaps it was his solemn tone or maybe his honest eyes. Maybe it was the way he picked up her case and put his hand under her elbow to help her across the dusty yard. Or maybe it was the way he met Matthias's dark eyes with a look of his own. Whatever the case, Mary believed him. And that belief gave her the courage to go inside with the preacher and marry the man who had killed her husband.

Katherine ejected the CD from her player and sighed. Poor Mary. How horrible to be so desperate you had to marry for necessity instead of love. What were Mary's choices, really? Back then, women didn't have careers, couldn't get an education. What would Katherine have done? She hoped not the same thing.

Tapping her brakes, Katherine took the Jeep off cruise and turned west off Highway 59, following the signs to Phillips, thinking of the unnamed ranch hand in the story. Obviously, he knew something of Thatcher, probably even how his first wife had died, but he hadn't stopped the wedding. Maybe he couldn't. If it had been Bradley, he would have simply paid old Matthias off or brought him up on murder charges.

But did that make Bradley any different from Matthias? The thought chafed her as she drove into Phillips. She was being too hard on him.

Katherine found the tiny Main Street quaint, with its old grocery store hosting coin-operated rides out front, a bookstore, and a corner saloon. She slowed for the light and saw a community park, then the bleachers of a school stadium and the low building of what she assumed to be the county school. To her left, the cutest diner fashioned from an old railroad car advertised the best pies in Montana.

Katherine pulled into the diner lot, parked next to a pickup that made her Jeep seem like a gnat, and got out. She stretched, and the fresh air tasted clean and pure. Maybe all she needed was a clear schedule without the foundation and her grandfather to dodge and even Bradley hovering over her.

The last thought sent a twinge of guilt. She'd call him tonight as soon as she got settled in with her uncle Richard.

The door jangled as she opened it, and she entered a small room that sucked her back in time to a bygone era—soda fountain stools along a Formica counter, orange booths along the wall beneath the windows. Two guys sat at the counter, their hats pushed back, boots resting on the bar rail. Another sat at the far end, dressed in oily coveralls, nursing a cup of coffee. And a woman and a young boy sat in a booth sipping malts. A jukebox spilled out country-western tunes, and the smells of french fries and hamburgers filled the space.

Presiding over it all at the counter stood a woman with her blonde hair captured in a high ponytail. She wore a pair of jeans and a bright pink T-shirt.

The woman glanced at Katherine, and for a second she looked like she'd seen a ghost. Her face drained of color, and her mouth opened. "What are you doing here?"

❦

Lolly had spent her life wishing for this moment and then revoking that wish, burying it deep inside, hoping it would never resurface.

She wasn't sure whether to cry or leap the counter and crush to her chest the beautiful Katherine Breckenridge. She was here, in the flesh, Felicia and Bobby's daughter.

Lolly could hardly breathe.

"What did you say?" Katherine frowned and approached the counter.

Egger Dugan, the local salvage-yard owner, set down his coffee cup. Quint and Andy, ranch hands from the Silver Buckle, looked up from their plates of burgers and fries, and Maggy St. John glanced at her from where she and her son, CJ, sat.

Oh no, had she really spoken her thoughts aloud? Lolly swallowed, forcing away those wishes, those buried hopes, because once upon a time she'd promised . . .

"I'm sorry, ma'am. You just don't look like you're from around here." Lolly put on her best Western accent and a wide smile, hoping it hid the thumping of her heart. "C'mon and sit down. What are ya hankerin' for? I've got my best rhubarb pie today."

Katherine was even more beautiful in real life with her dark brown hair—probably from her father, only on Katherine it looked like mink's fur, all shiny and sleek—and big hazel eyes. She had the Russell genes in her curves, long legs, and elegant fingers wrapped around the leather bag at her shoulder. She wore a pair of jeans, red cowboy boots, and a brown, cap-sleeve, cotton prairie blouse that made her seem like she'd walked off the streets of Robert Redford's Sundance Film Festival.

If only. But those had been Lolly's dreams—to be among the beautiful and famous of Hollywood—not Katherine's. It hit her that she didn't have the foggiest notion what Katherine's dreams might be.

Katherine sat down on a stool, then stared up at the menu board on the back wall. "What's good here?"

"Everything, of course." Lolly laughed, and her heart gave a small leap when Katherine smiled.

"How about a piece of that key lime pie," Katherine said. "And a glass of milk."

Lolly felt a strange sense of pride as she poured Katherine the milk and cut her the pie. She'd turned out all right. Beautiful, articulate, smart.

Seeing Katherine sitting in her diner, enjoying Lolly's cooking—well, it filled Lolly's throat. Never in her wildest, most hopeful dreams had she ever truly believed that sweet baby Kitty-Kat would grow up and find her way to Phillips.

Which brought her back to—"So, what are you doing here? Phillips isn't a regular stopping-off place." Lolly kept her tone light while filling Andy's glass of root beer.

"Staying at my uncle's place." Katherine glanced up at her. "Maybe you know him—Richard Breckenridge?"

Lolly didn't flinch. "Oh, sure. Everyone has heard of the Breckenridge Bulls. They're famous for their breeding. R. B. also raises sheep." She waved at Maggy and CJ as they left the diner.

Katherine dug into her purse and pulled out what looked like a folded page ripped from a magazine. She smoothed it out on the counter, and Lolly recognized it as the article detailing the incredible story of Nick Noble and Cole St. John. It also advertised the Silver Buckle's fledgling—and now nonexistent—dude ranch business.

"I'm looking for the Silver Buckle dude ranch," Katherine said, taking a bite of pie. "By the way, this is divine."

Lolly tried to ignore the way Katherine's words found soft soil and took a deep breath. "Thank you. And, uh, the Buckle . . . well, I'm not sure that they—"

"We work at the Silver Buckle," Quint said, wiping his mouth. "It's about ten miles out of town. You can follow us out if you want."

Lolly swallowed a strange spurt of panic. Not that she didn't trust Quint. No, her fear ran deeper. Katherine shouldn't be here, around these cowboys, this life. She was young—twenty-five by Lolly's knowing count—young enough to not know better.

"I don't think that—"

"Hey," Katherine interrupted her, wiping her mouth, staring at the wall behind Lolly. "Isn't that a picture of Bobby Russell?" She stood up, leaning over the counter to peer at it. "It's signed to his sister, Laura."

Lolly didn't have to look at the picture to see it—Bobby, astride a bucking bull, his arm high, his legs clamped around the animal's girth. One of his winning shots.

Katherine sat back down, eyes shining. She looked at Lolly. "Do you know my father?"

And just like that, Lolly knew she had to hustle Katherine out of town as soon as possible, or they were all in for a world of hurt.

CHAPTER 4

RAFE USED TO LIVE FOR FANS. Loved to hear them call his name, flirt with him, wear T-shirts with his face printed on their chests. Occasionally he took a group of them out for dinner, let them fawn over him. He wished Nick could have been there to watch.

Now, nearly a week since he'd destroyed his career, Rafe sat at the kitchen table with his laptop and wished everyone would leave him alone. From letters of encouragement to outraged parents berating him for leading their precious ones astray, fans barraged his Web site and filled his MySpace account with comment after comment, some even starting online brawls.

And if that weren't enough, he kept hearing, *"So, you owe me. And I need your help."*

"I can't help you," he'd said right before he'd hung up on Katherine Breckenridge. He couldn't remember ever being that big of a jerk. Then again, the old Rafe Noble had died, probably right beside Manuel.

Everything inside this Rafe just wanted to drop off the face of the earth.

"I'm going to catch up with Nick. He's fixing fences by Rattlesnake Creek. Do you want to join me?" Piper, Nick's wife, stuck her head in the kitchen doorway.

She and Nick had moved into the old hunting lodge on the hill behind the house. For a former journalist, she fit like a glove into ranch life, with the exception of her aversion to meat. According to Stefanie, Piper's freelance writing business had kept gas in the trucks and groceries in the pantry throughout the winter. These days, everyone pitched in to keep the ranch from going under.

"Nope," Rafe said, trying not to be sullen.

Piper gave him a sad smile. "Answering fan mail?"

"Hard to type with one hand."

"I can help you later, if you'd like."

Rafe shook his head. "Thanks. I think I'll just get some sleep."

"I have a two-way radio with me if you need anything."

He nodded. He'd have to be on his last breath before he called Nick or any of the Nobles for help. He closed his laptop, drumming his fingers on the titanium surface.

Thankfully, he'd found a good place to hide should someone— like a nosy reporter—come looking. Hopefully, they'd stop first at his old ranch in Texas, where he and sometimes Manuel had spent their off time between events. Rafe was renting it out to one of his bull-riding friends in favor of motels and life in the fast lane and hadn't lived there in nearly a year.

From the looks of it, that life had sped by him, leaving him in the dust. Or at least in a brace above his knee, an arm sling, and a very uncomfortable neck brace. Stefanie had the gall to get him a wheelchair, and he'd nearly rolled himself right off the porch when he arrived back at the Silver Buckle three days ago.

However, he couldn't deny that coming back to the Silver Buckle had been the right thing to do. Stefanie had been correct in reading his need to recuperate, find a quiet place. The ranch seemed unchanged in the five years since he'd left, with its simple, two-story log home, the barns for the horses and calves, and the fences that corralled the horses. Even the carved Silver Buckle sign over the long drive had waved in the breeze, welcoming him back as if he'd left yesterday.

Only the absence of his father, leaning against the porch, arms folded in silent greeting, evidenced the changes on the ranch. Although Rafe had been back for the funeral, he hadn't expected the silence that echoed in the house.

Or in his heart.

Wheeling himself out to the porch, he sat inhaling the breeze filled with the smells of sage and alfalfa from the fields. The Silver Buckle, eighty thousand acres of homesteaded land, sat in the shadow of the Custer National Forest, and from there, hills and meadows rolled out until they spilled into the hazy Bighorn Mountains to the west. The heifers that hadn't calved lazed about the winter field, just down from the house, their tails swishing off flies, unaware of their impending doom. The new calves had already been rounded up, castrated, tagged, branded, and sent to Kelly's field for the summer. Rafe remembered well the roundups from his youth and his overwhelming pride at wrestling calves into the dirt, hoping to hear his father's praise.

It seemed Bishop always had plenty for Nick.

Rafe ran his hand through his hair. He needed a cut and a shave, but he wasn't planning on having any interviews—at least for a few weeks. He tested his shoulder and felt hope at the minimal pain that spiked up his arm. So maybe he wasn't quite ready for a ride yet. But give him a couple of weeks to recuperate . . .

He spotted a plume of dust kicking up and searched for the source—Andy's dirty pickup headed back from town with the part for the carburetor. Rafe had spent the morning supervising from the porch as the two hands had tried to put the tractor back together.

A Jeep trailed Andy. The vehicles turned up the Silver Buckle drive.

Rafe sat in the chair, feeling almost defiant. He'd had more than one fan track him down at events, his home, even his hospital rooms. If they were toting home a fan, she'd see exactly the kind of hero she worshiped: Broken. Defeated. A sham.

Andy parked near the barn.

Quint got out of the passenger side and waved at Rafe. "Someone's looking for you."

Rafe didn't smile as the Jeep slowed and stopped in front of the porch. A pretty brunette sat behind the wheel, but he refused to be impressed. Instead he raised his chin.

She got out of the Jeep. She was tall and curvy, with brown hair that fell past her shoulders. Except for the aviator sunglasses, she looked like she'd just stepped out of some Western catalog with her jeans, flowery shirt, and bright red boots. Apparently, her version of Old West mystique.

A moment passed between them when he felt sure she expected him to greet her. He said nothing.

She stared at him, probably comparing the image before her with his most recent appearance in *America, Now!* Then she blew out a breath and worked up a smile.

He must really look rough.

"Hi," she said.

Rafe would have nodded, but his neck brace kept him from being that aloof, so he said, "Hello."

She edged around the Jeep, holding on to her handbag with what seemed like a bull-rider's grip. She looked him over with another long perusal.

Yeah, that's right. This is what happens when you fall off a bull.

"You okay?"

He raised an eyebrow. "Do I look okay?"

Maybe she was a reporter, wanting an exclusive on how it felt to watch your career vanish, along with your hard work and reason for living. Couldn't she see that he just wanted to be left alone, to wallow in his shattered life in solitude?

"No, I guess not," she said softly in answer to his question. She looked past him, toward Andy's truck. "Oh, boy."

Not quite the response he expected. "Something I can help you with?"

She tightened her jaw, and for a second he regretted his tone.

"I want . . ." She cleared her throat, then looked down at a torn piece of paper, as if it held a script. Then she folded it and slipped it into her back pocket with a small shake of her head. She looked up. "I know I didn't call in advance, but I was hoping . . ."

"Oh, c'mon—just ask."

"Huh?" She took off her sunglasses and stared at him. Big, innocent hazel eyes, hair tickled by the wind.

"Fine, you can have an autograph. But then I'm done. No interviews, no pictures. You leave, okay?"

Something sparked in her eyes. "I don't think you underst—"

"Listen–" what more did she want? a date?–"if you can't already tell, I'm out of the game. No more riding for me. I'm really sorry you came all this way, but I'm not in an interview mood. Now, I'll sign whatever you have . . . just don't tell anyone how you found me, okay?"

She stared at him a moment longer, and then anger sparked in her eyes. "Wow, you're really a piece of work."

Everything inside him tightened as if he'd seen his future flash before him. But he hadn't ridden bulls since he was a kid without learning to hide his wounds. "Don't you worry, sweet thing. I'll be back in the game in no time."

"I'm not your sweet thing."

And right then, like he'd been kicked in the head, he heard the voice, the one that had been haunting him. The one that still made him feel like he'd up and run off with her daddy's gold.

"It's you."

Katherine Breckenridge–she looked a lot less like the snarling coyote he'd imagined on the other end of the phone and more like a spooked filly.

As if to confirm his accusation, she turned as red as his father's Ford pickup. "Okay, I thought I could do this, but you're . . . such a . . . such a . . . I knew I shouldn't have felt sorry for you. You really are as nasty in person as you sound on the phone. Are all bull riders jerks, or do you have the corner on that market?"

So much for spooked filly. "I can't believe you had the gall to fly all the way–"

"Drove. I drove."

"*Drove* all the way from New York just to–"

"Actually, I flew to Rapid City and–"

"I don't care how you got here. You get back inside that Jeep, turn around, and head east." *And don't look at me that way.* He stood, hoping to put oomph to his words.

"If you'd only listen—"

"I'm calling the cops." He turned, bumping into his wheelchair. Pain shot into his brain, and he started to fall. His hand went out, hoping to catch the wheelchair, but it rolled back, and he missed.

He landed on his knee, his shoulder, his back. It slapped the breath straight out of him. He lay there, openmouthed, feeling as if he'd been kicked by a bull.

"Are you okay?" Katherine Breckenridge stood over him, with what looked like real concern on her face. "Let me help—"

"Go away!" Where the volume came from, he didn't know, but he pushed her hand away. "Get away from me!"

She recoiled. "You're hurt—"

"You just figured that out?" He pulled himself up, gritted his teeth as he staggered to stand.

"I just . . . I thought—"

"I'm flat broke. So you can do your vulture picking somewhere else." He stood, grabbing the porch beam to keep from falling.

"Can I help you?" Stefanie rounded the corner of the house.

Katherine glared at Rafe. Then she smiled and turned to Stefanie. "Yes, please. I was wondering if I can hire someone to show me ranch life."

Rafe glanced at Stefanie. "Hey, she's not—"

Stefanie held up a hand, wearing the same expression she'd had when she volunteered him to take her best friend to junior prom. "Yes," she said with a slow smile, "I think we can accommodate you."

John walked into the diner at his usual time, thirty minutes before closing, slid onto his regular stool, and ordered his usual, a Reuben.

Lolly gave him a smile before making change for the customer at the counter.

He'd lost count of how many years he'd been doing this, helping Lolly sweep up, then walking her over to her trailer, where they'd sit under the stars while she shared gossip she'd heard that day. He'd put his arm around her and lull himself into thinking that they were really married, that she wouldn't eventually shrug out of his embrace and disappear into her trailer while he drove home alone.

Back in the days when he had high hopes for them, he'd steal a kiss or two. Lolly had never truly yielded to him, however. But, strangely, although he spent quite a few years trying to stamp out the flame of illicit rumor, she did nearly nothing to defend her honor.

As if she didn't care.

It took him years to understand why and to accept the fact that she'd probably never say yes to his proposal. So John bought Reuben sandwiches instead.

She set down a piece of rhubarb pie in front of him and poured him a cup of coffee. "Did you get the truck fixed?"

"Nope," he said, cutting the pie. "Fixed the hole in the fence, though."

They could be talking about the weather for all the intimacy of their conversation. Or maybe, in ways, their conversation resembled true marriage, caring about the intricacies of the day, embracing the mundane, bearing witness to each other's lives.

"Lolly had some interesting company today," Egger Dugan said from the other end of the counter. He had the uncanny ability to know everything that happened in Phillips within moments, and Lolly's Diner was his personal dispatch center. He started his mornings with a cup of stiff coffee and ended his days eating the leftover pie. John had never seen him out of his coveralls and oily canvas jacket.

This time, however, Lolly didn't bite. In fact, she ignored Egger, pocketing a tip. "Want fries with that sandwich, John?"

Had he ever wanted fries with his Reuben? He frowned at her, trying to read her eyes, but they avoided his.

She took a washcloth and cleanser and went out to clean the booths.

John turned to Egger, raised one brow.

Egger took the bait. "Cute thing with a New York accent came in here. Recognized Bobby Russell's autographed picture to his sister." He glanced at Lolly. "I didn't know ole Bobby had a sister."

Lolly didn't even look up as she scrubbed tables.

Yeah, Bobby had a sister all right. A pang went through John at Lolly's obvious efforts to act as if the information didn't hit her like a two-by-four. "Who was she?"

"Richard Breckenridge's niece, I guess." Egger finished his coffee. "Went up to the Silver Buckle, thinking they was still running the dude ranch." He laughed, a deep rumble that ended in a cough. "Remember the trouble they had last summer, trying to start a dude ranch? Betcha Nick takes one look at her and sends her packin'."

John gave him a look. Last summer had been different

circumstances—and Nick had changed a lot since then. He didn't miss the sharp look Lolly gave Egger at his prophecy.

Then she went back to spraying, washing, cleaning. As though her past hadn't come knocking on the door today and shaken her world.

How John longed to get up, take the cleanser from her hands, and wrap his arms around her. To tell her that everything was going to be okay. That her demons weren't so huge that they couldn't be tamed by the right force in her life.

But he didn't. Instead he sat there and watched the woman he loved carry her burdens alone, hating himself for not being able to say the words he could so easily type on the page.

Lolly reached into a booth and came out with a book. "I can't believe Libby. She was glued to this thing for three days, then leaves it here." She tossed the book onto the counter, where it landed next to John. He saw the cover, well-worn, and hid a smile. At least *someone* was reading *Unshackled*.

He picked it up, flipping it open, enjoying reading the words instead of anyalzing them.

WYOMING, 1935

Mary stood at her daughter's bedroom window, watching the sky darken, wishing it would finally rain. Storms like these scared her the most. Not because of the dust that would pile up against the house and coat her clothes, her skin, the inside of her ears and nose, but because they frightened Rosie. And then she would cry.

Mary picked up her two-year-old and wrapped Rosie's legs around her waist, holding her head against her body, wishing she had more padding on her to soften the curves. Wishing that, when her daughter held tight, it didn't make Mary bite her lip to hold back the cry of pain. Apparently her ribs hadn't yet healed.

Thunder pealed across the sky, and Rosie trembled.

"Shh." Mary rocked the child, smoothing her coarse hair. *Please let Matthias be so soundly drunk that he won't hear the floorboards creaking above him.* She'd left him where he lay on the sofa, thankful he'd fallen there last night and not in their bed.

Tears burned her eyes, but she refused to cry. She'd cried enough for three lifetimes. And tears wouldn't water the land, feed their cattle, or bring Charlie back. She didn't have time for grief, with the cooking and cleaning and farm chores. She stayed busy by choice. It kept her out of the house.

Sometimes, more and more often, it brought her into conversation with Jonas. Yesterday he'd helped her mound the potatoes in her garden. He sang as he worked, usually hymns, sometimes songs of his own making, and as usual, his voice soothed the wounds inside her.

For all the years I thought I was worth nothin',
For all the times that I gave up on me,
For all the fears I hid that kept me from believing
    it could be,
Could I be worth the love that sets me free?

Sometimes just humming those words filled her with hope that she shouldn't give up. That someday she, too, might be free.

She had no doubts Jonas had heard the shouting last night, had seen the fresh bruises on her arms, her chin. She'd long ago stopped trying to hide them. He'd become her protector of sorts, helping her with chores, and twice, running out to the field, alerting her that Matthias was on his way home. More than once, he'd even knocked on the door, hat in hand, intercepting Matthias's savage mood.

Unfortunately, Jonas wasn't always around. Legally, she was Matthias's wife, and according to Wyoming law, Jonas couldn't interfere. Besides, with people starving all over the country, who cared if a man took out his frustrations on his wife? Certainly not Sheriff Denny, in whom she'd confided. She'd spent two days in bed after he'd told Matthias her accusations.

Jonas had fed her, and when he thought she wasn't looking, she'd seen anger cross his face. When Matthias went to town, Jonas silently rewrapped her bruised ribs, his eyes red-rimmed.

Jonas was in a prison of his own. Matthias carried the title on the land owned by Jonas's family—his parents and his six brothers and sisters. She often saw him standing in the barn entrance, staring at the house, fists clenched.

Perhaps that was why she found an easy, healing friendship in him. They both understood being trapped.

Lightning flickered, and right behind it came another peal of thunder.

Rosie shrieked, and Mary shushed her, singing softly. "Hush, little baby . . ."

"Make her shut up," Matthias bellowed from downstairs.

Mary stiffened. Thus far, he'd never harmed Rosie, but that didn't stop the toddler from shaking. "Shh," Mary said, trying to stave fear from her voice.

The lightning flashed again, and in that split second, she saw a silhouette in the doorway of the barn. *Jonas.*

Rosie's crying heightened.

"Shh, baby, shh," Mary said, moving in time with her hums.

Heavy footsteps thumped up the stairs. The door banged open. "I told you to shut her up!"

Mary refused to turn, even as she felt him lunge toward her. She kept her eyes on the silhouette until the last moment.

John closed the book, remembering the ache inside when he'd written that scene, hating the fact that he'd bound Jonas's hands. He'd purposely made Jonas watch while the woman he loved suffered, knowing he couldn't do anything about it because sometimes life worked out that way. He often wondered if the hands at the Big K had ever felt like that, watching John Senior go after his kids.

"Seems as if the entire town is reading that book." Lolly took Egger's plate away.

He tossed a couple of dollars on the counter.

"Maybe you should read it." John pushed the book toward her.

Lolly rang in the bill, slipped the cash into the drawer. "No. I don't believe in fairy tales."

As if her own words jarred her, she stilled and looked up at him. In that beat of time, something passed between them. A sadness or just the sense of inevitability.

Whatever it was, John knew he had his answer to the question he couldn't ask. "Right," he said softly. Of course she wouldn't believe.

He was getting up to leave when the doorbell jangled. In the doorway stood the shapely brunette Egger had described. But John—probably *only* John—saw so much more.

He saw Bobby, courage in his eyes as he faced down his bull, and Felicia, poised, beautiful, and full of hope. Most of all, he saw Lolly, her pride wounded and desperation lining her face as she stood in a dusty street.

And just as he'd done then, he came over to the brunette and tipped his hat. "Ma'am, is there anything I can do to assist you?"

~CHAPTER 5

"Sweet thing! He actually called me sweet thing! Rafe Noble is the most bullheaded, insufferable, arrogant guy I've ever met. If he thinks he's getting away with his lies, he's got another think coming." Katherine sat at the diner counter, stabbing at a chocolate malt with her straw and wishing she'd been able to string enough words together to tell Rafe what she thought of him to his face. Apparently she could only resurrect Wild Kat over the telephone. Or a chocolate malt.

It didn't help that he had blindsided her with his expression of defeat. Maybe he really didn't have any money. If his sister hadn't shown up and practically begged Katherine to return, she might have believed him. Stefanie obviously had a reason for wanting her to stay. All Katherine knew was that winning the bull-riding championship came with cash—lots of it. He was just trying to play her.

"What lies?" Lolly asked.

Katherine had discovered the diner owner's name shortly after sliding onto the stool in a puddle of despair. When Lolly asked her name, she'd debated a moment, then decided on Kat, liking the spunk she attributed to the nickname.

Now, reading Lolly's response, she realized she'd dissed the local hero. If Rafe Noble thought he could scare her away, he hadn't seen the daughter of Bobby Russell. Mr. Noble's surly demeanor wouldn't spook her. "Nothing . . ."

"So, how did he look? His sister said the accident roughed him up good," Lolly said, nursing her own malt.

"He's in a neck brace and a cast, stitches over his eye," Kat said. She didn't mention the tumble he'd taken on the porch. "He looks like he's been run over by a buffalo."

But it didn't diminish his overall stun power. If Kat were hunting for the quintessential cowboy, with a lazy smile, heavy-duty arms, and a physique that could wrestle cattle, she had to look no farther than Rafe Noble. Under different circumstances—say a cover shot and some airbrushing away of his snarls—the man could steal her breath. As it was, when she'd met him, her heart had gone galloping off into those green, wildflower-scattered hills, scared silly.

Until he'd called her sweet thing and offered to sign something. Like what? Her hand? She had a gut feeling that Noble'd had his share of interesting signings over the years.

"He won't be getting on a bull anytime soon," said the man next to Kat.

Kat glanced at John. He looked about forty and had warm brown eyes and short brown hair. He leaned on the counter, his jaw propped on one of his wide hands, suddenly looking very interested in her adventure at the Silver Buckle Ranch.

"I don't know why not. Seems to me that Rafe Noble needs

somewhere to put all that nastiness." Kat took the straw out of her glass and licked the ice cream from it.

"Sounds like you've joined the victims—there's a club, I think, of women scarred by Noble men." Lolly sipped her malt. "Especially Rafe. He's been in the bull-riding circuit since he was about eighteen, collecting fans and trophies, in that order. Rafe was born with a mile-wide streak of trouble running through him. I think they retired his detention chair at the school, and for years he was the sole street cleaner in Phillips. I still remember him on those hot summer days in his yellow vest, picking up trash for community service." She grinned and glanced at John, who nodded.

Lolly's smile faded. "After his mother died and Nick left, Rafe sort of ran wild. Didn't your dad hire him on for a while, John?"

"He worked for Maggy's dad—our trail boss—breaking horses. I remember Maggy saying that he didn't seem to have a lick of fear in him. Which can be a dangerous thing for a teenager, even worse for a man who rides bulls."

As they talked, Kat envisioned Rafe younger, with dark, shoulder-length hair, recklessness in his eyes.

She remembered reviewing an application for a grant to help fund an after-school program for at-risk kids. One of their case studies reminded her of Rafe. Yet hidden inside all that anger, defiance, and pain had lurked great potential because that kid—with the help of the program, encouragement, and hope—had gone on to graduate from high school and was currently in the military, serving as a medic. Helping people, just like Rafe could.

There she went again, seeing life's best possibilities instead of reality. But wasn't that why she'd trekked out here? Because Rafe had potential?

Please, Lord, let him have potential.

"I met his sister—she seems real nice," Kat said quietly. "Why did Rafe turn out so . . . ?"

"Rafe isn't as bad as he seems." John ran his fingers along the brim of his hat lying on the counter. "He used to volunteer as a teacher for the junior rodeos when he was in high school—got a real way with kids. And he did some charity work at a youth center with his winnings. I think he's just licking his wounds. He nearly got killed last fall at the bull-riding world championships."

She knew it—Rafe *did* have a soft side. John's words settled into Kat's thoughts. She'd always had her world handed to her on a platter. Even now, she lived a perfect life—well, mostly. But what must it feel like to have your dreams slip out like sand between your fingers? No wonder he looked so broken.

"My unsolicited advice to you," Lolly said, "is stay away from Rafe Noble. If you haven't figured it out by now, cowboys are a passel of trouble."

"Hey, now," John said. "Be nice."

"Okay, *some* cowboys are real gentlemen." Lolly glanced at John, and something friendly, even sweet, passed between them. "But Rafe is a special kind of trouble. Anyone who looks a bull in the eye and dares him to buck him off is going to ride right over you without a look backward."

Yeah, Kat had met *that* Rafe. As she left the Silver Buckle, everything inside her had wanted to keep driving and forget the idea that she could talk Rafe into anything. Especially after her brief stop at her uncle's ranch—the Breckenridge Double B. That hadn't exactly perked her spirits. She'd nearly beelined out of town. As she drove by Lolly's Diner though, she'd felt the strangest urge–maybe even a divine urge–to stop. Go in.

It seemed as natural as breathing to sit here on the barstool, pouring her heart out to the owner. "If you two can keep a secret . . . I'm here because I need Rafe's help. He destroyed something I was working hard on, and I need him to own up to it. Or at least help me figure out what to do next." She dug into her purse and set the ad for the Silver Buckle dude ranch on the table. "I have this idea . . . but I have to talk Rafe into it. I have to get him to trust me, to see that I really want to help both of us. And then convince him my idea will work."

"How are you going to do that?"

Kat smoothed out the wrinkled advertisement. "Not exactly sure. I guess . . . I'm going to wait for the right moment, let him see I'm sincere." She shook her head. What would her mother have done? Probably flashed him a smile, and he would have asked how many zeros to add. Kat didn't have a clue how to emulate that. "Thankfully, Stefanie is on my side, although I don't know why. Rafe wanted to call the cops, but Stefanie invited me back to the ranch tomorrow."

"Oh, Kat, I don't think it's a good idea to hang out with Rafe. He's not in a good way right now," Lolly said.

"Listen," Kat said, speaking to herself as much as to Lolly, "I need to do this. You don't understand, but it's my last shot."

Lolly looked down at her malt, stirring it. Kat had noticed that despite her age–she put her in her early forties–she had a youthfulness about her. A tease around her eyes and a sparkle in her smile. She liked Lolly, and her easy friendship seemed exactly what Kat needed, especially after her conversation at the Breckenridge ranch.

"But I have a bigger problem than Rafe Noble at the moment. I went to Uncle Richard's ranch today–"

"And he's in London." Lolly made a face. "I forgot earlier. Sorry, honey. He goes to London every June."

Kat nodded. "So, do you have any hotels in town?"

Lolly looked at John, who gave a small shrug.

"Nope," she said.

Kat winced. "I guess I can sleep in my Jeep."

"You're not sleeping in your Jeep–," John started.

"Maybe it's not meant to be," Kat said.

Lolly looked down, stirring her malt again. "Don't you have someone waiting at home for you? A . . . boyfriend, maybe?"

Kat's entire body tensed. She fished around for something that didn't sound like a lie. "Let's just say I'm here on business. And I can't go home until it's finished. Maybe I can go back to the Breckenridge ranch and–"

"You're staying with me." Lolly put a hand on Kat's arm.

Kat couldn't hide the relief that poured through her. "I'll pay you–"

"No, you won't. It'll be my pleasure." Something glistened in Lolly's eyes, something sweet and kind. It made the knot inside Kat's chest ease.

"I promise I won't be any trouble."

"Of course not. My place isn't very big, but I do have an extra room. I just need to change the sheets, fluff a pillow or two."

Kat noticed John staring at Lolly, his expression unreadable.

"Thank you, Lolly." She finished her malt, then picked up the ad. She opened her purse to tuck it inside and saw the picture of her and her father. A five-year-old's innocent happiness.

She took the picture out of her purse and ran her thumb over it. "Um . . . this may sound like a strange question, but you don't happen to know Laura Russell, do you? I see Bobby Russell autographed his photo to her." She nodded to the picture behind Lolly's counter. "If my aunt is still around, I want to find her."

Lolly picked up Katherine's empty glass and wiped the condensation from the counter.

"I know just about everyone in the county," John said slowly. "I'm not sure Laura Russell lives around here anymore." He put his hand on Lolly's arm. "Do you know, Lol?"

Lolly glanced at him. "No. No, she's not around here anymore."

Kat's hopes dipped. "My mother never talked much about my father," she said, deciding that she'd already told them about her present—why not her past? "But I always had a curiosity about how they ended up together and how he really died, beyond the reports in his obituary. I was really hoping my aunt Laura could fill me in."

Silence passed between them. Lolly finished her malt.

John fiddled with his hat. Then he said quietly, "I knew your father. He was my best friend."

The last time Rafe had eaten dinner in the Noble dining room, pine wreaths festooned the stained log walls and ivy wound through the wrought-iron chandelier. His mother, still alive but in her last season, had managed to pull together a roast with all the trimmings, homemade rolls, and red velvet Christmas cake.

The Noble family—whether purposely or unconsciously, he wasn't sure—avoided this room after Elizabeth Noble's death. His father certainly couldn't cook, and after Nick left home, they hadn't had much reason to celebrate. Stefanie took over running the ranch with Bishop, and Rafe ran away to join the rodeo circuit.

"Rafe, you're at this end, Nick at the other," Piper said as she carried in the roast and put it in the center of the table. Behind her, Maggy St. John and her eleven-year-old son, CJ, came in with fresh green beans and rolls. Rafe had known Maggy from the days when she'd been Nick's girlfriend. Sometimes it felt strange to see her married to Nick's best friend and co-owner of the Silver Buckle Ranch.

The smells had the power to make Rafe's stomach turn to knots. Or perhaps the twist inside came from the residual adrenaline from his fight with Katherine Breckenridge. He couldn't believe she'd actually followed him to his hometown of Phillips. How had she even known where to find him?

"It's Katherine Breckenridge from the hotel," he'd said to Stefanie. His voice was probably still echoing off the far hills. "She's here to ask for my money. Which I don't have because . . . I'm broke." Despite his tone, he had felt a little guilty when Katherine flinched.

"I just want to talk to him," Katherine had said.

Even though Rafe had stood there, barely balancing on his broken knee, in his neck brace, smarting from his recent fall–right at Katherine's feet–Stefanie merely nodded and invited the woman back for another go-round the next morning. If he could have, he would have thrown something. Anything to wipe that smug little smile off Katherine's face.

"I'll be back in the morning," she'd said.

Yeah, he'd show her around the ranch. Maybe lose her in one of the back fields.

"Are you going to ride bulls again, Uncle Rafe?" CJ asked, climbing into the chair next to him, yanking his thoughts away from the fact he'd been betrayed by people serving pot roast.

"Don't ask him that," Maggy chided him. "Sorry, Rafe."

Rafe ignored her and reached over, tousling CJ's hair. "You bet, kid. I'll be back on a bull before you know it." As fast as he could, in fact. Plenty of riders rode injured. And apparently, he needed the cash.

Nick looked up from where he was slicing meat at the end of the table. His mouth tightened.

"Go easy with the roast, Nick," Cole said, bringing in a pitcher of water. "What did it ever do to you?" Now that Maggy's husband, Cole, and Nick were on speaking terms again, they'd combined lands and worked them together, hoping to keep both their operations in the black. Their reconciliation after years of hatred still surprised Rafe, and he could admit it rankled him that they'd left him cleanly out of the operations of the Silver Buckle.

"Rafe's got some mending to do first, CJ," Stefanie said, pulling her chair out beside Rafe. "He's in no shape to be riding bulls."

"Yeah, but I'll bet he'll be back for the championships in Vegas, won't ya, Uncle Rafe?"

"For sure. I'll be back long before—"

"That's enough!" Nick stood and dropped his knife with a clatter onto the plate.

Stefanie and Maggy jumped.

Piper put a hand on Nick's shoulder. He shrugged it off. "Are you trying to get yourself killed?"

"Sit down, Nick," Stefanie said quietly. "Let's just give Rafe a chance to—"

"No. He's got to admit it—he's done. It's over. He's back on the ranch, where he belongs."

Rafe stared at his brother, at his wide stance in the place where Bishop used to sit, and the emotions he'd been trying for years to deny—to *expunge*—came roaring at him.

Sometimes Rafe hated Nick, and he knew the feeling was mutual. Hadn't Nick said that very thing on more than one occasion when they were growing up?

"Thanks, Nick. I appreciate the show of support."

Nick braced his hands on the table, breathing hard.

Silence filled the room, and Rafe could hear in it the pity, the word *failure*. Nick was wrong—he'd never belonged on the Silver Buckle.

"I'm not hungry." Rafe started to wheel himself away, but the chair hooked on the table, bringing with it the tablecloth. His mother's plates crashed on the floor at his feet, a hundred shards that in no small way resembled her shattered hopes for him. His hopes for himself.

Biting back his frustration, he wrestled himself out of the cursed chair to his feet. Maggy made a move toward him, but he pushed her away with a glare. Then he hobbled out of the room.

"What's wrong with Uncle Rafe?" CJ asked in his wake.

"Nothing that time won't fix," Stefanie said softly.

As Rafe rounded the corner and dragged himself upstairs, he knew that no amount of time would fix the broken places inside him. Because a man couldn't fix something that had never been whole to begin with.

Bracing himself on the hall walls, he worked his way down to his old bedroom, the one he once shared with Nick, while white-hot pain shot up his leg, nearly blinding in its assault. He pushed the door open and half lunged, half fell onto his twin bed.

He rolled onto his back and ripped the sling from his arm. He wanted to do the same to the neck brace, but the doctor's warning rang in his ears.

Rubbing his shoulder, he stared at the posters of legendary bull riders Lane Frost and Bobby Russell on the walls, the ribbons over his dresser, the dusty trophies. He'd seen Russell in action during a charity event in Billings once when he'd been about six. Bobby Russell had been the greatest bull rider to ever live, with three PBR championships and not an ounce of quit in him. One season he'd even ridden a bull with a broken leg. If Bobby could do it, Rafe could do it.

Of course, Bishop had called the man a fool. Rafe had a sneaking suspicion he did it in some warped attempt to curb Rafe's idol worship. But whom else did Rafe have to pin his gaze on?

And, no, Rafe didn't listen to the voices inside that taunted him with what had happened to both Frost and Russell. What could so very easily happen to him.

Rafe gazed at the ceiling, the dust layering the lantern light fixture, and the old memories flooded back as clearly as if he were again six-years-old and bedridden.

"He can't go, Lizzie. He's too fragile." Bishop's voice had drifted up from the kitchen, waking Rafe from his slumber. He stayed still, listening. "I don't want him getting hurt."

"The doctor says he's fine. He spends every hour in bed, dreaming of being out there with you and Nick, working the cattle. You even take Stefanie. Rafe needs to learn to ranch."

"He'll learn soon enough. When he's strong. Better."

Rafe had traced the neat, bright red scar on his chest. Six months old, it was just starting to fade, but it felt funny when he touched it. Like it was numb or something. He *was* better. Although his mom was right about him feeling fine, she had it wrong about him lying in bed all day.

Most days he sat at the window, waiting for Nick and Dad to ride out—wishing he were going with them—then he snuck down to the barn to help Dutch, the ranch boss, feed the bums—the orphaned calves. Sometimes he worked on his roping. Most often, he dreamed about riding the Black Angus bulls in the field above the house. Sometimes he wandered up to the fence and studied them as they raised their massive heads and watched him with their glassy eyes, chewing grass that hung out of their mouths. Once, he'd ventured into the field. When one ambled toward him, his six-year-old courage fled, and he'd hightailed it back to the fence. As he'd dived into the dirt, he knew it wouldn't be the last time he got near a bull.

Too bad Nick had been coming out of the barn and seen the entire thing. At eleven, Nick was already winning roping championships and driving the truck. He nearly split his side laughing at his kid brother sprawled in the grass and dirt. He laughed at him that night and the next day. In fact, Rafe couldn't remember a day until he hit about ten when Nick hadn't laughed at him.

They all laughed at him, really. The skinny kid with the hole in his heart. The fragile twin. The sickly one of the litter.

Bishop's runt.

Rafe clenched his jaw at the words. He hadn't believed the truth, that his father was ashamed of him, until the day—he'd just turned ten—his sheepdog Chigger gave birth to five pups. The last was born blue, and only because of Dutch's ministrations did the little runt start to breathe. Rafe sat with the pup in his lap throughout the night and tried to get him to latch on to Chigger's teat, but the little guy didn't have the strength.

The next morning Bishop came into the barn, stood above Rafe, his shadow cold as it blocked out the sun. "He's not going to make it, Rafe."

Rafe didn't look up.

Bishop crouched beside him, his big hand on his son's shoulder. He had always seemed huge to Rafe. Only later, when Rafe had grown up, did he discover that he was taller and wider than his father. Somehow, however, Bishop still seemed gargantuan.

"He's suffering, Son. You need to put him out of his misery. Look at Chigger—she's agitated, knowing he's not latching on. Take him down to the crick."

Rafe stared at him, horror sluicing through him. "No. He's . . . fine, Dad. He's going to be fine." He ran his hand down the pup's hairless, shivering body.

Bishop took a deep breath, and for a moment, Rafe thought—hoped—he might sit down beside him, help him nurse the pup to life. Instead, Bishop stood and retrieved a burlap feed sack. Bending down, he eased the pup out of Rafe's hands, then put the animal inside the bag.

"No, Dad—please—"

Bishop had seemed nearly . . . well, if Rafe didn't know better, he would have thought he saw tears edge his father's eyes. But Bishop Noble didn't cry. Not for a runt puppy.

"It's for the best. He's just a whelp." Bishop stood and, with a small shake of his head, walked away. "He's more trouble than he's worth."

A knock came at Rafe's door, yanking him from the past to the present throbbing in his leg, his empty stomach growling from the delicious smells downstairs. Sometimes he still felt—and apparently acted—like a little kid. "Come in."

Stefanie appeared, carrying a plate of food, a napkin, and silverware. "We can't eat all this. You gotta help." She stood there, waiting to be invited in, her dark eyes shiny, as if she might have been crying.

"Thanks, Sis," Rafe said, sitting up.

Stefanie sat down next to him on the bed and handed him the silverware. "He's just worried about you, you know."

"Nick always thought he could tell me what to do. Those days are over."

"He doesn't want you getting killed."

Rafe said nothing, cutting his roast.

"We need you around here, Rafe. I need you. Nick needs you."

"No, you don't." He took a bite of meat. "Did you cook this?"

She smiled. "Piper. She's turning into quite the chef."

"Delicious. Nick needs me about as much as Dad needed me."

Stefanie looked surprised. "How can you say that? Dad depended on you after Mom died. It nearly killed him to let you go off rodeoing—"

"Are you blaming me for Dad's heart attack?"

"No! Of course not. I'm saying it devastated him to have both his boys gone. He knew he couldn't stand between you and your dreams. What he couldn't figure out was why you hated the Silver Buckle." Stefanie handed him the napkin, and he tucked it in his shirt.

"I didn't hate the Buckle. I just didn't belong here. This is Nick's domain and your world. I'm not a rancher."

"Then what are you going to do? Because—and don't take this as a dare—you really can't be serious about riding bulls again." Stefanie touched his arm. "I don't want to see you end up permanently in a wheelchair . . . or worse, dead."

Something in her tone slipped beneath the anger he'd been nursing over the past week. It scared him too, as if there might be truth in that statement.

He couldn't give up bull riding. He figured it might be like giving up breathing. However, until then, he needed something to take his mind off his busted-up knee, his broken life.

"I know you're still pretty worked up about my inviting Katherine Breckenridge back here, but I think there might be a way for you two to work together," Stefanie said.

"She wants to leave me for the buzzards, Stef."

"She didn't look that scary to me."

Sweet and pretty, yes. Scary, no. But looks could be deceiving. "I don't have any money. You know that."

Stefanie looked out his window, where the night had begun to swallow the hills. "I think you owe her something. She said she had a plan. Just listen. Maybe you two can figure this thing out."

Rafe took another bite of dinner. "Fine. One day. She gets one day. And then I'll put her on a horse and point her back to where she came from."

CHAPTER 6

"DON'T TELL ME she isn't there, Angelina. I want to speak to her."
Bradley walked to the window of the penthouse suite overlooking
the Potomac River and rued the day he left New York. *Katherine,
what are you up to?*

She'd been acting strange ever since the doctor gave her an all
clear. As if she might know that something wasn't right inside her.
But leave town? She was becoming dangerously more and more
like Felicia every day. Unpredictable. But perhaps he could use that
to his advantage.

"She's not here, Senor Lymon."

"And she's not in San Francisco. You know where she is." He
hung up on her. *Where did you go, Katherine?* He'd left messages on
her cell, at the hotel in San Francisco, and on her home phone.
He'd even sent her an e-mail.

In the background, the television scrolled the stock report, and
his half-eaten supper evidenced his concern for her. That he'd blown
off dinner with a senator to call her made him nearly nauseated.

Well, he did have a fairly productive cocktail hour, topping it off with a rendezvous with a shapely brunette he'd met in the bar last night. He stared out the window. How he liked the energy here, the feeling that everyone eyed him twice, knowing he had connections to one of the richest men in America.

Someday people would envy him for more.

He hadn't thought it would be like this, the pressure from Breckenridge. Could he stand to be shackled to him for life?

Perhaps, what seemed like shackles actually meant freedom. A real future. Because money was freedom. It was opportunity.

An opportunity he might lose if Katherine left him. An opportunity he might have to be more creative with if he hoped to keep it.

Where are you, Katherine?

❧

Now this was a view Kat would never find in Manhattan. Miles and miles of rolling grassland, brushed by the morning wind, broken by a rugged gully or a scattering of pine trees, backdropped by the hazy purple Bighorn Mountains. And over it all, knots of fluffy white clouds scattered over an endless blue sky.

Okay, she might find this view on her TV, but it didn't come with the smells—grasses, loam, wildflowers, and even a tinge of sweaty, magnificent animal.

Kat closed the door to her Jeep, stood in the yard of the Silver Buckle Ranch, and just let herself breathe. *Grace and peace go with you.* She tried to let Angelina's words settle into her bones. *Lord, please make this day fruitful. Help me convince Rafe to help.*

Wouldn't it be nice if Rafe had awakened from a sound sleep with a burning desire to track down that very nice, needy Breckenridge lady he'd blasted off his property yesterday, apologize profusely, and offer to write her a very large check?

That was about as likely to happen as, well, as her learning to ride one of those bulls she'd passed on the drive to the Silver Buckle.

All the same, being here made her feel oddly hopeful, as if today God *would* change Rafe's heart. She already felt better this morning—no headache—and she was energized.

Funny, she should be exhausted. What with staying up past midnight listening to John Kincaid tell her stories about Bobby.

Bobby Russell had been a real-life, flesh-and-blood man who loved hamburgers and herding cattle and had once stranded his truck in the middle of Rattlesnake Creek. John had given him a voice, and Kat went to sleep with the sound of her father's laughter in her mind.

The only blemish in the evening had been when Kat asked how he died. Silence had finally forced John to say that Bobby had been thrown off a bull and broken his neck. Lolly said nothing and busied herself with cleaning menus. Kat felt again five-years-old and left in the dark.

Lolly fixed Kat up in a bedroom that had never made it past the eighties, with bright rose-colored floral wallpaper and a royal blue comforter on a daybed. It gave the trailer a cozy, even retro aura, and Kat slept better than she had in weeks.

The smell of breakfast from the diner had woken Kat, and she'd had a way-too-fattening and uncommon meal of pancakes and scrambled eggs. Not a yogurt in sight. She felt almost fortified enough to stand up to Rafe this morning.

As if on cue, Rafe emerged from the house and came onto the porch. No wheelchair or sling. He leaned against one of the posts, squinting into the sunlight. Although neatly dressed in a pair of jeans, one boot, and a red shirt, his hair looked as if he'd just rolled out of bed. Or as if he might be getting ready for a photo shoot. Especially the way he tapped his straw hat against his good leg.

She wanted to scream, *Get over yourself.* But his ego or longing for the limelight contributed at least in part to why her plan would work. The negative, of course, being his ever-so-sweet demeanor.

Kat straightened her hat, digging deep for a smile. "Hi," she said, approaching him. "How are you feeling this morning?"

"Like I got hit by a bull. You?"

"Like I spent the morning at a day spa. Refreshed, relaxed, and ready to learn about life on a ranch." She sweetened her smile.

He rolled his eyes. "Well, the first thing is—look out for manure. If you want, I can package some up for you for that spa."

"That won't be necessary, thanks." Clearly, Rafe's opinion of her hadn't changed overnight. "I know you don't like me—"

"That's putting it mildly."

"Listen, I can tell you why it's important—"

"And if you'd just listen to me—I don't have any money. So, you can go home."

So much for that bright and sunny day. Or changing Rafe's heart.

But as she stared at him, at the way he shoved his hand into his pocket and looked away from her, she knew—just knew—that he was trying too hard to be a jerk. *Please, please let my instincts be right.* "I'm not here for your money."

He looked at her.

"Well, I mean, I am here for your money, but it's for a good cause.

A great cause. There's this organization called Mercy Doctors that helps provide treatment to underprivileged kids–"

"There are a billion worthy causes out there. Why would I give a dime to yours?"

Kat stood, mouth open. And then, since he had the frightening ability to make her say and do things she'd never imagined, she said, "Because you crashed into my event that was supposed to raise money for said cause? Because there are children who might die because you had a beer or two for breakfast?"

Rafe winced as if she'd slapped him. For a second, she regretted her tone, her raised voice. He closed his eyes, and for the first time, she saw real emotion, even regret on his face. "I'm really sorry about that. I wish I could change it. But I can't."

"You can."

He opened his eyes, gave her a look that she knew had come from honesty. "I really don't have any money."

Kat nodded, rubbing her hands on her arms. She was wearing a short-sleeve pink T-shirt with *Cowgirl* spelled out in rhinestones as well as her red boots and a hat. Already, the sun kissed her pale skin. "That's what I'm trying to tell you. I don't necessarily want your money."

Rafe eyed her as if she might be an old-time snake-oil salesman and eased himself down to sit on the steps. He balanced his hat on his good knee. "I'm listening."

"First . . . do you run a real ranch or is it just for show?"

He shook his head. "You sure know how to make friends."

What was wrong with her question? She inched closer and saw that despite his growl, curiosity ringed his eyes. And he had gorgeous dark molasses eyes with long lashes. . . . *Honestly, get a grip.* "I was wondering because my plan includes cattle."

"What plan?"

"I don't want to tell you until I know if it will work. So . . . how many cows?"

"More than three thousand head."

"Is that a lot?"

"Depends on your point of view. The Lock-T out of Billings has nearly a hundred thousand and their own private city. We're sort of a one-family operation."

Kat sat next to him but not too close. "You ever taught anyone how to ride?"

"Hmm. You have anyone in mind?" Rafe flashed her a smile. "Sweet thing?"

"Stop. Really."

He gave her a long look, something he probably used on his female fans to make them swoon. "I'm not sure what to call you then. Annoying? Stubborn?"

She would hardly wobble under the smoldering looks of Rafe. Even if he did have a nice smile. But it wasn't like she was going to fall for him. She had Bradley, a man every inch as gorgeous as Rafe, not to mention his more substantial qualities, like patience, faithfulness, and a sense of responsibility. "How about Katherine?" she said, hating the hitch in her voice.

Rafe gave her another long look. "How 'bout Kitty?"

"Kat?"

"Kitty'll do." Rafe stuck out his hand and grasped hers.

She felt the calluses from his bull rope, the strength of his hold. Katherine might have melted under the pressure of his dark gaze, but *Kitty* only smiled. "Glad to meet you, Rafe Noble."

"I guess if I'm going to hear about this plan—and I'm not saying

I'm agreeing—I should show you around the ranch. At least Stefanie will be happy."

After three hours, Kat had learned exactly three things about Rafe. First, he had an enormous tolerance for pain. He refused help, stumbling along the fence line for support, then grinding his teeth for the few steps it took to get to the barn.

Second, Rafe loved animals. He might ride bulls, but he had a soft spot for anything with four legs that didn't have horns. He picked up the barn cats, petting them absently as he told her about their cattle, what the different pens in the barn were used for, the kind of horses they owned. He even told her about his former pets—a sheepdog, a mutt, a lamb, various chickens, and a hamster. The whole time, the cats rubbed themselves against him, purring. Apparently he was used to the attention because he didn't even notice. Purring—from all kinds of creatures—was probably second nature to him.

As the morning grew long, Kat got the sense that he'd morphed into media-tour mode, including turning the charm on overdrive. Clearly, if he couldn't scare her away, he'd sweet-talk her brain into knots. Deflect her from her goals.

Too bad for him, she was one step ahead of him. She put on her best smile and listened. After all, listening led to trust. Which would lead to him agreeing to her brilliant idea.

His demeanor led to the third thing she learned about Rafe: he oozed charisma. She noticed it in everything from the tease in his voice to the twinkle in his eyes. This made Rafe not only a bull rider but a star and the perfect candidate for his new job as a Breckenridge fund-raiser.

"Hungry? I think my sister-in-law's cooking lunch." Rafe leaned against the corral, arms propped on the rails, the wind in his hair. He'd shaved this morning, and his cologne, mingled with the scent of hay, gave him a real cowboy aura. Another weapon in his knock-'em-dead arsenal.

Oh, this plan of hers could work. It could *really* work.

"A little. I ate this morning at Lolly's. After my lodging fell through, she offered to put me up."

He raised an eyebrow as if waiting for her to continue.

Kat just looked at him.

After a moment Rafe said, "Lolly serves good food. You won't starve."

No. In fact, Kat couldn't believe her providence. Not only finding a place to stay but also someone who knew Bobby Russell. "Thank you for showing me around this morning."

He glanced at her out of the corner of his eye.

"You make a great spokesperson."

"So when do I hear about Kitty's 'great plan to redeem the world'?"

Kat laughed despite herself. "Patience, cowboy."

Rafe looked at her, and for a second, he smiled. A real smile that went all the way to his eyes. As if he might be enjoying himself just a little.

Perfect.

⚬⚬⚬

Lolly had to find that picture. She closed the drapes, darkening her trailer. Somewhere, probably in the last place she'd look but the first place Kat would notice, she'd put a copy of that picture of a five-year-old girl in little red boots, taken with her daddy. The one Aunt Laura had sent to Kat after her daddy died.

Lolly cupped her hand over her eyes, exhausted. She hadn't realized how bringing out the old stories would surface her own memories of Bobby's laughter, his raucous spirit. The way he'd been her hero time and again. She'd hardly slept last night, remembering the day he'd shown up in Sheridan with Felicia and a solution to her darkest nightmare.

She shouldn't blame Felicia for what she'd done to Kat. She'd defied her father in marrying Bobby, and as a widow with a child, Felicia couldn't take care of herself. She'd run from her pain and started over.

In some ways, Lolly had done exactly the same thing.

But if she didn't find that picture—and destroy it—everything she and Felicia had sacrificed might be for naught.

She'd emptied out her bookshelf and found nothing wedged in the pages of the ancient, yellowing romance novels she'd read long, long ago when she still had idealistic dreams. When she thought she and John might have a life together.

Good thing she quit reading.

Then Lolly had searched under the daybed—in the photo albums she kept hidden in Kat's room. She found nothing but grainy black and whites of her childhood and a few formal shots of Katherine over the years.

Finally, she shoved everything back under the bed—this time way, way back—and searched through her knickknacks, photos of her and John, a newspaper clipping of Lolly's Diner right after it opened. She stopped, amazed at how young she looked. She had been about twenty-three.

She was looking through a stack of postcards when a knock came at the door.

"Hello? Lolly?"

She shoved the postcards into a big manila envelope and kicked them under the sofa. "Come in."

Kat came in, looking sun kissed and happy, and flopped on the sofa.

Lolly tried not to cringe. Kat grew up in luxury, with servants and designer clothes, gourmet food. To see her sitting on the fraying green sofa Lolly had purchased for twenty bucks at a garage sale nearly two decades ago . . .

In fact, the entire trailer seemed like a dump, from the paneled walls with fake vines over the windows and the orange Formica in the kitchen to the green shag carpeting and the rusty fixtures in the bathroom. The place even smelled . . . old. Lolly wanted to crawl under her two-tiered plastic planter and hide.

The fact that she'd decorated Kat's room, well, for *Kat*, all those years ago felt ironic at best. Pitiful at worst. Only Kat's good breeding must be keeping her from running from the trailer screaming. She clearly had some acting ability because she looked comfortable, even content, as she kicked off her boots and curled up on the sofa, drawing an orange crocheted pillow onto her lap.

Lolly sat opposite her on an old La-Z-Boy. "How was your day?"

"It was a good day. Very good." She wore a dreamy expression. "Did you know the Silver Buckle is nearly a hundred-years-old? The Nobles' great-grandfather homesteaded it—it's been passed down through the family. It's huge too—eighty thousand acres. It even has petrified rocks and an ancient Indian burial ground. Rafe is going to take me to see them."

The way she said Rafe's name had all of Lolly's instincts rising. "Rafe was nice?" *Please, no!* Because a nice Rafe meant a scoundrel Rafe. Which would lead to a brokenhearted Kat and a very, *very* angry Lolly.

"The perfect gentleman." Kat drew her knees to her chest, and her smile dimmed. "But he was just putting on an act. I wasn't fooled for a second, and most of all, I'm not impressed. Rafe is still trouble—trouble wrapped up in a lot of charm. And I'm going to corral it and use it for good, despite his best efforts to stop me."

A streak of relief went through Lolly.

Kat ran her fingers through her hair. "I felt bad for him, though. He was in lots of pain but wouldn't admit it."

"He's a cowboy; they never admit they're in pain." Lolly had John to prove that. He'd never admitted how she'd broken his heart, but she saw it in his eyes and it grieved her. Sometimes she wished they could just move away, start over. But she'd already done that once. She wasn't going to do it again.

"I think he's starting to like me. Which means he'll agree to help me raise money for my foundation."

"I've never met anyone quite as . . . optimistic as you, Kat." Lolly meant it in a kind way.

But Kat's smile dimmed. "My friend Cari says I like to see the best in every situation to the extent that I don't really see reality. Yes, I want to get Rafe to help me, but a part of me wants to find a way under that steely exterior, get him to see that there's more to his life than moping around his ranch."

Did Kat think she could somehow heal the hurts that Rafe Noble had been nursing his entire life? "Kat, I don't think–"

"He calls me Kitty." She smiled. "No one has ever called me Kitty before."

That's not true, Lolly started to say but held her tongue. "Be careful. Rafe's got charm, but under all that sweet talk and glitter is a man who's broken many hearts."

Kat looked over at her and laughed. "Oh, I'm not going to fall for him. Rafe is just a means to an end. He's nothing more than a cowboy with a million-dollar smile to me." She swung her legs off the sofa, stood up, and stretched. "Trust me, I'm going to get every dollar I can out of that smile."

Rafe knew what Kitty's great plan was–to drive him crazy. He had tried his best to wipe that hopeful grin from her face. He'd tried to bore her to tears with the history of the ranch. Distract her with mindless facts about beef cattle. Even see if he could scare her by putting her next to big animals like a horse.

She acted like she'd been adopted and raised by Gulliver's Houyhnhnms.

Nope, evidently Kitty had every intention of sticking around to drive him insane with mindless questions about the ranch until she deigned to reveal her plan, which probably entailed him writing a check with five zeros.

Rafe knew her type–fund-raisers were all the same. They'd act like they're your friend and then hit you low when you weren't looking with some heartrending story about misery in Somalia.

He was on to her. And if by tomorrow–okay, yes, he'd invited her back to the newly created Silver Buckle Ranch for Tourists—she didn't start talking, then . . . then . . .

What?

A smart, honest man would admit he'd enjoyed the day. Once they got past the snarling part. Even if she'd made him bleed with that comment about the accident.

Rafe should at least listen to her bright idea—and not just because he'd enjoyed her company. Maybe it was her smile or the way she listened to his stories about the ranch without filling in the gaps. How she didn't reach out to baby him, even though, much to his chagrin, he'd grunted in pain right in front of her. Tomorrow he'd dig out his old crutches from high school.

In fact, she didn't gush much at all. No fawning, no, "Oh, Rafe, you're just so brave. I'm so scared every time you get on a bull." There was just a quietness about her that had caught him off guard and made him smile.

Kitty didn't ask him once about the sport. She talked about life on the Silver Buckle. A life he'd forgotten or, rather, pushed from his mind.

As he showed her around the place, reminding himself of the things he'd learned, he'd felt the knot of despair in his gut begin to uncoil. As if, for a little while, he could forget the mess he'd made of his life.

"What was your favorite part about growing up on the ranch?" she'd asked as she fed the horses alfalfa snacks.

Instead of mentioning the days he spent with his nose pushed up against the window watching his dad and Nick ride out together or helping his mother tend the kitchen garden or sorting the cattle while Nick herded them into the corral, Rafe said, "I love winter, watching the wind swirl up over the drifts. The smell of summer alfalfa, my mother's canned peaches. I love Sunday afternoons playing Parcheesi."

"I play Parcheesi," she'd said quietly, giving him a smile that made the entire day seem way too short.

Yes, he could think of worse ways to earn his keep than to spend all day in the company of a beautiful woman.

And she *was* beautiful, in a simple, not-trying way. Kitty wasn't bone skinny like so many of the women he knew; she had curves. The silly cowgirl outfit worked for her, especially with her easy smile and the twinkle in her pretty eyes. Her full and expressive lips intrigued him, and he found himself wondering . . . and then reminding himself that she was trying to take him for all he had.

Oh yeah, they had the makings of a real friendship.

Still, being with Kitty Breckenridge put him in such a decent, noncombative mood that when he joined Nick, Piper, and Stefanie for supper, he managed to have a real conversation about ranching and the stock market without throwing a jab even once.

As he went to bed, laying an ice pack on his aching shoulder and another on his knee, he felt better than he had in months.

He couldn't wait until tomorrow.

CHAPTER 7

"HAVE YOU EVER ridden a horse?" Rafe couldn't believe Kitty had talked him into saddling up a mare, but she could be persuasive. She had this way of making him think he'd thought of the idea when all along he knew she had come to this party with an agenda.

Her tenaciousness rivaled his own, something he hadn't counted on. Or perhaps something he had *begun* to count on over the last couple of days. Frankly, he'd stopped asking. Mostly because he had simply begun to enjoy her company. And the distraction from his current list of problems.

He'd spent yesterday picking wildflowers, watching prairie dogs and meadowlarks, showing her the new calves, demonstrating how to feed the orphans, and generally listening to himself talk about ranch life in a way he hadn't known he even remembered. Today, however, he'd lost the battle of talking her into exploring Silver Buckle land from the inside of his truck.

Kitty had simply turned a deaf ear to this coaxing and instead hung around the corral, holding out treats to the horses, all the while saying,

"What's your favorite horse, Rafe?" and "How old were you when you started riding?" and "Did you ever ride a bronc in the rodeo?"

Someone should shoot him, because he found himself answering her.

He finally chose the most docile mare in the corral and let Kitty stroke her velvety nose and run her hands down her neck. She just smiled at him, and good grief if he didn't find himself going out to the barn, picking up a saddle, and balancing on one leg as he threw the blanket and saddle over the mare and tightened the cinch. The mare barely moved as Rafe explained to Kitty how to mount her.

Then, to his shock, Kitty put her foot in the stirrup and swung up. She looked so natural sitting there that for a second he couldn't think of anything to say.

She answered his question about her previous riding experience with a cryptic, "Nothing that actually breathed."

Hmm. He whistled to his old roan, and the horse trotted over, letting Rafe halter him. Pulling the animal close, he mounted the rail, leaned over him, and threw his bad leg over the bareback animal. He grabbed the mane and scooted up, the familiarity of being on a horse oddly healing.

"We'll start with a walk. Just urge her forward. She's a smart horse; she'll respond to you." He gave his own horse a nudge, and the roan trotted out. Without the leverage of both his legs guiding the animal, Rafe knew he'd be in trouble, so he slowed the animal to a walk.

Kitty followed. "This is kind of fun."

Of course it was. To her, picking wildflowers and throwing bread crumbs to prairie rats was the president's ball. She even stuck a handful of pink roses in her hair.

But he had to admit that sitting in the sunshine, watching an antelope and her fawn graze had made him feel the breath in his lungs for the first time in . . . well, since he was six, waiting for the hole in his heart to heal.

If he didn't watch out, he may just have the same problem in the future.

They rode down the road to the gate. Kitty reined her horse, got down, and opened it. She waited as Rafe urged his horse through, leading hers, then closed the gate behind him.

"Always leave a gate how you found it." She remounted. "I read that in a book."

He found himself smiling. Again. He probably smiled too much lately. They walked the horses through the hay field, and he pointed out the bulls grazing in the field above the house.

"Do you read a lot?" Rafe asked.

"Yes. Mostly . . . Westerns."

He glanced over at her and saw her face redden slightly. Cute.

"Do you read?"

"Sometimes." Until recently, he hadn't read a book in a year or two. "Why do you like Westerns?"

"The heroes are always chivalrous, always fighting for the women they love."

"I don't think real life is like that. If a woman doesn't want me, I'm not going to go charging bullheaded into her life, trying to change her mind." Then again, he couldn't remember the last time he'd had to do more than wink at a woman to get a date. Maybe he'd keep that tidbit to himself.

Kitty wore an inscrutable expression. "Why not?"

"If she doesn't show me she wants me, then apparently I'm not worth her time."

"Maybe she just . . . wants you to put some effort into it."

Rafe harrumphed.

"Don't you think that a man should fight for the woman he loves?"

"A woman should give a guy the benefit of the doubt. Even if he doesn't say it, he still cares about her."

A soft smile creased her lips.

Rafe spurred his horse out ahead. She made him say the stupidest things.

"You sure you never rode a horse before?" he asked as they crossed into another field. Cows lounged on the table, content, well fed. The smell of silver sage spiced the languid breeze.

She laughed. "I used to go down to the carousel in Central Park and I'd ride the horses, pretending they were my own herd."

"I'll bet you had a horse named Shadow or Beauty or Princess."

"Hornet. Fastest stallion in the West."

"Of course."

Kitty nodded. "Actually, my dad was a cowboy. But he died when I was young, and my mother traveled a lot, so I grew up in the care of my grandfather. Or rather, my grandfather's money. Mostly I stayed in various boarding schools. The closest thing I got to ranch living were postcards from my aunt Laura, pictures from *National Geographic*, and the carousel."

"Sorry about your dad. That must have been tough."

She gave him a kind smile. "Thanks. Probably the mystique of his life only fueled my desire to learn to ride and rope. It made me wonder how much cowboy I had in me."

He let his gaze run over her. She occasionally took her hat off and fanned away the gnats gathering about her face. He noticed a few bites on her arms and the tan line on her fair skin where her sleeve cut across her arm. A smattering of freckles over her nose had appeared over the past few days, and she smelled good, a fresh scent that tangled his thoughts and left him thinking of her long after she'd gone for the day.

"I think you have plenty of cowboy in you, Kitty."

Her smile vanished, and she swallowed, averting her eyes.

He felt it too—something that pulsed between them. "So, tell me about this organization—the one I owe half a mil to."

She looked over at him, and for once he didn't see accusation in her eyes. "It's called Mercy Doctors—well, actually, that's the organization we support. You owe money to the Breckenridge Foundation, an organization founded by my mother. We're the sole funding agency for a Mercy Doctors hospital in Guadalajara, Mexico."

"Are you a doctor?"

Kitty wrinkled her nose at him, gathering up all those freckles. "No. I just help doctors. I have a very helpful degree in English, which completely qualifies me to run a million-dollar organization." She shook her head. "Lately, I haven't been very good at my job."

"I doubt that. From where I sit, you're pretty good at talking people into doing things." Rafe expected a smile but didn't get it.

"I wish. I love helping people, but for all my hard work, it seems like I'm not making a difference. It's not enough." Kitty twirled the reins between her fingers. "I just wish I could do one amazing thing that would . . . I don't know, make me feel like . . ." She shrugged.

He could finish her sentence for her. Like her life mattered? That there might be a reason she—or he—was here on earth?

"Do you ever feel that way? Wanting to do something amazing? be someone special?"

Only all his life. "I used to. But it's too late for me."

"It's never too late to do the right thing."

Apparently she didn't live in his eight-second world of life-ending bull wrecks. He slowed his horse to walk beside hers. "Wanna tell me your brilliant plan yet?"

Kitty smiled at him. "Do you come out here a lot? It seems like the perfect place to leave your hectic life behind."

"I haven't really been back since I left home to rodeo. Mostly it's been pit stops since then."

She reached out and patted her horse's neck. "How am I doing?"

His mind blanked out, and he just stared at her.

Kitty raised an eyebrow. "Riding lessons?"

"Oh. I think you have walking down. Maybe we should try a trot if you're ready."

"I'm ready." She grinned. "You're a good teacher. Just like I hoped."

Everything inside Rafe went very, very still. Was she . . . flirting with him? He'd had women flirt with him before, but this was different, sweet even. He'd forgotten what it felt like to have a normal conversation with a woman who didn't have bull-riding stars in her eyes. Until three days ago.

Yes, Kitty most definitely had flirted, because her face reddened in a way that had nothing to do with the sun.

Rafe looked away. He hadn't felt this flustered with a woman since he'd been eighteen and signing his first autographs. "Thanks," he mumbled.

She took a deep breath. "It smells incredible out here. I always dreamed about the smell, but I never imagined it would be so fresh. I can't get enough of it. Thanks for showing me around, giving me a chance to get to know you."

Sure, he could ride a foaming-at-the-mouth bull, but put him next to a nice woman and he wanted to run for the hills.

Rafe urged his roan past her, unsure what to do. When he looked back, she smiled at him, and a cold sweat prickled on his neck.

He'd known her only four days. No one could change a person's world in that short a time, regardless of how beautiful and positive and easygoing. What's more, he wasn't the kind of man who fell in love. Infatuation, yes. But not the kind of love that makes a man do stupid things. Like ride bareback through a field of wildflowers with a busted-up knee.

Oh, brother.

His world had been shaken; that's all. Kitty and her mystery plan served as a very healing distraction from his miserable life. Which was exactly why his heart suddenly double-timed in his chest. He swallowed away the tinny taste and angled their path toward another gate, not exactly sure where to lead her next.

Kitty opened and closed the gate again without asking. When she remounted, she said, "You mentioned something about ancient burial grounds."

The ancient burial grounds. Yes, yes! He forced his voice to idle. "Yeah, right. They're over this knoll."

"I read that this area isn't too far from where Custer had his last stand."

The late afternoon sun hung low in the sky, right over the

Bighorns, pushing through the pine trees, between shadows. He pointed west. "Custer National Forest is off in that direction. And beyond that is where the Battle of Little Bighorn took place."

"I've never been there." The wind knocked her hat back on her head.

"I have. I can hear the ghosts sometimes. It's a somber, very . . . dark place."

She turned to him. "Do you have any ghostly places here? any battles that took place on Noble land?"

Rafe gave a wry chuckle. "You don't know the half of it." He instantly regretted his words. Some territories weren't open to exploration, and he meant to keep it that way. He clicked to his roan, rode down the ridge.

Kitty said nothing as she followed. The shadows deepened as they rode into the gully, and nothing passed between them but the sounds of a meadowlark and the horses' hooves on rocks.

He led her up a hill to a small grove of pine trees. "When we were kids, we'd find arrowheads and other Blackfoot artifacts here."

She dismounted and handed Rafe the reins, then began walking slowly, hunched over.

"What are you doing?"

Kitty looked at him, and the sun caught the twinkle in her eyes. "Finding an arrowhead, of course."

Of course. Because ancient relics concealed by time and weather could be easily dug up. "This spot has been picked clean of any old memories."

He heard whistles and saw below them a small herd of cattle moving slowly in the direction of Cole's land. Nick and Cole came into view, followed by CJ, on drag. Poor kid. After Bishop had finally let Rafe ride with him, Rafe had spent plenty of time behind the herd, eating cattle dust.

Rafe lifted a hand. Cole waved back.

Nick, however, broke away from them and trotted up the knoll.

"Hey," Kitty said to Nick as he came close.

He tugged on the brim of his hat. "Ma'am." Then he turned to Rafe. "What are you doing out here?" He looked pointedly at his braced leg. "I thought you were supposed to stay off that."

Rafe felt about six-years-old, lying in the dirt while his brother laughed at him. "Unless you're blind, I'm off it."

Nick lowered his voice. "I can appreciate what you're doing here. But don't wear yourself out."

"Yes, sir," Rafe snapped.

They stared at each other for a long time until Nick turned his horse and trotted back down the hill.

Kitty stood there, petting her horse's nose. "He seems worried about you."

"He's not worried. Just bossy. He doesn't like the fact that I might have a life off this ranch." In the settling silence Rafe heard his anger. Old battles indeed.

She ran the reins through her fingers. "Why did you start bull riding?"

Her question caught him off guard, and at first, he didn't answer, just let the smells and colors of the approaching dusk fill the silence. But maybe because it had taken her so long to ask, he found an answer.

"First time I rode a bull, I was eight. I made Stef rope a steer and fastened a bull rope around his chest and hopped on. Landed in the dirt in about point-six seconds. In that blink of time, I felt . . . strong."

Kitty met his eyes, her face solemn. "Like a cowboy."

More like a man. But he nodded.

"So are you going back to bull riding?"

"No. I'm done." The words, said aloud instead of rolling around his chest, bit at him. The sooner he accepted it, the better. His bull-riding days—his *life*—were over.

"Because you're hurt?"

Rafe guessed that was one way to look at it. He certainly hadn't been responsible with his successes, and deep down, he wondered if he simply didn't deserve to do what he loved anymore. Maybe this was God's way of punishing him, of reminding him he was truly just a runt. "Doc says that if I ride I could get . . . well, it's not *if* I get hurt, it's *when.* And how bad." He turned his gaze on Nick, Cole, and CJ as they herded the cattle from view.

"You going to help run the Silver Buckle?"

And spend his days following in Nick's shadow? "No, I don't think there's room here for me."

Kitty resumed her search for arrowheads. "Seems like a pretty big place. A place to find peace, even some grace. Maybe heal you enough to start over, do something with your life that makes a difference."

He took a breath. "Even all this can get crowded. The land might look peaceful, but the winter storms rattle you down to the inside." The honesty in his own words surprised him. Then again, Kitty was unlike any woman he'd ever met. "Most of all, the Buckle isn't mine. Never was. My dad brought up Nick to run it, and I just . . . don't fit."

She bent over and dug into the soil with her finger. "Is that why you left? Because Nick was in charge?"

Rafe watched as Cole and Nick disappeared into a draw. The shadows seemed longer now; the sun a ball of fire, dying as twilight stretched out overhead.

"Nick wasn't even around when I left." He patted his horse's neck. "Actually, I left because–" he wasn't sure why, but he suddenly *wanted* to tell her–"my mother died, and the place felt so . . ." *Ghostly.*

She stood, a sad look on her face. "Quiet?"

He lifted one side of his mouth. "Maybe. Or maybe I didn't have a reason to stay anymore. I needed to find my own way. And I was good at bull riding."

"It gave you the room you needed to make your own name."

Rafe glanced at her, startled by her words. They made it worth the risk he'd just taken. "I guess I wanted to live up to the name I had."

He saw her ponder his words. "Yeah, I know what you mean."

He frowned, ready to ask her what she meant.

"Hey, I found one!" Kitty pried up a small, flat, chipped stone. "It's not perfect, but I think it's a real arrowhead." She handed it to him.

He took it and ran his thumb over it, then met her gaze. Fear coursed through him when he saw a gentleness in her eyes that made him feel like he'd gotten thrown from a bull–disoriented and undone.

"See, I told you I'd find one. You never know what treasures you might find if you look hard enough."

The sun had come down enough to fill the gullies and bring out the gold in her eyes, and for a second he was caught right there, unable to breathe when she looked at him like that.

Yeah, treasures.

Lolly didn't need an episode of *Dr. Phil* to spot the signs of infatuation in the way Kat arrived home, glowing and buoyant. Lolly would have liked to wrap both her hands around Rafe's neck and squeeze.

When Kat came out of the bathroom, she looked so young standing there in the hallway that Lolly had a hard time remembering she was twenty-five and old enough to fall in love and have her heart broken by a reckless, bent-for-destruction cowboy.

Just like her mother.

"I don't suppose anyone answered my ad for Laura Russell yet, did they?"

Kat had put up an ad on the diner bulletin board: *Searching for any information pertaining to the whereabouts of Laura Russell. Please leave message with Lolly Stuart.* Lolly had to stare at it every hour of the day.

Laura had vanished twenty-some years ago, hadn't been heard from since. And she wasn't going to reappear, if Lolly had anything to say about it.

"Sorry, kiddo. Nope."

"Oh, well." Kat stretched her arms over her head. "It's funny. I'm so tired, but I've got energy like I haven't felt for months. I guess it's getting away from the stress back home, but it's as if I've been freed from a cocoon."

Lolly looked at Kat's tanned cheeks, her wavy hair hanging in carefree tangles. Yes, maybe she did look as if she'd metamorphosed from the pale, upset, one-nerve-shy-of-unraveling woman who'd appeared in her diner to strong and healthy.

"I can't remember the last time I didn't go to bed with a head-ache nagging in the back of my head."

"That's the Big Sky for you. Takes away the knots," Lolly said, remembering her own knots. "How goes your big project?"

Kat smiled. "I've got Rafe champing at the bit. I knew if I let him get to know me, know that I'm not an impulsive, desperate woman, he'd listen. And it always helps to have an aura of mystery. I'm going to spring it on him tomorrow." She stood up. "Good night, Lolly."

Lolly stretched out on the sofa as Kat disappeared into the bed-room, then grunted at a bump between the cushions. She reached for it and shook her head. That stupid book. She'd seen it at the diner, but how had it migrated to her sofa?

She snuggled into the pillows, opening the book to a random page. Two lines. She'd give it two lines, and if it didn't hook her by then . . .

Mary knew that someday Jonas would have enough. That he'd escape the ranch and find his own way in the world. She just hoped—falsely, it appeared—that he'd take her with him.

She loved him more than the very breath in her body. From sunup to sundown, she lived for their snatches of conversation, the moment when he'd look up from his work and smile at her, his blue eyes warming, humming a new song, one that told her more than she'd ever dreamed.

For the times you've heard that you were nothing,
For all the wounds that you thought God couldn't see,

*For all the ways I've tried to tell you that you can count
  on me,
Please believe you're worth the love you see.*

Jonas had never actually said he'd written the song for her, but she knew it. She saw it in the small gestures, like the way he swept her kitchen and brought in the eggs. In the carved horse he'd made for Rosie and the flowers he left on the sill.

Thankfully, Matthias hadn't noticed. He never noticed anything but if she served his breakfast late or went to bed without him, even if he was passed out on the sofa. He didn't notice the clean house—an impossible task—or his clean spittoon. Didn't notice how Rosie ran from him, hiding herself and her doll. How she no longer cried for her mother in the night.

He also never noticed Mary's plans for escape. How she'd secreted away egg money for years. How she learned to drive. How she'd packed an old carpetbag and hidden it in the barn, waiting. Waiting for *this* day, when he was soundly drunk, and she was smarting from the marks he'd left on her arm last night.

Why hadn't she told Jonas of her plan? She'd thought . . . well, *he* noticed everything. He noticed when she hid her face from crying, noticed when Rosie wandered off into the fields. He'd even seen her drive the car into the flower bed that day Matthias went to Sheridan on the train. Certainly Jonas noticed the bag in the barn.

"Mommy?" Rosie said from the kitchen table. "Is Daddy sick?"

It made her ill to hear Rosie speak of Matthias as daddy. Charlie had been her daddy. And she wanted Jonas to be her daddy. "Yes, baby. Shh . . . eat your porridge."

Mary knew that when Matthias drank whiskey, he slept for hours, even more than his gin nights. "Stay here," she said and opened the back door. Perhaps Jonas was sleeping late in the barn.

But when she climbed to the loft, her heart fell. His spot had been cleaned out. She gritted her teeth against a rise of fear. She'd made it this far without him. . . .

Screams from the house made her jerk, and she nearly fell off the ladder. She ran to the house.

Matthias had her little girl by the arm. "She woke me."

"I'm sorry." Mary went to her, but he yanked the five-year-old away.

Rosie hit the doorway like a rag doll and cried out.

"No, Matthias, please!"

"I've had enough of her noise and your blubbering. This time, she's going to learn to obey." He raised his fist.

Mary leaped at him with a cry she didn't realize she had in her.

Surprised, Matthias whirled, eyes wide. He backhanded her and she hit the table. He turned back to Rosie, struggling against his grip, her tiny fingers raking to free herself.

"No!" Mary shouted.

Matthias made a fist and swung.

She didn't hear the screen door squeal. And she felt, more than heard, the anger as Jonas roared. He launched himself at Matthias. They went down with a house-shaking thud.

Mary ripped Rosie from Matthias's grasp. She tucked her daughter close to her body, hiding her eyes. Yet Mary watched, horror filling her in small gasps.

Jonas slowly backed away from an unmoving Matthias. He turned to her, breathing hard, saying nothing.

"What . . . ?" She looked at Matthias. His head was tilted at a strange angle. "Oh . . . my . . ."

A beat passed as realization sunk in. A crow cawed from outside. The early morning birds chirruped. But inside Mary, everything turned shadowed and deathly still.

Jonas crouched before her. "Are you okay?"

"Is he . . . is he dead?"

Jonas wet his lips, his breathing uneven. He glanced back at Matthias. "I didn't—"

Mary put a hand over his mouth. "That's right. You didn't. He fell. Maybe I pushed him. You weren't here."

Jonas touched her wrist, then gently pulled her hand away from his mouth. He put his other hand on Rosie's back. "Mary, no . . . this isn't right."

Something inside her snapped. She could even hear it—the band of control that had kept her from taking a frying pan to Matthias's head. "He tried to kill me over and over, and . . . and . . . he would have succeeded. If not me, then Rosie!"

She began to crumple, and Jonas was right there, taking her into his arms, wrapping her tight in the embrace she'd longed for.

He rocked her, shaking slightly himself. "It's going to be okay, Mary. I promise."

She closed her eyes, holding on to him, needing to believe him now more than ever.

Finally, she blew out an unsteady breath and backed away from him. She turned away from Matthias, from the last five years. "Why didn't I just leave him?"

Jonas framed her face with his hands. "Mary, . . . listen, I was going to ask you today to . . . to come with me. I'm ashamed of myself, but I couldn't watch anymore. I had to do something, and the only thing I could think of was taking you and Rosie away from here." A line of sweat filmed his forehead, trickled down his face. "You're going to call the sheriff and tell him what's happened. I'll turn myself in."

"No!" With the word, something inside Mary shifted. As if dormant, the inklings of her old self—the suffragette she'd been in Chicago, the woman of strength Charlie had met and married—awoke and began to break through the parched soul she'd become. She heard her old voice returning and, with it, her dream of running her own ranch, owning her own land. Creating a life for herself and her child. In fact, her brain conjured up a scenario so quickly that it frightened her. "You're leaving, all right, just like you planned."

"I'm not leaving without you." Jonas took her hand. "I want us to start a new life, away from here and all this desolation and pain. Come with me . . . please?"

Mary stared at him, this man who had saved her life, and felt the tender shoot of hope wither under the hot breeze. "I . . . can't."

He flinched.

Tears filled her eyes, and she pushed his hands away. "If I leave with you, trouble is only going to follow. They'll blame you or me, and we'll never have a life."

"No—"

"I can't marry you, Jonas. And I think you should leave . . . now." Everything inside her wanted to scream, *No! Take me with you!* But running would only lead to suspicion. Maybe even to prison. And to Rosie without a mother. Or worse, Jonas in the electric chair. "Leave, Jonas. Go live your life."

He stood, staring at her with so much hurt on his face that she wanted to howl. "I'll be back for you, Mary. Believe that."

She closed her eyes. And she held on to his words with all her strength.

Lolly closed the book, angry that she'd let herself get hooked this far into the story. The clock read 3 a.m., and she wanted to read more. But her eyes felt gritty, her body buzzing with exhaustion.

She could kill that B. J. King for evoking in her the exact emotions she'd been trying for twenty-plus years to escape. Helplessness. Fear. A misplaced guilt. It was as if he—or she, the author's gender wasn't listed—had crawled inside her heart and knew her story.

Once upon a time, she'd had a dream. Like Mary, she'd been sidetracked by a man. She hadn't dreamed of ranching, however—far from it. Her dreams had bright lights and fame attached to them. They even had a name: Hollywood.

The thought of her back then, idealistic, packing her bags for California, made Lolly nearly nauseated. The closest she'd ever come to Hollywood was her collection of movies stacked under her DVD player. Movies with heroes like Jonas.

In her wildest dreams such a hero walked into her life. Loved her enough to rescue her from her dreary world.

She hadn't harbored those kinds of dreams for a long time. Nowadays, she simply hoped to live out her life in Phillips and keep Bobby's daughter from falling in love with a man who could derail her life.

Lolly set the book on the coffee table, turned out the light, and tiptoed to bed. She watched the darkness pass into light, afraid to sleep, sure that the nightmares would come . . . and with them, the memories.

CHAPTER 8

"WHERE ARE WE GOING?" Not that Kat really cared. She raised her face to the sun as she followed Rafe across the open field. In the distance, a bull bellowed what sounded like a painful moan. The first time she heard it she'd nearly screamed.

Rafe had laughed, a low, rumbly chuckle that sounded real. It gave worth to the three days she'd spent trying to pry the image of the broken, smelly cowboy at the Breckenridge Hotel from her mind, in hopes of seeing the man behind the magazine cover.

The man who had begun to trust her.

Today she'd even brought along the pictures of her trip to the clinic, just in case he didn't believe her, and a well-thought-out game plan.

If he didn't bite, she'd hang up her hat as Kitty—how she'd grown to like that name—return to New York, then begin plan B or perhaps C, which she'd figure out on the way home.

"I want to show you something," Rafe said.

Rafe looked devastatingly charming today in a black GetRowdy

T-shirt with a bull on the front, his ratty straw hat, a pair of jeans, and chaps that ended above his knees. He'd called them chinks. It wasn't lost on her that he'd dumped the neck brace and discarded the crutches in some manly attempt to act less incapacitated. She hoped he'd be in shape in plenty of time to help her make enough money to save lives.

Lord, please help me find the right time, the right place today....

"What field are we on?" Kat asked.

"Lizzy's field. We keep the bulls here during the summer."

"Who's Lizzy?"

He didn't look at her when he answered. "My mother. This land belonged to her family."

She watched his jaw, now covered with a few days' dark whisker growth, tighten. Something inside her chest tightened too.

Three days and everything about Montana had seeped into her soul, starting with this beautiful land. She could name the flowers that colored the fields—the pink prairie roses, the purple pasque-flowers, yellow bells, and blue flax. The wild blue irises and white yarrow that Rafe said could be turned into herbal medicine. She even found beauty in the cactus, the prickly pear that grew close to the ground, wide and dangerous yet beautiful with its yellow blossoms. In the air, she smelled the bite of the black sage and the fresh alfalfa growing in the far-off field.

She knew that a contented cow lay upon the ground, swishing her tail, and an agitated, unhappy cow wandered, bellowing. And that if a cow and calf were separated, they'd return to the last place they nursed to find each other.

"I think you have plenty of cowboy in you," Rafe had said. That had found all her vulnerable places. Today she believed it too.

Her trek out west had been a good idea—even if Rafe turned her down. She wished she could figure out how to bottle this healing magic and sell it back home for the good of Mercy Doctors.

Rafe urged his horse to a trot, then a canter, and Kat followed, liking how she eased into the motion, rode with the animal. A thousand times better than Hornet. The thought made her smile.

Rafe glanced back now and again, and once his lips twitched, as if hiding a grin.

They slowed, riding along a trickle of stream, then up a grassy hill covered with tall grasses, a stripped and whitened fallen tree, a tumble of rock. To their left, a grove of fragrant overgrown trees—not pine but something else she couldn't place—caught the breeze and the dark green heart-shaped leaves shimmering in the sun.

Rafe reined his horse, climbed down, and dropped the reins over one of the branches. Kat watched as he stripped a sprig of leaves from the tree. The fragrance smelled at once strong, earthy, and fresh. He handed it to her.

Kat took the sprig. "What is it?"

He smiled, and with him looking up at her like that with those dark eyes, a sweetness filled her. "Balm of Gilead."

"Like in the Bible? The stuff renowned for healing?"

"It's not exactly the same stuff as in the Bible but our American version. Native Americans have been using it for years. Only thing is, it's not native to Montana. We're not sure where it came from. My mother used to come out here to Gilly's Bluff, strip off the leaf buds, and use them to make a paste. She called it Gilly salve and used it like an antibiotic ointment and sometimes on burns."

Rafe stripped off another sprig, smelled the buds. "She even made this black paste with it, hoping it would cure her cancer. Heard of this fellow up in Miles City who ingested it, and his stomach cancer was cured." He shook his head. "Funny thing is, the paste hurts. But the longer you leave it on, the better it works. Gets down to the bottom of the wound, to the infection and takes it out from the roots. When it's over, you're healed. Or supposed to be."

Kat watched him as he talked, the way he took a leaf in his hands, rubbing the furry underside with his thumb.

"Obviously, it didn't work for her," he said softly. "But she loved the smell. Cut these sprigs and put them all over our house. When I was little, she used to rub Gilly salve on my chest, and I'd go to sleep with that smell in my nose, thinking of her smile."

Kat got down from her horse.

"The stuff probably didn't work at all. It was just . . . the love she put into it that made it powerful," he said.

Kat stood behind him. "Reminds me of the mud Jesus used when He put it on the blind man's eyes. The mud wasn't the healer—Jesus was." She touched Rafe's arm.

Rafe didn't pull away, but he didn't look at her either. "I was thirteen when she died."

Kat said nothing, just closed her eyes.

"I like these trees," he said.

She let herself simply breathe for a moment. "Me too."

The wind found them and caught up the fragrance of the Gilead, mixing it with Rafe's leather and hours-in-the-sun scent, the lilac soap she'd used this morning, and the sage and yarrow.

"May God's grace and peace go with you," she murmured.

Rafe tensed. "What?"

Kat startled, opening her eyes. "Oh, it's something someone said to me as I left. Grace and peace. Sort of a blessing, I guess."

He frowned at her, then looked at the branch. "Yeah."

She stepped away from him and sat on the ground. "I see God here better than I've ever seen Him before. From the colors and delicacy of the flowers to the landscape that can't make up its mind to the sky that seems to stretch from the first gasp of wonder to the next and beyond." She lay back onto the grass, tracing the clouds in the endless ocean of blue. "Yeah, I like this place."

She heard him sit beside her. Silence passed between them, but she didn't feel the need to fill it. She just watched the wind push the clouds across forever.

"My mother said that she loved this land because she knew she was never alone. She could always see the face of God," Rafe said quietly. "She was a believer and spent as much time in church as out, dragging us with her, even if it didn't take."

Kat glanced at him, hearing more in his tone than what his words said. "You can't live out here and not believe in the God who made it."

Rafe stripped off one of the branches and tossed it away. "I believe. Even made a confession of faith, as the preacher put it, during a revival." He stripped off another branch. "But God's not interested in a guy like me."

Kat willed back the sadness that rose in her chest. "That's not true. God has good plans for you." In fact, she knew it, right down to the core of her being.

"You sound like my mother. Before she died, she told me . . ." He threw the entire branch away. "Nothing."

Kat looked over at him. "Obviously it was something. You don't have to tell me, but the thing is, your mother was right. For some of us God asks for big things—give a kidney, forgive a hurt, ride bulls, maybe even raise millions of dollars. And the rest of us are to do the so-called small things, the unglorious things—put supper on the table, rub balm on a child's chest, believe in the good things. It's the same God doing the asking, which makes it all important. The Bible says to work out your salvation with deep reverence and fear, because God is at work in us, to give us the desire to obey Him and the power to please Him. It's no small thing to have the Creator of this big sky at work in your life, on your side, giving your life purpose, regardless of what He calls you to do."

Rafe got up, paced away from her, then turned, pinning her with his eyes. "Not sure my life has a purpose, Kitty."

Everything inside her wanted to tell him how yes, his life could have a purpose. She could even see it—not the polished tuxedo-wearing, wide-shouldered guy but the man hunkered down with the kids treated by Mercy Doctors, telling them a story, encouraging them to fight the good fight. She took a breath, met his gaze, and put it all right there in her eyes. "I'm sure it does. One day at a time, it does."

Rafe stared at her. "It doesn't matter anymore, anyway. I've lived my life my way, and that's the way it's gotta be."

Kat watched as he turned and ran his hands over his horse's neck. She sat up, drew her knees to her chest, aching right down to her toes. If only he could see what she saw—a man who could be so much more than he believed of himself.

"Even when my mother was so weak she could hardly walk, I'd find her on the porch in the morning, watching the sunrise. Said it gave her peace."

"I would have liked your mother," Kat said, surprised at the sudden wetness in the corner of her eye. "My mom, she sorta slipped out of my life right after my dad died. I'm not sure why."

"How old were you?"

"About six."

He crouched, picked up a rock, and tossed it in his hand. The movement seemed so natural, and it hit her that she'd begun to know him. Sense his moods, even his restlessness. For all his lazy wandering around the ranch, answering her inane questions, he had a vibration about him, an ever-present hum that told her he liked a challenge. He'd just gone down for a short count; that's all. She had bigger challenges in store, if he just stuck with her.

"My dad died about a year ago. But our family really crumbled long before—when Mom died. Nick took off for college, and I started rodeoing. Life was never the same."

"I'm sorry," she said.

He lifted a shoulder and threw the rock in a high arc.

"Thanks for being so nice to me, Rafe," she said quietly.

He flashed her a smile. "Anything to get out of writing a big, bouncy check."

Even though she knew he meant it in fun, it made her throat tight because she'd seen a big crack in Rafe's spit and polish. Under his charm and even despite his growls, she'd found a man worth knowing. A man who needed a friend.

She wanted to be that friend so much it scared her.

"Rafe, do you want to hear my bright idea?"

Kat knew she had his attention by the way he sat down beside her.

"I'm listening."

She took a deep breath. "I read about this new pastime in

Hollywood. All these actors and rich people are enamored with the West. It's all the rage for urban cowboys to come out and experience a real-life roundup."

He opened his mouth to speak, but she held up her hand. "Maybe we could invite your bull-riding friends—if they would be willing to come and do an exhibition—and I'll invite my donors. They'll have a real-life dude ranch experience—learning to ride horses, searching for arrowheads, and even taking home a balm of Gilead sprig—whatever it takes. It'll be better than any gala dinner because they'll taste and feel like real cowboys, just like you showed me this week."

Again his mouth opened, but she put her hand on his arm to stop him from interrupting before she got it all out. "All you have to do is say yes. I'll put the whole thing together." She couldn't help but glance in his direction. "Please?"

Rafe sat there, rubbing his fingers over the rim of his hat.

She saw—no, *heard*—him swallow. *Please, Lord, help him see the vision.*

"I'm not so sure I shouldn't just stay in hiding."

She saw embarrassment on his face, and it made her hurt deep inside where she'd begun to care for him. "Listen, we both need good press right now. It's all about spin. Please?"

Rafe tapped his hat on his leg. "I don't know. Let me soak on it for a while. I'm not so sure that bringing New York to Montana is going to work."

Disappointment weighted her chest. She'd wanted him to say it was a great idea. But at least he wasn't running her off his land. "Thank you, Rafe. I can't tell you what it would mean to me, to Mercy Doctors. I promise you'll be glad if you agree."

He smiled, and she noticed something unfamiliar and sweet in his eyes. "If I say yes, will you take back what you said about bull riders being jerks?"

"You remember that?"

He put his hat on and winked.

"I think maybe I could bring myself to do that. But I don't want you to get too confident, cowboy," she teased. "You'd still have to earn your keep to impress me."

His smile dimmed, and she saw a hint of challenge in his expression. "C'mon then. I'll teach you how to gallop."

She needed that, just so she could catch up with her foolish, disobedient heart.

They rode back to the Silver Buckle in spurts of walk, trot, and gallop. Kat lost her hat twice and probably most of her good sense.

"See you tomorrow, Kitty," Rafe said quietly, leaning on the porch rail as Kat waved good-bye.

She pushed the gas pedal of her Jeep to the floor, kicking up dirt. Turning on the radio, she cranked the volume, and a country music song swelled from the speakers. She didn't know the words—something about mud and tires—but she tapped out the rhythm on her steering wheel.

If he saw her, Bradley would probably check her into a clinic for a psychological overhaul.

Odd that she hadn't gotten ahold of him. She'd left a message the first night at Lolly's, conveniently leaving out her current location. She guessed that he'd been busy in meetings, and the time difference between Montana and New York kept her from trying again. It also hadn't helped that she'd forgotten her charger. She'd turned off her phone to save power in case she needed to call home.

Home. Maybe, just maybe, there was some truth to Lolly's

warning about Rafe's charm and his many victims. Because five days after meeting him, Kat was thinking as much about her next excursion with Rafe as her crumbling charitable foundation and even the man she'd left back East.

But that was because Rafe seemed to enjoy her company. He greeted her on the porch each morning as she drove up, watched her leave each afternoon. They were friends. Just friends.

Kat slowed as she came closer to town. The sunset was starting to darken the town, and a piece of pie called to her. That and Lolly, who had become more than a friend to her with her willingness to listen and occasional warnings and stories about Rafe.

However, the stories only made Kat want to know him more, get behind that outlaw smile, speak truth into that parched soul. She attributed that to the Kitty persona, because while she'd been accused of being a Florence Nightingale before, she'd never had an interest in bad boys.

And she didn't have an interest in Rafe. Not really. Besides, she didn't even like arrogant, swaggering guys, did she?

Most of all, she wasn't going to make the same mistakes her mother made. Look how her life had ended up after falling for a bull rider.

Lord, help me be a real friend to Rafe. Yes, I need him, but even more, he needs You. Help me be someone who blesses him, who shows him Your grace, who is a balm of Gilead—the touch of love in his life.

She pulled in to the lot in front of Lolly's Diner and spied John's truck. Again. She couldn't be sure if he came in every night to tell Kat more stories of her father, or if he was there to see Lolly. Even Kat could tell the man was in love with Lolly. Only Lolly didn't give him even a smidgen of encouragement.

If Kat had a man that smitten, that good-looking, that willing to wait for her, well, she'd at least give him a smile.

But she wouldn't dare give him her heart.

⁂

"How are you feeling this morning, Rafe?" Stefanie came out to the porch, holding a cup of coffee. "Waiting for Kat?"

The sun had lifted over the eastern horizon, filling the rolling prairie with rose gold. He could already feel the scorcher the day would be. Birds sang, however, putting a cheery tone into the morning.

But he didn't exactly need a meadowlark's song to feel cheery.

Rafe lifted a shoulder to feign nonchalance.

Stefanie gave him a wry smile. "Admit it—you like spending time with her. And she seems nice."

Oh, she was more than nice. She was . . . refreshing. And annoying the way she lingered in his thoughts. She even dredged up old, once-upon-a-time dreams about a wife and family and living here on the ranch. Ancient, buried desires that still had the power to draw blood when dug up. It didn't help to have to watch Nick and Piper tease each other, then amble up to their home on the hill every night. Maybe there were some people who didn't get to fall in love and grow old with the woman they love. Like Manuel. Like himself.

He could hardly believe he'd taken Kitty to Gilly's Bluff yesterday. He hadn't meant to open up his own wounds, but he found himself saying things around her . . . things he hadn't told anyone else.

"Yep," Rafe answered his sister. "Kitty's real nice."

"What are you two up to today?" Stef said, sitting next to him.

"I'm going to be working with a couple of new horses down at Maggy's; you could bring her over, and we'll show her how we break them."

And help her gather another harebrained idea for her so-called Hollywood dude ranch? But maybe, if done right and if Stef and Nick agreed, the idea could work. And, yes, some people would pay good money—really good money—to see him ride. Only, he didn't ride anymore. But his friends did. . . . He hoped they were still his friends after his recent all-around less-than-friendly behavior.

"Stef, I saw this ad in a magazine—something about the Silver Buckle being a dude ranch for rich people. Do you still think that's a good idea?"

She gave him a long, very strange look. "Oh, thanks for bringing that up. I don't think it's very nice of you and Nick to laugh at my ideas. For a long time I was the only one trying to keep this ranch together, and I was grasping at straws." She threw out her coffee. "You might want to remember that if it weren't for my dude ranch then Piper wouldn't be here, would she?"

"I didn't mean anything by that."

"I think you should focus on how you can help Kat get out of the mess you got her in." Stef stood up and stormed into the house.

"Stef!"

The door banged again, and she came out, jangling her keys. "I think you need to wipe that giddy, teenage, love-struck smile off your face and start facing your responsibilities." She marched down the steps.

What burr did she have under her saddle? "Stef, what did I say?"

"You know, you're not the only one with big dreams, Rafe!" Stefanie got into her pickup, slammed the door, and drove off.

What big dreams did Stef have? He knew his—or had known them until Kitty walked into his life. Maybe his big dreams just looked different suddenly.

And did Stef say *love-struck*? A guy couldn't fall for someone in a week's time, could he? Besides, Kitty just wanted him for her project. Her friendship, his feelings, weren't real.

None of it was real. Not the warmth in Kitty's smile as she drove up and got out of the Jeep, looking like a dream with her long brown hair. Nor the crazy way his heart leaped when she said, "Hey, you going to teach me to rope?" Not her sweet, clean, freshly showered aroma as he coiled the rope and fitted it into her hand, showing her how to hold it.

No, it simply wasn't real, the way she looked at him with those incredible eyes and softly said, "Can you show me?" Nor the sudden desire that rushed into his chest, filled his throat, cut off his breathing as she said, "I think this should definitely be included in the dude ranch list of activities."

As long as none of this was real, then neither were the ramifications of his stepping close behind her, wrapping his arm around her, holding her hand, and showing her how to flick her wrist so the loop twirled around her head. She giggled, and he swallowed hard at how well she fit into his arms. She came to about his nose in height. If she were to turn . . . just a little . . .

Kitty threw the lasso, and the loop landed around one horn. "I caught him, Rafe!"

"Good throw," he said, stepping back and shaking some sense into himself before he got them both into trouble. What was he thinking? They should go watch Stef and Maggy work the horses . . . and he'd stay on the other side of the corral.

"A man's gotta think before he acts, Rafe. Life isn't handed to you on a platter. You have to work for it."

Bishop's voice found him from across time, and Rafe was again sitting in the detention hall as his father picked him up at school. Disheveled, with a trickle of dried blood on his split lip, he knew that the other kid looked a lot worse. Just once, he wished his father might look beyond the troubled kid he saw to the one inside who'd been trying to keep the fourth-grade bully from scaring the second graders.

But Bishop never looked that far. He shook his head and told his ten-year-old to get in the truck.

Rafe had learned one thing from those days: pretty girls like Kitty didn't pick the runt of the litter. No matter how he masked it—with his charm or his bravado—someday she'd figure out he was more trouble than he was worth.

"I did it again!" Kitty yanked back on the rope, now having encircled both horns with her lasso. She fairly glowed. "Did you ever try roping in a rodeo?"

He shook his head. "I left that to Nick. He won the National High School Rodeo Championship in team roping."

"So you decided to ride bulls instead? Isn't that harder? more dangerous?"

"Maybe that's the point."

She narrowed her eyes at him, and he let that statement, that very vulnerable, why-did-he-say-that-again statement hang there without comment. He was turning into a regular gusher of information around her.

Kitty turned back and wound up the rope, getting ready to give it another go. "Now hold still, little fake steer."

Rafe shook his head, but she glanced at him, her eyes twinkling.

She nailed the dummy steer again, and he felt the strangest leap of joy.

"I think I'm ready for something tougher. Maybe some steer wrestling. Or bull riding."

"Uh, I don't think so, cowgirl." He reached out to take the lasso from her.

"Why not? If you can ride bulls, why can't I?"

He gave her a pointed look. "Well, are you tough?"

"I'm tough."

"Can you take a little pain?"

Kitty thought about it for a second, then nodded.

"Are you afraid of a challenge?"

She grinned. "I'm here, aren't I?"

His mind went back to their first meeting. Yes, she had some spine.

"Did I ever tell you that my dad was a bull rider?" Kitty looked away from him. "His name was Bobby Russell."

Katherine Breckenridge was Bobby Russell's . . . daughter? Rafe tried to register this information. This beautiful woman was the daughter of his hero? "You're Bobby's *daughter*? Why didn't you say that in the first place?"

She shrugged. "I didn't know it would matter. Besides, I didn't want to mention that he was in your profession."

"I know he died. I was a huge fan."

"Really? So you saw him in action?"

"Yeah, a couple times. He even signed . . . my poster."

She giggled, apparently pleased by this. "I met John Kincaid; evidently, they were good friends. My dad even worked on his ranch back in the early days."

"I didn't know that. Hey, you wanna see Bobby's poster? I had it signed when I was six. . . ." Oh, brother, he sounded like he was *still* six-years-old. The eagerness in his voice made him want to pull his hat down over his face.

"Oh, I'd love to!" Kitty's enthusiasm made him feel as if it might be okay to still be a child and infatuated with a hero.

She followed him into the house and moved behind him patiently as he dragged himself up the stairs. Rafe had never let a woman see his room before, and he hesitated at the door, glad he'd given it a once-over this morning. Still, it felt odd to let Kitty see the trophies, the ribbons, and—*oh no*—the tumble of Westerns by the side of his bed that betrayed his lack of a social life.

Kitty stood quietly in the doorway, staring at the poster of Bobby above his bed.

He definitely felt like a kid again, but he was profoundly glad he'd never taken the poster down. Then again, last time he'd been home for any length of time, he'd been sixteen and lived and breathed bull riding.

"Bobby Russell was an incredible rider," Rafe said, standing slightly behind her and resting his hand on the doorframe. "I have a videotape—"

"Of him riding?" Kitty turned slightly to look up at him. "Can I watch it?"

She consumed his thoughts, and the fact that she was Bobby Russell's daughter . . . well, she had bull riding in her blood too, didn't she? Besides, she smelled so good and stood close enough to . . .

Rafe couldn't stop himself. He leaned down and kissed her. Gently, just enough to satisfy his curiosity and the desire he'd been avoiding all week.

Kitty didn't move or kiss him back, but she didn't pull away either.

Rafe closed his eyes, losing himself in this moment, feeling that painful longing he'd lived with for so many years ease. She tasted of coffee, her lips soft and sweet and opening slightly. . . .

Kitty. Sweet Kitty. He braced his hand over the door, using the other one to cup the back of her neck as he deepened his kiss. Yes, this was a thousand times better than any meaningless kiss from a fan. This was real, and something—

She put a hand on his chest and pushed just a little.

Rafe pulled away, his breath tight, a smile tipping his lips until he saw her eyes wide, her face nearly white.

He'd kissed plenty of women, but none of them had ever acted as if he'd done something to be strung up for. "I'm sorry, Kitty. I just . . . I lost myself there. I didn't think . . . I'm . . ." He looked away, running his hand through his hair, kicking himself. He should have asked, shouldn't have assumed that those smiles meant anything beyond . . .

What had he been thinking?

He'd do better next time. Much better.

"I think I should go." Kitty ran down the stairs.

"Kitty, wait! I'm . . . sorry."

She was already gone, evident by the squeal of the front door. Clearly, there wouldn't be a next time.

The door banged shut, and he jerked, bringing himself firmly back to reality.

So much for happily ever after.

~CHAPTER 9

KAT MADE IT as far as the Jeep before she stopped to let her heart catch up. What had she done? She felt sick, traitorous, and horrified, because for a moment there, she nearly put her arms around Rafe and kissed him back.

Oh, did she want to kiss him back. To free herself in the embrace she'd been wondering about for days. To feel that smile on her lips, those arms around her. To be held in a way she imagined Rafe might hold a woman—like he meant it. Most of all, she'd never had the world stop, never felt herself tingle from head to toe when she kissed Bradley.

Bradley's kisses were tame. Controlled. And while Rafe's kiss had been even more so, the feelings it evoked in her had been anything but tame. Apparently she had more of her mother in her than she realized.

Guys like Rafe equaled trouble. Aside from his propensity to crash into things, like buildings, the ground, and bulls' hooves, he lived and breathed danger. Rafe belonged in the guts-and-glory world of bull riding. After spending the past few days with him, she didn't buy his I'm-not-going-back line for a minute. Everything in that scenario screamed *broken heart*! No, thank you.

The only kind of bulls in her world were a good day on Wall Street. Kat had a nice, calm, safe life. And a *sort of* fiancé!

But she saw the way Rafe looked at her. Especially when he thought she wouldn't notice. It warmed her, clear down to her toes. No one, not even Bradley, had ever looked at her like that, and it made her feel free. Cute. Brave. Special. Desirable.

The fact that such a look came from Rafe Noble, of the smoldering good looks, dangerous smile, muscled arms, and sweet brown eyes, made her truly feel like Kitty Russell, cowgirl.

Yes, she needed to leave—not just the Silver Buckle but Montana—and hightail it back to reality in NYC.

"Kitty! Don't leave."

See, this is what hesitation cost her. She shouldn't have stopped by her Jeep to assess the damage to her heart but instead jumped in and floored it. Because the minute she took one look at Rafe as he half limped, half hopped after her, she knew she'd be sticking around. She wasn't exactly sure why.

"Kitty!" He touched her arm and turned her. "I'm so sorry. I don't know why I did that. I just . . . you . . . you're so pretty and you're here, and you . . . you're Bobby Russell's kid!"

"You kissed me because you like my father?"

He opened his mouth, then frowned and shook his head. "I, uh . . . no . . . I mean . . ." He sighed. "Listen, let's start over. You surprised me; that's all. I'm sorry. I saw your smile and the way you looked at those posters, and I wanted to—"

"Impress me. I know." Kat smiled at him and he smiled back.

His eyes found hers, and she saw a tinge of embarrassment flood over him.

Imagine that. She'd discovered a guy who just wanted the girl to like him.

"I don't suppose that kiss impressed you at all?" Rafe looked at his boots, then at her.

"Oh, honestly, are you in junior high?" She laughed, shaking her head. "Yeah, okay, it was nice. *Sort of* impressive."

He rolled his eyes. "What does a guy have to do to impress you, Kitty?"

Stop being the man you think I want and be the man inside. Only, wasn't that exactly what he'd been doing? She lifted a shoulder. "I'll know it when I see it. But that kiss is not happening again."

He held up the Boy Scout sign. "I promise to behave myself."

"Oh, sure. This from a man who rides bulls for a living and drives his truck through my favorite hotel."

His smile dissipated. "You ever going to let me live that down?"

Kat gave a small, slow nod. "I am. Right after we raise half a million dollars."

She meant it as a joke, but sadness filled his eyes. He reached out as if to take her hand, then dropped his arm to his side. "I'm going to help you raise that money. Even though I've made a few mistakes in my life, I'm not that guy anymore. Not really. So your answer is yes."

Yes? *Yes?* "Oh, thank you! You won't be sorry!" Everything inside her wanted to throw her arms around him, but instead she did a sort of happy dance, because that seemed a million times safer.

Rafe was dead-on. He wasn't that man who'd stumbled out of his totaled pickup at all. This Rafe Noble—the sheepish, adorable man before her—was much, much more dangerous. An arrogant cowboy she could dismiss. A man who let her see his insecurities, his needs . . . well, that might be more than she could say no to.

How did his life get so complicated? A week ago John was just a simple rancher, with a secret life as a Western romance writer, holding on to the unrequited love of the local diner owner, trying to sell the nearly bankrupt ranch his father had left him—okay, so maybe his life had always been a little complicated. But this morning's news that the production team had moved their arrival date up to tomorrow, along with last week's arrival of Katherine Breckenridge, daughter of Bobby Russell and ghost from Lolly's past, made him feel as if his life might be imploding.

How was he supposed to keep Katherine from discovering the truth that Lolly so desperately—he could read it all over her face—wanted to keep hidden? More than that, how would his sudden rise to fame change Lolly's life?

Probably the best thing for Lolly would be for him to exit her life—and fast.

But John was a sorry man with an addiction to a beautiful blonde diner owner, so he headed for Lolly's at his regular time, sat in his regular stool, and ordered a Reuben. No fries on the side.

Lolly plunked down his order and a Coke and snarled, "I'm tired and it's all your fault."

He wasn't sure what to make of that as she took Egger's empty plate and waved to the two hands from the Silver Buckle. She did look tired. Bags shadowed her eyes, but she could still make his heart stand still.

He needed her in a good mood for the bomb he planned to drop tonight. Namely, that his Realtor had found an interested buyer for his ranch. If he took the offer, in less than a month he'd close on the property and move. To Malibu. He already had a Realtor on the hunt for a condo—he liked the sound of that word—or a small beach house.

Maybe he'd even buy a yacht.

By this time tomorrow, his secret would be out. The production crew would be arriving in the morning. Just in time for the Fourth of July parade and rodeo this weekend.

Talk about being exposed in front of the entire town. A Western romance writer . . . perhaps he could ride a bull or something right before they made that announcement.

If he didn't drop the news on Lolly first, it could only add fireworks to the already volatile event.

"Great sandwich, Lol," he said.

"Cody made it," she snapped, looking up from where she cleaned tables. "Why didn't you just take that book home with you?" She moved to the next booth, then turned and pointed to her temple. "He's in my head!"

John put down his sandwich. "Who's in your head?"

Lolly came over and threw the dishrag down on the counter next to him. "Jonas, that's who. He won't leave me alone."

John barely stifled a smile. "Yeah? Uh, who is Jonas?"

She rolled her eyes, shook her head, and flopped down on a stool. "A dumb book character. I started reading Libby's book a couple of nights ago, and now I can't get the story out of my head. I've stayed up really late every night reading."

"You have?" He fought another grin.

"Yeah, 'cause I'm sucked into the story."

"So it's good."

She sighed. "Very good. No wonder everyone's reading it. B. J. King is a great author. Now I'll probably be required to get all his—or her—books."

"I think it's a him." John hid a smile. Most definitely a him.

"Well, I don't know how a guy did it, but I felt as if he crawled inside my head or maybe my heart and probed around. And Mary and I have nothing in common."

"Who's Mary?"

"The main character. Except we do sort of think alike. And Matthias—oh, what a jerk. I can think of a few things I'd like to do to him."

John raised an eyebrow, hoping he could pull off casual and not stupid.

"I was so glad Jonas killed him."

"Jonas killed someone?"

She closed her eyes tight. "You probably think I'm crazy."

John let himself smile. "Yeah. But that's okay. I've thought that for a long time."

She opened her eyes and gave him a mock glare. "It's just a good book. And it's getting better. Mary talked Jonas into leaving, and he went to work on a ranch in South Dakota, waiting for her to write to him and tell him that she's settled things with the sheriff. In the meantime, Mary tells the sheriff what happened, saying that Matthias slipped, and now she's running the ranch, which is starting to turn a profit since Mary let all the tenants run the land with the smallest cut for herself. She's a pretty smart businesswoman."

"Hmm," John said. "Reminds me of someone."

She wrinkled her nose at him. "The thing is, Mary won't send for Jonas. And since he's afraid of pushing her before she's ready, he won't return without her word. But now he's going to war!"

"Calm down, Lolly. I'm sure there'll be a happy ending."

She threw the dishrag at him. "How do you know? He could die—and Mary will be heartbroken."

She would? For a second, John couldn't breathe. Couldn't think. He swallowed, wishing with everything inside him that she wasn't talking about the book but . . . herself. Finally he found his voice. "What do you think will happen?"

Her hair had started to whisk out of her ponytail, and she tucked it behind her ear. "I . . . don't know. Sometimes life doesn't turn out happily. I guess I need to be prepared for that."

Oh no you don't, Lolly. He folded his hands on his lap and cleared his throat, not sure exactly how to respond. He knew she blamed herself for the curve ball life had thrown her. But she hadn't the slightest inkling that he knew her secrets . . . so how was he supposed to speak the truth he longed to say? Words! He was a master of them, yet there they were, piling up in his throat, bottlenecked.

She deserved to be happy, but she didn't believe it. Just like Mary didn't.

"So, how is any of this my fault?" he choked out.

Lolly took a deep breath, then looked away. "Jonas reminds me . . . of . . ."

John's world stopped as he watched her, praying, holding his breath, wanting to reach his hand out to her. *Yes, Lolly?*

She put her hand over her eyes. "Nothing. I'm being silly. It's just a story; that's all. I'm tired and probably reading too much into it. It feels like I know her—the main character—even though it's set in the Depression, and I feel all the things she feels. Hope the things she hopes."

John looked at Lolly, and deep inside he ached to tell her how he'd written the book, how he'd wanted to be Jonas. Her hopes could become reality. In fact, he felt the words breaking free. . . . "Lolly, I have to tell you—"

The door jangled as it opened, and Lolly turned. "We're closed."

"Oh, sorry," said a tall, wide-shouldered man, perhaps in his early thirties, with blond hair that hung long enough to scrape his shirt collar and a layer of dark, three-day whisker growth. He looked like a lost trucker, but he wore sunglasses despite the late hour, and something about him struck a chord of familiarity inside John.

He realized why at the same moment Lolly got to her feet, gaping. The same moment the man removed his glasses and gave the woman John loved a slow, movie-star smile.

"Good evening, ma'am," said Lincoln Cash.

And with that drawl, John knew that any words from him were already too late.

❧

Bradley had been worried. Now he just felt anger. Or, perhaps, panic. Katherine had all but disappeared off the planet, with her millions in inheritance and his future at stake.

He had to find her before she did something stupid. Like donate everything she owned to charity. Or worse, decide that she didn't want to marry him.

"I don't know," Bradley repeated to Walter Breckenridge, hoping his voice held steady over the phone. He lay on the bed, still in his clothes. Light sliced through the dark velvet curtains, evidence that he'd slept long and probably hard.

In fact, he couldn't remember exactly when he'd returned to his room. He recalled leaving the gaming table flat broke. Things got bleary from there.

Bradley cleared his throat. "I left countless messages on her machine and her cell phone. I've even e-mailed her. She's not answering, not picking up her mail. I don't know where she is."

"Find her," Walter said. "I don't know what has gotten into her, but all these trips to Mexico and now she's gone and disappeared. I'm afraid . . ." Behind his sigh, Bradley heard history and Walter's deepest fears that Katherine might follow in Felicia's unstable footsteps. "It's the stress of this confounded foundation. She's bent on seeing it through until it breaks her."

"I agree, sir," Bradley said, putting believability into his voice. Walter Breckenridge saw only what he wanted to see, which could work in his favor. "When I find her, maybe I should take her away on vacation, something to soothe her nerves."

"You need to find her first. But, yes," Breckenridge's voice softened. "Anything to keep her from . . ."

"I understand, sir. I'll take care of her. I promise," Bradley said.

"I knew you would, son," Walter said, enough relief in his voice for Bradley's hopes to soar.

He couldn't ask for a more perfect scenario. Breckenridge giving him permission to disappear with his granddaughter. His very valuable granddaughter, whose mother had once had a very convenient breakdown. Like mother, like daughter.

Bradley closed his cell phone and ran a hand through his hair, noticing again how thin it had gotten. Another fallout of the past year.

He walked to the bathroom and stared at the mirror. He'd barely slept in two days, and it showed on his face, in his red-rimmed eyes.

Two days holed up in a hotel room in DC had netted him roughly . . . zero. Actually about three hundred thousand zeros if he did the math.

What if Katherine was hiding from him? What if she knew?

His bourbon glass sat on the counter, half full, and he downed it fast, then wiped his mouth with his shirt. One way or another he'd find her and end this.

Katherine, where are you?

⁂

Sweat slicked Rafe's body as he twisted in his sheets. It was just a dream. Just a dream.

But it felt, tasted, and smelled so frighteningly real. He could hear the crowd gasp, smell the earthy odor of animal sweat, taste panic welling up in his throat.

Manuel's face hovered above him, his eyes wide as he tugged Rafe's protective vest. "Get up, man!"

Then memory cut into fragments, each moment sliced out and driven into his soul to elicit the most pain.

PeeWee's hooves centering above them. Slamming down.

Pounding into Manuel at the base of his skull, separating his brain stem from his spine.

Manuel slumping against Rafe.

Rafe throwing his arms around Manuel as another jackhammer hoof found Manuel's temple, grazing Rafe's protective vest.

The screams from the crowd as PeeWee spun away, distracted by the other bullfighters.

Rafe, rolling over, his head still swimming, not sure what had happened, sickened by the blood that wet the dirt, his hands, his clothes. Seeing then that it belonged to Manuel.

He forgot any other pain. Forgot the explosions inside his chest, the burn in his knee. He just hunkered over Manuel, trying somehow to put him back together, hold back the blood, or shake him to consciousness. Manuel's lifeless eyes looked up at him. Through him. Shattering Rafe to the core.

Rafe stumbled out of the ring on his own power—or the power of his grief—and followed Manuel's stretcher to the ambulance. He came to life when Lucia threw herself at Manuel's body and screamed. Rafe grabbed her, held her with everything he had in him, wishing he could come unglued too and that someone might hold him.

Lucia crumpled and he went with her to the ground, holding her as she shook. He wanted her to hit him, to call him names, to hurt him. Please.

"No!" Rafe's own voice woke him, and he lay there in his room in the quiet predawn, listening to his heart beating against the walls of his chest. The images lingered, and he opened his eyes, orienting himself.

Oh, what have I done?

Rafe pushed himself to a sitting position with a groan. His

shoulder had since stopped throbbing, and his neck felt nearly normal, although stiff. His knee, however, could blind him with pain if he focused on it.

He headed to the open window. The sun hadn't yet scaled the horizon to the east, and shadows outlined the gullies of Buckle land. A hint of rain scented the air; Rafe drew that into his lungs, wishing it could wash away the despair that dogged him.

Manuel's death hadn't exactly been his fault, but it felt like it. Rafe had done a stellar job of making himself suffer, right up to the point where he'd managed to rack up charges for reckless driving. Notification of his court date had arrived in the mail yesterday, courtesy of his agent—or rather *former* agent, according to the letter attached to the police report—along with the bill for services and the legal documents suing him for breach of contract and loss of income from said agent.

He had also received a packet from his attorney that not only cataloged his outstanding to-date fees but included a list of the irate victims and their claims. Starting with the Breckenridge Hotel.

Unless he got back on a bull, he could kiss his life—the fans, the bright lights, the cars, the clothes, the ranch in Texas, all of it—good-bye.

Then again, did he want that life, anyway?

After pulling on a pair of track pants, he went downstairs. At this hour, the house was quiet, reminding him of the days before he turned eighteen. He'd rise early for a weekend rodeo trip, then gather his boots and hat and tiptoe down the stairs, hoping not to wake Stefanie or his dad.

He usually found his father sitting in his reading chair, in the nook of their family room, with his Bible open and his glasses perched on the end of his nose. Sometimes wearing his ratty red bathrobe or a pair of jeans and a shirt. But always with his Bible.

Rafe stood in the silence of the family room, seeing in his mind's eye the great Bishop Noble looking up from his reading, giving his son a long look, and saying, "Remember, Rafe, you're not out there alone."

For some reason Rafe had always thought that his dad had meant that in some ethereal way, that his father would be with him. How he'd hated that. Bull riding belonged to him, not his dad or any of the other Nobles. Rafe alone could muscle past his fear to hang on to a bull. He didn't need his dad's help—through his thoughts or prayers or otherwise.

He'd usually held back that stream of words, nodded, put on his hat, and hit the road, heading for freedom and a life away from the Silver Buckle.

Now, Rafe limped over to his father's corner, noticing the pictures stacked on the side table. One of his mother, Elizabeth, sitting in the leather chair in front of the giant stone fireplace, an enigmatic smile on her lips. Another of Stefanie on one of the stock horses she'd trained and a picture of Nick from his graduation.

Rafe picked up the fourth photo, one he'd never seen before. He was on a bull and wearing the turquoise chaps that he'd thought made him a rhinestone cowboy. He must have been nineteen. Funny, the shot looked like it might have been taken at the Cripple Creek Invitational during the long stretch of time he'd barely spoken to his dad. Confused, Rafe put the picture down.

Bishop's black leather Bible sat on the seat of the chair as if he had just left it there. Rafe hesitated, then picked it up. It felt soft and even heavy in his hands. He sat in the chair and flipped the book open to where Bishop had laid his last bookmark, noting the scribbles in the margins, the highlighted portions of Psalm 35.

Without thinking, Rafe sat down and read the passage. *"O Lord, oppose those who oppose me. Fight those who fight against me."* He stared at the page a long time before noticing Bishop's cross-reference scrawled above it: Romans 8:1.

Curious, he turned to it. *"So now there is no condemnation for those who belong to Christ Jesus."*

Rafe had been a Christian most of his life, thanks to his early Sunday school years, and he felt plenty of condemnation. Kitty's words had only confirmed it. If God had a purpose for Rafe's life, he'd done a spectacular job of ignoring it. For him, there was nothing left *but* condemnation.

He closed the Bible and set it on the table, accidentally knocking his picture to the floor. He picked it up and turned it facedown on the book as he pried himself out of the chair.

"Remember, Rafe, you're not out there alone." His father's voice thrummed in his thoughts as Rafe balanced himself along the long leather sofa, then shuffled into the kitchen. His father had been wrong. Rafe had been alone. Very alone. Even here, when he'd returned to the ranch. He'd never been a part of this land, this life.

All the same, somehow over the past week everything had changed. No longer did the Buckle seem like a noose around his neck. Rafe had begun to see it with a new freedom. With new eyes.

Kitty's eyes.

He'd seen the lavender beauty of the pasqueflower tucked into Kitty's hair and the funny expressions of the prairie dogs as they poked their heads above their holes. He saw the joy of learning to understand a horse for the first time and even the old thrill of landing a lasso around a steer's horns. *"I caught him, Rafe!"*

Yes, she certainly did.

When he'd kissed her—despite her cut-and-run reaction—he'd felt something open in his heart that both scared and exhilarated him. Then she'd added tease and her smile, forgiving him and—so shoot him—he couldn't get Kitty out of his mind.

Rafe dumped out the old coffee filter, added new coffee grounds and water, and sat down at the table waiting for it to brew.

What if he really didn't go back to bull riding? Despite his words to Stefanie, he hadn't seriously considered it. What if . . . what if he . . . *stayed* here and helped his brother and sister ranch, built a new life? That had a sort of purpose, didn't it?

And what if that life included Kitty?

He'd gotten hit in the head one too many times. What did a guy like him have to offer the heiress of the Breckenridge fortune?

That thought brought him up short. Exactly why was she here, if she had a trust fund of millions?

The bigger question might be: did he want her to leave? Maybe he should trust her and her little plan. With her excitement—he still smiled at the image of her dancing—and spunk, they could pull it off; he knew it. At the core she was every bit Bobby Russell's kid, which meant that she had the inner fiber to tackle what life put in front of her.

Including starting over with a broken cowboy. Didn't she say she loved it here in Montana?

If a guy was patient, perhaps he could get her to stay.

Rafe got up and poured himself a cup of coffee. Black, just in case all his synapses weren't firing. As he sipped it, leaning against the doorjamb, the sunrise gliding over the prairie grass, the idea found firm soil.

Rafe would talk Kitty into staying. Then maybe, finally, the nightmares would slink back into the night.

For the first time since his life crashed down around him, he knew exactly what to do.

⚜

"I think I was kidding."

"No, you weren't." Rafe stood behind Kat, blocking her quick escape, so she just froze in the entrance to the Buffalo Saloon.

"I am not riding that."

Across the room, the bar owner inflated the cushion around a rawhide-covered mechanical bull, one of the few nods toward the twentieth century in this whiskey- and smoke-saturated room. In the corner, a jukebox whined out a country song.

"Yes, Kitty Breckenridge, aka Russell, you are. You have it in your bones. And I believe in you."

"Okay, so a small part of me wanted to learn to ride a bull, but really, Rafe–"

"Hey, if you want, we'll add it to our list of activities for our high-paying guests." He wound his arm around her waist and pulled her into the room.

Daylight streamed through the windows, and at this hour, only two weary guys looked up from their beers. She'd never even been in a real-life bar before, especially one that looked like it should have spittoons on the floor. Bradley would be horrified.

That thought made her yield to Rafe's pressure. Maybe she

didn't want to do everything expected of her. Maybe she wanted to ride a bull, just like her dad.

"Can you make it not throw me off?"

Rafe raised one dark eyebrow.

"Okay, but if I get hurt—"

"You won't get hurt. I'll be with you."

"What, are you going to ride behind me?"

He led her around the tables, carrying a small bag. "Do you want me to?"

Kat stopped, stared at him. "Would you?" Despite the fact he'd ditched his crutches and his neck brace and looked rather sturdy— not to mention cute in a pair of well-worn jeans, a denim shirt, that ratty hat pushed back on his head, contrasting with his clean-shaven chin—she could probably knock him over with two fingers.

"Of course."

She didn't know why, but those words found all the places in her heart she'd been trying to bulwark and ripped them to shreds. "I think I can do this alone."

He dropped the bag he carried on a table. "Me too."

Kat blew out a breath. "What's in the bag?"

"Supplies." Rafe opened the bag and pulled out a long rope with a sort of handle loop in the middle, a bell attached at one end. "This is the bull rope. The bell is so that it's weighted at the end and falls off easily when it's loosened. The mechanical bull has one, but I thought you should know what you'll use and what to do when you face a real bull."

Right. Hardy har har.

He handed her a leather glove. "Put it on."

"Only one?"

"You only need one hand. And you're right-handed, so . . ."

She put it on. It swam on her.

He took out a roll of white medical tape and tightened it down on her wrist.

"Nice."

"We're just getting started."

Kat picked up the rope. "Is this yours?"

"Mmm-hmm," he said, taking out a pair of spurs.

She turned over the rope and saw an extra layer of padding. "What's this on the bottom of the loop?"

"Sheepskin. I sewed it on to help protect my knuckles."

She fitted her hand into the hold. Somehow, with her hand wrapped around it, she had the image of Rafe gripping this very rope as he hung on for dear life, riding the bull. Doing what he loved. Emptiness welled within her, an echoing chamber as she realized all he'd lost.

He pulled up a chair to sit on, leaned over, and fastened one of the spurs onto her boot.

"Do I need those? I'm pretty sure he's not getting away." She nodded to the headless bull in the middle of the padded mat.

Rafe glanced up at her. "You're not going to get much grab on a mechanical, but they're generally for holding on."

He put the other spur on, tightening the strap down over her boot. Then he pulled out from his bag of tricks a shorter length of belt. This he wrapped around the boot, right above her ankle. "We don't want those boots coming off during the middle of your ride."

"Oh no, that would be bad."

One edge of his mouth turned up. "Now touch your glove."

She reached into the palm, noted its dark, shiny surface, its stickiness. "What is it?"

"Rosin. It's on the rope, too, and it'll help you hang on."

"That's important, I think."

Rafe smiled. "Okay, lean over and touch your toes."

"Excuse me?"

"Listen, it's almost guaranteed that the bull will rattle every joint in your body and that you'll pull a muscle if you're not loose, so you need to be as limber as you can be. Stretch out; jog in place; breathe deeply to get the oxygen to your brain, deep inside."

"You're serious."

He stared at her. "Yeah, what did you think? We just run out there and hop on the first available animal? This is a sport, Kitty, just like football or soccer."

"I don't know. I guess I thought it took more guts than . . . than . . ."

"Brains? Is that what you're getting at?"

"No!" *Maybe.*

But she'd lit his fire. "Guess what? We study these animals. We know how the bull we draw stands in the chute, whether he leans or squats, if he throws his head around or tries to hook you. I know how he leaves the chute, if he blows out hard or stumbles out and explodes seconds later. I know if he likes to break legs against the side of the gate, if he spins to the right or the left, and if he throws inside or outside of the spin. I know if he walks on his front feet, which means he kicks up and takes an extra step before his back feet land. And I know if he stays in one place or if he travels down the arena. Most of all I know if the bull is going to try to kill me when I get off."

Kill him? Panic wound around her throat and tightened. She never wanted Rafe on another bull again. Ever.

Then again, if he didn't, he wouldn't be much use as a fundraiser, would he?

Kat had to work to unclench her jaw, and she blinked away the burn in her eyes. Then she lifted her arms above her head and began to stretch.

Rafe turned away to talk to the bar owner.

She put her leg in front of her, leaned over it, stretching her hamstrings, her thighs. Perhaps she didn't need him to ride bulls. Just to flash that charming smile.

Or better yet, she didn't need any of it. Maybe she should . . . stay. Start a new life. She hadn't exactly turned her mother's organization into a stellar success.

No. She couldn't give up on Eva. Or kids like Carlos.

"Kitty, you about ready?" Rafe held a pair of fringed turquoise chaps. He buckled them around her waist and behind her thighs.

As she stood there, something strong and brave swelled inside her.

"Introducing the amazing Kitty Russell," Rafe said.

Silly, stupid tears. "Point me to the bull."

He shook his head, but she saw a gleam in his eyes. "We're ready," he said to the slim guy manning the controls.

The operator nodded, as if New Yorkers risked their necks in his establishment every day of the week.

She walked across the padded surface and climbed onto the rim under the mechanical beast. The thing seemed twice as big as the horse she'd ridden yesterday. Rafe held out his hand and gave her a leg up. And then she was on the bull.

"Put your hand into the loop there."

She reached for the rawhide rope.

"Palm up, Kitty. It's not a shopping bag."

She glared at him but changed her hand position.

"Now, scoot up real tight on your rope. This is where you position your legs."

Kat leaned back and braced her legs around the bull.

"Lean forward, up over your rope."

She hunkered down, feeling like an idiot.

"Now, remember, be smarter than the bull. The bull—or Big Red, as we call this guy—will move back and forth, not unlike a teeter-totter. The only thing is, you're riding both sides, and it's spinning too."

A teeter-totter? "Rafe—"

"In order not to get your arm jerked out of socket, you need to think ahead. When the bull's backside is up, your arm is a brace. Push your shoulder forward and jam your fist into the bull's back. Keep your chest out, your neck tight, and your eyes on the head of the bull. Don't look away, and go where his head goes."

Kat tried to mimic that movement.

Rafe rubbed his eyes, his jaw tight.

"See—"

"Shh. When the bull's backside comes down, you'll need to hunch forward a little to keep balance. Stay up on or at and over your rope. Pay attention to your left foot position. Most riders buck off into or toward their riding hand, so you want to clamp down on your left side to keep balance. Also, remember your free arm is there to help you keep your balance. Don't let it dangle like a fish."

"No dead fish."

"Please listen. I'm trying to help."

So was she, because the adrenaline inside her was already launching her off the bull, and everything about this felt surreal. "Rafe—"

"You can do this." He looked so earnest that for a crazy moment she believed him.

Her smile faded because right then, she felt it, everything that she'd been feeling about him and her frustration at his inability to see exactly what God had put inside him.

Perhaps he saw the same thing in her. Which made a lump larger than Big Red form in her throat. Maybe Kitty Russell wasn't a fantasy.

Maybe she was real.

"When you're thrown, try to land with most of your weight on your feet and hands. If we were in the arena, I'd tell you to then run as if your tail is on fire, but I'm thinking Big Red won't go after you. Much."

Kat tried to smile.

Rafe touched her leg. "It's all about attitude. You were born to do this. It's inside you—a rhythm, a beat. You'll get it."

"How long do you plan to keep me up here?"

And there it was, a capital *T* for trouble in his eyes.

She swallowed and nodded at the operator. "Ride 'em, cowboy."

CHAPTER 10

"WHY ARE WE making potato salad for three hundred?" Kat sat at the table in the kitchen of the Silver Buckle, cutting her tenth onion.

"Because I'm suddenly in charge of the Fourth of July picnic, which has to be the best one in the history of time." Piper ran her wrist over her forehead. "Apparently, people in this town think I can cook."

"You can't? Because Rafe says you're a great cook."

"Rafe is delusional. His taste buds have been knocked out of place one too many times." Piper dropped her cut potatoes into the pot. "Feel better? I know I'm always game for a good cry."

"Oh, very funny." Kat had given up trying to hold back the tears long ago and let them run freely, nearly blinding her. It did feel cathartic. A release of all the pent-up tension—and guilt—of being around Rafe.

Although she'd drawn the line between them and Rafe hadn't crossed it, that kiss—*his* kiss—remained in her thoughts like a brand.

That and the feeling of her heart taking flight outside her body as she rode Big Red over and over. So the machine had been on one of the lowest settings—she'd stayed on for eight seconds. When Rafe caught her as she swung down, she knew she'd broken through a sort of invisible wall and suddenly learned to breathe.

Yep, Kat needed therapy because she was painfully addicted to the Silver Buckle and Montana . . . and especially Rafe, who'd made her believe in herself. She'd kept returning every day, wearing the red boots, learning how to rope and herd cattle. She was just doing research for their big event, of course.

Tomorrow she was going to get another lesson from Stefanie on her horse-whisperer techniques. Kat had watched for only an hour, but even she could see that Stef had a way of gentling horses that seemed almost magical. As if she were trying to understand the animal, to get inside its head and coax it into letting her ride it.

But the head Kat wanted to get inside at the moment belonged to Lincoln Cash, Hollywood heartthrob and the biggest thing to hit Phillips since the dawn of time. What was Cash doing in Phillips, Montana, anyway?

She supposed Bradley might ask the same thing about her. Could she help it if her cell phone was on its last blip of power? She'd turned it off, hoping to save the battery for an emergency. Okay, she could have borrowed Lolly's phone to call. If she wanted to.

Kat was in serious denial, because the idea of talking to Bradley weighed like a rock in the pit of her stomach. She didn't even want to imagine how angry he'd be at her weeklong vanishing act. What was worse, she hadn't yet located her aunt. No one had even hinted about the flyer, and every time she mentioned Aunt Laura, John and Lolly looked like they might be asphyxiating.

Which was how she felt when she thought about leaving. Now that Rafe had agreed to help her, it would probably happen soon.

It was strange how in little over one short week, she felt like a different person. Kitty Russell. Connected to Bobby Russell, her father. Rafe gave that connection to her. She imagined that Bobby had possessed the same maverick smile, twinkle in his eye, and confidence that drew people like a flame.

No wonder Kat's mother had defied her own father to marry Bobby. In a way, knowing Rafe made Kat understand her mother better. All those questions about how Felicia had ended up with Bobby vanished when Rafe pulled her close for that kiss, which it would behoove her to wipe from her memory.

What if she stayed another week, like she'd originally planned? She wasn't ready to return to the pace of New York. Besides, her boots were just getting broken in.

"Do you think he's nice?" Piper pushed the last pile of potatoes into the boiling water and topped the pot with the lid.

"Who?"

"Lincoln Cash. I heard he's been hanging out at the Kincaid place." She raised an eyebrow. "I think I'm going to have to do some investigating."

Rafe had told Kat that Piper was an award-winning reporter. Until she met Nick Noble. Apparently the Noble men had that sort of effect on a woman—made her reconsider everything about her life and turned her upside down and inside out so she'd never be the same again.

"He's probably nice," Kat said evenly. "I mean, everything I've read about him seems nice. Until recently, he was into supporting charitable causes."

"I'm going to find out why he's here." Piper wiped her hands on a towel.

With Piper's words, an idea formed, and Kat blurted it out. "Have you ever heard of a Laura Russell?"

Piper adjusted the flame on the stove. "No. But I haven't lived around here long."

"She's my aunt, the sister of my father, Bobby Russell. A long time ago, she sent me a letter postmarked from Phillips. I was hoping that she might still be in the area."

Piper stirred the potatoes. "I'll ask around. See what I can dig up."

"Thanks. I appreciate it." Kat added the onions to the bowl, then wiped her eyes.

When she looked up, Piper laughed. "I think you need to look in the mirror. You have mascara running down your face."

"Great," Kat said. She went upstairs to the bathroom and noticed that across the hall Rafe's door was closed. He'd gone up to shower earlier, and now the scent of his soap lingered in the room. She peered into the mirror and attempted to resurrect her appearance with a wad of wet tissue.

"You're beautiful even with raccoon eyes."

Kat turned to find Rafe standing in the doorway, buttoning his shirt. Wow, did he look good in gold, nearly as good as in red. It picked up the flecks in his eyes. . . .

He had reached the middle button when she saw it—a scar down the center of his chest, thick and faded. His hands stopped moving as he noticed her stare.

"What happened to you?" she asked, moving closer, reaching out.

He caught her wrist before she could touch him and stepped back. "It's—"

"Is it from a bull?"

"No." He cleared his throat and finished buttoning his shirt. "Stefanie and I are twins, and she was born with a good ticker. I had a hole in my heart."

He met her eyes, and in his gaze Kat saw an embarrassment she didn't expect. "I had surgery when I was six to fix it."

"Are you okay? Is it safe for you to ride?"

He ran his thumb under her eye, where moisture still remained. "Depends on who you talk to, but, yeah, my heart's fine. Don't worry."

But a *hole*? "How serious was it?"

He frowned. "I almost died. Twice. But that was before surgery."

"I'll bet that was scary for your parents. And even Nick. He's what, three years older than you?"

"Five." At the mention of Nick, Rafe's eyes hardened. "I'm sure Nick didn't care one way or another."

"Of course he would care, Rafe."

Rafe was already turning, heading down the stairs.

And just like that, it made sense. Rafe, born with a hole in his heart. Nick, his older brother, who obviously still cared about him and his health, judging by his words the other day on the range. Rafe, who didn't stop at roping but became a bull rider as if trying to prove something. To his father? To Nick? To himself?

Like a cattle prod to the brain, she got it. Rafe rode bulls not for the glory or the women or even the money.

"I guess I wanted to live up to the name I had," he'd said. If anyone

could live up to the name Noble, Rafe seemed the perfect candidate. Aside from his mishap in New York, he'd been a gentleman, kind and patient. Add in all that bravado and grit, and he seemed noble down to his toes.

Kat, better than anyone, knew what it meant to want to be worthy of a name. She'd longed to be a Russell most of her life but had not known it until the first time she'd ridden Big Red.

Lord, please show me how to help him. Up until now, the idea of her somehow cracking open Rafe's hard exterior and getting him to help fund her cause had been her sole mission. But what if God had sent her here, using her own desires to intersect her path with Rafe's?

For however long she might have.

Lord, make my time with him count. For whatever Your plan is.

She followed Rafe down the stairs and to the kitchen. He moved in a rolling gait now that his sore knee was healing. He hadn't combed his black hair, and it lay curly and tousled on his head. Too easily she remembered his head bent forward as he wrapped his muscled arms around her and taught her how to rope.

"I can't believe what this town is doing for this actor. What's his name?" Rafe stole a hard-boiled egg.

"Lincoln Cash. Don't tell me you haven't seen any of his movies." Piper poured the potatoes into a colander and steam rose, filling the room. "He's been nominated for an Academy Award."

Rafe opened the fridge, pulled out the pitcher of iced tea. "Oh yeah, I think I met him once. At a charity event. Big blond guy?"

Piper put the pot back on the stove with a clunk. "You've met him?"

Kat felt another tug of hope. Rafe knew celebrities. People they could invite to their Western soiree.

Rafe poured himself a glass of iced tea, then glanced at Kat. "I have to take off. But you'll be there tonight, right?"

Let's see . . . the town was having a picnic, a rodeo, a street dance, and fireworks. Hmm, sounded boring. "Of course I'm going to be there."

Rafe gave her a wide smile, adding a wink. "Good. See you tonight." He limped out the door, a *ker-thump* to his wobbly step that echoed the one in her heart.

"Where's he going?" Kat asked as she watched him climb into an old cherry red pickup and back out of the yard.

Piper lifted a shoulder. "Wouldn't say, but he went into town yesterday too after you took off."

The question dogged Kat as she helped Piper make the potato salad and later load it into the truck with the barbecue ribs. Piper looked very Western in her jean jacket, boots, and skirt, and Kat made a mental note to stop by Lolly's trailer and change. No particular reason why.

Nick came out of the house, putting on his hat. "Sorry I'm late, honey." He wore a pair of black jeans and a white dress shirt that barely hid his hard-work physique and complemented his dark hair and eyes. They made a cute pair, Piper and Nick. Watching Nick pull Piper into his arms, Kat wished she might find a man who loved her with such a public display of affection.

Perhaps she hoped for a man who loved her all the time, not just when he scheduled romance into his planner.

Kat got into the Jeep and followed Piper and Nick into town, chiding herself for her criticism of Bradley. So he didn't have Rafe's strength, his dazzling smile, or the tease in his eyes. So Bradley didn't make her feel like her world spun on its axis. He was a good man who loved her. She would call him as soon as she got back to the trailer.

Kat looked up and noticed a tumble of thunderclouds. It had been threatening to rain for two days, and she wished the sky would open up and drench the parched hills. *After* tonight, however. After she and Rafe sat under the fireworks in a clear sky . . .

Yeah, she should call Bradley right away.

Piper and Nick turned off at Main Street, and Kat pulled up to Lolly's trailer. No sign of Lolly as she went inside, but she figured her hostess was at the diner, feeding a crowd. Or even napping. Twice in the last two days Kat had returned to find Lolly sprawled on the sofa, asleep. The poor woman worked too hard. Kat had every intention of surprising Lolly with a large, anonymous gift when she left.

Checking the clock, she turned on the shower, then rustled through her suitcase for a clean, semidressy outfit. She chose a white tank top to show off her new tan, a wispy ribbed black cardigan, and a blue silk georgette skirt that fell right below her knees. She'd add her black sandals, let her hair loose, and forget she was nearing the end of her life as Kitty Russell.

She emerged from Lolly's trailer to the smell of hot dogs grilling from the tent in the community park. Walking to the stoplight in front of Lolly's, Kat stood there, soaking in the aura of the festivities that ran the length of the five-block street. Police had barricaded Main from Lolly's down past the feed store, and on one end, a band complete with fiddles warmed up. She recognized a tune about fishing she'd heard on the radio during her ride from Rapid City. In the feed store lot, someone was judging the bike parade. The kids with their decorated spokes and seats made her recall a bike parade held in Central Park and how she'd pressed her nose against the window of her grandfather's limousine, wishing.

She crossed the street, heading toward the giant white tent behind the feed store. Passing a wooden sign naming the community park after a local hero, she entered the tent, surprised at the crowd. Children ran between legs of adults—nearly all of whom wore cowboy hats, boots, and jeans. Of course, she'd overdressed.

She spotted Piper, who was standing next to Nick. He was listening to a portly man in a white Stetson.

Piper waved Kat over. "Get yourself a plate of food. Lolly donated her best rhubarb pies."

"Where is she?" Kat asked.

"Cooking, maybe?" Piper gestured toward her husband with her fork. "Nick's talking to the candidate for senator. He's running in the primary against the incumbent."

For a moment, Kat had the impulse to introduce herself, mention her charity. If Bradley were here, he'd have the man in a conversation, already vying for a donation. "Have you seen Rafe?"

Piper grinned, then glanced at Nick and lowered her voice. "I saw his truck at the rodeo stands."

Kat turned, intent on heading for the stands, when she felt a change in the crowd. As if everyone had taken a collective breath.

Before her, the crowd parted.

Into the tent walked Lincoln Cash, Hollywood hunk. And beside him, grinning like she might be his tour guide, her blonde hair done up, wearing a skirt, boots, and a jean jacket, Kat's hostess . . . Miss Lolly Stuart.

John wanted to get on the fastest horse in the county and ride into the sunset at full gallop. But because this was the twenty-first century, he planned on leaving by BMW, driving as far as he could on a tank of gas before he slowed to feel the sting of watching the woman he loved turn adoring eyes on the man who would play Jonas Strong. John's character. The one *he* created.

John stood at the far side of the tent with Dex Graves, the director of *Unshackled*, and tried to ignore Lolly as she nearly floated into the tent beside the superstar. Like she belonged there all along.

Give him five minutes with Cash and John would rearrange that pretty-boy face. Cash didn't have the first idea how to make a woman like Lolly happy. Then again, apparently John didn't either.

He downed his fruit punch, then crumpled the cup in his fist.

"Everything okay?" Dex asked, finishing off his barbecue rib.

"Fine," John said. "So are you about done shooting the pictures?" They'd done location shots for most of the day, and although Graves planned on filming at the studio in California, he wanted sweeping scenery footage to plug into the background. The fact that it hadn't rained in nearly a month added to the parched-ground aura the director wanted.

John felt parched. Every minute he spent with Cash only made him relive that moment when the actor had walked into Lolly's life and swept her off her feet. Even if Cash had acted momentarily stymied by her offer of free pie, he'd recovered well. Lolly had stood at the counter, leaning on her hand, stars in her eyes, letting Cash see her charm.

John had wanted to strangle him on the spot.

Then Cash had to say, "I'm here working on a film," which turned Lolly's curiosity meter on high.

"What kind of film?" she'd asked.

"A Western. A historical romance." Cash took a bite of pie. "This is delicious."

"I love romantic Westerns," Lolly had said, blushing slightly.

John wanted to get up, wave his arms, and shout, "Since when?" But he figured the sooner he slunk out of the diner, unnoticed by Cash, the better. He'd rather be run over by buffalo than leave Lolly alone with Cash, so he sat in the back booth and sulked as Cash told her about the story—enough for Lolly to realize that it was the same one she was reading—the same one she hadn't yet finished. John forgot to breathe for what seemed like ten minutes until Cash refused to give away the ending.

John would let the man live for that small favor.

John died inside when Lolly said to Cash, with a sort of deep, longing sigh, "When I read the part of Jonas, I instantly thought of you."

Now that wasn't fair, not at all.

Only when Cash left had John come out of hiding. But did Lolly notice how he quietly swept the floor and wiped down the tables? She didn't even sit with him on the porch but went inside her trailer to read that confounded book. It seemed she'd suddenly developed a case of bookworm.

John hadn't returned to Lolly's since, afraid of what Cash might be telling her. According to Cash, he'd eaten dinner there the last two nights. He "liked the company," he'd explained when Dex asked him why he wasn't dining on the catered food at the Big K.

Sure, John had thought. He did too.

It seemed, however, that Cash had been tight-lipped about his daily activities, because no one had looked at John twice tonight. He half expected a twitter of laughter. Big John Kincaid, local romance writer.

He was already packing his bags, physically and emotionally. It would help make his exit easier if Lolly hadn't looked so radiant tonight. Dressed in a brown prairie skirt, a pair of boots, and a tank top under her jacket, she looked about twenty, especially with her blonde hair up and soft around her face. And her smile—oh, his chest hurt.

"I'm going over to the rodeo grounds," John said to Dex, pitching his cup into the trash.

And do his best not to get into a brawl like Jonas did and lose the woman he loved.

"Dig in deep, hold tight to the wool, and remember it's okay to be afraid," Rafe said as six-year-old Tyler Riggs mounted the ewe. The boy panted but wore a gaming spirit in his eyes. "You can do this, sport."

Tyler nodded, and Rafe freed the ewe. She ran out into the yard, bleating. Tyler dug his heels into her girth, hanging on with all his strength. Seconds later he was sprawled in the dirt.

Rafe hobbled over to him, along with Tyler's dad. The little guy had begun to whimper, his lower lip trembling. Grant Riggs picked up his son and dusted him off.

Rafe leaned toward him. "It's okay if it hurts, kid. That's part of riding. But you did it—you stayed on for nearly five seconds! That's a win!"

Tyler looked up at him, big eyes glistening. He swallowed and forced a smile. "Really?"

Rafe tugged his hat down. "You betcha. Get over there and get your ribbon!"

Tyler jogged to the fence, where the staff of the Little Tyke Rodeo had a ribbon waiting. Everyone got a ribbon today.

Even Rafe, who wore one that said *Rodeo Instructor* on his shirt. He'd been to dozens of rodeo clinics over the years, but he never tired of the littlest buckaroos trying their hand at mutton bustin'. Their fearful eyes, their sense of triumph, even when they hit the ground, reminded him of when he'd been young, dreaming big.

Too big.

"Me next!" A little girl with long brown braids and freckles on her nose climbed the gate.

Rafe glanced at her mother, who shrugged. "Why not?" He opened the gate. "We're an equal opportunity stain maker." He leaned over. "What's your name, cowgirl?"

"Sammy."

"Sammy, you ever ridden a ewe before?"

She shook her head.

"Okay, then, listen close." Rafe explained the basics—how to dig her hands into the wool, grip her legs around the animal's body. "You ready?" he asked as he lifted her onto the animal. She felt so small, so light. A bird.

"I'm ready!" Her high voice, rife with enthusiasm, made him smile.

He opened the gate, and the ewe rocketed out of the chute.

Rafe watched as little Sammy glued herself to the animal, fighting to stay on until she'd nearly dragged the animal over with her.

"Good job, Sammy!" he hollered, hopping over to her.

She stood up, fairly glowing. "Let's do that again!"

Rafe laughed. "We'll see. Go get your ribbon."

Sammy took off, and her mother waved her thanks to Rafe.

What might it be like to have a little girl like her, with long brown braids, freckles on her nose?

"Rafe!" Stefanie stood at the corral, one leg up on the rail. She wore a pair of straight-leg jeans, a black T-shirt that showed off her tan, and her long black hair loose under a straw hat. "I brought you supper."

Rafe ducked through the gates. "Thanks." He took the plate of baked beans, potato salad, and a brat and walked over to his father's red truck. Looking past her to the crowd in the parking lot, he scanned for–

"She's talking to Lincoln Cash."

"What, oh, who?" He forked some beans into his mouth.

"You know who. Kitty. Lolly was with Cash, and I guess she wanted Kitty to meet him or something. They're sitting in the stands."

Rafe didn't respond, taking a bite of potato salad. He knew Cash better than some and certainly better than he'd let on to Piper and Kitty. His gaze explored the stands. Sure enough, Kitty sat with Lolly and Cash. Cash's hands moved in wild gesticulation. Probably turning on the charm, like he did with all the ladies.

His potato salad stuck in his throat, choking off his air supply. He swallowed it, then looked at himself. Dusty from his jeans to his once-clean gold shirt, he wore a knee brace and had practically hobbled out of the corral.

Rafe supposed that next to Lincoln Cash he might seem . . . less than star quality. Even a has-been. Cash might be feeding Kitty lurid stories of a former, yet too-recent, Rafe Noble.

Rafe set his plate on the tailgate, his appetite gone. He wasn't a has-been. Yes, he might have a few chips, be one step slower, but if Kitty thought he couldn't be a champion again . . .

He turned to Stefanie. "Tell Kitty to keep her eyes on the bull riders tonight." He dropped his plate into the garbage before Stefanie could respond and headed straight for the rodeo officials.

Hang on to your hat, Kitty, because Rafe Noble, GetRowdy bull-riding champ, has a show for you tonight.

❧

"He's going to do *what?*" Kat sat in the stands, trying to comprehend Stefanie's words, tossing the what-ifs through her brain.

What if Rafe rode a bull again and got hurt? What if she told him how she felt, how she had turned into a fan of the real Rafe Noble, and begged him not to ride? What if she stayed here, started a life as Kitty Russell?

She didn't want to think about the what-ifs.

Kat looked for Rafe in the cluster of cowboys by the announcers' booth. "Why does he suddenly feel the need to risk his neck? Is it the money?"

"I doubt it. The prize tonight is a whopping two thousand dollars." Stefanie glanced at Lincoln Cash, and Kat thought she saw a slight blush on her face. "He was just eating dinner, and he looked over, saw you, and all of a sudden, he's GetRowdy's famous bull rider in action."

Kat had thought Rafe looked more like the poster boy for the Boys & Girls Clubs. She'd watched him help the kids ride the sheep, and she'd turned all gooey inside.

She needed to get some media out here to shoot footage of

him playing with the kids. She even had visions of flying some of the healthier Mercy Doctors patients to the Silver Buckle so Rafe could teach them to rope. The fresh air and wide spaces certainly wouldn't hurt their treatment. She knew Rafe would make the perfect Breckenridge Foundation fund-raiser. Soon he'd know it too. If he lived that long, the idiot.

"He's going to hurt himself," Kat said almost to herself. Rafe's words the day he'd taught her to ride the bull zeroed into her thoughts. "He could get killed."

Stefanie shook her head. "He's about as hardheaded as those bulls he rides."

"What's wrong with him?" Lincoln Cash asked.

"Rafe's injured—or at least was injured," Kat answered, not elaborating on the circumstances behind Rafe's wounds. It didn't matter anymore.

"He had knee surgery just a couple of weeks ago," Stefanie added.

"Are we talking about Rafe Noble? bull rider?" Cash asked.

"You know him?" Stefanie asked.

Kat stood up, searching for Rafe. Why would he—?

"Rafe and I are old friends. He consulted on a movie I did a few years ago. If I remember right, he and I were interested in the same makeup artist." Cash smiled.

Kat looked at Lincoln. Did Rafe think that Lincoln might be interested in . . . her? Now she was really making leaps.

Which was why his ego had kicked in. "Excuse me," she said, stepping down the bleachers.

"Kat . . . ," Stefanie said.

Kat ignored her, a strange feeling moving her legs, gathering momentum. That stiff-necked cowboy. He had nothing to prove. Not to her at least.

She lengthened her stride as she wove between horses and trailers toward a group of riders attaching numbers to their vests. Beyond them, at the contestants' table, she spotted Rafe arguing with a judge.

"I'll pay the fee tomorrow; you know it. Just let me draw a bull tonight." Rafe leaned against the table. Kat knew him well enough to hear the pain in his drawl.

She didn't pause to think, just let her emotions drive her right into the conversation. "He's hurt, and he shouldn't ride," she announced to the judge.

"Kitty, get out of here." When Rafe's dark eyes narrowed at her, she recognized the bull rider she'd met the first day on the ranch. The one in pain, with rawhide around his heart, who was still gritting his teeth against the truth that his bull-riding days were over. The one bent on impressing the girls.

Impressing her?

"Excuse us," Kat said to the man and looped her arm around Rafe. "I need to talk to super cowboy here."

He glared at her, but she smiled at him and tugged him away from the judge.

"What are you doing here?" Rafe hissed, balancing himself on the rail of a metal corral.

"What do you think? Trying to keep you from permanently injuring yourself. The fact that you have to brace yourself on this gate should tell you something."

"It's eight seconds." His voice had lost pitch, and he clenched his jaw, as if trying to stem a flow of words.

Kat noticed a few onlookers and motioned toward the privacy behind a horse trailer.

To her shock, Rafe followed her, refusing to acknowledge the pain on his face. In the shadows of the trailer, his expression softened, and with it, his tone. "I can handle eight seconds."

Kat lowered her voice. "Eight seconds . . . to prove what?"

"I'm not trying to prove anything. I just want to ride." Some of the fight had gone out of him, but he obviously wasn't ready to let go yet.

"You're not ready. Anyone can see that." She gestured to his leg. "Just because you can haul yourself onto a horse doesn't mean you can hang on to a bull. Thanks to you, I know you need more than brute strength for that."

His eyes flashed. "What are you saying?"

Kat looked at the healing scar over his eye from where he'd hit the windshield, at his broad shoulders, at the way a muscle pulled in his jaw and decided that she hadn't come out West just to rescue her foundation.

She put a hand on his chest, touching his shirt. "Listen to me. I believe in you. I know you could ride any bull out here tonight, could stay on and probably even win. I believe you are exactly that stubborn and tough. But I want to two-step with you tonight, and that's going to be tough if you're taken out on a stretcher. And I'm not real interested in dancing with John."

Something flickered in Rafe's eyes, something so needy it swiped her breath from her chest.

"What about Lincoln? Do you want to dance with him?" He said it so softly that she might not have heard it, but she'd known—no, *hoped*—all along that this wasn't about bull riding. Or maybe it was about losing his life and not knowing how to get it back except by riding a bull.

"I don't want to dance with Lincoln Cash," she said, smiling. "He's just playing a part. You're the real cowboy here."

Rafe looked away.

"You don't have to be a bull rider to impress me." Kat took a step closer, suddenly feeling like she'd been waiting for this man—this *moment*—her entire life. Feeling both brave and terrified at the same time. Feeling like she'd finally found the person she wanted to be. Kitty Russell, daughter of the champ.

She smoothed Rafe's gold shirt. "I'm already impressed," she whispered.

Rafe snaked out his arm, wrapped it around her waist, and pulled her close, so close that she could see the different shades of brown in his eyes, his long lashes. Even the hope hidden by his danger-ous smile. "So, if you don't want me to ride, how are you going to stop me, Kitty?"

She swallowed, searched his face, her heart in her throat. "I don't . . . I . . . uh—"

He kissed her. Really kissed her, pulling her close, tight to him, as if she might be his very breath.

She kissed him back exactly the same way. As if a veil had been pulled from her eyes, she knew the truth. She was falling hard for Rafe Noble. Not poster boy Rafe but the Rafe who had helped her connect with her father, the Rafe who sat with her and named wild-flowers, the Rafe who petted kittens and still missed his mother, and the Rafe who was still trying to close up the hole in his heart. With everything inside, she wanted to stay and help that wound heal.

She put both arms around his neck and deepened her kiss. Rafe.

He smelled of leather and hard work, and his arm around her felt strong enough to hold her there in his embrace forever.

"Kitty," he said as he pulled away. In his eyes she saw everything she'd been denying for a week. He gave her the softest of smiles. "Yeah, that will stop me."

She grinned. "Good. Now, come up and sit with me in the stands. And then take me to the street dance."

The smallest spark of sweet danger lit his expression, and it sent a ripple of delight through her. "I dunno. . . . I think I suddenly want to ride again. . . ."

"Rafe!"

He gave her a very naughty grin. "Stop me?"

"Oh, you are trouble, aren't you?"

"You know it, sweet thing." He threaded his fingers together behind her back, trapping her.

Kat ran her fingers against his five o'clock shadow and knew the last thing she could stop was the way her heart went tumbling out as she kissed him again.

⁂

Lolly froze at the registration table, watching elegant, successful, wealthy Katherine Breckenridge make the same mistakes as her mother.

Lolly managed a shaky breath and turned away from the scene, feeling weak. She couldn't let Kat do this. Rafe was exactly the wrong type of man for her. He could never make her happy, not long-term. Sure, he had a smile that could tangle her mind and make her believe he hung the moon, but that didn't mean they'd get married and ride off into the sunset.

Rafe would chase his dream. Kat would follow him, be disowned by her grandfather, and discover that love doesn't pay the bills. Rafe might even start drinking—hadn't Lolly heard wild tales about him?—and take out his losses on Kat.

At best, Kat would wind up in a one-horse town, seeing her dreams sift between her fingers, dropping into bed at night in a tiny trailer with an air conditioner on the fritz.

Fighting the scream building inside her, Lolly strode back to the stands, where Stefanie talked with Lincoln Cash.

Kat needed to leave Phillips. Yesterday, it appeared.

Why couldn't men be like Lincoln Cash? Handsome, polite. And three nights in a row he'd arrived at the diner asking for a piece of pie. He'd even joked of offering her a job as his personal pie maker.

But Lolly wasn't a fool. And she wasn't about to let a silly dream make her change her name, her address. Still, his attention resurrected old dreams—the ones she'd entertained as a starry-eyed seventeen-year-old en route from South Dakota to Tinseltown.

She stood at the bottom steps of the stands, and a thought—one John would approve of—struck her. What if God had brought Kat out here to Lolly's territory so Lolly could keep her from making the same mistakes her mother had? To keep her from that heartache?

Lolly was just climbing the stairs when she saw John enter the stands. She started to raise a hand to him but stopped when she saw him in conversation with Dex—she remembered Cash introducing her to the director of *Unshackled* in the tent. Why would John be talking to him?

She lowered her hand, confused, as she watched them find a

seat together. John looked miserable, however. Much like that time she'd told him she wouldn't marry him.

"Lolly, I love you. Please marry me." She remembered too well that night. And the way she'd started to cry, glimpsing happiness, knowing it would never be hers.

She scooted into her place beside Cash. Stefanie sat on the other side of him, lost in one of his stories. For a second, Lolly couldn't help but notice what a striking couple they made—Lincoln with his blond hair, blue eyes and Stefanie with her dark eyes, black hair. And something about Stefanie's smile . . . Lolly'd had a smile like that once.

Her gaze went back to John, and a pang went through her. Had she even told him good-bye last night? Or had that been the night before? She'd been in such a hurry to read the next chapter of *Unshackled*, delighted that she now had a face to put with the Jonas character.

Although she'd thought Lincoln would fit the part, it wasn't his blue eyes and blond hair she saw when she read about Jonas.

"Did you find them?" Stefanie asked, leaning past Lincoln to snare Lolly's attention.

"Uh . . . yes." Lolly made a face, not sure how to tell—

"Here they are."

Lolly followed Stefanie's gaze, speechless at the way Kat held Rafe's hand. The way she glowed. The way she looked as if her life was perfect.

Oh, boy, did she have heartache in front of her.

~CHAPTER 11

KAT WASN'T SURE which part of the night had been her favorite. Rafe's voice in her ear as he taught her about bull riding, about the scoring and technique as she sat next to him in the stands, holding his hand. Or two-stepping with him, if a bit awkwardly, at the street dance. Or sitting now on a blanket, her back against his chest as they watched the Fourth of July fireworks on the Phillips football field.

Maybe all of it. Every single moment of the fairy-tale night.

He had such strong, tough hands. Full of calluses yet tender as he rubbed his thumb over her hand. She'd seen that tenderness in his eyes when he two-stepped with her and felt it in his arms as he wrapped them around her.

"I can't decide what I like more, the fireworks or the stars," Kat said.

"Mmm, I know what I like," Rafe said, his lips brushing her neck.

She wrapped her arms around his biceps. "So, are you glad I stuck around and annoyed you into helping me?"

"Did I really say annoyed?" He laughed. "Thank you for not giving up. I think . . . I needed your help to see the truth." He ran his hand down her arm. "I don't know how I can live without bull riding in my life . . . but maybe I could if you stuck around."

He'd really give up bull riding for her? But what would it mean for her to live here in Montana? What would happen to the Breckenridge Foundation and Mercy Doctors?

The fireworks popped, sprays of red and blue, turning the sky into a carnival.

"I went to Mexico—that's where Mercy Doctors have their clinic. I met a boy named Carlos." Kat faced Rafe and ran her hand over his forearm, over the muscle defined there. "He was dying of cancer, and although it was excruciating, he barely made a sound. Only his eyes . . . they followed me around the room, and sometimes, when he thought I wasn't looking, a tear would leak out. On the night he died, he asked for me; he wanted to thank me. But I hadn't done anything. Nothing to save this boy's life. I'd cleaned him up, prayed for him, but in the end, he died all the same."

"Kitty, you can't expect to change the world."

"Actually, I'd be happy changing just one person's life. Just one. Which is why your help means so much. Maybe I'm not a failure at this fund-raising stuff after all."

Rafe twirled a lock of her hair between his fingers. "You're not a failure. You're the amazing Kitty Russell." He picked up her hand and wove his fingers into hers. "I need to tell you something. About six months ago a friend of mine was killed by the bull I was riding. I sort of blamed myself." His Adam's apple bobbed in his throat, and she wanted very much to lay her head on his chest. "I hit my lowest point when I crashed into the hotel. It was a bad day, and something inside me just snapped. I didn't mean to do it, and for a while, I wished I'd never woken up in that hospital bed."

Fireworks spattered the inky sky.

"Rafe—"

"Let me finish. I'm not a good man, but . . . I want to be. Around you, Kitty, I want to be. I've been thinking about what you said . . . about purpose. And grace and peace. Well, I feel that when I'm with you." He winced slightly as he said it, and she knew what his admission had cost him.

Kat hadn't expected that. Worse, she hadn't expected how good it would feel, just to sit here with him, to hear the hope, the healing in his voice. She knew that there had been a real hero under all that barbed wire. "Rafe, you are a good man." She touched his chest. "When I look at you, I see a man who fits his name. You know what I think?"

He covered her hand with his, looking at it.

"You've been your own worst enemy. I don't know what you're fighting, but I believe you're more than you think you are."

A cry of delight from the crowd caught her attention, and she watched a red cluster bleed down the sky.

"Are you saying you heard my inner cry for help across the space-time continuum and came running?" Rafe gave her a wicked grin, but around his eyes, she sensed the slightest edging of chagrin.

She wet her lips. "No. A cry—" she swallowed, knowing how stupid she was about to sound—"a cry to be loved for the man you are. Not the man you pretend to be."

Rafe's smile vanished. A strange emotion played across his face, and for a second she stilled, praying she hadn't gone too far.

"Maybe you're right. Maybe . . . I'm just looking for someone who won't flinch when they see the truth."

Kat touched her hand to the side of his face, then leaned close and gently, ever so gently, pressed her lips to his. "I'm not flinching, Rafe Noble," she whispered. "In fact, I believe in you."

He smiled at her. "I believe in you too, Kitty."

She sank into his arms, letting everything become fuzzy and sweet as he kissed her, hiding herself in Rafe's intoxicating embrace, refusing to accept that tomorrow just might show up.

She wasn't going home; that much was sure. She knew it as Rafe drove her back to Lolly's trailer and kissed her good night at the door. She hadn't felt this right in months, years even. So immensely far from the person she'd left behind in New York nearly two weeks ago.

Was it already two weeks? She watched Rafe drive away, something inside her wanting to sing. She hadn't talked to anyone at home in nearly two weeks, particularly Bradley. The fact she hardly felt guilt should have been a red flag, shouldn't it? Bradley didn't love her—not like Rafe did. At least she *thought* Rafe loved her. He hadn't told her as much, but she could see it in his eyes.

Bradley never looked at her that way, which meant he'd find someone else someday.

Going to her room, Kat noticed that light snuck out of the crack under Lolly's door. She didn't want to bother her but felt restless as she tucked herself into bed. She picked up her copy of *Unshackled*, lying facedown on the nightstand, and began to read.

Mary stood at the window, watching the twilight puddle in the washes of her land, turning the sage silver, the prairie grass a dark green. Cattle lounged on a table that would make them fat by fall and hopefully turn another profit for her growing ranch. The years without Matthias had been healing years. For the land. For herself. Charlie and Jonas would be proud of the ranch she'd built.

The smell of the fresh-cut hay hung in the heavy August air, and she inhaled, wondering how yet another season had gone by without being in Jonas's arms.

Seven years since he left. The breadth of it felt engulfing as she realized how far she'd come from that day when Jonas told her that he would come back. That she should hang on to his words.

Her grip had begun to weaken. Yet she could only blame herself.

She heard movement downstairs and knew that Rosie had returned from her after-dinner walk. That her daughter found joy in the land the same way as her father—her real father—had brought Mary peace.

"Mama?" Rosie called from the bottom of the stairs. "Mr. Lewis is here to call on you."

Mary sighed, turned away from the window, and went to the door. "Thank you. I'll meet him downstairs."

Tall, churchgoing, proper Erland Lewis owned land just south of hers. A man from wealthy stock in Boston, he wanted to try his hand at ranching. His enthusiasm made her smile. He might be a tenderfoot, but he was devoted and he liked her. With the right response from Mary, he might even love her.

Her smile faded. She closed the door. Then, turning to the writing desk, she sat down and pulled open the chocolate box. She remembered when it had appeared in her mailbox, along with a sweep of emotion so strong that it lingered long after the taste of the chocolate. If she closed her eyes she could still imagine Jonas, with his brown hair, kind eyes, strong hands, writing the letters now stored in the box. Hundreds of them, filled with his life, his words.

She slid one of the earliest letters out to read it again.

My dearest Mary,

I hope this letter and the few dollars it contains for your sustenance might convey my longing to be with you. I have found work at a meat-packing plant outside Sioux Falls and am preparing for the day when we might be together. I long for you more each passing day. I wait patiently for your word to return. Through my parents, I heard the sheriff affirmed that Matthias's death was an accident and that it had rained on our land. I hold out hope that it will again turn green and become a place in which you might prosper.

Around here, the army is recruiting for fliers who might serve with the Brits. I've given this some consideration in light of our circumstances. Trust that should I enter the service of our country, I do this with full intention of returning to you. Soon, I hope.

My love to Rosie. Know that you are in my prayers, sweet Mary.

Yours,

Jonas

Mary folded the letter. He promised he'd return as soon as she beckoned. But she hadn't, fearing the sheriff's suspicion.

So she waited for the right moment when she could at last feel peace and believe that she deserved to be happy.

Soon, I hope, he'd written.

Soon. That word hung in her mind, a word of hope and heartache. A word she longed to hate, that she turned to in the dark of night when she felt frail and alone.

Putting the letter back into the envelope, she placed it on the desk and removed the white telefax from the air force.

If they had been married, it might have been sent to her. But the news came through Jonas's mother, evidence that Jonas had betrayed his intentions about Mary to his parents.

Missing. How could Jonas be missing when he took up so much room in her heart? She could feel his hand in hers as he helped her out of the hennery, smell his earthy, male aroma, taste the sweetness of desire when he looked at her. She heard his laughter, his tenor singing the songs now playing in her heart, and saw the look of fury on his face as he'd protected her from Matthias.

He couldn't be missing.

"Jonas, come home," she whispered. "It's time."

She heard a tap at the door, and a second later, Rosie opened it and stuck her head in. "Are you coming down, Mama?"

Mary found a smile, nodded.

Come home, Jonas. Soon.

Kat closed the book. She knew exactly how Mary felt. Rafe took up so much room in her heart that she could trace his face in her sleep. And as she set the book on the nightstand, she knew that she wasn't going to let him go or leave him, like Jonas left Mary. No, she'd found where she belonged.

Lolly stood in the darkness, listening. Kat had arrived home less than an hour ago, laughing and buoyant. Lolly stood in the shadows not breathing as she watched Rafe kiss her good night. *Please, please, go home, Rafe.* While she knew that Kat had been raised with a list of dos and don'ts, so had she, and even good girls can fall to the temptation of midnight kisses and murmurs of love.

She'd slipped into her room, breathing relief when Kat came inside alone. Now, Kat's deep breathing suggested she'd finally fallen asleep. Lolly felt like a thief. Or a traitor. But this was for Kat's own good. If Kat had the good sense she was born with, she'd figure that out . . . in time.

Lolly eased open the door. Kat's purse, a cute pink bag that looked completely out of place here in the forgotten spaces of Montana yet perfect for her life back home, lay on the floor, her cell phone bag attached to the handle.

Lolly snagged the purse and tiptoed from the room. The cell phone still had juice, and Lolly stood in the dark hallway, opening the contacts menu. Then she scrolled down until she located *Bradley Lymon.*

Kat had no idea what her little vanishing act off the planet had stirred. Lolly could hardly believe it today when she'd turned on the midday news and seen a shot of Kat, then the impassioned plea by her boyfriend, Bradley Lymon, at a press conference begging for her safe return. Pleading for her safety.

Something Lolly wanted more than Katherine could imagine. She knew what it felt like to fall for a charming cowboy. But Bradley Lymon represented security. A future.

Lolly wrote down the number and slipped the phone back into the bag. Tucking it into Kat's room, Lolly snuck into her deserted diner.

Standing at the wall phone, she dialed, hearing her heart thunder in her chest.

A sleepy, confused voice answered. "Hello?"

Lolly took a deep breath . . . and told Bradley Lymon exactly what his girlfriend was up to in eastern Montana.

***

"I believe you are exactly that stubborn and tough." Rafe heard Kitty's words over and over as he sat on the porch, watching the dawn of a new day. A new life. He'd kissed plenty of women but never like he kissed Kitty. He showed her exactly how he felt, how she had become part of his world in a frighteningly short period of time, and how he had no intention of letting her walk out of his life.

"I don't know how I can live without bull riding in my life . . . but maybe I could if you stuck around." Had he really meant that?

He'd hardly slept all night, thinking about kissing her today on the bluff or tonight on a blanket under the stars near the balm of Gilead trees.

He must have knocked more than a few cells loose from his brain, because he was actually thinking about the *m* word. Perhaps she'd only said that he had nothing to prove to keep him off a bull, away from injury, but somehow he believed her. He didn't have to prove anything to Kitty. And that felt oddly freeing.

"Where's Kat this morning?" Stefanie asked as she joined Rafe on the porch. "She's late."

"She had some calls to make." Rafe blew on his coffee, trying to hide his grin. "Something about business back home."

Stefanie nodded, then sat beside him. "Got this in the mail yesterday." She held out an envelope.

Rafe glanced at the return address. Mexico. He slipped his thumb under the flap and opened it.

He struggled to decipher the Spanish words. Although Lucia was nearly fluent in speaking English, running the ranch and taking care of Manny left her little time to learn how to correspond in another language. Most of the time, Rafe read her letters with a Spanish-English dictionary. "It's from Lucia. I think it says something about Manny. And his being sick." He looked up at Stefanie, who hadn't moved. "His leukemia is out of remission."

"Oh, Rafe, I'm so sorry."

He put down the letter, and she picked it up and read it. "It says more than that. Good thing I got good grades in high school, because according to my rusty Spanish, she's on her way stateside."

He stared out toward the sunrise as it bathed the yard and his truck. Shadows still filled the gullies that edged the driveway. "I told her if she ever needed anything that she could find me here, through you, and I'd take care of things." He raised his gaze to hers. "I made a real mess of my life and now theirs."

Stefanie put her hand on his shoulder. "It's going to work out. Like Dad always said, you're not in this alone."

"Thanks. I appreciate your support."

She gave him a small smile. "I think Dad was talking about God."

Rafe stood. "God isn't on my side. Not anymore. You should have figured that out by now."

Stefanie said nothing as he headed toward the barn.

Bradley's cell phone went to voice mail on the first ring, which told Kat he'd shut it off. He was probably in a closed-door meeting with one of her grandfather's partners. Or maybe the big man himself.

Hopefully they weren't discussing her and the abysmal state of the foundation's finances. It was a temporary situation she fully intended to fix. With Rafe's help.

She elected not to leave a message, closed her phone, and dropped it onto the bed. She'd slept in this morning, but after rolling in long past midnight, she'd decided that Rafe needed the extra sleep also.

It took all her effort not to get up at the crack of dawn and drive out to the Silver Buckle to tell Rafe exactly how she felt about him.

She'd never had to play hard to get and wasn't even sure how to do it. Most of the men she met were naturally scared off by her grandfather.

Dressing in a pair of jeans and a T-shirt, Kat went over to Lolly's for breakfast.

Lolly smiled at her, a restraint in her greeting that bothered Kat.

Kat slid onto a stool. "Coffee, please. And do you have any leftover pie?"

Lolly poured a cup of coffee. "Eggs are better for breakfast."

"I'd rather have pie. Blueberry."

Lolly said nothing as she turned away.

"Morning, Kat."

Kat turned to see Nick, Rafe's older brother, sliding onto the stool beside her. She tried not to bristle, but some of Rafe's attitude had rubbed off on her. She wasn't sure why, but there was bad blood between these two. "Good morning, Nick."

Nick motioned to Lolly for a cup of coffee. She put that and a bagel down in front of him. "I saw Rafe's truck drive in pretty late last night."

Kat's face heated, and it didn't help when Lolly gave her a dark look as she plunked down a piece of blueberry pie.

"Not that I'm babysitting," Nick added, buttering his bagel. "Actually, he's been easier to be around since he met you. I'm thinking you're good medicine."

Lolly raised an eyebrow, and Kat matched it. "Really."

Nick nodded, took a sip of coffee. "Rafe has had a rough few years. With Dad dying and then his friend Manuel, he's taken it hard. Now he's being sued and losing his career. . . . I guess I'm just trying to say thank you."

Kat took a bite of pie, washed it down with coffee, and wiped her mouth. "Thank you?"

Nick swallowed a bite of his bagel. "For being his friend and giving him something to reach for."

"I think she's more than his friend," Lolly said.

Kat glanced at her, surprised at the venom in her voice. Apparently, this meddling in other people's business was part of that so-called small-town charm.

Nick smirked. "Maybe."

"I think she needs to go home before she gets hurt."

Kat's fork stilled in midair.

Nick put down his cup. "What exactly do you mean by that, Lolly?"

Lolly crossed her arms over her chest.

Silence settled upon the diner—all three other patrons had looked up, listening to this exchange. Kat wanted to duck under her stool and crawl out.

"You know what I mean," Lolly said evenly. "Rafe's not exactly the relationship type. His reputation with the ladies stretches from here to Wyoming and beyond."

"I don't think it's that bad."

"The tabloids are saying he was drunk when he drove into that hotel."

"Lolly, that isn't—"

"And Kat, here—she's already got a man."

Everything inside Kat dropped to her knees, including her stomach, complete with the pie that had turned rock hard. How did Lolly . . . ?

Lolly raised her chin, although the faintest blush betrayed her.

"No, I don't," Kat said softly. At least not the one she wanted. Besides, Bradley no longer laid claim to her heart, if he ever had.

Nick turned to stare at Kat.

"I don't," she mumbled. "Not really."

"Define *not really*," Nick said.

"I . . . Before I came here, I was dating someone."

"I read that she's engaged."

Kat glared at Lolly, then stood. "I'm not engaged, and I think you should stop listening to rumors."

Nick's hand on her arm stopped her. "Walk with me," he said in a tone that didn't brook argument. He glanced at Lolly, then got up, put on his hat, and walked out the door.

As if under some spell, Kat followed.

The heat of the morning sucked away her breath, and Kat shaded her eyes with her hand as they walked down Main Street. Sweat formed between her shoulder blades.

"My brother and sister are twins," Nick said as he shoved his hands into his back pockets. "And Rafe was born with a heart defect."

"I know. A hole in his heart. I saw his scar."

"Then you can also guess how hard it was on my parents. My dad especially. They nearly lost Rafe twice, and I'd guess that there might have been some bargaining with God during those early years. It took a very long time for my father to let Rafe on a horse or out into the fields. It used to rankle me how he'd let Rafe stay at home reading books or helping my mother while I worked the ranch. I'm ashamed to admit that I called him a baby for too many years."

"Rafe's one of the toughest men I know," Kat said.

"Yeah, he is. But I didn't figure that out until after I was long gone and he'd started riding bulls. At first I thought he did it to spite my dad. Then I wondered if it might be about me."

"You?"

He shrugged, and that movement let her see his regret. Could it be that Nick wasn't the bad guy after all?

"I was a horrible big brother. I taunted him, made him feel weak. Even now, I can't figure out a way to tell him that I want him to stick around. It comes out . . . just like my father. In negative speech that sounds like I'm daring Rafe to go back to bull riding. I think, in a way, Rafe also rides to prove something to himself. Although I don't know what."

Kat said nothing, but she remembered the look on Rafe's face when she'd seen his scar and the way he'd tried to talk his way onto a bull last night. Yeah, his riding was as much about making some sort of peace with himself as it was earning his spurs with his big brother. She rubbed her arms, not wanting to surrender his secrets. Still, she had to put words to what she'd been sensing all week, if only to help herself sort it out. "I don't think Rafe even knows why he rides. He just has to. Maybe it's in his blood."

Nick responded with a chuckle that had nothing to do with humor. "The problem is, Rafe is in bad shape. It's not only his knee; it's his neck, which has hairline fractures. Every time I remind him of this, he thinks I'm taunting him." He shook his head. "When you walked into the picture, Stef and I thought we had a chance to get through to him. Convince him that we wanted him around."

Kat wasn't sure what to say.

"I think my brother is falling for you. Stef and I are all for it, especially if that means he stays out of trouble. I don't know how you feel about him, but Lolly's wrong. As far as I know, Rafe's never had a serious girlfriend. Never really been in love—"

"And you're afraid I'm going to break his heart."

A shadow of that truth brushed over Nick's face.

A feeling filled her chest; it was so overwhelming that her eyes burned, moistened. "If it makes you feel any better, I'm—"

"Katherine, I can't believe I found you. What were you thinking, disappearing like that?"

Kat froze at the voice behind her, the heavy New York accent so out of place on this dusty street corner. Then she slowly turned and tried to find a smile for her almost fiancé, Bradley Lymon.

CHAPTER 12

"OH NO, WHAT have I done?" Lolly watched through the diner window as Kat turned white and her expression changed from that glow she'd carried over the past few days—thanks to Rafe—to defeat as she stared at Bradley Lymon. Well attired, even if a bit rumpled, in a silk suit, the man must have chartered a plane the second he hung up the phone with Lolly.

"What's that, Lolly?" Lincoln Cash, who'd entered the diner shortly after Nick had ushered Kat out, looked up from his pile of eggs.

"Nothing." Only, by the look on Kat's face, it was something. Something so oddly familiar that it brought a rush of memory too painful to be ignored.

Lolly pressed a hand to her stomach, aware that she might be ill. "Excuse me." She went into the back room, then closed herself into the bathroom. Staring at the reflection in the mirror—the age lines and the tiny scar on her chin—she refused to listen to the past.

She ran cold water, splashed it on her face, then braced her hands on the sink and drew a deep breath. She wouldn't allow her fear to spill over into Kat's life. Exiting the bathroom, she smoothed her apron, nodded to a perplexed Cody, and returned to the counter.

"More coffee?" Cash said.

"Sure." She grabbed the pot, poured him a cup. Outside, Nick had vanished. Kat and Bradley, however, still stood on the sidewalk.

Lincoln glanced over his shoulder. "Looks like a lovers' quarrel to me." He took a sip of coffee. "This is the best coffee I've ever had—and I've been all over the world." He reached out, and when he grabbed Lolly's hand, she nearly jumped. His blue eyes caught hers. "I can't believe that a beautiful, smart, talented woman is hidden out here in the hills. If you're willing to listen, I have an offer for you."

⚜

"I *did* call you," Kat said, wishing Bradley would stop pacing in the middle of Main Street for the entire town to watch. Nick had left—or slunk off, depending on the viewpoint. She had a sinking feeling he was flooring it back to the Silver Buckle to tell Rafe . . . what? That she'd lied to him? led him on? fabricated her feelings for him?

"I never got any messages!" This wholly-in-touch-with-his-feelings Bradley had the power to frighten her with his deep frown, his eyes boring into hers. "I was worried sick!"

"I called you the day I left and told you I was going on vacation—"

"Cari booked you a room at a spa in San Francisco—a reservation you didn't show up for. Can you imagine how your grandfather and I felt? I thought you'd been kidnapped."

Kat gave a derisive laugh. "As if Grandfather would pay the ransom."

Bradley didn't join in her self-deprecating humor. "I would have."

Kat's smile vanished. "Listen, Bradley, I'm sorry. I am. I just needed to get away."

"To Phillips, Montana? What's here? A hot spring? Maybe a five-star resort that isn't yet on the map?"

At his words, the door to the diner opened, and Lincoln Cash walked out. Kat looked up at him and gave him the barest of smiles. He nodded to her, greeted Bradley.

Bradley watched him go with a frown. "Is that Lincoln Cash, the actor?"

"Yes, and as you can see, there is more to this little town than you give it credit for."

"Okay, so why are *you* here?" Bradley's voice had lowered, and he blocked the sun, a shadow of anger and confusion.

"I came to . . . save the Breckenridge Foundation. I have a plan."

"Does it involve that guy—the same one who drove his pickup through your hotel?"

"Yes. He's going to help me raise the money. We—"

Bradley let out a word she'd never heard him use before. Then he said, "So it's true."

"What's true?" Kat stared at his shiny loafers, now dusty from the street. Amazing how good a man looked in cowboy boots.

"That you've been *kissing* another man."

How had he found out? But did it really matter? Kat took a breath and gave the slightest nod. "I found someone . . . who . . ."

What? Understood her? With whom she wanted to spend the rest of her life herding cattle, roping steer, or watching kill himself in the rodeo arena? ". . . who taught me how to live like a cowboy."

"So you paid him in kisses?"

"Don't be crude. I was just trying to keep him from killing himself." The words came out with a tone of indignation, yet Kat felt as if she'd betrayed everything she felt for Rafe, everything that had been real and alive and incredible between them. She glared at Bradley. "Don't overreact. It's not like we're engaged or anything."

A muscle pulsed in his neck. "Let me fix that." Then, as she stood rooted, he dug into his suit pocket and pulled out a ring box. He opened it, and the solitaire stone in white gold sparkled in the sun. "You've had nearly two weeks to think about it. What's your answer?"

Kat looked up at Bradley as her eyes watered. "Maybe you should ask me first. Who knows what I might be agreeing to?"

He shook his head even as he got down on one knee on the hot pavement. Then, holding up the ring, he ground out, "Katherine Russell Breckenridge, will you marry me?"

⁂

"These pictures turned out perfect, John." Dex leaned over the digital stills he'd taken over the past three days. "Everything I need to create scenery and texture for the sound stage. Thanks for letting us use your ranch."

"You know that the story takes place in Wyoming during the dust bowl years, right?" Sometimes John felt as if he might be talking to a cloud for all the impact he made on Dex.

The director smiled and nodded. "Don't worry, John. Everything is copacetic."

John managed a smile, watching out of the corner of his eye as Dex's assistant loaded the truck. Which meant, hopefully, that Lincoln Cash would also be leaving.

Finally, he'd have Lolly to himself again. But after spending a week in the attention of Lincoln Cash, would Lolly even notice John?

"Why don't you come with us?" Dex's question jarred John back to the moment. "I have a meeting with the producer tomorrow, and you two can go over the screenplay, work out any last glitches. You're leaving soon anyway, right? We'll send a mover out; he can pack up the place, send your stuff to California."

"I don't know. . . . It seems too soon. . . ."

"You told me you've been waiting to do this for fifteen years. Now's your chance. Besides, didn't you say your Realtor found you a condo on the beach in Malibu? Can't buy without doing a walk-through." Dex brushed past John and walked over to his assistant. "Hey, don't put that on the truck. I'm taking that with me. . . ."

John stood in the kitchen of his family's home, listening to his father's voice. *You'll never leave, Johnny boy. You'll always be a rancher, Son. Get that through your head.* For the most part, the voice had spoken the truth. He'd stayed. But not because he couldn't escape.

Marry me, Lolly. Maybe twenty years was too long to wait.

Especially when she so easily rejected him for a wannabe cowboy.

Dex returned, tore his new cowboy hat from his head, and wiped his brow. "I don't know how you live out here in this heat."

"Me either," John said. "Hold up while I pack a bag."

"She's not there." Rafe put the phone down after listening to it ring thirty-seven times. He wanted to allow Lucia ample time to answer just in case she might be on the far reaches of her ranch.

"What if she's on her way to Texas or even here?" Stefanie propped one hip against the kitchen counter.

"There's nothing I can do about it now. Even if she does come, I don't have two pennies to give to help Manny." He sat in the chair and ran his hands through his hair. By throwing himself over Rafe, Manuel had given him a second chance at life—no, he suddenly realized, God had given him a second chance at life—and what had he done with it?

He couldn't bear to answer his own question.

"They still have time left on their one-year visa from when they visited last fall."

"I'm sure they're fine, Rafe," Stefanie said, putting her hand on his shoulder. She looked out the window. "Nick's back from town."

Rafe watched Nick's Silverado pull up. He got out of the truck and stood in the yard for a moment before turning to the barn. A few minutes later, Rafe heard the sound of hooves as Nick rode his horse from the corral. So much for riding fence together.

Rafe checked his watch. "I thought Kitty might be here by now."

"Maybe she got hung up in town."

With the way this day was going, for all he knew, her good sense had returned with the dawn, and she was packing her bags.

"I'm going to check on the horses down at Maggy's," Stefanie said, picking up a two-way. "Call me if you need anything."

Rafe put his head down on the table, wishing that somehow he could travel back in time and make things turn out right. With him protecting his best friend and Manuel still alive to care for his son.

Rafe's own behavior since that day made him sick. He didn't deserve the grace of living, of being happy. Of loving someone as incredible as Kitty.

Rafe limped out toward the barn. The horses in the corral nickered to him. He fetched an alfalfa cube from the burlap bag hanging in the barn and fed it to the animals through the rails.

The squeak of brazen prairie dogs in the land south of the house and the buzz of cicadas across the fields only amplified the silence in his heart. Where was Kitty? He could use her optimistic spirit right now. Maybe he should go to town. But he'd never had to chase a woman, and he wasn't about to start.

"A woman should give a guy the benefit of the doubt. Even if he doesn't say it, he still cares about her."

His words, dredged up from memory, stung. Surely Kitty knew he cared about her. He'd told her he would give up bull riding for her, for pete's sake.

Rafe rubbed the blaze on one of the quarter horses as that thought found fertile soil and germinated. He *did* care about her—more than cared, in fact. Next time she came by, he'd tell her.

Grabbing a halter, he opened the corral and whistled to his roan. The horse responded and stood still for him as he slipped on the halter, led the horse into the yard, then used a stump to spring himself up, bareback.

There was something about riding alone that always helped him clear his thoughts. When he returned, he might discover that this morning had simply been one of his many nightmares and he was still sitting under the star-strewn big sky with Kitty in his arms.

⚜ CHAPTER 13

KAT HAD JUST left Bradley standing on the sidewalk, holding out a ring.

"He should have asked nicely," Kat said to no one as she drove toward the Silver Buckle. "He sounded like he was *forced* to propose."

Wait. Grandfather hadn't . . . wouldn't . . . She wasn't such an embarrassment that her grandfather would have to *bribe* someone to marry her, was she? Just because she wasn't cover-girl beautiful like her mother didn't mean she couldn't be beautiful in her own way.

Had Rafe called her beautiful? She couldn't remember.

In fact, Rafe had said *nothing* about his feelings for her. He believed in her, called her amazing, and wrapped her in his arms and kissed her like she'd never been kissed before. Then again, he'd kissed plenty of women before, so it wasn't passion or his heart she felt in those kisses but a man with plenty of practice.

No, he'd never said he loved her. Not that she expected him to after only two weeks, but . . .

Yet Bradley had—many times. Just because Bradley didn't hold her like he'd never let her go didn't mean he didn't love her. He used words and gestures, like gifts and phone calls and flying two thousand miles, to show her how he felt.

She wiped a tear as it trailed down her cheek.

"Why are you here?" Bradley's words made her wince.

The answer felt far bigger than she imagined. She'd come out here at the end of her rope, hoping to put together her future, perhaps find pieces of herself in the past. Instead she'd discovered she had a lot more rope to work with than she realized.

She wasn't just the heiress of the Breckenridge fortune. She could ride a horse, rope a steer (okay, a dummy steer), feed calves from a bottle, two-step, ride a bull, and even talk a man out of risking his life.

But she couldn't seriously consider throwing away the life she knew, the life God had given her in New York, a life of meaning and responsibility, for the unknown—an unknown that could backfire into heartache and pain.

"I know if the bull is going to try to kill me." In a moment, she saw Rafe crushed, pale, unmoving in the dirt, a bull breathing over him. Trying to *kill* him.

Kat pulled over, her heart thumping. She couldn't watch him die.

But didn't he say he wasn't going to return to bull riding if she stayed?

Even she, a woman who'd known him for only a couple of weeks or so, could see the lies he told himself. Rafe would quit bull riding right about the time he started ballet dancing.

Lord, I don't know what to do. I think I'm falling in love with Rafe.

But I have this sick feeling he doesn't love me. And what if he goes back to bull riding?

She'd end up like her mother, that's what. Heartbroken. Unable to love even the daughter Bobby had given her. Making that daughter feel as if . . . Kat cupped her hand over her mouth. As if she was a terrible reminder of all she'd lost.

No wonder Felicia never came home, had left Kat's care to Angelina. She couldn't bear to be around the daughter who only reminded her of her grief.

Kat got back on the road, wiping her chin. *Katherine, pull yourself together.* The last thing she wanted was for Rafe to see her unraveled. He knew the Kitty who smiled and encouraged and laughed at his jokes. And she desperately wanted him to give her a reason to stay.

At the Silver Buckle, she got out of the Jeep and slammed the door. The horses in the corral lifted their heads. The wind brushed the prairie grass, gathering momentum, lifting the sweat from the back of her neck, then dying down to nothing. "Rafe?"

No answer.

Kat didn't expect him to be waiting on the porch, but it would have been nice to see his smile, to reassure herself that these past twelve days hadn't been just a dream. She walked to the house, up the porch stairs, and stood outside the screen door. "Knock, knock?"

Still no answer.

The door squealed on its hinges as she opened it. She stood in the deserted kitchen, hearing nothing from the rest of the house. A fly lifted from the bowl of apples on the counter. "Rafe?"

Kat closed the door behind her, trying to figure out what to do. Bradley, for all she knew, still stood on the street where she'd left him, and it wouldn't take long for him to get directions to the Silver

Buckle. She had never treated anyone so rudely in her life. Well, maybe once. A bull rider who had owed her so much.

And given her back more than she could imagine.

The breeze ruffled the edges of a letter sitting on top of the kitchen table. Kat noticed the Guadalajara postmark and frowned. Mercy Doctors had a clinic there. She picked up the letter and, knowing full well she was snooping, read the Spanish script.

Dear Rafe,

You promised that if ever I had a need, I could write to you. I know that you are busy on your tour, but because of your love for us and your promises, you should know that Manny's leukemia is back. This time, the doctors say that he will not survive. Rafe, I am afraid. I need you and so does Manny. So we are coming to you as soon as I can arrange our travel.

You are in our thoughts and prayers daily. Manny sends his love.

Always,
Lucia

Kat read the letter again, a knot forming in her throat, blocking off her air supply. Who was Lucia? And what kind of promises had Rafe made?

He *loved* her?

Her legs turned weak, and she reached out for a chair. Was Lucia a former girlfriend? What if . . . what if Manny was Rafe's . . . *son?*

Kat sat in the chair, putting the letter back on the table with a shaky hand and smoothing it flat. She and Rafe never talked about the past—she sensed he hadn't wanted to delve into the glory days that only reminded him of his losses. But she should have asked about his relationships with other women. With Rafe's attention this past week, she just *assumed* . . .

Good grief, he was a professional athlete. That should be some sort of siren right there.

Kat closed her eyes, orienting herself. She needed to leave. Clearly, she and Rafe lived in two different worlds. Worlds that could never be combined.

"Kat?" Piper's voice startled her.

She wiped her cheeks and found a smile. "Hey, Piper."

"I didn't think I'd see you this soon. You'll never guess what I found out."

Maybe that I have a boyfriend who came looking for me and proposed on the street this morning in front of the entire town? Kat braced herself for the answer.

"I found Laura Russell."

⚜

Lolly stood in the tiny, outdated family room in her trailer, her heart racing. The sounds of the diner lunch rush, with banging dishes and Cody calling out orders, drifted out the back door, needling her thoughts, but all she could hear was Cash's offer to hire her as his personal chef.

"Come with me," he'd said. He'd said more, of course, about the life she could lead, the home she'd have, and the stars she'd meet. Finally, after twenty years, she'd finish the dream she started. So it wasn't stardom, but being Lincoln Cash's personal cook certainly had a sparkle to it. And she'd break free of the South Dakotan girl from Mobridge who'd followed her dreams to tragedy.

She could start over and build a new life. A new Lolly. Maybe this time she'd become . . . Eliza. Like Eliza Doolittle, who changed her fate by changing her speech and telling herself that she wasn't a trollop, then summoning the courage to become the person she dreamed of.

But what of Kat? Lolly sat on the sofa, her hands over her face. What if Kat chose to stay? Lolly couldn't leave, either. She'd spent her life watching over Kat from afar, keeping a promise. She couldn't abandon her now. Especially if Kat married Rafe Noble.

By the looks of things, Bradley wasn't the knight in shining armor Lolly had hoped. She recognized the look on his face when Kat deserted him on the street. A look she'd seen the day she'd walked out of Randy's life so long ago. A chill brushed through her.

She rubbed her eyes, wishing she knew what to do. Wishing she could call John. She'd missed him the last few days, and suddenly his absence crept up on her and took away her breath. She needed to talk to John. He'd tell her what to do. About Kat. About Cash.

John would help her sort it all out. He'd been her dearest friend for twenty years. She could trust him—*should* have trusted him— because John, unlike so many others, had never betrayed her.

She picked up the phone and dialed his number. It rang six times before it flipped over to voice mail. "John, it's Lolly. . . . Can you . . . can you come by when you get this?"

Hanging up, she sank back into the sofa. She heard the bell chime and Cody's voice as he announced an order up. Thankfully, her part-time waitress knew how to cover the floor, but responsibility tugged at Lolly. She should return to her life. The life that had given her a home and a purpose.

Instead, she closed her eyes. Then grabbed the pillow on the sofa.

Under the pillow lay B. J. King's book. Lincoln would make the perfect on-screen Jonas. And she'd told him so. But as she'd devoured the story, only one man filled her mind as the real Jonas character.

John.

Missing him made her open the book.

"Mama, he's waiting."

Rosie poked her head into the Sunday school room of the chapel. She looked so beautiful at eighteen that it took Mary's breath away. How she wished she'd had the courage to make this decision years ago when Rosie could have had a proper father. But Mary had made the mistake of waiting, of believing that someday Jonas might return.

She'd waited too long to let hope drive her decisions.

Mary surveyed herself in the mirror. So different from the young, too-innocent bride who'd married Charlie in front of friends and family in Chicago. She wasn't foolish enough to believe that she had any chance at a bright future. She'd tried survival—with disastrous consequences. She'd take contentment and be as happy as she could.

"Mama, you're beautiful," Rosie said, coming up behind her. She carried a nosegay of orchids and handed Mary her bouquet, then gave her a kiss on the cheek. "I'm happy for you."

Mary enveloped her daughter in a hug. "At least I'll have someone to keep me company while you're back East."

Rosie's acceptance to nursing school in Chicago had made Mary realize just how alone she might be. The next time Erland

Lewis had come to the door with his hat in his hands and suggested marriage, she accepted.

A lifetime was too long to wait for true love, wasn't it? To
believe the words to a silly song, promises made in emotion.

For all you're worth, I'll stand here for a lifetime,
For all you're worth, I'll sacrifice it all,
You can know that you're a treasure,
I'll show you how to measure,
You can look into His eyes for all you're worth.

"Oh, honey, don't cry." Mary wiped her gloved thumb across
her daughter's face.

"I just want you to be happy, Mama. Really happy."

Mary smiled, but a hollowness inside threatened to engulf
her. She swallowed it and pressed a smile on her face. "Erland
is waiting."

Lolly hurtled the book across the room. It hit the kitchen counter, bounced against the microwave, and finally landed on the floor.
"You're not supposed to marry Erland!"

Her voice, thundering through the quiet room, startled her. As
did the sweep of emotions that threatened to drown her. Jonas
was worth waiting for; didn't Mary see that? Just because he didn't
return . . . or had he been killed?

See, this was why she didn't read romances. They made her hurt
all over. Mary *did* deserve a happy life. She'd tried to make the right
choices for her daughter, protecting her despite the cost to herself.
And when she finally healed enough to let Jonas in her life . . . he
didn't come for her.

"Please, don't let her marry the wrong man." The words felt strange on her lips, and Lolly let out a harsh laugh. Not only had she taken these characters into her heart, but she was now, what, *praying* for them? God didn't care about characters in a book. He barely cared about real people . . . especially people like her who messed up life so badly that they didn't deserve a second chance.

Lolly definitely needed to get back to work, to reality and her world. Maybe she wasn't living happily ever after, but at least she had contentment.

<hr />

Kat's world changed with Piper's words. She stared at her, her open mouth drying. "You . . . found her?"

Piper's blonde hair was pulled back from her face into a long ponytail, and with her sleeveless blouse and cutoffs, she looked every inch a rancher. Except for the gleam of resourcefulness in her eyes. "Yep. Went down to the local newspaper and did some hunting." She slapped a folder down on the table. "You'll never believe this story."

Kat opened the folder and took out a copy of a newspaper article dated the year before she was born.

MAN SENTENCED TO TEN YEARS FOR ASSAULT
By Cicely Sturgis, staff reporter

SHERIDAN–WYOMING COURTS MADE HISTORY TODAY WHEN THEY SENTENCED RANDY MORRISON, LOCAL RANCH HAND AT THE BAR T, TO TEN YEARS IN PRISON

FOR THE ASSAULT OF HIS WIFE, LAURA RUSSELL, SISTER
OF PBR CHAMPION BOBBY RUSSELL.

MORRISON, 26, PLEADED GUILTY LAST MONTH TO
CHARGES OF ASSAULT IN THE OCTOBER 12 BEATING
OF HIS ESTRANGED WIFE. IN EXCHANGE FOR HIS PLEA,
MORRISON AVOIDED A MUCH LONGER SENTENCE, SAID
DEPUTY DISTRICT ATTORNEY FRANK WINCHELL.

MORRISON AND HIS 18-YEAR-OLD WIFE HAD BEEN
SEPARATED FOR TWO MONTHS WHEN THE ATTACK
OCCURRED AT HER RESIDENCE, THE PROSECUTOR SAID.
RUSSELL IS CURRENTLY FIVE MONTHS PREGNANT.

PROSECUTORS SAY THIS IS THE FIRST SUCH
CONVICTION IN WYOMING.

Kat put the article down, took a deep breath, and looked at Piper.

She wore a grim look. "I called the *Sheridan News,* and as a professional courtesy, they gave me the reporter's number. She's retired, but she still remembers the case. She faxed me a copy of her research file, which included the police report. It's pretty ugly. He broke her jaw and was trying to kill the baby, which he claimed wasn't his."

Kat ran her finger down the article. "What happened to Laura? And the baby?"

Piper pulled out a chair. "According to Cicely, she left town right after Morrison went to prison. Her brother was on tour, so Cicely thinks maybe she went to live with him. But I did a search and came up with nothing. No report of her or even a birth record of the baby."

"Did the baby die?"

Piper lifted a shoulder, then reached over to take her hand. "I'm sorry I couldn't do better."

Kat stared at the folder. "A year after my dad died, Laura sent me a letter from Phillips. Bobby worked for John during his rodeoing years before he met my mother. I thought with John Kincaid and him being friends, maybe they were from here."

Piper shook her head. "As far as I can tell, Laura Russell never lived in Phillips."

"Well, I guess that answers that." Kat rose from the table. "Thank you, Piper, for all you did to find out about Laura. I . . . uh . . . Could you please tell Rafe that I stopped by? Or on second thought . . ." She put her hands to her head, feeling the slightest inkling of a headache. Or maybe it was just the tears welling inside, wanting to break through. "Don't tell him. Just . . . oh, I gotta go."

Piper stood up. "Are you okay?"

She forced a smile. "Yeah. I'm . . . great. Thanks for everything." For some reason, she reached out and pulled Piper into a hug.

Piper hugged her back, and when she released her, she looked concerned. But Kat offered nothing and Piper only followed her as far as the porch, watching as she got into her Jeep. She lifted a hand as Kat pulled away.

Kat waved in return, then turned away from the Silver Buckle and drove back to Bradley.

⫷CHAPTER 14

RAFE TRIED NOT to let the fact that Kitty hadn't shown up eat at him, but he found himself sitting at the old burial site, searching for another arrowhead, as if trying to recapture that moment when she'd gotten inside the darkest places of his heart. Sure, he'd tried to peg her as someone who just saw what she wanted, like his fans. But Kitty wasn't a fan. Or rather, she was much more than a fan. She believed in him, not for his status or his gold buckles but for . . .

What? Why exactly did she believe in him? What did he have to offer a lady like Kitty? She was sunshine and grace in his life, and he was . . . trouble. He threw a handful of grass into the hot wind and felt it splatter back onto his legs. In the distance, he spotted Nick and CJ riding the fence line in Kelly's field. It figured that Nick would round up his son—the one he hadn't known he had until just a year ago.

Rafe wondered what it might be like to have a son to ride with in the hot sun, to dazzle him with stories of triumph in the rodeo arena. Triumph . . . and tragedy.

He swallowed past the burn in his throat and climbed to his feet. His horse stood in the shade, munching the grass. Rafe walked over and wrestled himself to a mount.

He spotted Piper sitting on the porch as he rode up to the house. He waved to her, put the animal into the corral, then joined her.

"Kat was here." Piper didn't look at him.

Rafe let those words just sit. He stared out past Buckle land to the drying, chafed hills. "How long ago?"

"About an hour." She gave him a long, troubled look. In the short time he'd known Piper, he found her to be complicated, even secretive. But when it came to family, she also seemed fiercely loyal. "I got the sense that she wasn't coming back."

Rafe tried not to let her words jar him. "That right?"

Piper nodded.

"Maybe I should—"

"My keys are on the table." She winked, the slightest smile on her lips.

Rafe went into the kitchen, glancing at a manila folder as he retrieved the keys. He came back out on the porch. "What's in that folder?"

"Something Kat asked me to find. A lady named Laura Russell."

"Bobby's sister."

"Yeah. Evidently she got a letter from her postmarked from Phillips. She wanted to track her down." Piper shook her head. "Laura married the wrong guy, and it derailed her life. She sort of dropped off the planet."

Rafe thumped down the porch and into Piper's truck, pulled out, and headed toward town. Her words sat in his brain like the oppressive heat. *She married the wrong guy, and it derailed her life.*

He pushed the words from his mind. What did Piper mean—that Kitty wasn't coming back? Why would she leave? He vividly recalled last night's rather ardent kiss outside Lolly's trailer, his hand braced over Kitty's shoulder, her arms around his waist. He hadn't wanted to let her go, but deep inside he knew that if he had a prayer of starting over, he had to be the kind of man she deserved.

Not that he hadn't been sorely tempted to charm her back to his truck and take her out to Gilly's Bluff, where the stars seemed close enough to touch. Especially with the way Kitty smelled and her curves fitting so well in his arms.

But Kitty made him want to be a different man. A better man.

He stopped in front of Lolly's trailer. *Please, Kitty, be here.*

As he got out of the truck, he heard voices inside.

"We'll talk about it when we get back to New York."

Rafe recognized Kitty's voice but not the strained tone. He stepped onto the porch.

"We'll talk about it now. I want to know, Katherine."

This voice Rafe didn't recognize, but through the screen door, he saw a tall blond in a mussed and slightly stained gray silk suit. He stood, arms folded across his chest, his hands in fists. "Will you marry me or not?"

Somehow, out of all the things Rafe expected to hear, it wasn't another man asking to marry his Kitty.

He wasn't sure whether to storm in and grab the man by the throat and toss him out on his tailored backside or snatch Kitty and run for the hills. He did neither, as his muscles wouldn't move.

Kitty sighed and said, "Yes, Bradley, I'll marry you."

Thankfully, she didn't throw herself into Bradley's arms and kiss him passionately. . . .

Wait a second. She'd been standing in this very place, kissing *him* passionately only twelve hours before.

"What do you mean you'll *marry* him?" Rafe threw open the screen door and found himself inside Lolly's trailer before he could rein in his heart.

Kitty looked up from the bag she was lugging from the back bedroom. For a split second, Rafe thought he saw relief or hope on her face, but it vanished in a mask of anger. "What are you doing here, Rafe?"

"Trying to find you!"

"This is that cowboy? The one you . . . you *kissed*?"

Kitty flinched. "Yes. Bradley Lymon, meet Rafe Noble."

"Her fiancé." Bradley didn't hold out his hand. "You can leave now."

"Over your dead body, Slick. Kitty, what's going on? Did you just say you'd marry this . . . used car salesman?"

"I'm an attorney."

"Worse. Kitty, c'mon." Rafe couldn't believe the sound of pleading in his voice. But by the look on Kitty's face, it made a dent, because she dropped her bag and stood there, her eyes filling. "Take it back. You don't belong with him." *Please, Kitty, you know where you belong!*

"She certainly does, and stop calling her Kitty. Her name is Katherine, and we're getting married. And by the way, I've been planning to propose for weeks. We're only making it formal now."

Rafe stared at Kitty, and the wretched look on her face confirmed the truth. A fist of pain tightened in his chest. "You were engaged? What about—" he swallowed, hating how his voice hitched— "believing in me? That was a pep talk, wasn't it? To get me to agree to help you."

"It's for the kids," she mumbled.

She could have screamed it for the way it broadsided him. *For the kids?* "Was it all a lie?"

She didn't answer.

Rafe rounded on Bradley. "And you're the bloodsucking lawyer trying to bankrupt me!"

"You're the cowboy who drove into the hotel." Bradley matched him decibel for decibel, about one inch from his face.

Rafe didn't flinch, and everything inside him got very, very quiet. Kind of like it did right before he got on a bull. "I don't want to hurt you. . . . Well, I do, but I won't if you back away. Slowly."

"Go ahead. Take your best shot. I'll add that to your list of charges."

"Bradley, stop."

Rafe narrowed his eyes, stepped back, and turned to Kitty—no, *Katherine.* "So what were you doing, Katherine? You figured if you couldn't get me to agree with you on principle, you'd attack my emotions, make me think that you . . . forget it."

"No! I-I just knew that you weren't the jerk I talked to on the phone, and I wanted to give you another chance to do the right thing. I didn't realize that . . . that I would . . . that we would . . ." She covered her face with her hands.

"Are you even related to Bobby Russell? How do I know that isn't some sort of story?"

Kat looked at him, something terrible on her face. Then she picked up a ceramic lamp and threw it.

He dodged a second before it crashed against the wall, shattering into a dozen tiny pieces.

"Katherine!"

"What's wrong with you?" Rafe snapped.

Kitty's face paled. "Sorry, I . . . It's just . . . you make me so angry, Rafe. You're so, so . . ."

"Much trouble?" Rafe glared at her. "I know why you came here, Kitty. Or at least why you stayed." His voice lowered, and he took a step toward her. "You wanted to see what it might be like to win the heart of a bull rider. To break free of the high society ball and chain and live a real life." He took another step. "To be in the arms of a man who doesn't live in a three-piece suit, who makes you feel alive." He curled his hand around her neck, and although everything inside him called him a jerk—she'd at least been right about that—he yanked her toward him and kissed her hard.

Even in that moment, he wanted to take her into his arms and soften his kiss. Show her exactly how he really felt, despite her betrayal. But he wouldn't let hope take over again, so he just kissed her with the desperation that he couldn't seem to tame.

She pushed on his chest, and as he let her go, she slapped him. A real doozy that rang his chops. He didn't even blink.

"Get out!" she cried, choking back a sob.

"Thanks, sweet thing. It's been fun," he said as Bradley pushed him out the door. He righted himself on the porch rail before he went over it. "By the way, you can take your dude ranch back with you to New York City, where it belongs." Then he thumped down the stairs.

Bradley stood on the porch, eyes dark. Inside, Rafe heard Kitty crying.

And he knew then just what he had to offer her. A broken heart.

He slammed the door to the pickup and nearly took out a stray dog as he peeled out and headed back to the Buckle.

Nick was riding in when he pulled up. Rafe didn't look at him as he got out, but he felt Nick's eyes burning with disgust. Out of his peripheral vision, Rafe thought he even saw a small, pitying shake of his brother's head.

Rafe slammed his way upstairs, banged open his bedroom door. The entire house shook. Crossing the room, he ripped his Bobby Russell and Lane Frost posters off the wall and grabbed the box of videotapes he'd dug out for Kitty. He took his trophies, his ribbons, his two championship buckles, and the scrapbook he'd kept for himself over the years and shoved them into his PBR duffel bag. Then he threw them all over his shoulder and stormed back downstairs.

Piper, Stefanie, and Nick stood in the kitchen, holding a pow-wow of concern.

He ignored them, marched back out to Piper's truck, threw the bag in the back, and roared out.

He took the back roads to the burial mound, driving as fast as he could without dropping one of the axles. He stopped at the bottom of the hill, lugged out the bag, then muscled himself up the hill.

He threw sticks and twigs together, and taking a lighter he'd found in Piper's glove compartment, he knelt and lit a blaze.

The flame crackled as it devoured the sticks, then the kindling, and finally the larger pieces of wood he added for fuel. The flame showed no distinction between the fragile and the hearty, biting into the wood with tongues of orange, red, and yellow.

Rafe opened the duffel. Instead of dumping the entire thing on the flames, he pulled the items out one by one. His posters. They burned in a second, curling into tight balls. The ribbons, which sent out an acrid odor. The scrapbook. The fire started on the edges, burning away the accomplishments, the defeats. Then the tapes. The smell of plastic burning made his eyes water and sent black smoke into the now bruised sky. The trophies would take hours to fully burn, but their plastic mounts deformed and caved in on themselves immediately. Finally, the buckles. He dropped both of them into the flames, feeling his throat thicken.

He closed his eyes, smelling a bull's hide, dirty and sweaty, feeling the adrenaline spike through his body, the jarring as every muscle, every bone screamed in pain. He felt the rush of relief as he let go and rolled off the back hip of the bull, found his feet, and ran to safety. He heard the crowd roar.

The flames crackled, spitting and popping as they devoured his life. The bull rider. The man Kitty claimed she believed in.

Rafe drew up his good knee, crossed his arms atop it, buried his head in them, and for the first time since his mother died—even during Manuel's funeral, even in the dark months that followed—Rafe let himself cry.

※

Lolly wiped the last of the tables, filled the salt and pepper shakers and the ketchup bottles, and even prepared the coffeepot for the first brew in the morning. Still, she refused to turn off the neon Open sign just . . . because.

John hadn't shown up yet. And she'd called him twice. John never—well, until the last few days—missed closing up the diner with her. She'd even made his Reuben, leaving it to warm under the lights.

She poured herself a cup of decaf and leaned against the bar. Waited. Sipped. The second hand clicked toward ten o'clock.

She put her cup down. Coffee sloshed onto the counter. "John Kincaid, where are you?"

As if summoned by her very words, a dark figure crossed the plate glass of her diner, outlined by the neon lights. Finally.

She turned her back to him, not wanting him to see her expression. The fact that after twenty years of friendship seeing him could still induce feelings of joy should tell her something.

Yeah, that she was turning into a silly romantic. She grabbed a rag just as the door clanged open. "'Bout time you got here. Your Reuben is getting stale."

"I wasn't aware I ordered a Reuben."

Lolly turned, but even the sight of handsome Lincoln Cash couldn't replace the grin that had vanished from her face.

He slid onto a stool. "What's the matter? You look upset."

"I'm fine." She smoothed her apron, dredged up a smile. "We're closed."

"Not even a piece of pie for your favorite patron?"

She waggled her finger at him. "If you weren't voted one of America's sexiest men, I'd boot you out in a second." She slid him a piece of cherry pie and filled a cup with coffee.

He dug in. "Delicious, Lolly. I'm telling you, no one makes pies like you."

She managed to keep her smile, but as the clock ticked past ten, she knew John wouldn't be joining them. Again. She felt like crying, but she blamed it on that stupid book and the way she had wanted to yell at someone all day. She wiped up the coffee she spilled, then dumped the cup into the sink.

"Seriously, Lolly, what's the matter?"

"Nothing." She turned on the faucet hard, and the water splashed her apron as it ricocheted off the cup. "Oh!" She stepped back, and her eyes filled as she lunged for the faucet. She missed and got a spray full in the face. "No!"

Then arms came around her, and deft hands turned off the faucet, stopping the deluge. She covered her face as Lincoln turned her into his chest and held her.

She felt foolish sobbing, but she couldn't stop.

"Shh," Lincoln said, rubbing her back. "Shh. It's okay. I promise."

"No . . . it's not." Lolly stepped back from him, wiping her face with her apron. "It's really not."

Lincoln apparently didn't have to search far for his on-screen charm, because he took her hand and pulled her to a booth.

She sat opposite him, grabbed a napkin, and blew her nose. "Sorry."

Lincoln shrugged. "Women. Crying. I get it."

"You don't understand. I've made a complete mess of things. I think. But I don't know. . . ." Her words ended in a sort of wail.

Lincoln took her hand.

"I'm emotional because . . . well, you're going to think this is so silly."

"Try me."

"I'm still reading *Unshackled*—"

"Say no more. I'll bet you're at the part where Mary marries Erland. When I read that scene, I suggested the book to my producer. He liked it enough to commission a screenplay by the author. At least it turns out—"

"Don't tell me!" She slapped the table, and he laughed. "Did you cry at that part too?"

He frowned at her. "Uh, it's still a romance. And I'm a guy." But he winked.

Lolly shook her head. "The thing that gets me is that after all this time, she *knows* who she's supposed to marry, yet . . . she still chooses the wrong guy."

"But she hasn't heard from Jonas in years–even before the war. He might be dead."

Lolly shook her head. "No, she'd know if he was dead. His mother would have told her. And she'd feel it in her heart."

"I just can't get why she didn't write to Jonas sooner, ask him to come home."

Lolly wadded up the napkin. "Because she didn't want to drag him into trouble. What if the sheriff decided to enact some payback? She loved Jonas enough not to want him hurt."

"Don't you think he deserved to make that decision?"

Lolly shrugged.

"Even more incredible, after all this time, Jonas loves–"

"Don't tell me!" She lunged for him, as if trying to cover his mouth.

He laughed. "Okay, okay. But seriously, he hasn't heard from her for what, twelve years and he *still* loves her?"

"So I take it he's not dead, then."

Lincoln made a face. "Sorry."

Lolly held up a hand. "No, that's okay. I figured something had to happen–I still have fifty pages left."

"What gets me," Lincoln said, "is that she honestly believes she doesn't deserve to be happy. That somehow her mistake in marrying evil Matthias should doom her forever."

Lolly stared down at the wadded-up napkin.

"That's not true, you know."

Lolly didn't look at Lincoln. "Sometimes you can't escape your mistakes. They show up, and just when you think you might redeem yourself, you make them worse. Like Mary did when she married Matthias." Like she did to Kat when she called Bradley. Because deep in her heart, she knew something wasn't right. Something about the way Bradley looked at Kat. . . . It couldn't be just her imagination, her past rising to haunt her, could it?

"I guess it's getting away from the stress back home, but it's as if I've been freed from a cocoon," Kat had said. Lolly had felt the same way when she'd arrived in Phillips, but she'd been running from a life gone bad. What was Kat running from?

It was time for the running to stop.

She cleared her throat. "Lincoln, I can't accept your offer. Not yet at least. I have some unfinished business. Then maybe I can consider it. Let me think about it, okay?"

"I don't know how I'll live without you," Lincoln said. "But, yes, take your time."

"You'll manage."

He chuckled and got up, heading for more pie. "By the way, if you want to know the ending of the story, you should ask John."

Lolly froze. "Why would I ask John? He hasn't read it."

Lincoln opened the pie case. "Of course he's read it. He wrote it. And the screenplay, which is incredible." He cut himself a piece of pie.

"John . . . *John* wrote the book?"

Lincoln put the pie back in the case and reached for a fork. When he caught her expression, he stopped. "You didn't know? I thought you knew. . . ."

Lolly was already halfway to her trailer. She threw open the door and crossed the room to the kitchen, where she retrieved the book and opened it.

B. J. King. Big. John. *Kincaid.* Could she be more blind? And no picture, of course, but a short author description: *B. J. King, author of twenty novels, lives on a ranch in Montana.*

Twenty novels. One for every year she knew him.

Or rather, didn't know him.

Lolly threw the book across the room again.

ᵀ CHAPTER 15

NOT EVEN SEEING the wife and child of his best friend could lift Rafe out of the black hole that consumed his life. He stood on the driveway watching Lucia and Manny climb out of the small Cessna that Nick piloted, and as he smiled and opened his arms, he felt strangely sapped of joy, of hope.

Manny wrapped his skinny arms around Rafe's neck as Rafe lifted the boy off the ground. "I'm so glad to see you, Uncle Rafe!"

Rafe hugged him back, meeting Lucia's eyes as she walked toward them. "Me too, Manny."

How would he ever tell them that he couldn't keep his promises to pay for Manny's health care? His legal bills had soared to crushing heights, and he'd had to put his Texas ranch up for sale. Soon he'd have nothing but a pair of old boots, his bull rope, and his Stetson.

He put Manny down and gathered Lucia in his arms. "Welcome to Montana, Lucy."

A petite woman, Lucia laid her head against his chest and seemed even more fragile than he remembered.

Nick came up behind them, toting their duffel bags. "I'm putting them in your room, Rafe, right?"

Rafe nodded, aware of the pitying smile Nick gave him. In the last two weeks he'd been the recipient of much pity from his family, who seemed to dodge him or treat him with a sort of he's-ill-so-keep-your-voice-down mentality.

He wasn't ill, for pete's sake. Just . . .

He wouldn't call it heartbroken. Maybe angry. Or even sad. But not heartbroken. Because a man had to have been in love for his heart to break. And he hadn't loved Kitty.

He wasn't the type of guy who could fall in love in two weeks.

"How's your knee?" Lucia asked as they turned toward the house. She'd seen him on crutches plenty of times over the years, and he appreciated the casual way she asked, as if it had simply inconvenienced him between events.

"Good. I can walk on it now, and the doctors expect a decent recovery." Sort of a lie. No one knew that each night he wrapped it in ice, gritting his teeth against the pain. That any recovery would be less than what he needed.

"Are you going to talk to the sports doc, get an athletic knee brace?"

They'd reached the house, and Rafe kept a straight face as he climbed the porch stairs. "Dunno." A brace would mean that he planned on riding again, which he didn't. Yes, deep inside he hadn't really thought his career was over, but after Kitty . . . well, maybe he wanted it to be. He wanted that Rafe to die and had no desire to resurrect him.

"How's Manny feeling?" He caught sight of the boy standing at the corral, his hand out to one of the horses, feeding it an alfalfa treat. His black hair blew in the gentle wind, and he laughed as the horse's lips tickled his palm.

In that moment, he looked so much like his father that it took away Rafe's breath.

"He's tired. And they're still looking for a bone marrow donor. Seems as though we are always on our knees, praying for something." Lucia gave him a small smile. "But Manuel is looking out for us; I know it."

Rafe never exactly understood their religious beliefs, but the thought that Manuel might be in heaven rooting for them . . . well, that might be a comfort to Lucia, but it made him want to slink away in shame. "Yeah," he said.

Nick came down the stairs. "Your suitcases are upstairs, second door on the right. We're glad to have you, so make yourself at home."

Lucia touched Rafe's cheek, a gesture she'd often used to reassure Manuel that she believed in him as he dodged bulls for a living. "Just being here is enough."

Rafe gave her a half smile and stepped away from her touch.

Piper had planned a cookout for Lucia and Manny's first night at the ranch, with barbecue ribs and biscuits that seemed to be an inside joke among her and Nick and Stef. They grilled the ribs over a grate and cooked the biscuits in a cast-iron pot. Sparks shot into the inky, cloud-covered sky.

Rafe made out only one or two determined stars as he leaned back against a log, his stomach churning with hunger. "How long before it's ready?"

Piper stood above the fire, armed with an oven mitt, a barbecue fork, and a don't-push-it look. Apparently dinner would be ready when it was ready.

Manny sat down next to Rafe. "I found this in your room," he said, handing him an arrowhead. "Where did you get it?"

Rafe took the arrowhead, rubbing his thumb against the sharp points. He'd forgotten that Kitty had given it to him after their first ride. "There's an ancient Native American burial ground on our land. I can take you there, if you want." He pushed the point into his thumb. Pain shot down his hand.

Manny nodded. "Remember you said last time that you'd teach me how to ride a bull. Can we do that too?"

Lucia sat down on the other side of Rafe. "I don't think that's the best idea right now, Manny. Wait until you're feeling stronger."

Manny's chest rose and fell with a dramatic sigh. "I might never feel better. And I don't want to die without knowing."

Manny's words hit Rafe right in the center of his chest.

Lucia reached across Rafe and took Manny's hand. "You'll learn, Manuel. I promise you'll have time."

Manny gave her a long look, then a soft smile. "I'll just watch Uncle Rafe then."

Lucia glanced at Rafe.

"Uh, the thing is, I'm not riding . . . right now."

"'Cause of your leg?" Manny asked.

"Yeah, 'cause of my leg." Rafe dropped the arrowhead into Manny's palm. "We'll go hunt for those tomorrow, okay, pal?"

Manny nodded as he climbed to his feet and skipped off toward Dutch, who had just pulled out his harmonica.

"That's not true, is it?" Lucia's voice, so soft he could barely hear, made him wince. "You quit riding because of Manuel."

Rafe glanced at Piper, hoping it might be time to eat. She had drawn the pot of biscuits off the metal grate and was now slicing them. "That part of my life is over. I don't want it anymore."

"I've been watching your headlines, Rafe."

Rafe threw a piece of grass into the fire.

Lucia turned to face him, her long, dark hair shiny in the firelight. "I know you're . . . upset. But do you want to know what I think?"

He looked away.

"I think that you were born to ride bulls. That it's a gift God gave you, just like He gave Manuel a gift to fight them."

"I hardly think that God gives the spiritual gift of bull riding."

"Do you think that anyone can get into a ring with a bull and hang on . . . even enjoy it?"

Rafe glanced at Piper, his stomach growling as she pulled the ribs from the fire. "Bull riding doesn't change people's lives . . . at least not in a good way."

"Now you listen to me, Rafe. Manny needs you to be his hero, and I don't care if you never get on a bull again, but he does. So, if you care at all about my son, about Manuel's son, you'll give him the courage to fight, even if it's only for the next few weeks."

Rafe stared at Lucia. Behind her words, he heard Kitty. *I just wish I could do one amazing thing that would . . . I don't know, make me feel like . . .*

He mattered. That God had been right in sparing him.

"It's no small thing to have the Creator of this big sky at work in your life, on your side, giving your life purpose."

Rafe watched the flames spark into the dark vault of night.

Ever since Manuel's death, he'd been riding for the eight seconds in time that he might pay back the grace Manuel had given him in saving his life.

Only, he could never quite fill his account. And he certainly wasn't using his *gift* for good. Sure, he impressed his fans, but when he really had the chance to impress someone, to do something good and decent with his life . . .

He put his hand on his face, right where Kitty's hand had left its imprint. He wasn't going back to that life. Not now, not ever.

"I believe in you. . . ."

For pete's sake, would she get out of his head?

"I'm not sure what kind of encouragement I can give him, Lucy."

"But you'll try, right?" Funny, the expression on her face matched Kitty's right before he acted like the jerk of the century. Relief? Hope? It didn't matter. Not anymore.

He got up to fetch his plate of ribs.

"Katherine, I can't believe you're wearing those again." Cari came into Kat's penthouse office carrying a stack of files. She plunked them down on the cherry table Kat used as her desk and pointedly stared at the red cowboy boots. "They don't go with anything."

"I like my boots," Kat said. Wearing them helped her believe the time she'd spent in Montana hadn't been a dream and that she had changed, become stronger, despite the cavern inside her that grew with each passing day. "And call me Kat." She pulled the stack of files toward her. "What are these?"

"Donor reports, the latest accounting figures, two possible sponsorship leads, and your schedule for this week." Cari set her bag on her desk.

Kat scanned the figures. She'd returned home to find the auditors still neck-deep in her files and to bear Cari's cool reception. It took a bowl of popcorn, a couple of yogurt shakes, and hours on the sofa describing every juicy detail for Cari to forgive her.

Bradley, despite his victory, treated her as if she might have been recently released from Attica. It made the ring on her finger seem cold and clunky. Especially when her grandfather called and offered his congratulations. He'd triumphed in his efforts to turn Kat into the society girl her mother had run from. Yet she'd run to the same life Kat longed for.

But unlike her mother, Kat had been living a fantasy. Rafe Noble would break her heart—one way or another—and prudence demanded she turn back to the one man who made sense.

"What happened to the Roosevelt grant? It comes in every year about this time," Kat asked, shuffling through the files.

Cari shook her head.

"And the Winchells always do their year-end giving in July."

"Kathe—Kat, while you were on your jaunt, the press wasn't friendly. Although two donors have stepped up after your engagement announcement . . . well, maybe I should draft a letter to Mercy Doctors, telling them not to expect funding for this quarter."

The children in the clinic in Guadalajara filled Kat's thoughts. She pressed her fingers to her eyes. So much for her not being a gigantic failure. "Do you have any ideas?"

"I don't know. Your grandfather called this morning. He wants you to attend a board meeting this afternoon." Cari hitched a shoulder, her expression offering little in the way of encouragement.

Swell. Kat sighed, opted to ignore the accounting, and instead opened a file on possible corporate and private sponsors.

The Breckenridge Foundation needed a leader who knew how

to ask for help and get it. Someone who could speak for those who didn't have a voice. Apparently that wasn't her.

She closed the file, pushing away the image of Rafe at the rodeo, helping a six-year-old hold on to a sheep. The way Rafe picked up the child, dusted him off, tickled him to make him smile. Make *her* smile.

"Stop."

Kat frowned at Cari.

"You're doing it again. Thinking about *him*."

"I'm not. I'm just—"

"I see the look in your eyes." Cari perched on the side of her table, one trim leg swinging. "And I saw you surfing the Internet for his name yesterday."

Kat rubbed her forehead, feeling that nagging headache like residue in the back of her head. Two weeks at home, and she felt nearly as old and exhausted as when she'd left. "I saw something in Rafe that made me believe he was more than just an arrogant bull rider."

"You wanted to bring it out. Save him. Give him a second chance."

"Is that so terrible? To want to make a difference in someone's life not because I'm a Breckenridge with a bank account but because I'm . . . me?"

Cari folded her hands over her chest. "You can't change people— especially a surly guy with an attitude."

"He changed me." Kat stared at her hands, the calluses there now beginning to fade. "I never felt more like myself than when I was with Rafe."

"You never felt more like the girl you have always wanted to be."

Cari took her hands, running her finger over Kat's calluses. "But you're not that Kitty girl. You're Katherine Breckenridge."

Kat pulled her hands away and folded them on her lap.

Cari sighed. "Okay, listen to me well, my friend. I know I've never been on his side, but Bradley was really worried about you when you were gone. Nearly frantic. I couldn't believe he held that press conference, offering a reward for your safe return. And announcing that you were his fiancée. I thought you said he hadn't proposed. I hate to admit it, but you have a good thing going with Bradley. Don't mess it up."

Bradley. Kat leaned back in her chair. She didn't bother to correct Cari's false assumption of being left in the dark about their engagement. It didn't matter anymore. "He wants to elope to someplace exotic."

"And you?"

What did she want? A big wedding with a dazzling gown, maybe a five-tiered cake and a thousand guests all crammed into the Breckenridge ballroom? Her throat tightened. "I want to two-step."

"Oh, brother." Cari got up, shaking her head. "I'm saying this for your own good. Rafe doesn't want you. If he did, he'd be here or at least in the lobby. We both know he isn't shy about making a grand appearance."

Kat gave her a dark look, but Cari's words silenced her. Rafe didn't want her.

And Bradley did.

Yes, Rafe had been right—she wanted a man who made her feel alive and bold. And she probably spent too much time back in that magical night when he'd made her believe she'd won his heart. But she also wanted a man whose world changed with her smile. Like her mother had done for her father. He'd practically ridden up on a white stallion to steal away the woman he loved.

Kat Breckenridge was not her mother, Felicia. Apparently, she didn't have her mother's powers, because Rafe certainly hadn't followed her to New York and shown up on a white stallion, begging for a second chance.

Rafe may have changed her, but Kat hadn't changed Rafe one iota. That had been clear in the way he'd kissed her. She'd simply been a game for a man who needed some entertainment in his life. He probably never even intended to help her raise a cent for her cause.

Kat massaged her temples, wishing her headache would ease.

"Head still hurt?" Cari got up, poured Kat a glass of water, and grabbed her prescription bottle. "I'm getting worried about you."

Kat took the glass. "They're worse than before. If it's possible, the longer I sleep, the more exhausted I become. Bradley brought in a doctor a few days ago. He didn't know what's wrong." She swallowed two pills. "And these Vicodin don't seem to make a dent."

"Go lie down. I'll call you in time for the meeting."

"No," Kat said, picking up the folder. Because if she did, she'd only dream of the cowboy she'd let break her heart.

❧

"John vanished, Piper. Just like that. *Poof!*" Lolly snapped her fingers, but the sound of dishes clanking in the kitchen behind her swallowed the effect. Still, she felt his disappearance right down to her heart.

No one had to know that she had finally driven to John's place last week to find his cattle gone, his house empty, and his hired hand packing his truck for his new job at the Lock-T in Billings. Or that she'd returned home and cried herself to sleep.

Or that she couldn't bear to read the end of the book, because she just knew that Jonas would never show up. And even if he did, Mary had waited too long, had pushed him away and chosen the wrong man.

"I doubt he's vanished, Lolly. I haven't seen any crop circles lately or UFO sightings in the paper. And the earth hasn't opened up, at least not between here and the Silver Buckle."

"Then where did he go?"

Behind her, Cody dinged the bell, signaling order up, and Lolly retrieved Piper's Caesar salad.

"I don't know. Maybe on vacation."

"With his cattle? his furniture? His place is up for sale. Why would he sell?"

Piper shrugged, but the question nagged at Lolly. She remembered the day John had shown up in his three-piece suit, looking like an usher at a funeral. Why hadn't she joined him in Sheridan? Maybe then he would have trusted her enough to tell her the truth. About himself. About his intentions.

"Did you know he's an author?"

Piper looked up from her salad. "No. Really?"

"Yeah. He wrote that book everyone is obsessed about— *Unshackled.*" Lolly stalked to the end of the counter to take Quint's order.

"Coffee with sugar, please," he said, his attention on the television screen. "Hey, look, it's that Kitty who was here."

Lolly watched a very pale and ungroomed Katherine being

led out of the Breckenridge hotel surrounded by . . . police? Lolly
turned up the volume.

". . . hospitalized after her recent disappearance. Sources close to
Miss Breckenridge suggest an addiction to prescription medication,
which raises questions about the recent loss of Breckenridge Funds.
With rumors of the Breckenridge Foundation being dissolved, her
lawyer and fiancé, Bradley Lymon, had this to say."

The screen flashed over to Bradley, and Lolly's stomach knotted.

"Katherine is overwrought with recent stock market losses that
have damaged her charity fund, which led to her recent disappearance. With time, we expect a full recovery." The interview ended,
and the camera caught Bradley taking Katherine's arm, helping her
into a limousine.

"She's sick?" Quint said.

Lolly barely restrained herself from throwing the sugar container
at him.

"No." Piper put down her fork. "Something's not right here. Kat
didn't seem sick or depressed at all—"

"Of course she's not." Lolly felt as if someone had scooped her
out from the inside, taking with it all her hopes and dreams. "She
was wearing her red boots," she said quietly.

"Yeah," Piper said slowly. "She really liked those boots."

Lolly stared at Piper and saw the wheels in her head turning.
Almost before she could keep up, Piper's gaze went to the picture
hanging on the wall, the one taken on the day of Lolly's grand
opening, twenty years prior.

Lolly stood, hands folded over her chest, with one foot up on
the steps to the dining car.

Wearing a pair of bright red cowboy boots.

❦

Rafe sat in the wingback chair in the quietness of his father's bed-room listening to memories. To his mother's weak voice, quiet as she summoned him into the darkness of her room during the last days of her cancer, telling him what kind of man she hoped he'd be. He'd stood by her bed, held his mother's hand wrapped in frail, broken skin, and believed her.

Rafe stood up, flicked on a light. He couldn't sleep here. Not tonight. Not ever. He'd moved in here after Manny and Lucia's arrival but managed to spend every night on the family room sofa. He grabbed a pillow and the bedspread and went downstairs.

The moonlight filtering in through the windows gave the room eerie angles, cutting across the leather sofa, over the coffee table, against the stone fireplace. Rafe threw the pillow down on the sofa, then followed it, curling up as he pulled the bedspread over him. He lay there in the darkness, listening to the old house creak. From the kitchen, the ancient faucet dripped into the porcelain sink. He got up, found a washcloth in the drawer by the silverware, and wadded it into the sink, then returned to the sofa.

The ceiling fan whirred above him, lifting the covers of the cof-fee-table magazines. He grabbed a hardcover book, flattening them to the surface. Upstairs, the toilet ran. Someone forgot to jiggle the handle again.

He closed his eyes. And just like that, as if tormenting him, Kitty returned. Her screams of fear, then of triumph as she rode Big Red. Her smell as she yielded in his arms. The hurt on her face as she'd slapped him.

Throwing off the bedspread, he sat up. He wore his track pants and an old T-shirt, and despite the heat, a chill brushed through him. Yep, the woman was haunting him.

Rafe stood in the milky darkness. His gaze fell on the stack of books on his father's reading table. He went over and dug through the pile, looking for one that might hold his attention. He found a Ralph Compton book, but he'd read that. He'd read the Elmer Kelton Western also.

Rafe slid into the chair, moving the Bible from the table where he'd left it nearly a month ago. He hesitated before he opened it to where he left off in the Psalms. *"O Lord, oppose those who oppose me. Fight those who fight against me."*

Yeah, he could use some old-fashioned, sword-wielding fighting right now. Against the Breckenridge family and Manny's leukemia and even his own mistakes. Rafe didn't follow his father's cross-reference to Romans this time, not needing the self-condemnation.

Instead his gaze went to a passage on the opposite page, Psalm 32. *"Many sorrows come to the wicked, but unfailing love surrounds those who trust the Lord."*

Rafe knew about sorrows, but he'd never considered himself particularly wicked. But maybe wicked didn't mean what he thought. Maybe it simply meant someone who lived . . . the way he'd lived. For the moment. For the ride. And he certainly couldn't put himself into the trusting God category.

"Remember, Rafe, you're not out there alone."

Apparently the voice in his head wasn't paying attention to his life, because sitting here in his parents' home, afraid to sleep in the bed where his mother had died, the weight of Manny's fears on his shoulders, and nursing what felt like the biggest hole he'd ever had in his chest, Rafe felt very, very alone.

"I believe in you." How he wanted to purge Kitty's voice from his thoughts.

After two weeks away from her, he could admit that maybe she *had* been healing to his broken spirit. At least the time spent with her had kept him from letting his despair drown him. He supposed he should be thankful for her, sort of like the balm of Gilead—healing despite the pain. Being with her had made him believe that he could perhaps be the man his mother had hoped for. Be the man he thought he saw in Kitty's eyes, however briefly.

"You've been your own worst enemy. I don't know what you're fighting, but you're more than you think you are."

As if remembering her hand touching him, he pressed his hand against his chest, felt only the beating of his heart.

Had Kitty been right? He picked up the Bible and followed his father's scribbles to Romans. *"So now there is no condemnation for those who belong to Christ Jesus."*

The enemy inside told him that he couldn't be forgiven. It told him that he had disappointed too many—his mother, Manuel, Lucia, even Kitty. The enemy screamed that he was just Bishop's broken, feeble child. That he could never be a Noble. The enemy declared that if God got a good look at him, He would flinch.

The words written in the margin leaped at him: *Fight for me, O Lord.*

Could it be that Rafe's father struggled with his own voices, inadequacies, and even his fears of losing his youngest son?

What would it be like to have the God of the universe fighting for him and holding on, even when Rafe tried to break free? What might it be like to have the Almighty believe in him, as his mother had? As Kitty had?

He'd seen more in Kitty than just her sweet smile. In fact, he'd glimpsed the smile of God. And if Kitty hadn't flinched at him, maybe God wouldn't either.

Rafe closed the Bible, set it on the table, and rubbed his hand on it. "Fight for me, O Lord," he whispered into the stillness of the night.

He stared at his hands, feeling something inside break. Behind it, the flow, fresh and whole, of something he hadn't even known he thirsted for. "Fight for me, O Lord," he repeated, this time in a voice that sounded strangely young, even desperate. His eyes burned, and he let them fill, let the tears run down onto his unshaven face.

He closed his eyes. "Fight for me, O Lord."

CHAPTER 16

IF HE EVER had a kid of his own, Rafe hoped his expression matched the one Manny wore as the Buckle's two hands unloaded Rafe's mechanical practice bull into the barn.

"It looks like a giant saddle." Manny came around the side, running his hands over the faux cowhide.

"This one is specially shaped like a bull—see the hump where the shoulders would be? And the handhold on it is like my bull rope. It's a little old, but it works." Rafe motioned for Quint and Andy to move it into the center of the barn as he retrieved the mattress pads. "I bought it used off a seasoned bull rider about five years ago, and it helped me train for my first championship when we couldn't buck out some bulls because of bad weather. Good thing I didn't sell it with the rest of my spread, huh?"

It was about the only thing left of his Texas ranch he hadn't sold. As soon as Manny left, it would go up on the auction block too.

"Can I ride it?"

Rafe moved the red padded mattresses in place on the floor around the bull. "If you don't tell your mother."

Manny grinned and climbed aboard, holding on to the strap and lifting his left hand high. "I'm not supposed to touch the bull with my free hand, right?"

Rafe plugged the extension cord he'd run from the house into the control box. "First of all, you're about fifty feet off your rope, which means when his head goes down it'll be easy for you to go over his shoulders, and you'll flip off the second after I turn this machine on."

He walked over to Manny, then pushed his body up against his rope. "Second, you need a glove." He pulled his own glove out from beneath his belt and handed it to him.

"It's got your initials on it."

"This is my lucky glove, Manny. So I got a good feeling about this ride." It had also been the glove Kitty wore when she'd tamed her bull. But he didn't add that.

Manny grinned, two gaps between his teeth showing as he pulled on the worn glove. He worked his hand back into the rope. "What about the rosin? Don't you have to use that to get it all sticky?"

"That helps when I use the bull rope. But for practice, it's just you and your grip. Now, let me see you set your spurs."

Manny leaned back, drew his heels together forward on the bull's body.

"You don't have to spur him, but it'll help you stay on or regain your balance if you slip to one side or the other if you hold on with your legs."

Manny nodded.

"Ready?"

"Let's do it."

Rafe bit the inside of his cheek to keep from smiling at Manny's serious expression. He turned the speed to the lowest setting and flipped on the power switch. The bull body began to turn, gyrate, switching positions as it spun.

"Whoo-hoo!" Manny spun once, then added his free hand to the grip, holding on as his face whitened. He flew off, landing on his back on the mattress. He lay there, dazed, blinking.

Rafe turned off the machine, his breath stuck in his throat. "You okay?" He crouched beside Manny. "Just lie there for a second and catch your breath."

Manny nodded, but a smile came over his face. He sat up. "That's fun, isn't it?"

Rafe pushed down his hat. "Yeah, it is." Most of the time. Unless it costs lives. But watching Manny, he couldn't shake from his memory Kitty astride Big Red, holding on with all she had. Would she still be holding on if he hadn't shoved her out of his life?

Wait—she was the one agreeing to marry another man. Besides, she hadn't loved the real Rafe, just the bull rider she saw on the outside.

Yeah, and if he said it enough, maybe even *he* would believe it.

He grabbed Manny's hand, pulling him to his feet. "So, do you want to give it another go?"

"I want you to do it."

Rafe stared at Manny's shiny eyes, recognized a fan in his smile, and couldn't say no. Just one ride . . .

"Let me show you how to work the switches." He brought Manny to the box, dialed the knob up to medium high. "Hit this when I tell you to. When I get thrown, turn it off."

"You won't get thrown."

Rafe laughed and patted the kid on the shoulder.

Although constructed of plastic and padding, the bull felt so familiar that a dormant adrenaline shot through Rafe, one he hadn't felt in months. His knee wasn't wrapped, so he put on his glove and pulled himself in tight, hoping his strength hadn't sapped so much that he would fly right off. He lifted his left arm. The pain from his accident still made him wince. But he could do this. For Manny, he could do this.

"Hit it!"

The bull jerked, violent and rude. Rafe met it with oomph. He braced himself, finding his center seat. Sometimes he could sense the bull's direction, anticipate the movements. But he'd set the machine to operate so the bucking came randomly, impossible to read. Thankfully, a mechanical bull didn't have hooves or a head to butt against to give him a concussion. Still, he could just as easily get thrown and end up with a broken neck, back, or other bones.

"Go, Rafe!" Manny yelled.

Rafe zeroed in on keeping himself tucked in, using his free hand for balance, and staying on.

A timer sounded—the eight-second mark—and Manny turned off the ride. "You did it, Uncle Rafe! You stayed on!"

Rafe sat there, breathing hard, his pulse pounding. The muscles in his arm shook, and he couldn't release his grip. Slowly, he opened his hand, letting the blood rush in.

"Good ride." Nick leaned against the barn door.

Manny bounced toward Nick. "Wasn't that cool?"

Nick narrowed his eyes at Rafe.

Rafe steeled himself. He didn't really care what Nick thought.

"Yeah, that was cool." Nick stepped into the darkness of the barn. "Manny, can you go into the house for a minute? I think Piper is trying a new cookie recipe."

Manny vanished, and Rafe sat there on that giant fake bull, looking at Nick and wondering what he meant.

"You're really going to do this?"

Rafe took a breath, looked at his tingling hand. "I'm just trying to encourage Manny." He brought one leg over the front and slid off the bull. "I'm going to sell the machine after he leaves."

Nick nodded and looked at his boots. "Okay, I gotta say something—"

"I know. My bull-riding days are over—"

"I want you to start riding again."

Nick could have pushed him over with a wild iris. "What?"

"I'm tired of you being ornery, and if you getting back on a bull is going to snap you out of this, then . . . well, Stef and I are behind you."

"I'm not ornery."

"Oh, really? Wasn't that you out in the yard late last night roping that dummy steer?"

"I need the practice." Rafe worked off his glove. "I'm just going through a rough patch."

"You've been going through a rough patch for about ten years. It's time you and I had a talk." Nick pulled off his hat, ran his hand around the rim as if trying to find the words. "The truth is . . . I was always jealous of you. You were Dad's favorite. He didn't ride you like he did me. He didn't make you feel like you let him down or that you weren't good enough—"

"Were we in the same family? I distinctly remember Dad choosing you to ride the fence with while I sat at home and helped feed the bums."

"It depends on how you look at it. But this is the important part: when you started riding bulls, I was really angry at you."

"Why?"

"'Cause I couldn't. I tried once . . . and it wasn't that I didn't have the strength to stay on. I was too scared."

Rafe stared at him. Nick stood two inches taller than him, with wider shoulders, stronger arms. He had Noble written all over him. Rafe had simply never caught up, in every way that mattered.

"Maybe I'm crazy," Rafe said, finding a smile.

Nick didn't match it. "No, you're not crazy. You're driven. Only, I never could figure out why. Until Kat said something—"

"I don't want to talk about her—"

"For better or worse, she saw something in you I never saw. She said that she thought you rode because you have to. Because it's in your blood."

Rafe unplugged the electrical cord. "Not anymore."

"I'd like to think that kind of courage is in my blood too." Nick gave a wry smile. "I'd like to think I could face a one-ton bull or even my own fears like you do." He paused, putting his hat back on. "Maybe I'm a fan."

Rafe gave a disbelieving harrumph, coiling up the cord.

"I think you should start riding again. For all of us."

Rafe's chest screwed up into a tight fist. He couldn't meet Nick's eyes, so he dropped the cord and moved toward the door.

Nick stepped in front of him. "I'm sorry about Kat, Rafe. She reminded me a lot of Mom."

Rafe stopped. "Yeah, she did, didn't she?"

Silence passed between them.

"You know she's in trouble, right? Piper said she saw on the news that she was hospitalized for depression. And that the Breckenridge Foundation was being dissolved."

Kitty's laughter, her easy smile as she'd followed him around the ranch and watched prairie dogs, drifted through his mind. "No, I don't believe that." Only, something had grabbed his chest and slowly begun to squeeze.

"I thought so." Nick smiled, something very big brother in his expression.

Rafe glared at him, then brushed past him and strode toward the house.

With her disappearance, Katherine had played right into Bradley's hands. Especially in the wake of her foundation's financial plunge. He couldn't ask for a better scenario. After all his sacrifices, his gambles, he would finally cash in.

But time hovered like a buzzard. It wouldn't take long for her grandfather to round up his own list of specialists. Bradley had been forced to accelerate his agenda.

He opened a bottle of mineral water, grabbed Katherine's orange bottle of prescription medicine, and knocked on her door. She'd been in seclusion since her psychiatric checkup last week– something he'd arranged through a friend who would sign off on Katherine's unstability. Like mother, like daughter.

"Katherine?"

She lay with a sleep mask over her eyes. Beside her, an old scrapbook lay open.

"Honey, are you awake?"

She ripped the mask from her reddened eyes. Her brown hair hung in a stringy mess, and with the fatigue on her face, she looked about eighty.

He didn't comment. "I have your medicine."

She held out her hand, and he dropped in two pills. "Thank you." She drank it down with the water he handed her.

Bradley sat on the bed. Put a hand on her leg. "Have you thought any more about getting away? We could even get married while we're there. How about Bermuda?"

She gave him a small smile. "Sure. Whatever you want, Bradley." Then she pulled the mask back over her eyes and rolled to her side.

See, it could be easy. He just had to keep it simple. Bradley kissed her hand, then let himself out the door.

* * *

Lincoln Cash made the best Jonas that John could ever imagine. He captured Jonas's quiet frustration as he watched the woman he loved suffer, his patience as he prayed for her healing. John had originally written the book only from Mary's point of view, but when the director suggested he write the screenplay from Jonas's perspective too, the scene came alive.

The biggest surprise came when Dex told John they'd be shooting the ending scenes first. He didn't care how they shot the movie. He simply wanted it over, so he could return to Phillips, to Lolly. In his wildest dreams, she'd close up her diner and move west with him.

And if she didn't, the hole in his chest told him that there might be a reason he hadn't yet found a condo in Malibu or anywhere else.

As Lincoln acted out the scene, John remembered how he'd

written the chapter, how he'd poured his own frustration into Jonas's thoughts.

Jonas blamed himself for this moment. He stood outside the church, listening to the organ music filter out as it played the prelude to the ceremony. He never should have left, never should have let his fear stand in the way of his heart. And now . . . well, he'd already lost her, hadn't he?

Then again, had he ever had her, really? A frightened, desperate woman. Of course she'd turn to the one person who had shown her kindness. But had he ever told her how the moment she'd walked into his life, everything changed? How he'd stayed five more long years on the ranch just to see her every morning?

He should have killed Matthias the first time he touched Mary. But back then, he'd been a meeker kind of man. He liked to tell himself that if she'd given him but one hint of encouragement, he would have stolen her away, but he couldn't be sure of that truth.

Instead, he'd given her what he could, hoping she heard not only his love but God's love for her through his songs.

For all you're worth, I'll stand here for a lifetime,
For all you're worth, I'll sacrifice it all,
You can know that you're a treasure,
I'll show you how to measure,
You can look into His eyes for all you're worth.

Jonas wet his palm, slicking back his hair, knowing he must look different. Prison camp had etched scars into his body, not to mention his psyche. And if he hadn't taken the rage home, he might have stood here two years earlier instead of wasting time in Leavenworth.

But he couldn't be sure of how she would have reacted. She'd never written, not even once.

He probably had no right to return, even now. But he couldn't let her just . . . go. Not until he knew.

Jonas walked up the steps and eased open the church door. Slid into the back pew. He stayed long enough for the bride to walk down the aisle. And then, quietly, he slipped out the back.

And walked away in silent, gripping pain.

"Cut!" The command yanked John from his thoughts.

Lincoln came over and sat in the chair next to him. "I love this scene. It's nearly as good as the final one."

John nodded.

"Dex says you haven't been back to Phillips since you pulled out a month ago. You're still looking for a condo?"

"Haven't found the perfect one yet." He'd turned down twenty. They just didn't feel right.

Cash leaned back. "You'll be glad to know that you're not the only one moving west. Lolly's coming out to live with me."

He said it so casually, so confidently that John had the sudden urge to leap out of his seat and strangle him. Instead he took a deep breath. "Really?"

Cash stood up, readying himself for the next scene. "She had to think about it, but she called yesterday and told me that she'd be willing to help me out. And, of course, I told her I couldn't live without her."

John watched him walk away and hated the man with every cell in his body.

⊰❧⊱

"I don't want to talk to anyone!" Kat crammed the pillow over her head, hoping to drown out the knocking, pretty sure that the sound was amplified three times over because of her migraine.

Maybe she was depressed, like Bradley said, because she hadn't had one clear, happy thought since leaving Montana. Her head pounded, and over the past weeks, she only felt worse with each passing day. Or maybe it was that the board of directors had frozen the accounts of the Breckenridge Foundation, pending their decision to dissolve the charity.

Which she'd responded to by . . . hiding. Yes, it felt as if she'd given up. She spent her days locked in her darkened room, seeing only Bradley and occasionally Cari, who brought her food and the daily news. With all the articles about Kat and her dismal finances and state of mental health mercifully clipped out.

Her only consolation was that when she married Bradley, she'd inherit her trust fund. And then she could support Mercy Doctors herself. At least for a while.

"Go away!" Kat said, turning on the television and scanning the channels. She stopped at a commercial of a girl riding a horse.

The door of her bedroom cracked open. Light spilled in. Kat winced.

"Okay, that's enough." Angelina came into the room, flicking on the light and opening the curtains. "You're not a mole. Pity time is over." She turned and raised an eyebrow at the magazines piled on Kat's bed. Her gaze landed on the scrapbook. "Oh, Katherine."

Kat reached over to close it. There were too many unanswered questions, the kind that kept her awake despite her pounding brain. Like what had happened to the baby Laura carried? And why didn't she have her mother's powers to win the man she loved? The questions only made her feel worse.

Angelina sat on the bed and touched her hand as she closed the scrapbook. "I know you're looking for something to make you feel better, but you're not going to figure out what you're missing, because there isn't anything missing."

Sighing, Kat muted the television. Why did Angelina have the power to look right into her soul? Kat tried hard to stare at the TV screen.

"You know what made your mother beautiful? what made her a person who drew people to her?"

"Her blonde hair? size-two figure? blue eyes?"

"No." Angelina grabbed the remote from Kat's hand and turned off the television. "It was what was on the inside. It was the fact that she loved God, and it showed on the outside. That's what people saw."

"I love God."

"Of course you do. And you need to trust that. You need to trust that He is at work in your life." Angelina got up and pulled the sheet back, exposing Kat's three-day-old pajamas. Kat lunged for the covers, but Angelina ripped them clear off the bed. "Enough of this nonsense. You have children who are depending on you."

"They put their trust in the wrong person. I can't do this. I'm a fund-raising flop."

"But God isn't, and He's the one Mercy Doctors needs."

"Thanks for that vote of support."

Angelina smiled. She sat down next to Kat, took her hand. "The one thing that you share with your father is your grit, as your mama put it. You won't give up. And that is a good thing. But I will say the same thing I said to your mother. When God says be still and know that He is God, He's telling you that He has everything in His hands."

"You told my mother that?"

Angelina cupped her hand over her cheek. "More than once. Especially after your father died. Grace and peace go with you–it means that God knows what you need and will give it to you today and tomorrow. It also means that God is pleased with you, Katherine Russell Breckenridge. You are His, and that is what makes you amazing."

Kat placed her hand over Angelina's. "I'm so tired."

"I know, child. Stop trying so hard to change the world, and let God change the world through you. Be still, trust in His grace, and you will experience His peace." She leaned over to press a kiss to Kat's forehead. "Now, you have a friend who wants to see you. But I told her that you need a shower first."

Kat wrinkled her nose. "That bad?"

"I'll be airing out the room while you clean up."

By the time Kat emerged from the shower, Angelina had changed the sheets, freshened the air, and even left a bouquet of fresh flowers on the bureau.

Cari was sitting on the bed, feet folded under her. "Hey, nice to see you up and fit for society."

"I'm not sure I'm fit, but at least I can live with myself." Kat sat next to her. "What are you doing here?"

"You need to see this." Cari took out a current issue of the *New York Times* from her bag.

Kat shook her head. "If it's another article about—"

"Just read it." Cari turned to the sports section and handed it to her. "Maybe *he'll* be there."

PROFESSIONAL BULL RIDERS COME TO MADISON SQUARE GARDEN
AP Newswire

NEW YORK—FOR THE FIRST TIME IN ALMOST FIFTY YEARS, PROFESSIONAL BULL RIDING RETURNS TO MADISON SQUARE GARDEN. GETROWDY PROFESSIONAL BULL RIDING ASSOCIATION ANNOUNCED THE INCLUSION OF A BIG APPLE STOPOVER DURING THE RIDE FOR THE GOLD TOUR.

"I THINK IT'S PERFECT TO HOST ONE OF AMERICA'S FASTEST GROWING SPORTS IN ONE OF AMERICA'S PREMIER CITIES. WE'LL HAVE THE BEST BULLS, THE BEST BULL RIDERS, AND THE BEST FANS," ORGANIZER PETER FRANKLIN SAID. "ADD TO THAT THE PYROTECHNICS AND THE ROCK AND ROLL, AND IT'LL BE AN EVENT NOT SOON FORGOTTEN IN NEW YORK."

THE TWO-DAY EVENT WILL FEATURE THE TOP FORTY RIDERS AND BULLS IN THE INDUSTRY.

Kat set the paper on her lap and smoothed it over her legs. "Why did you show this to me?"

Cari swiped the paper from her lap. "Says here the event is over

Labor Day weekend." She looked over the top. "Should I get tickets, or are you planning on competing?"

"Funny. No, thanks. People die in these events." People like Rafe. Thankfully, he wouldn't be riding.

"I think impending doom is part of the attraction." Cari folded the paper.

"We're back to the days of the gladiators. Man against beast. Let's see . . . gladiators and lions, cowboys and bulls?"

"And blood."

"I don't think it's about blood, Cari. People want to see bravado. Courage." Rafe's words came back to Kat. *"You wanted to see what it might be like to win the heart of a bull rider."*

So maybe she *had* fallen for the idea of taming a bull rider and getting inside that tough outer core to find the softy within.

She'd found it. Even if Rafe never wanted to admit it. Yes, she'd fallen for Rafe because she couldn't get past the fact that with him she felt alive. Since leaving him, she'd felt as if she might be slowly withering away. It had nothing to do with migraines, fatigue, or her increasing sense of despair over her foundation.

And everything to do with something sweet dying inside her.

"So you're saying the attraction to bull riding has nothing to do with the lineup of good-looking cowboys." Cari winked.

Kat threw a pillow at her, and Cari ducked. Yeah, Rafe had power in that rugged smile.

Her face must have betrayed her emotions, because Cari touched her hand. "Are you sure you don't want to call him?"

Kat got up, sat on her chair, and pulled on her red boots. "He told me that he thought he could live without bull riding if I stayed in his life." Then he'd kissed her while fireworks exploded above her. But she didn't say that.

Cari's voice fell to just above a whisper. "Then why don't you go back to him?"

In the silence, Kat heard the answer creep in, the one that had always been right behind all their conversations, all their emotions. An answer she'd known but refused to admit.

"Rafe is wounded. He's got a hole in his heart the size of Montana, one that he's had all his life." She studied her friend's perfect hair, perfect makeup, perfect attire, and with a rush she knew exactly what it felt like to have a gaping emptiness inside. "But I can't close it for him, regardless of how much I long to or try. Although I might ease the pain, eventually I won't be enough. He's got to go beyond himself and his good looks and the adrenaline of flirting with death, go beyond his fame and fans and even me if he wants to find healing. He needs to see that God has a good plan for Rafe Noble, one that He intends to use. Only then will Rafe understand how much God loves him."

"Sounds like you've done some pondering on this." Cari met her gaze.

"Until Rafe figures out who God made him to be, he'll always be looking for something bigger than the emptiness."

"Looking, perhaps, for the real Rafe Noble?"

Kat grabbed the newspaper. "You know, I've been trying to do things my mother's way for too long. It's time for the Kitty Russell in me to have a go at planning the soiree of the year."

CHAPTER 17

RAFE EXHALED TO the count of ten as he raised his injured leg against the weight, strengthening his knee. His entire body shook, and the pain had morphed into needles encasing his body.

"Now, that's what I'm talking about," Nick said, leaning against the cement wall of the smelly high school weight room. He went over to sit on a deadweight machine. "I spent way too many hours in here."

Rafe lowered his leg. "Feel free to work up a sweat."

"I have to pick up some supplies at the hardware store." Nick grinned at Rafe. "I'll be back in an hour."

"Don't hurry." Rafe leaned back on the padded surface of the weight machine. He needed to get his own wheels and soon, because with his dad's truck half apart in the shed waiting on a part, he'd had to rely on Nick or Stef to drive him into town every day. However, those small gestures went a long way toward healing the broken places inside.

Rafe caught his breath, sat up, and repeated the exercise.

Once upon a time, he'd had a trainer to help him bounce back from injury. But he couldn't afford a trainer or Nautilus machines. So he'd begged Nick's old football coach for the keys to the high school weight room.

He'd never played football, leaving that to Nick. But as a thirteen-year-old, he'd stood outside this room watching as Nick pumped up his muscles to become even more of a superhero to his scrawny brother.

"Maybe I'm a fan."

Rafe repeated another rep. Breathing hard, he didn't hear the footsteps. He looked up, surprised to see Lolly Stuart standing by the door.

"Hey, Rafe."

"Lolly." He grabbed his towel, stood, and caught his breath as fatigue rushed over him. He should slow down a little. He wasn't sure why he spent every day at the gym or riding the mechanical bull except that the old habits made him forget—at least for a while—everything he'd lost.

Lolly continued to stand there, arms folded over her brown T-shirt.

"Can I help you?"

"I made a mistake." She pursed her lips. "I should have . . . I should have left it alone."

Rafe frowned.

Her tone turned angry. "I'm the one who called Bradley Lymon. I'm the one who sent him out here."

Well, Lolly didn't cultivate a reputation for meddling without reason. Rafe shrugged, then went over to the bench press. "I would have found out about him sooner or later. Besides, Kitty and I would have never—"

"Stop, Rafe. I know what I saw. Kat had feelings for you."

Yeah, feelings of pity. He lay down on the press, then planted his feet on the floor. "Like I said, it doesn't matter. She's gone. I'm over her."

"Sure, you are." Lolly walked over to him. "I'll spot for you."

Rafe took the weight off the mount and lowered it.

"She's in trouble, you know."

Rafe blew out a breath, raised the weights. "I know," he huffed. He lowered the weight, breathing hard. "Not my problem."

"She made you *her* problem."

Rafe lifted the weight again, blowing out, and lowered it. "No, she saw me as a way out of her problems."

"She wanted to help you, encourage you."

"She wanted to use me for her own purposes."

"Her purposes might have been good for you. She saw beyond the flashy Rafe to the man inside, and she knew you needed a friend."

Oh, she'd been a friend all right. "I was just a summer fling before she married Slick."

"Have you ever thought that she doesn't really want to marry Bradley, but she doesn't feel like she has a choice? Maybe she doesn't believe you want her. Maybe she needs a better offer."

That was the problem. He wasn't the better offer, regardless of how much he wanted her. "What do you want, Lolly?" Rafe ground the words through his clenched teeth as he pushed the weight up and held it, his arms shaking.

Lolly gripped it and helped him place it back on the mounts.

He let his trembling arms drop.

"Piper told me that you were working out, that you wanted to show Manny you could still ride."

Rafe sat up and looked at her. "I can still ride. I'm just . . . waiting for the right event."

"I might have found it." Lolly pulled an envelope from her pocket and handed it to him. "Make her believe you want her. It may be what you're looking for." She walked away without another word.

His crazy heart leaped as he looked at the New York postmark. He had so many problems that one letter from Kitty wouldn't change anything.

But he pulled the letter from the envelope anyway and found an invitation to a charity event—his kind of event from the looks of the bull on the red-and-black glossy front. Inside, a listing of the bull riders, the ones with whom he'd competed and partied. His old life. He looked at the dates—Labor Day weekend, the day before the GetRowdy Bull Riding invitational at the Garden. An event that, until last year's accident, he had fully planned to compete in.

And the purse . . . he knew then what Lolly meant. A cool five hundred thousand dollars. Rafe closed the card, tapped it against his sweaty leg. *I can still ride.* He stood up. For a moment the world spun as the blood left his brain.

He *could* still ride. Only this time he'd do it with purpose. Because although he'd turned her down, the plight of the Mercy Doctors hospital—brought home because of Manny's recent turn for the worse—kept haunting him.

He wanted to help Kitty. Even if she no longer wanted him in her life.

⁂

"Have you finished the book yet?" Piper came into the diner and dropped a manila folder on Lolly's counter.

"Leave me alone." Lolly served Egger his roll and orange juice.

Piper smiled. "Finish the book, Lolly."

She handed Piper a menu and shrugged, like the book didn't sit on her kitchen table, calling to her, taunting her, reminding her of all she'd lost. So John had left. She would too. Leave and start a new life. Thanks to Lincoln, her future had already been put into motion. She spilled ice onto the counter as she poured a glass of water. "When are you leaving for New York?" Lolly asked.

"Tomorrow. Rafe went early with Manny and Lucia to get ready for the event. He wanted Manny to meet the riders his dad worked with."

"How's he feeling?"

"Rafe or Manny?"

Lolly set the water before Piper and wiped the counter. "Both."

"Manny's doing okay. Getting weaker. As for Rafe, he's been working out all hours of the day and night, riding that big black mechanical monster in the barn. I didn't know so much training went into bull riding. I thought they just got on and prayed."

"He's a pro. He's going to do great."

Piper took a drink. "Nick believes in him."

"When does Manny head home?"

"Right after the event in New York. Manny needs more treatment, but his father didn't have life insurance, so they're out of money. Lucia is going to sell the ranch, but they mortgaged it for Manny's first round of treatments, so even if she does sell it, there's not much left."

Lolly picked up the folder Piper had set on the counter. "What's this?"

"Something I had my friend Carter dig up." Piper took it from her. "Listen, it's just a theory, nothing for sure, but I thought you should know."

"Know what?" Her suspicions sparked, and she shook them away.

"I thought Bradley Lymon looked familiar, and now I know why. Years back, I did a research piece on people who used psychiatric conditions, like hallucinations and delusions, as criminal defenses. Sort of like research into the temporary insanity plea."

"Were you thinking of using it?" Lolly smirked.

"Don't get me started. Anyway, I came across a rather sensational case in Pennsylvania from fifteen years ago. A patient had Cushing's syndrome, and the symptoms eventually turned into full-blown psychosis."

"Yikes," Lolly said.

"It gets worse. The patient killed his wife in a fit of hallucinogenic rage."

Lolly handed a menu to a rancher who sat down two stools away. "Gives new meaning to the old-fashioned blood test."

Piper nodded. "The world gets smaller. The defendant had a public defender, a rookie, fresh out of school. You'll never guess who that might have been."

Lolly nearly poured coffee on the counter. "I have this sick feeling you're going to say Bradley Lymon. Why is that?"

"Here's the creepy part. He was engaged to be married. Three weeks after the wedding, his wife had a heart attack and died."

Lolly set down the coffee and steadied her hands on the counter. "That's very sad."

Piper pushed the folder toward her. "Or . . . frightening. I called in a few favors and got her autopsy report. The Pennsylvania ME faxed it to Carter a couple days ago, and he sent it with some more research. They found elevated levels of potassium chloride in her system."

Lolly opened the folder, but the chart inside meant nothing to her. "And that matters because . . . ?"

"Potassium chloride is used in the treatment of Cushing's syndrome."

"Piper, your brain works differently than mine . . ." In fact, Lolly wasn't sure she liked how Piper's brain worked at all. Ever since Piper had eyed the picture of Lolly's opening that formerly hung on the wall, she'd acted odd, asking her seemingly innocent questions about her life before Phillips, commenting on old family recipes she might have used. Deep in her heart, Lolly knew that Piper *knew*.

"Let me give you a few more dots to connect. Bradley Lymon's deceased wife was former Senator Frank Hiller's daughter, of the Pennsylvania Hillers." Piper leaned forward, lowered her voice. "Lymon inherited two-plus million dollars from her death."

Oh. Lolly's eyes widened. "*Oh.*"

"Yeah, *oh*. It seems to me that if I were, you know, related to Kat, like an aunt or something, I might put a Closed sign on my front door and head to New York. Just in case she needs someone to check up on her. I remember her saying that she had never felt better than when she was here."

"I thought she was talking about the fresh air." Lolly shot Egger a look as he raised his empty coffee cup for a refill.

"Maybe. But some of the symptoms of potassium chloride poisoning are fatigue, confusion, weakness, anxiety, and one source even mentioned headaches."

In all of John's daydreams about this moment, when he stood on the deck of a condo overlooking the beach and the rolling surf of the Pacific Ocean, feeling the salty air film his hair and watching the sun dip into the far reaches of the horizon, Lolly stood at his side. Sometimes she held his hand. Sometimes she wore a ring. Always she looked up at him, eyes shining.

Never had he imagined he'd stand here alone with his real estate agent hovering behind him to seal the deal.

"Gorgeous, huh?" the Realtor said, clapping him on the back. "It doesn't get much better than this."

John could argue that point. No, Montana didn't smell like the ocean or lull a man to peace with the rhythmic sounds of waves combing the shore, but it had its own beauty, the way the sky stretched so far it took him beyond himself and back again, making him realize the magnitude of God. This view didn't include the smells of pine and aspen, the sound of cicadas, the sight of contented cows sleeping in the sun. It certainly didn't include the soft smile Lolly gave him at the end of a long day. How he missed a Reuben sandwich.

"The seller is highly motivated. He's moving east and is ready to negotiate. It's got a mosaic fireplace, a garage, three bedrooms, and a rooftop Jacuzzi." The real estate agent continued to list the amenities.

But the condo didn't have Lolly.

He'd been planning this moment for years, decades even. Even though Lolly hadn't decided to join him didn't mean that he'd throw it all away.

Then again, John hadn't asked her, had he? Not really. He'd been waiting until he knew she wouldn't break his heart again.

But what was he always telling his characters? Big dreams were worth the risk. He'd been hiding for too long, not only his identity as a romance author—an award-winning, wealthy romance author, no less—but as the man who knew Lolly's secrets and loved her in spite of them because she was worth it. Which is exactly what he told Jonas when he redeemed him from prison camp and sent him stateside. What he told Jonas after he'd done time for a barroom brawl fresh off the boat from Europe, delaying his return to Mary for two long years, just in time for her to walk down the aisle. What he'd told Jonas when he'd given him his song.

Just because Mary had made mistakes—mistakes that she said should condemn her for life—didn't mean Jonas, or John, had to listen. And he didn't have to listen to Cash's words about Lolly.

It was time to write the ending to his own Western romance and fight for the woman he loved. A good romance didn't let the wrong cowboy get the gal.

"John, what do you say? Do you want it?"

He smiled. "Yeah, I want it." He brushed past the Realtor, went into the main room, turned, and took in the view. The pier stretching out into the ocean, kids playing in the sand. Maybe, someday, even kids of his own? Yeah, he wanted it all—the condo and the dream and the woman he loved. Enough to give it his last and best shot.

Just like Jonas.

⚡CHAPTER 18

FOR ONCE, KAT knew exactly what footwear matched her outfit.

"Trust you to create an event where you can wear your red boots," Cari said as she met Kat in the lobby of the still-being-reconstructed Breckenridge Hotel. "They go well with the black pants. And I love that vest." She reached out to touch Kat's fringed, red leather vest.

"Stiletto cowboy boots? Where'd you get them—Italy?" Kat said, taking in her friend's leather skirt and silk shirt.

"These are 100 percent longhorn calfskin from Dallas." Cari turned her leg, highlighting the cactus and sun emblem up the side. "I think I can see the fascination."

"I told you they're comfortable." Kat gave her a sly smile as they maneuvered around the construction zone and up the stairs to the ballrooms.

Waiting to escort them, Bradley stood at the head of the stairs, dressed in a pair of boots, an orange shirt, and jeans. He'd even conceded to a black, flat-topped Stetson, although for some reason it didn't have the charm of Rafe's beat-up straw hat.

It would have done Kat well to stop comparing Bradley and Rafe. Bradley would never be a cowboy, but Kat didn't expect to see Rafe showing up to support her Daredevils and Dreams event. For all she knew, he didn't even know about it.

Thanks to GetRowdy's enthusiastic cooperation and their need to create buzz for a Western event in a non-Western town, she and Cari and a small army of volunteers as well as the GetRowdy publicity department had pulled together the fund-raiser in little over a month. Cari had moved heaven and earth, and they'd both called in every favor they had outstanding to create the invitations, publicity, entertainment, food, and celebrity hot list.

Rafe had told her that she couldn't bring New York to Montana, so she brought Montana to New York instead.

She hoped Lolly had gotten the invitation she'd sent. She missed her listening ear, the way she felt at ease with their friendship, even though she'd known her only a couple of weeks.

By the looks of the attendees and the music spilling out into the foyer, the party had already started. With the buzz they'd created about the GetRowdy riders coming to town, New York had rodeo fever, and Kat had sold tickets faster than she imagined. Apparently even a five-star dinner didn't hold a candle to hobnobbing with men who wrestled animals that could turn them to dust. However, Kat still had to raise over five hundred thousand dollars in donations to pull herself out of the red.

Thanks to GetRowdy's involvement, she'd also managed a lineup of country singers, anxious for their pictures and names to appear in the next GetRowdy ad campaign. Currently, a bluegrass band filled the hall with banjo and Dobro music, and Kat pushed away memories of the Fourth of July street dance in Phillips.

She'd decorated the outside of the ballroom with life-size photos of GetRowdy's championship riders in all their bull-riding glory. She knew exactly where Rafe's picture hung, could see the grit of his teeth, the look of determination on his face, the muscles bunching in his arm. She'd stared at it a good long time as she directed the caterers to set up for their barbecue ribs and sweet corn.

Next to those photos were her own blown-up shots of the children suffering in the Guadalajara clinic—the same children who would benefit by Mercy Doctors' help.

"Why are all the GetRowdy riders lined up against the wall looking as if they're in a war zone?" Cari asked quietly as she waved to a congressman trying to clog with one of their hired dancers.

"They're probably shy." Kat kept her hand on Bradley's arm but scanned the crowd for a glimpse of Rafe. She didn't know why she was hoping he would attend. She hadn't heard from him, and she refused to ask GetRowdy. The last thing she needed was to stir up speculation and rip the scabs off her wounds.

"Shy cowboys? I can fix that," Cari said, heading for her prey before Kat could warn her to stay far, far away.

Bradley's hand encased hers as he led her to the dance floor. "Good job, Katherine. I'll bet this event brings in everything you need to put the foundation back in the black."

She glanced at him. Even in his hat, he looked like an attorney from the East Coast. What had Rafe called him? Slick? Kat quirked a smile. "Thanks. But I'm going to need a lot more than that to keep Mercy Doctors in business."

"Are you sure that's a good idea? You've been so tired lately. Maybe you should—"

"Give up and let my mother's hard work go down the tubes?"

They'd reached the floor, but Kat backed away, refusing to dance with him. "This meant the world to her."

"No, it didn't. Don't lie to yourself. The foundation is in trouble, and you've been pouring everything you have—your time, your money—into this charity only to see it crumble. And now you want to indebt yourself on a gamble that you can get it back up and running. Please wake up, Katherine. Your mother wouldn't want this for you. The only reason she ran Mercy Doctors is so that she didn't have to come home."

Kat stared at him, a horrible ball of anger igniting inside her. Without thinking, she slapped him—hard enough to attract the attention of everyone around her. A few couples stopped dancing.

Horrified, Kat stared at the red mark on his cheek, the look of fury on his face. The Katherine Breckenridge she knew would never have hit anyone, but she'd struck a man twice in the past two months.

She looked at her trembling hand, then back at Bradley. "I'm sorry."

He tightened his lips and forced a smile that looked anything but friendly. "No problem."

By the way he took her hand and walked her toward the door though, she knew it *was* a problem. "You're hurting me."

"Kitty, are you okay?"

Bradley stopped.

Kat stood there as Rafe simply materialized before her eyes. He cleaned up well. From head to toe, he looked exactly like the man she remembered in his shiny black boots, jeans, and a patterned black silk shirt that matched his equally dark eyes. Instead of his straw hat, he wore a black Stetson, and when he bent his head and tugged on the brim in greeting, she saw a tiny arrowhead tucked into the band.

And that, more than anything, left her without words. *This isn't the real Rafe,* Kat thought, scrambling to gather her defenses. *This is the arrogant bull rider with a chip on his shoulder.*

"Hello, Kitty," Rafe said softly.

She nodded and met his eyes, and for a second, she saw something . . . different. A fresh spark of life. A little bit of tease.

"What are you doing here?" Bradley growled.

Rafe glanced at him. "I was talking to the lady."

"I was talking to you."

"Listen, Slick, I'm not here for a fight. I'm here for the cause." Rafe pointed to his picture on the wall. "See, there I am."

Bradley didn't look. "Well, Katherine is fine, and we're having a chat."

"Seems to me that you're taking her away from all the fun." He turned that thousand-watt gaze on her again, and it was all she could do not to melt into a puddle. But she was here with Bradley. Her future husband. Who still had a tight grip on her arm. "You been okay, Kitty?"

"I'm . . . okay."

"Let's go, Katherine." Bradley yanked her through the double doors of the ballroom and down the hall.

"What?" Kat said.

"You slapped me in front of all our guests."

"I'm sorry, Bradley. But what you said . . . it wasn't true."

Bradley blew out a breath. "All right, I've been willing to put up with this phase for the past two months, but apparently I'm the only one with all my brain cells working here." He bent close, his voice tight. "Your mother started the Breckenridge Foundation out of spite. She didn't want your grandfather getting his hands on the money she owed him, so she plugged it all into a charitable organization. She could never admit that she wasted her life on a no-good cowboy."

Kat stared at him, unable to keep up.

"Your mother didn't even have custody of you; did you know that?"

The breath sucked out of Kat's body. She couldn't understand it, but she felt the truth in his words. No wonder her mother had looked at her with such sadness.

"I can't believe I'm the one telling you this." Bradley shook his head. "After your dad was killed—by a *bull*—your mother lost it. She was hospitalized for a while, and during that time your grandfather got custody of you. He'd already disowned Felicia for marrying the scum she did, yet he was willing to take care of you. When your father died, he left Felicia his prize money and his life insurance, which amounted to nearly a million dollars."

"Grandfather wanted it."

"Of course he did—he was taking care of you. But Felicia gave it all away to the foundation. She didn't have a cent of her own; everything belonged to the foundation. Your grandfather gave you the penthouse and let her stay there, but it belonged to you, even from the beginning."

Kat sagged against the wall. "Why did he do that?"

Bradley glanced back into the ballroom. "Because Bobby Russell was as much trouble as Rafe Noble, and your grandfather didn't want her to destroy her life by marrying him."

"Bobby Russell didn't destroy her life."

Bradley stared at her, an incredulous expression on his face.

"She was a supermodel, someone who traveled to Paris and Milan on a regular basis. She knew every designer in the industry and could have started her own fashion company. Instead she supported Bobby, and they lived off her salary while traveling the world to go bull riding. During those years with him, she lost her contacts, her momentum. She gave everything up for a man who risked his neck every time he went into the arena. And for what? So she could watch him die?"

Kat flattened herself against the wall, a heaviness in her chest so thick she thought it might crush her. "How do you know all this?"

"Your grandfather. Did you know that Bobby punched him? When he went to your grandfather's office to ask for Felicia's hand in marriage, Walter gave him the only answer that made sense—*no*— and Bobby broke his nose. Security hauled him out of the office, and your grandfather sued him."

"Which is why he needed my mother's support."

"She was foolish and bought into the dream that she and Bobby could live on love alone." Bradley's last words held a mocking tone.

Kat closed her eyes, trying to hear the truth behind his words. Loving Rafe Noble could have been the biggest mistake of her life.

"Thankfully, Katherine, you're not your mother. You don't have to work; you don't have to throw away your life spinning your wheels."

"The Breckenridge Foundation helps people!"

"Mercy Doctors will find another bleeding heart to fund them. Don't think for a minute that their work really makes a dent in the suffering in this world."

Kat put a hand to her head, feeling her headache knocking against the back of her skull. Sometimes she felt so very, very tired.

Bradley put his finger under her chin, lifted her head. "I know you're trying, honey. And I know it's a good cause. But it's wearing you out—even you can see, can't you? It might be time to acknowledge that you need to let go."

She sighed. "Maybe."

"Yes," he said, pressing his lips to her forehead. "Listen, sweetheart, I have people I need to meet in there. But afterward, let's leave. Get away, just like we talked about. Get married in Bermuda, maybe? You tell me when and where. I don't care. I just love you and want you to be happy."

Kat forced a smile. It wasn't too late. She didn't have to love Rafe Noble. She *could* find happiness, find a man who wanted to be with her. "Okay, Bradley. Tomorrow. We'll leave tomorrow."

"That's my Katherine, the one I know and love."

"I thought her name was Kat."

Kat turned, and a rush of joy went through her as Lolly Stuart, flanked by Piper and Stefanie Noble, strode down the hall.

A dark expression crossed Bradley's face. "What are you doing here?"

Lolly looked as if she'd done some shopping, wearing a pair of designer jeans and a patterned silk shirt over her black tank top. Kat smiled when she saw her red cowboy boots.

"We were invited," Lolly said.

"Of course you were." Bradley glanced at Kat. "Who didn't you invite?"

She made a face. "Quint and Andy?"

Bradley shook his head and strode back inside the ballroom.

Kat watched him go, hating how hurt he looked. But she needed to talk to her friends, because after tonight she'd never see anyone from Phillips again.

Lolly wrapped her arms around Kat. "How are you?" She pulled back, holding her at arm's length.

"Good. Tired. I'm so glad you came."

"Of course I did. In fact, I have to talk to you about something–"

Screams from inside the ballroom cut her off.

Kat stared past her. "Oh no, not again."

⚜

Kitty had looked so good that Rafe felt as if she'd slapped him again. Her hair loose and curly, those hazel eyes wide with surprise, looking every inch a cowgirl in her red boots and fringed vest. It took everything inside him to let her walk away–no, to let Slick pull her away into the hall.

It's none of my business.

But, oh, how he wanted it to be his business. From the second he saw her, he knew. He'd never truly heal from the hole she'd made in his heart.

Rafe had watched her go, then walked over to the rib table, stared at the offerings, and decided his stomach just might not handle it. He picked up a glass of soda instead.

"Are you Rafe Noble?" The question came from a curvy brunette in a pink fringed vest over a white GetRowdy T-shirt. He recognized stars in her eyes.

"Yep," he said.

"I thought so!" She looked him over. "They said you were on the injured list."

He glanced around the room for Kitty. "Do I look injured?" he asked, the old Rafe finding his way through the hurt.

She giggled and shook her head. The band had fired up a new tune. "Wanna dance?" she asked, grinning.

For a second he debated it. But the last time he'd danced, Kitty had been in his arms. . . .

What did he care? Kat had a fiancé. He was free and single, and his fans had obviously forgiven him for his mistakes. Still . . . "No, thanks. I gotta ride tomorrow. I need to save my strength." He gave her a wink to go with his lame excuse as she made a face and walked away.

But inside, it felt right. He was a new man, and although the world didn't know it yet, they were about to meet the new Rafe Noble. The one who stayed out of trouble, who treated women with respect, who didn't embarrass himself or his family. He fully intended for this event to be his "back on the bull" debut—had even talked his agent into another go-round. Maybe he could even earn enough to pay for Manny's medical costs.

The former Rafe Noble had wanted to impress the world with his smile, his fast living, his charm. But over the last month, he'd found healing—no, acceptance—like he'd never known in the words of his father's Bible.

He'd met a God who listened when he cried out for mercy, like David, wanting to break free of the sins that sometimes felt as if they'd choke him. *Fight for me, O Lord.*

It would help if God could do some fighting for him in Kitty's heart. He'd probably read too much in the way she lit up just for a second when she saw him. . . .

Music did little to drown the hum of conversation. In the center of the room, one of his cronies rode a mechanical bull while a ring of women clapped. He shook his head, remembering the old days.

But he didn't want that—not now.

He'd searched the crowd for Kitty, wondering if she'd returned from her powwow in the hall and nearly bumped into a couple in conversation. "Sorry." Turning, he felt someone bump him, and his drink sloshed out—right on Slick. "Sorry—"

"You shouldn't have come here." Bradley pushed Rafe.

Rafe stumbled back. "Hey!"

"Stay away from her." Bradley kept on coming.

Rafe heard warning sounds in the back of his head. "Calm down. I'm not here to get into a fight."

"I'm not a *bull rider*, Noble, but I did box on my Harvard team, and I know I could teach you a lesson."

Rafe hid a smirk. "I'm sure you could—"

Bradley hit him right across the jaw.

Rafe's head jerked, and it took him a second to realize that Bradley had gotten the drop on him. The drink went flying. Did the man not know he was in a roomful of Rafe's buddies? Bradley popped Rafe on the chin. Pain exploded across his jaw.

"C'mon!" Rafe put up his fists. "I don't want to hurt you."

"I want to hurt you." Bradley swung again.

Rafe dodged him and landed a right punch on Bradley's nose. The man's head snapped back.

"That's enough!" Rafe spat.

Bradley launched himself at Rafe.

Rafe grabbed him, turning. They went down sideways, Rafe rolling to the top. Bradley seized him around the neck, but Rafe landed a punch in his kidneys. He pinned Bradley's neck to the floor. "What's your problem?"

"You're my problem." Bradley elbowed Rafe in the face.

Rafe's nose started to gush. He bent into Bradley, sent an uppercut to the man's jaw, and followed it with a left punch just above his kidneys.

Bradley writhed beneath him. He kicked out, trying to catch Rafe across the chest.

Rafe rolled away and sprang to his feet, the agility of watching for hooves in his peripheral vision making him quick. "Get up, you jerk!"

"No!" Kitty appeared between them. She knelt next to her beloved Bradley, wiping his bloody nose with her hands as he got up. She turned to Rafe. "What did you do?"

The world slowed as she came into focus. Rafe stared at her and at his bloodied, sore hands. "Kitty, I didn't mean for this to happen."

She picked up Bradley's hat and glared at Rafe. "Of course you didn't. You never mean to destroy my life, do you? It just happens." She looked so broken then, blood on her vest, her eyes shiny. "Please stay away from me."

He stood there, breathing hard and feeling hollow as she pulled Bradley's arm over her shoulder and led him away.

"You really know how to add life to the party, don't you?" Nick said, clapping him on the shoulder. "Some comeback."

"Here," Piper said, handing him a wad of napkins. She wrinkled her nose as she looked at his eye. "I think you're going to have a shiner for those cameras tomorrow."

Just what he needed to convince the world that he wasn't the same Rafe Noble.

"Let's get you cleaned up and back to your hotel," Nick said. "I think your work here is done."

⚘CHAPTER 19

"I CAN'T BELIEVE he punched me!" Bradley sat in Kat's bathroom, holding a washcloth to his nose, which thankfully hadn't been broken.

"Just pinch it. . . . No, don't lean back." Kat knelt before him, lifting his shirt. "You said he hit your back?"

"Yeah. A couple times. I can't believe you were with that jerk for two weeks."

"Twelve days, and he wasn't like that." She probed his skin, watching for a wince or broken blood vessels. "I think you're going to be okay."

"I want charges filed."

Kat leaned back into a sitting position. "I don't need any more negative press for the Breckenridge Foundation."

Bradley looked at her, and she raised her hands in surrender. "Okay, so . . . maybe you were right. I should just give up." She felt it all then, his words and how suddenly everything made sense. The reality of it rushed at her, and she put her hands over her mouth. "My mom really didn't want to be here, did she? Not with me."

Bradley shook his head. "But you still have your trust fund."

"I don't care about the money. I wanted . . . I thought she . . . well, that her noble causes were so great they were worth the sacrifice. That God wanted her to do it. And I felt like He wanted me to do it too."

Bradley looked at the washcloth. "I don't know about God, but I'm tired of this thing running your life. Please let your grandfather take over the charity. He'll run it the way it should be, and I promise that you'll still be involved."

Kat drew up her knees, then lowered her head onto them. She was tired. So *very* tired. Of everything. Of watching her hard work turn to a fiasco. Of trying too hard to be and do something that she'd never get right.

"Katherine, Lolly Stuart is here for you." Angelina appeared in the room holding a bowl of ice and a clean washcloth.

Lolly. She'd left her and Piper and Stefanie in the hallway. "Let her in. Thank you."

Kat got to her feet. "Will you be okay?"

Bradley nodded, checking his nose in the mirror. "I'm going to get cleaned up, then go back downstairs."

"Are you sure?"

"I promise not to let Noble jump me. Again. I'll see you there." He grabbed her hand as she made to leave, smiled up at her. "Tomorrow night, okay?"

Kat nodded, dredging up a smile. Tomorrow this would all be over.

Lolly stood on Kat's balcony, staring at Central Park. "This is a view I never thought I'd see," she said.

"It's a beautiful evening." Kat stepped out onto the balcony and sat in a rattan chair, leaning her head back.

Lolly turned. "Headache?"

She nodded. "It's just stress. After tomorrow, things will be better." It was smart to turn the charity over to her grandfather. He could probably double their money in a year. Or he'd simply absorb it into the empire of his company. She rubbed her temples.

"Are you sure?" Lolly knelt in front of her. "You don't look well."

"I could use a piece of pie."

"I wish I could give you one."

Kat closed her eyes, seeing Lolly's Diner, hearing the laughter, the easy conversation. "Who's minding the restaurant?"

"Missy Pike. She and her kid sister Libby waitress for me, and Missy has wanted to buy it for years, so we worked out a deal. Kat . . . well, I'm not going back."

Kat opened her eyes. "Why?"

"I have another offer."

Something in her tone made Kat sit up and study the way Lolly stood up, so solemn, and began tracing the railing with her finger. "Did John propose?"

Lolly's face drained of color. "Uh, yeah, he did, about twenty years ago. But I wasn't ready to say yes, and . . . John left town right about the time you did."

"Oh. I thought you two . . ."

Lolly shrugged. "It's too late for us." Even Kat could tell the smile she produced came from a place of resignation. "I've decided to be Lincoln Cash's personal chef."

"That's a pretty big move. Why did you decide—?"

"Because I'm tired of waiting for my happy ending! Because this is the way it's going to be."

Kat raised her hands in surrender. "Lincoln is a lucky guy, getting all that pie. I was just saying, I thought you and John had something."

"Well, we don't. We have nothing. I thought we did, or maybe I didn't see it and let it die. But it's over, and I have to get used to that. If John ever loved me, there's nothing left now." Lolly lifted a shoulder. "This is best for everyone."

"I invited Lincoln to tonight's event. He's in town getting ready to promote a new movie. He might stop by later, according to his press agent. He didn't make it to my last event . . . although Rafe did a great job of totaling that one also." She pushed the memory of watching him hit Bradley from her mind. Why had she expected anything different?

"Kat, I came here because I have to talk to you about something." Lolly paused. "You can't marry Bradley."

"What?"

"He's trouble—"

"Stop. Rafe's the one downstairs beating people up. He's the troublemaker—"

"Rafe loves you."

"Rafe loves Rafe. And I can't compete with him or his profession. I don't even think I want to."

"He's changed. He's not the same guy—"

"I'm marrying Bradley. Tomorrow. Rafe is out of my life."

Lolly shook her head.

"What?"

She sighed. "You're just . . . so much like your mother."

Suddenly, something inside Kat simply snapped. "I am *not* like my mother. I don't even look like her. And I'm not beautiful or smart or fashion savvy. Most of all, I'm not going to make the same bad choice she made."

"Yes, I think you are."

Something in the way Lolly said it, her voice low and even shaky, made Kat pause.

"You're going to marry a man who is going to hurt you."

"That's Rafe, not Bradley."

"No, not break your heart—I mean *hurt* you. Piper thinks that Bradley might be poisoning you—"

"What?"

"Listen to me, Kat. Bradley had a first wife who died."

"I know all about his first wife. She had a heart attack. He didn't poison . . ." A chill went through Kat, and her heart thumped hard against her sternum. "Bradley wouldn't hurt me. Besides, I don't know what you're talking about. Bobby Russell didn't hurt my mother. He loved her."

"I'm not talking about Bobby."

Kat wrapped her hands around the arms of her chair. "Who *are* you talking about?"

Lolly didn't answer. The wind had picked up, a cool breeze for September, curling her blonde hair around her face.

Kat stayed silent, tucking her hands between her knees. The sounds of traffic lifted from the street. As the sun had begun to set, drizzling Central Park in shadow, the city came alive, neon signs lighting up Fifth Avenue all the way down to Times Square.

"I knew your aunt Laura."

Kat stared at her.

"In fact, I *am* your aunt Laura. I know I said I didn't know her, that she didn't live around Phillips. And that's sort of the truth because when I moved to Phillips, I changed my name from Laura Russell to Lolly Stuart. I couldn't have my past following me."

Headlines flashed through her mind, and Kat saw again the news file. "You didn't want him—your husband—following you."

"How did you know?"

"He broke your jaw and killed your child. Piper found the news article. I'm sorry, Lolly. We weren't trying to invade your privacy. If I'd known, I never would have asked Piper for help. But I was just so desperate to find you. I wanted to hear the story, to know what happened."

Lolly sank into a chair. "It's okay. I should have known Piper had found it. She seemed like she knew, anyway."

"Bradley already told me what happened. I know why my mother didn't want me."

"Oh no, Kat, that's not true." Lolly reached out to touch her but pulled back. "That's just not true."

"No, you're probably right. Maybe my mother did want me. But she'd had enough pain in her life, so—"

"Listen to me. Felicia loved you the best way she knew how. She didn't want you growing up poor or getting sick in one of the countries she worked in. Bradley was right—she didn't have a choice. But not because of why you think."

"I . . . don't understand." Kat stood up, rubbed her forehead.

Lolly took her hand. It was so warm, so firm that Kat found herself sitting back down, caught in the pain in Lolly's eyes. "You need to know that Felicia and Bobby were deliriously happy. They adored each other, and Felicia never regretted a minute of loving Bobby. No, he wasn't exactly the man Walter Breckenridge would have chosen for Felicia, but she saw something in Bobby that not many got close enough to see—a goodness, a desire to be a better man. They started supporting charities while Bobby was riding, because of all the needy kids they saw during their travels. They loved children, Kat. And they adored you. Bobby always said that your smile was his reward for coming home. I remember the day I snapped that picture of the two of you; he'd just purchased those red boots and that cowgirl outfit. Although you probably don't remember, you adored him back."

Kat's eyes began to fill at Lolly's words. "I thought I did. I have those remnant feelings every time I see that picture."

Lolly's voice grew soft. "Your world ended when he died—as did Felicia's. It was horrible. He got bucked off—not a big deal, but the animal went after him, kicking him in the head. He never wore a helmet, and his hat offered little protection. He went into a coma and never woke up. Felicia kept him on life support as long as the insurance covered it, but that topped out and they were going to move him to a convalescent home, give up on him. Finally, Walter flew in, and he made her a terrible deal. He told her that he would fund Bobby's medical care . . . if . . ." Lolly licked her lips and blew out a breath. ". . . if she'd let him raise you."

Kat wasn't quite sure she was breathing, because everything had turned deadly quiet around her.

"He wanted to raise his granddaughter the way he thought she should be raised—as a Breckenridge, not a Russell. Felicia was distraught and broke and at the end of her rope, so she agreed."

Kat took a shaky breath.

Lolly seemed to match it. But her gaze never let Kat's go. "Bobby hung on another five months, and then his heart gave out and he died. Felicia shattered. That's when she found salvation and became a Christian. She took her inheritance and the life insurance money and donated it to the Breckenridge Foundation. I think she did it because she couldn't forgive herself for the choice she'd made—choosing Bobby over you."

In that moment, Kat wasn't sure she could forgive her either.

Lolly reached out and this time touched Kat's knee. "Felicia spent her life making that organization work. The fact is, she loved what she did. She told me that in a way it was like Bobby was there with her. She said that every day she spent with Bobby was a day of grace from God. And she figured she could extend that grace to just one more child, just one more day. But I don't think she ever recovered from losing Bobby . . . or you."

"Bradley said they had to hospitalize her."

Lolly nodded. "Not for long, but yes, right after Bobby died. She was under suicide watch. That's when Walter filed for your name change."

"I always thought that I had done something wrong—that she blamed me for my father's death."

Lolly touched her face. "No, Kat. She never blamed you. She may have blamed herself over and over, but she loved you."

"Then why didn't she fight for me? If I had a daughter, I'd never give her up."

A fragile pain crossed Lolly's face. "Kat, the reason your mother didn't fight your grandfather is because if she did, he would have uncovered the truth."

"What truth?"

"Felicia wasn't your biological mother." Lolly took Kat's hand. "And Bobby wasn't your biological father."

Kat slid her hand out of Lolly's, her chest tight. She leaned back in her chair, both hands on the arms. "Oh . . . oh . . ."

"You were adopted, only not legally. We had a fake birth certificate drawn up by a lawyer in Phillips who Bobby paid off."

"Oh . . . I . . ." Kat put a hand to her throat, hoping it didn't close off. "That baby . . ."

"Yeah."

"Your baby."

Lolly nodded.

"It didn't die, did it?"

Lolly shook her head slowly. Then her face crumpled and broke, and she held her hand again to her mouth, her breath catching. "Oh, Kat, I'm so sorry. I was young and scared of what Randy might do to me–or to you–if he got out of jail. So I pretended the child died and gave her–you–to Bobby. I promised that I'd keep that secret. That I'd never interfere in your life."

Kat could barely see, what with her eyes burning and the terrible clenching in her chest.

Lolly hiccuped a breath. "That's why I moved to Phillips. It was after Bobby died, and I needed to be near you, near where Bobby is buried. I pledged that even though I promised not to interfere, I'd still watch over you from afar. Your uncle Richard Breckenridge would occasionally drop morsels about you now and again, never realizing I lapped them up like a starving dog."

Kat closed her eyes. And that's when she felt Lolly's hand on hers, warm against ice-cold.

"I'm so, so sorry. I should have told you years ago but definitely when you came to Phillips. I just didn't want . . . I didn't want you to hate me."

Kat opened her eyes. Hate her? A tear dripped off her chin as she saw for the first time Lolly's hazel eyes, the full lips, the face shaped so much like her own. Except for the blonde hair, she felt as if she might be looking into a mirror. A reflection that made her feel whole and perfect and . . . found.

"You . . . you're my . . . my *mother.*"

Lolly put a hand over her heart. "I'm your mother, Kat."

That woman could destroy everything he'd worked for. Bradley stood beside the French doors, listening to Katherine and Lolly's conversation, feeling his world shake.

Did Walter Breckenridge know that Katherine wasn't a blood heir but the daughter of a convict and a line cook? What would the old man do if he found out?

He rubbed his eyes, thinking fast as he crept out of the penthouse. He'd have to accelerate his plans even more. Their marriage. Katherine's devastating suicide.

Smoothing his shirt, Bradley surveyed his appearance in the elevator mirror, confident he'd obliterated all traces of the fight with Noble. And a profitable fight it had been, just as he'd hoped. He nodded to the bellboy who greeted him as he exited, remembering the look on Noble's face when Katherine turned on him. Perfect.

Now he needed to finish what he'd started.

But first he had to shut up that waitress.

John stepped out of his Cessna, where he'd landed it at his deserted ranch. The new owners hadn't taken possession yet, but it looked as if it had been abandoned for centuries. Tumbleweeds filled the yard; a fence hung open; a windmill squeaked in the wind. His ranch hand Crockett had left a month ago after loading the last of the cattle to market, and Cole St. John had purchased his stock horses.

John walked to the house, opened the door. It swung wide and bumped against the wall where the coatrack used to be. The sound echoed in the empty kitchen, through the family room with the overstuffed cattleman print sofa he'd left behind, down the worn carpeted hallway to the vacant bedrooms, and back to his soul.

The movers had forgotten to grab the aerial shot of the Big K off the family room wall. A legacy abandoned.

Only, not abandoned. Purged. If John listened hard enough, he could hear the old voices. But why do that? This land, this life was a part of him. However, he no longer felt bound by it. No longer bound by the fear or his father's prophecies. This land no longer belonged to the man who had to confine his heart to the written page.

"I am leaving. I am gone." His voice sounded bold, filling the room, and he smiled. "I am free." It sounded silly for him to say it like that, but he felt this unshackling of himself from the past and from the memories that had told him who he'd been.

And this unshackled Big John Kincaid would go after the woman he loved. He would simply tell her, "Lolly, I love you and I want to marry you. Still." Just like that. After all, nothing else had worked. Not years of waiting patiently, his listening ear, the friendship, the way he supported her dreams. Nothing.

Please, God, give me the right words.

He closed the door behind him when he left and didn't look

back as he uncovered his truck and backed it out of the barn. Even his hired man hadn't wanted the beater, so John planned to drop it off at Egger's junkyard. He drove past his empty fields, smelling the arid prairie grasses, the scent of animal on the breeze. Feeling the dust and wind on his face. Funny, he'd already forgotten the scent of the ocean.

He pulled up to Lolly's. Her trailer door was locked tight, the geraniums on the porch needing water. Going around the front, he entered the diner.

Quint and Egger sat at the counter. Libby stood behind it, a coffeepot in hand.

The smells of french fries and burgers greeted him like an embrace. He tipped his hat to Libby and slid onto a stool beside Quint.

Quint nodded to him.

John smiled.

Libby plunked down a cup in front of him. "Loved the book." She waggled her eyebrows at him. "Especially the ending."

Heat rushed into his face.

"Order up!" Cody's voice from the kitchen accompanied a bell.

Libby turned away and retrieved a plate of meat loaf and potatoes.

"So, when we have lady problems, I guess we should give you a jingle?" Egger stuffed a bite of pie into his mouth. He glanced at John with a small smile. "Reckon we should call you the King of Love."

"Hey–"

"Just messing with ya." Egger forked another piece of pie. "Hey, Libby, this ain't Lolly's, but it's close."

Libby refilled the coffee cups. "Thanks. She gave my sister her recipes before she left. Missy's planning on overhauling the entire menu, with the exception of the pies."

"Where's Lolly?" John barely kept the panic from his voice. When Cash said she'd be joining him soon, he didn't expect—

"She went to New York. Some fancy event Kat was hosting."

John sipped his coffee, trying to wrap his brain around the news. Did Kat know about Lolly? Why would Lolly give up her secret now? Unless she too was breaking free of the shackles in her life. *Finally.* "When did she leave?"

"Yesterday. Took a flight outta Sheridan," Libby said.

"When's she coming back?" John asked, pointing to the meat loaf special on the board.

Libby wrote down the order. "She's not. She's selling Missy her place and her trailer. I'm not sure where she's going."

John stared at his coffee, then looked at Libby. "Hold that order. I'm not staying."

❧

The house echoed with silence when Mary closed the door. Shadows darkened the room as the last flickering of sunlight disappeared beyond the hills. Loss swept through her.

Closing the door with her heel, she walked into the kitchen, filled a vase with water, and put the bouquet in it, hoping it wouldn't die before Rosie returned.

"Thank you, Mama," Rosie had said today as she hugged her good-bye outside the church, climbing into a Hudson Hornet with her new husband.

Mary had searched Franklin's eyes, watched him over the weeks he worked on their ranch, and finally given her blessing.

Having seen love, she could now recognize it on the face of others.

Perhaps that was why she'd stared at Erland years ago on that awful day and said no. No, she couldn't marry him. She wouldn't give away her heart for second best, because she had known what it was to love someone, and Erland deserved better.

She set her hat on the table and climbed the stairs to her room.

Now, better than anyone, Mary knew the different sides of love.

Charlie had been the love of her youth, passionate, hopeful. A love that had taken her by the hand and set her dreams afire.

Rosie had been unconditional love. Love that depended without shame. Love that hoped without reserve. Love that shared her pain without condemnation.

Even Erland's love—the kind of love that made her look at herself with new eyes. Eyes of compassion.

But perhaps the love that had changed her the most had been the love unspoken. The love she'd had for Jonas. The love that had set her free one day at a time. Loving Jonas, even unrequited, had allowed her to dream. To survive. To build. It was only the power of hope that kept her love alive, the places in her heart still left untended, yearning for more. But that power made her believe that even after all these years, despite the fact that she'd never written, Jonas would keep his word and appear on her doorstep at the right time.

She picked up her Bible from the bedside table and flipped it open to the letter inside. The one that began "Dear Jonas, . . ."

Slipping the letter inside her dress pocket, she put the Bible back on the table.

The moon had begun to rise as she hiked out onto the prairie, across her land, into Charlie's land. Oddly, it bathed the mound she'd tended with care, as if illuminating her destination.

She knelt before the grave. Put her hand on the mound. The grass wove through her fingers, light and cool, and she dug her fingers into the dirt.

"She's married, Charlie. Our little girl got married today. I wish you could have seen her—she was so beautiful." Mary drew up her knees under her dress. "I saw Erland there with his new wife, Esther. They look happy."

She sat there in silence, listening to her memories. "I miss you," she said finally. "I know you always wanted me to be happy, Charlie. And . . . I am."

She got up and moved away from the grave, taking out the letter.

Dear Jonas,

I know I should have written years ago, probably a week after you left, begging you to return to me. But I simply couldn't, and I think you know why. I said I was afraid for you and what would happen, but in the end, I was afraid for me. Afraid to lose myself yet again in hopes of finding a life. Afraid that for all you would be to me, there would always be the fear inside, that wounded place that someday I'd end up exactly where I was when Charlie died. Alone and without hope.

Somehow, just holding on to your promise, I began to live again. To break free of my mistakes. To live each day just a little more free than the day before. Your love gave me the courage to learn to live, to dream, because I believed that you'd return. And now I am hoping you will. I am ready.

Yours,

Mary

Folding the letter, Mary ripped it slowly. Then she cupped the pieces in her hands and let the wind take them.

A knock at her hotel room door yanked Lolly from the book. Lincoln. He'd left a voice mail for her, asking her to meet him in her room, but he had yet to show up, and it was getting late. She much rather wanted to be with Piper and Stefanie, convincing Kat not to marry Bradley. But she supposed this was how her new life would look.

She yanked open the door to find a room service cart topped with a dozen red roses in a crystal vase. A card tucked inside had her name scrawled on the front. Strange. "Lincoln?" Or maybe it should be "Mr. Cash?"

Lolly took out the card to read it. *To my best gal.* She looked out into the hall again, puzzled. To her recollection, she was nobody's best gal. Or at least, not of the man she hoped to be. She brought the roses inside and set them on the table, then touched one of the velvet petals, Mary's actions still heavy in her mind.

Lolly understood, probably better than anyone, why Mary had torn up the letter. How the friendship and gentle presence of a constant love might set someone free even from afar. She pulled out one of the roses and smelled it.

Oh, she might as well admit it—she harbored the crazy hope that John had sent these. That he missed her as desperately as she missed him.

If only she, like Mary, hadn't been too afraid, too broken to accept John's proposal. But like Mary, she'd needed to find her footing and learn to live again.

Yet John had never left. In fact, if she were to take a good look at their friendship, he'd been all the faces of love to her—the one that believed in her dreams, the unconditional love that hoped despite her coldness to him. He made her see herself through his eyes. Capable. Even beautiful. Deep inside, she wanted to believe he'd always be there, waiting.

The flower slipped from her hand. *Unshackled* wasn't Mary's story. It was *hers*.

Set in a different time, with different players, John had written her story from her point of view. A story of a woman with dreams, of tragedy and mistakes. A story of a woman shackled in shame and a man whose love gave her the strength to break free and create a new life. And to allow herself to believe she could be happy.

John *knew*. All this time, he knew about her past and loved her anyway. When he couldn't tell her he loved her . . . he wrote it. But he'd left town just like Jonas.

"Please, Jonas, don't give up on her!" Lolly snatched up her book. She flopped down on the bed, tears hot in her eyes.

She didn't even sense the presence behind her until it was on top of her, pressing her down into the bed, pushing the air from her body.

CHAPTER 20

"YOU'VE LOST YOUR mind, Piper!" Flanked by the two women who probably had the least to lose by the truth, Kat still couldn't comprehend their words. "Bradley is not trying to *kill* me. That's absurd."

Then again, now that the event had wound down, the musicians packed up and all evidence of Rafe's fight cleared away, she had to agree, this night had been full of crazy moments. Like Rafe showing up, looking as if he'd walked off the pages of her favorite Western and then turning Bradley's nose to hamburger. Her long-lost *mother* appearing on her doorstep. Or Bradley phoning to tell her that he'd pick her up tomorrow afternoon for their getaway. For their *elopement*.

And now Piper and Stefanie here in her penthouse, per Lolly's instructions, barraging Kat with insane accusations about the man she loved. Or thought she loved.

Yes, *of course* loved.

She couldn't be with a man who had to be leashed every time

he went out in public. Besides, Rafe didn't want her. If he did, he would be here fighting for her, wouldn't he?

The last thing she wanted was to end up like her mother or . . . her *aunt*, living with broken dreams.

"Read the evidence for yourself." Piper thrust the manila folder at her.

Kat looked at it as if it might contain anthrax. "No. I refuse to believe it. I know Bradley. My grandfather trusts him, and he wouldn't hurt me."

"You said yourself you felt better than you had in months when you were in Montana," Piper said. "Could it be because the drugs were finally being flushed from your system?"

Kat put a hand to her head, rubbing at the faintest claw of a headache. "I was stressed before I went to Montana, and coming back hasn't been a picnic."

"Maybe you should have stayed." Stefanie leaned against her dressing table.

"I couldn't stay. I have a life here. Responsibilities," Kat said. "Besides, Rafe doesn't care for me."

"That's the craziest thing I've ever heard," Stefanie said. "Rafe is falling hard for you."

"Oh yeah, I can tell by the way he's sending me flowers and serenading me from the balcony." Kat winced at the apparent hurt in her tone. "Rafe is back in his life, surrounded by fans, and I certainly don't belong."

"Listen," Stefanie said. "I know my brother and he's different. After you left, he—"

"Turned into a whiskey-drinking ladies' man?" Kat shucked off her red boots, tossing them into the dressing room.

"No, that was *before* you met him. The new Rafe is different. Focused. And he's all about helping Manny."

"Manny?" Kat folded her arms and stared out the window, surprised at the bitterness in her voice. "Who is he, anyway? Rafe's . . . son?"

Silence ensued in the wake of her words.

"Whatever he is, obviously there is a commitment between Rafe and Lucia, whom he loves *oh, so very much*." Okay, now she sounded like she might be about thirteen and in the middle of a jealous crush. "It doesn't matter—"

"It does matter," Piper said softly. "Manny is *Manuel's* son—Rafe's friend who died."

Oh.

"He has leukemia. And Rafe is trying to raise money for his expenses because he doesn't have insurance and lives in some village in Mexico without decent medical care."

Oh.

"Rafe's just trying to give the kid hope. He's going to ride in tomorrow's invitational, hoping to earn the purse to pay Manny's expenses."

"He's riding to help Manny?"

"Yep."

Kat felt a hand on her shoulder and turned. Stefanie stood there, flanked by Piper. "The truth is that . . . okay, we don't have any *solid* proof about Bradley." She glanced at Piper, who apparently didn't share that sentiment. "But something's not right. And we're worried about you. Even if we're wrong, you don't belong with Bradley."

"Bradley is exactly my type."

"Bet he doesn't like your red boots, does he?" Stefanie said.

"No one is saying you don't have a great life here," Piper said. "But is it the life you're supposed to live? Just because something is good doesn't mean it's right. We can surround ourselves with a million really good things and miss the one excellent thing we're supposed to do with our lives."

Kat rubbed her arms, turned back to the darkened skyline. "You know, all I really wanted to do was live a life that mattered and carry on where my mother left off."

Piper joined her at the window, staring out at the night. "Maybe you should *start* where she did."

Kat frowned at her.

"By loving a good man."

The words hung in her mind as Piper and Stefanie took up residence in her guest rooms, like the cavalry to her rescue. A glance at the clock told her that Lolly was either still meeting with Lincoln or had decided to turn in. Kat lay on the bed, watching the lights of the city.

"Loving a good man."

She sat up, pulled her scrapbook onto her lap, and ran her fingers over the eight-by-ten glossy of Bobby. Oh, he had been gorgeous. No wonder Felicia had fallen for him. She turned the pages until she found the photo booth snapshots. The one of Felicia laughing and looking gloriously happy.

She turned more pages and saw her baby photos, the ones with her and Felicia and with all three of them—Kat, Felicia, and Bobby—together. She carefully took out one of the pictures, hoping to find the date. She found an inscription instead: *My darling Kitty on her first birthday.*

Kat tightened her mouth. Her mother called her Kitty? She'd never heard anything but Katherine. She remembered Felicia showing up at Christmas when Kat was nine, a stuffed horse in hand. She had stayed for most of the afternoon, playing with Kat on her bedroom floor. And at her graduation, waving from the crowd, grinning. Right before Grandfather took her back home to Manhattan.

Kat continued turning pages until she came to Bobby's obituary and the picture of him astride his final bull, before he fell off and they lost him to his profession. Rafe had a picture like this.

"So are you going back to bull riding?" Their conversation the day she'd found the arrowhead came back to her, and for a few seconds, she was caught in that moment, in the smells of the ranch, and in the smile of a guy who'd made her feel like his girl.

"No. I'm done."

Oh no, he wasn't. And she'd known it even then.

"Seems like a place to find peace, even some grace," she'd said. *"Maybe heal you enough to start over."*

Kat hadn't known then that her words had been for her as well.

She had found peace, even grace, in Rafe's world. She'd found a part of herself she didn't know existed. Not her courage or even her ability to embrace the land . . . but her heritage. A heritage of courage and commitment. Felicia *and* Lolly, mothers who had been brave and strong and who had sacrificed for the child they loved.

She pressed her hand to her mouth as she felt her eyes burn. She'd been trying so hard to be like her parents, to measure up to their world. And why?

So she might believe she too deserved the happily ever after she saw for everyone else. Tears leaked out, and she let them fall. *Lord, please tell me what to do.*

Kat let the words from the verse she'd paraphrased to Rafe find her heart, her soul. *Work out your salvation with deep reverence and fear, because God is at work in us, to give us the desire to obey Him and the power to please Him.* God in her.

God, giving her the identity she so craved.

Maybe her entire trip to Phillips hadn't been for Rafe . . . but for her, to show her that she wasn't a Breckenridge or a Russell. But God's girl, just like Angelina had said.

Perhaps the more Kat understood her identity as a child of God, that He created her and loved her, the more she could be free to be the person He'd created her to be. Without having to prove anything. To impress anyone.

"Stop trying so hard to change the world, and let God change the world through you. Be still, trust in His grace, and you will experience His peace." Angelina, as always, the voice of truth in her life.

What if choosing the excellent thing wasn't so much about her actions—always striving to be and do the best—but rather receiving the acts of grace and letting her life rest in Jesus' hands?

"Every day she spent with Bobby was a day of grace from God," Lolly had said about her mother.

Kat had to confront Bradley; she knew it. But she couldn't truly believe that Bradley would ever hurt her. Not really. Earlier when Kat had read Piper's "proof," it just seemed a horrible coincidence. Even if it wasn't true, the real question hovered in her mind: did Kat count a day with Bradley a day of grace, a gift from the Lord?

She already knew the answer, hoping that maybe even wannabe cowgirls got a happy ending.

Sometimes Bradley had to believe that fate loved him. Yes, things had gotten more complicated, but he'd dealt with that last night. He'd spent the morning packing, envisioning the life that would be his as Katherine's husband. How sad that soon after their nuptials, Katherine's depression would overtake her.

Bradley pulled up in the limo and called the helicopter waiting on the roof, instructing the pilot to wait while he went upstairs to Katherine's penthouse. He'd phoned thirty minutes earlier, wanting to surprise her, and Angelina informed him Katherine was packing. Now that was his good little Katherine.

He pressed the elevator button, then smoothed his tie. Soon he'd be living in a penthouse instead of a cramped one-bedroom apartment.

The doors opened to the top floor, and he used his key card to enter. "Katherine? Are you ready to go?"

He closed the door behind him, hearing the click but nothing else. He did see, however, two large bags by the front door. Frowning, he crossed to her bedroom, knocked on the door. "Katherine?"

No one in the dressing room.

"Hello?" Angelina said, entering the room. "Are you here for Katherine's bags?"

"Where is she? We had a . . . date."

"She went to the bull-riding event."

He rubbed his eyes. "Okay. Thank you, Angelina."

He strode to the window and stared out for a long, long time. He had worked long and hard for this.

Enough games, Katherine.

"I'm still not sure I should sign off on this, Rafe. You had surgery two months ago. And if you land wrong . . ." Doc Wilson strapped the knee brace on Rafe's leg, checking one last time for fit.

"C'mon, Doc. You've seen me worse off than this." Rafe forced a smile, hoping the doctor couldn't see the pain pulsing in his brain, needling his common sense. He shared Doc Wilson's concern, but short of hog-tying him, nothing could keep him from riding today. He planned on staying on for eight seconds and all three go-rounds and winning that purse. He hoped it would be enough to help Manny live to be a hundred and ten.

"You look like you've been in a fight." Doc flashed a light into Rafe's eyes, making him blink. "Up to your old tricks?"

Doc had been privy to a few of Rafe's darkest moments—when he'd shown up at an event hungover or broken after he'd ridden one too many times, fighting to keep his demons away.

"No, I'm clean." Rafe looked away, hating the fact that he'd been the kind of guy who even had to say that. "In fact, I spent the morning at cowboy church." He'd raised a few eyebrows from the regulars who knew that Manuel had been trying for years to get Rafe to the pre-event meetings.

"All right then. Let me see you set your spurs."

Rafe drew up his knees and put his heels together. He clenched his teeth to keep out the moan.

"Okay, you're good to go." Doc helped him off the table. "Ride safe, Noble."

Rafe hobbled out of the room toward the lockers. Already he could feel the adrenaline in the air, a tension that mounted every minute until the event. GetRowdy had an explosive, roof-raising fireworks-and-country-music intro designed to deflate tension among the bull riders as much as to ignite the audience. Rafe could hear the sound guys rolling the videos for a sound check as he walked through the tunnels toward the staging area.

Last night GetRowdy's bulls had been unloaded and put in pens on one end of the Garden floor. The earthy smell of their hides mingled with the dirt floor, adding a rough-and-ready aura to the scent of big city that embedded the cement walls and pervaded Madison Square Garden. Rafe could almost close his eyes and believe he was back on the Buckle, riding the mechanical. Almost. Except for the shallow murmur of excitement from the gathering fans that would grow as time for the event neared.

Usually, GetRowdy held their events in the evening, and Rafe had an entire day to manage his nerves, center himself, think through his ride millisecond by millisecond. Today he'd had about three hours, most of which had been consumed by Nick's pep talk, Piper's endless barrage of questions about bull riding, Stefanie's worry over his leg and shoulder, and an hour of hymn singing and preaching.

Not a bad way to spend the morning. Especially when the preacher read from Psalm 40: "'Please, Lord, rescue me! Come quickly, Lord, and help me.'"

God had been doing a lot of saving, of fighting with and for Rafe Noble over the past month, chipping away the man on the outside—the cowboy who lived to impress—to free the one on the inside. Rafe was beginning to like the man in the mirror.

As he'd walked out of the hotel on the way to the Garden, he kept his eye out for Kitty. Not that he expected to see her, especially after the glare she'd given him at the party.

Yeah, his fists had done a decent job of killing any hope that he might win her back with good behavior. So much for showing her the new Rafe. Obviously, Rafe, with God's help, still had some more work to do.

He had to purge her from his thoughts if he hoped to have a prayer of not getting killed this afternoon.

Rafe entered the locker room, where Nick waited with his gear. He nodded to a couple of buddies and joined Nick. "All clear."

"Did you bribe the doctor?" Nick asked.

"He told me I was aces to go, no bribery needed. I'm going to be fine." Rafe pulled on a black snap-button shirt, rolling up the sleeve of his right arm to his elbow. Then he buckled on his chaps, a fancy pair of buckskin fringed in red and black, tipped with gold. He'd had them made two years ago for a photo shoot.

"Vest," Nick said. "Don't forget the vest."

Rafe put on the protective vest, thumped it a couple times, and grinned at Nick. "Feels good to be back."

Nick shook his head. "Dad would kill me."

Rafe laughed. "Let's go see what bulls I drew." He put on his black hat, the one that matched his chaps, grabbed his bull rope, then exited into the hall.

A low hum rolled through the arena as the stands filled. With the noise, his adrenaline began to burn. He loved this part the most. The anticipation igniting inside him. The challenge that filled his veins. He blew out a hot, eager breath.

Okay, so maybe he *had* been born to ride bulls. He wouldn't exactly call it a spiritual gift, but he could use it for good, right?

"You don't have to be a bull rider to impress me." Kitty's words dug into his brain.

He shook them away. This wasn't about impressing anyone. Today was about being true to himself.

Nick searched for Rafe's name on the sheets posted by the office. Usually Rafe knew his bulls days ahead of time and researched them until he knew their every move, their disposition, and their weaknesses. Kitty's event had thrown him off his game.

"You sure you're up for three rides?" Nick asked.

"Gotta be if I hope to win."

"Will your points count toward the finals?"

Rafe nodded, not sure how he felt about the finals in Vegas. Especially if PeeWee would be there.

"First ride's on a bull named Yellow Fever."

"I know him. He's a fighter, but I've stayed on him."

"Second ride is a bull named Clean Break."

Big Brahman bull. "Yeah, I've heard of him. Haven't ridden him, but he's got a 90 percent buck-off rate." Rafe made a face. "Good news is that he scores points if I can stay on him."

"You'll stay on him," Nick said almost absently as he read the third name to himself. He paused.

"What?"

"Rafe, we can figure out another way to help Manny. I know you think this is a God thing, but it's not too late to pull out. Besides, I have a feeling the doc would feel a whole lot better if you—"

"Who am I riding?"

"You drew PeeWee." Nick's expression was stony, as if holding back the emotions Rafe felt, not wanting to acknowledge their power.

Rafe went cold. The kind of cold he'd felt that night in the arena in Vegas. The kind of cold that should have made him hesitate, back down. That could have saved a life.

The cheers of the crowd filled the silence between them, and in it, Rafe felt the old Rafe—who just wanted to get it done and escape—trying to claw back to life. *Fight for me, O Lord.*

"I'll be all right," he said without looking at Nick. "One ride at a time."

Nick stuck his hands in his pockets. "I guess I should go find our seats." He wore an expression that Rafe hadn't seen since . . . he'd been six-years-old. It looked a lot like fear.

It rattled Rafe so deeply that for a second his voice left him. He could only nod.

Nick nodded back. Then he grabbed his brother in a quick one-arm hug. "Good luck," Nick said stiffly and walked away.

Rafe watched him go, his throat burning.

He could do this. He *would* do this. Heading out to the door of the arena, he looked up toward the seats reserved for family, to the right of the chutes. Stefanie and Piper sat with Nick's empty seat between them. Lucia and Manny waved to him. Rafe gave a thumbs-up, breathing in the moment between now and when they all found out he was riding the bull that had killed his best friend. He wouldn't look at them the rest of the night, not until it was over.

He tried to ignore the disappointment of not seeing Kitty. But what had he expected? That she'd show up to wish him well?

If he remembered correctly, last time she'd used kisses to talk him out of riding. Good grief. She was like a burr under his saddle, irritating. If he kept it up, he'd get himself killed.

Rafe headed to the stage as the music started, dredging up memories, feelings, nerves. He lined up behind the other bull riders as the organizers from GetRowdy motioned them toward the stage.

The riders would stand in full regalia, holding their bull ropes in darkness while the music accompanied video of their rides. Then in an explosion of triumph, fireworks would light up the stage, backlighting the riders.

In the past, Rafe devoured the moment, the thousands of screaming fans, the rush of his hot pulse on fire to ride, to go man to beast.

Now he stood there as the crowed erupted, and all he could do was pray.

⚜CHAPTER 21

THIS COULD NOT be happening. John leaned forward in the taxi, speaking to the driver through the opening in the plastic panel. "Can you drive any faster?" He wasn't sure what his hurry might be–Lolly wasn't waiting for him. But maybe he could find her before the words that had been building in his chest all night–as he'd taken the red-eye to LaGuardia–died in the glaring truth that he was too late.

Just wait until he got near Lincoln Cash–the makeup artists wouldn't have to manufacture a shiner or a busted lip.

"We're in a traffic jam," the driver said.

John could see that. For once he longed for the five-block, one-stoplight simplicity of Phillips, where to find the woman he loved he just had to walk into the local diner. When had life gotten so complicated?

About the time he'd decided to hide his life instead of letting Lolly inside his secrets. He'd been so afraid she'd reject him–the Western romance writer–that he'd refused to risk. And without risk, there couldn't be reward.

"Perfect love casteth out fear." John knew that. He wrote Jonas around that very thought. The only problem was he didn't take the story home, into his heart. Up to now, loving Lolly had been about his needs, his fears. If he really loved her, he had to tell her, regardless of his fears of her laughing at him or running away again. If he loved her, her reaction couldn't change that. He'd keep on loving her. Because true love didn't back down. Didn't give up. Didn't move to Malibu.

"I'll give you an extra twenty if you find a shortcut."

The cabdriver shook his head, but he flipped on his blinker and moved into the left lane.

John's cell phone rang. He'd never had one until last month, and for a second, he thought the Brad Paisley song might be playing on the radio. When the jingle cycled through to repeat, he knew it was his back pocket.

The caller ID listed *unknown.* He flipped it open. "Hello?"

"John? Lincoln here."

Lincoln? Oh, how convenient. "Lincoln, you'd better not be in—"

"I'm in the hospital."

"What happened?"

"It's not me. It's Lolly."

"Lolly? Is she okay?"

"She was beaten up. From what I could get from the EMTs, she has a couple broken ribs, some internal bleeding. The cops said that she wasn't raped, but whoever did it left her to die. She has strangle marks around her neck."

John gripped the back of the seat, feeling dizzy. *Beaten up? Strangled?*

"She's in ICU at Mount Sinai Hospital. They won't let me in

because I'm not family, but I figured you were the closest thing. You need to come to–"

"Yeah. I'm the closest thing. And I'm here in New York." John leaned forward to the driver. "Mount Sinai Hospital as fast as you can." As the driver wove through traffic, switching lanes, John asked, "How'd you find me?"

"I called Dex to get your number, and he said that you were headed to Montana."

"When did it happen?"

"They don't know. Probably late last night."

"How'd you find her?" John asked, hating that Lincoln had been the first to be there for her.

"We had a meeting last night, but I couldn't get ahold of her. I called again this morning, and she still didn't answer, so I stopped by her room. When I knocked, I thought I heard a funny sound. I got the management, and we found Lolly beaten on the floor."

"Stay with her. I'll be right there." John closed the phone. He leaned forward and said to the cabdriver, "Whatever it takes, just get me there—now."

❧

Kat thought she might be ill. The smells of popcorn and hot dogs only made her swimming stomach clench, and a layer of sweat prickled her forehead. Had Felicia endured the same gut-spilling fear every time Bobby got on a bull?

Kat rose from the box seats and walked to the railing, where she held on for dear life. On one of the big monitors, she watched Rafe in the chute, and everything inside her wanted to throw herself at his feet and beg him not to ride.

Instead, like some sort of gawker, her gaze stayed glued to his movements, the way he ran his gloved hand up the end of his bull rope to rosin it and how he wrapped the rope around the bull, then wedged his hand under it, pulling the end tight, hitting his fist so he could tighten his grip, wrapping the rope back across. She'd seen a previous rider get hung up, tossed about like a rag doll, and she'd gasped along with the crowd, her shoulder aching with each torturous second.

Rafe had dislocated his shoulder just over two months ago. *Please, please watch over him, God.*

He hit his vest twice, then put his hand on the rail.

Kat held her breath.

Rafe looked straight at the camera. His expression stilled her. Before, in his videos and photos, she'd been mesmerized by his smirk and a wildness in his eyes that almost made the event into a game, a battle for his enjoyment. That was probably why he rode with such recklessness, a trait that had earned him every bit of his scoundrel image.

But this Rafe had a resoluteness around his mouth, a fierceness in his expression that made everything inside her thrum with power. Maybe Rafe *had* changed.

He nodded.

The bull exploded from the chute and jerked Rafe forward, throwing his head back. The dulled horns barely missed his face. Kat winced. The bull twisted his back end one way, his front another while Rafe moved with him in brilliant anticipation.

"Go, Rafe," Kat breathed. Excitement roiled inside her.

The bull twisted in a new direction. Rafe pitched forward. Looked unseated.

Kat's hand tightened on the rail.

But he hung on, his arm high, his heels tight on the bull's neck.

The crowd roared.

The clock ticked past six seconds.

"C'mon, Rafe!" Kat screamed.

The bull took Rafe around twice more.

Kat glanced at the monitor close-up. Rafe wore his fight face, but she saw pain in his gritted teeth. She especially knew how well he could hide it, which meant he had to be in agony.

"Rafe," she moaned, her hands to her mouth.

The eight-second buzzer sounded.

Kat jerked with the sound, then exploded in cheers as Rafe cleared the bull, rolling off the animal's back and landing in the dirt. "Yes! *Yes!*"

The roar from the stadium drowned her voice as Rafe found his feet, took off his hat, and waved to his adoring audience. But Kat recognized the forced smile and the way he limped to the rail.

"He's hurt!" Hot tears burned her eyes, and she whisked them away as she made her way out of the box. "I knew he'd get hurt!" She thundered into the hallway, furious, wanting to hit someone or grab Rafe by his vest and . . . and . . . Kat slammed her open palm against the cement wall. "That . . . bullheaded–"

"I'm so glad I found you." Piper said. "Kat, are you okay?"

Kat wiped wetness from below her eyes. When was she going to learn not to cry over that man? "I'm fine."

"Wasn't Rafe incredible?" Piper grinned at her.

"Yeah, just great. He's hurt, you know."

"He looked okay to me."

"He's really hurt! Did you see him limp out of the arena? The fake smile he gave to the crowd? It's probably his knee, but it could be his shoulder or his back. You know the doctor told him never to ride again, but no, does he listen to reason, to the smart people in his life?" Kat clenched her fists. "I just want to—"

"Oh, you do have it bad. Okay, this is good." Piper grabbed her by the arm. "Come on. Sit with us."

Kat yanked her arm from Piper's grasp. "No. I'm not going to see him. It'll just distract him, and frankly I don't know what I'd do to him. I'm too angry."

"That's the Noble men for you. Make you angrier than you've ever been in your life. Which also makes you love them more than you've ever loved anyone in your life."

Kat stared at Piper. It was true. She'd never been this angry at Bradley because she'd never loved Bradley to the point of feeling his dreams, his fears right in the center of her chest. "Piper, I'm so scared he's going to get killed out there. I don't know if I can take watching him again. I don't think I can do this."

"You can't stop Rafe from doing what is in his heart. He's going to ride or not ride, because God put that in him." Piper began to walk. "When I met Nick, I hated him. I thought he'd done something . . . terrible. But the more I got to know him, the more I saw in him everything I needed: compassion, a sense of justice, a spirit of sacrifice that took my breath away." She stopped and turned, and Kat saw tears in her eyes. "I thought I was going to lose him too, but I had to believe in him, in his heart. Ultimately, I had to trust that God would deliver him. Nick had been broken, sort of like Rafe. And the only thing that could heal him was doing what God had created him to do."

"Like ride bulls?"

Piper lifted a shoulder. "Or something else. Come with me. There's someone you have to meet."

Kat followed her through the corridors, down two levels until they came to the section for family and special guests. She spotted Stefanie sitting beside Nick, cheering for the contestant now landing in the dirt and scrambling from the horns of a bull.

It struck her that knowing Rafe had given her something else she'd never had before. A family.

The Nobles, rooting for each other, hurting together. Wow, she wanted that more than she'd ever realized.

Kat stopped on the steps, watching the action in the arena. The bullfighters distracted the bull, then let it chase them back to the pen. They leaped onto the gate at the last second.

It never occurred to her that the bullfighters might be in more danger than the bull riders—and they did it without the glory.

Her conversation with Rafe under the balm of Gilead tree came back to her, the one about God using some people for big things—like riding bulls—and others for the so-called small things—like saving the lives of bull riders. She remembered her thought, and now it swept through her with a new breath: *It's no small thing to have the Creator of this big sky at work in your life, on your side, giving your life purpose.*

God had created Rafe to ride. She saw it on his face—in both the old Rafe and this new one. If she loved him, she'd have to love this loud, messy, dangerous life.

A life where every day with Rafe might be a day of grace.

"Kat, I want you to meet Manny and Lucia." Piper's voice cut through her thoughts, and she found herself standing at the end of the row as Piper sat down next to Nick and put her arm around a young boy with short black hair and eyes alight with excitement.

"Hi," he said.

"Hi," Kat said, holding out her hand.

"Are you Rafe's friend?" he asked.

"Yes," she answered. At least she dearly hoped so.

Manny's mother smiled at Kat. "I'm Lucia. Rafe speaks highly of you."

He does? He did? Something about Lucia's sly smile, her dark eyes sprinkled with a friendly spark of mischief told Kat that Piper and Stefanie had shared a few of her secrets. And that she'd been wrong about Rafe and his relationship to Lucia.

"Nice to meet you," Kat said, crouching on the steps. "Are you in town long?"

The stands erupted around them as another rider stayed on his bull. Kat glanced at the scoreboard. She didn't know how to read the scores, but she saw Rafe's name listed in the top three and holding.

"We're leaving tomorrow. Our visas are about to expire, and we have to go back to Mexico," Lucia said. Sadness touched her eyes.

Piper's words about Manny's disease throbbed in Kat's thoughts. Manny's green GetRowdy T-shirt did nothing to hide the bones in his shoulders, and Kat noticed his gaunt, flushed face and a scattering of bruises on his arms. "Where in Mexico do you live?"

Lucia spoke over the roar of the crowd as the announcer introduced the next rider. "About fifty kilometers from Guadalajara, in the foothills of the Sierra Madres." She glanced at her son, and in that moment, her fears flashed across her face. "We had hoped to stay here, but . . ." She forced a smile. "Rafe's going to win for us today, isn't he, buddy?"

Manny nodded as he clapped for the next rider.

Kat didn't have the heart to suggest that even if by some miracle Rafe won the event, the cost of Manny's medical care would far exceed the purse. But maybe . . .

"Have you ever heard of Mercy Doctors? They travel to villages and have a grant program in partnership with St. Jude's to bring kids to America for treatment." She didn't add that because of her recent turn of events, the Mercy Doctors clinic that might have been able to help Manny might have to close its doors.

Before Lucia could answer, Kat heard Rafe's name over the loud-speaker.

"He's up again!" Manny said, pointing to Rafe as he settled in on his bull in the chute.

"This one's named Clean Break," Nick said. "He's never ridden him."

Kat sat on the stairs, her chest on fire. It hurt every cell inside to watch him climb aboard, but a new exhilaration had replaced the fear. If anyone could hang on, Rafe Noble could. He knew what he was doing. He was born to be a modern-day gladiator.

Still, she held her breath as Rafe rosined his bull rope, heating it with the friction of his glove for a better hold. Then he wrapped it into his grip, clenching his fist into a tight ball. He blew out, pounded his vest, and gripped the rail. Kat thought she saw his lips move. Then he looked straight into the camera, straight into her heart, and nodded.

The bull erupted from the chute. Clean Break arched his back and hit the ground in a bone-jarring, four-footed landing.

Kat clasped her hands together on her lap as Piper, Nick, and Stefanie cheered.

Clean Break bucked again, twisting his back legs to one side, his head to the other. Rafe wrenched back. He braced his arm, his face stony and tight.

"C'mon, Rafe!"

The bull landed, threw his weight forward, his head back. The horns skimmed a breath away from Rafe's head.

The crowd gasped.

Kat's hands burned.

Clean Break went airborne again, all four hooves leaving the ground. The landing shook Rafe's hold.

Kat's back teeth ached.

The bull twisted again. Rafe lost his seat, flipped out over the back end.

Kat covered her mouth, holding in her scream.

He landed inches from Clean Break's hooves.

"Get up!" Kat yelled in tandem with about ten thousand other people.

Rafe lay there, curled, paralyzed as the bull rounded on him.

"Get up, Rafe," Nick growled loud enough for Kat to go cold.

The bull took a bead on Rafe, lowered his horns.

A bullfighter took the horns on his padded shorts as a couple of cowboys rushed in. Rafe leaned on them hard as they dragged him out.

The animal trotted into the chute, as if satisfied with a job well done.

Kat sat in horrified silence. On the monitors, the camera caught Rafe sitting down, his face tightening in pain. He touched his knee, then leaned back, blowing out hard, covering his eyes with his gloved hand.

Beside Kat, the Nobles barely breathed.

Rafe tore off his hat and threw it. His expression scared her as he pushed himself up from the stool, shoved away the EMT trying to help him, and turned toward the cameras. He smiled and waved to his adoring fans, his eyes full of danger.

As Kat watched him, as the crowd cheered, she felt something breaking inside. She knew this Rafe Noble all too well, had seen those eyes before. The day Rafe Noble, at the end of his rope, had driven into the hotel and fallen at her feet. Broken. Defeated.

"How badly do you think he's hurt?" Stefanie said, her tone matching the fear deep inside Kat.

"I don't know." Nick took off his hat, ran his hand through his dark hair, and looked at Kat.

A look, it seemed, that contained everything. The hope that she'd somehow change Rafe's life. The fear that he'd lose his brother to something beyond his control. And even, somehow, Rafe's desire to do something powerful and good with his riding.

"I'll go check on him." Kat stood, and it hit her. "Where's Lolly?"

Nick frowned. "She's not with you?"

"She mentioned having a meeting this morning," Piper said, "although I don't know with whom."

"Maybe she's with Lincoln," Kat said, remembering Lolly's almost angry explanation of his job offer.

"Who?" Piper asked.

"Lincoln Cash. She's moving out to Hollywood to cook for him."

If Kat had sprinted out to the middle of the ring and jumped on a bull, whooping in the air, it would have had less effect than these words. Stefanie looked like she'd been slapped.

Piper shook her head. "No way would she move away from Phillips to be with Lincoln. She loves John."

"Everyone knows she loves John," Stefanie added, as if Piper needed confirming.

"John loves her too," Nick said, shrugging when his wife looked at him.

"Then why did he leave?"

Nick held up his hands in surrender.

Piper got up. "Where's Bradley?"

Kat gave her a look. "He's been calling me on my cell all morning." She didn't add that she hadn't picked up one of his calls, not sure how to tell him that they weren't leaving together. Now or ever.

Piper pushed past Nick and Stefanie, came out to stand on the steps near Kat. "I'm assuming you could probably track down Lincoln Cash's cell number."

"Uh, sure." Kat dug into her pocket, produced her cell. "Call my assistant, Cari. She can find just about anyone."

Piper grabbed the phone. "Stay put. I'll find her." She turned to Kat. "And tell Rafe that we're rooting for him."

❧❧❧

Rafe gritted his teeth so hard that he thought his molars might crumble and limped back to the locker room.

The EMT walked beside him, a little skittish and visibly peeved after Rafe had nearly taken his head off. Like it or not, this was the real Rafe Noble. At least if he wanted to survive it was.

He'd taken the ride too seriously. It had ceased to become a sport, an adrenaline high, and had become something that gave him purpose. Something he put his heart and soul into.

The more he cared, the more it hurt when he wrecked. As soon as he hit the ground, the fear rushed through him, and he was back in the Las Vegas arena, watching the hooves crash down on his best friend.

Paralyzed.

Defeated.

He opened the door to the locker room and pushed the EMT back. "Leave me alone."

"Let me look at your knee—"

"Stay away from me." He slammed the door behind him. The last thing he needed was to have someone see him shut down and weep at the pain.

Thankfully, the rest of the contestants congregated out in the hallway, watching the other riders, helping them mount the bulls, giving pep talks. Technically the bull riders might be competing against each other, but the real opponents were the bulls.

Rafe leaned against his locker, breathing hard. He'd felt his knee rip when that bull switched directions on him, and it tore further when he landed.

In the past, Rafe would have sworn. Instead, he sent his fist into the lockers. The entire row shuddered.

He closed his eyes, frustration sweeping over him, and crumpled to the floor.

"You lost your hat."

Rafe didn't look up as he shielded his face with his hand. "What are you doing here?"

He heard Kitty walk toward him. She climbed over the bench and sat on it. "I brought you your hat."

He reached for it, not looking at her, staring instead at those ridiculous red boots. "Thanks. Now leave me alone."

"Oh no, you're not getting it back," she said, snatching the hat away. "I want you to sign it. For my Rafe Noble collection."

He frowned, anger the easiest emotion to latch on to. Did she think his sitting here on the floor might be for her amusement? Did she not figure out that his entire body screamed in defeat? that he might have damaged his knee beyond repair?

No, more than that, that if he wanted to ride again, it would have to be on PeeWee, the bull that could finish him off?

"Gimme my hat."

"No." Kitty put it on her head, made a face. "I suppose the smell will make it sell better on eBay. Rafe Noble's hat from his last ride."

"That wasn't my last ride," Rafe snarled, not sure where those words had come from because . . . well, yes, it had been.

"Your fans might agree, but I know when I see quit. And you have it written all over you."

He lunged for his hat. Kitty jerked away and he fell back against the lockers.

Her smile dimmed. She took off the hat, rubbed her hand along the crown, and fingered the arrowhead he'd stuck in the band. "You know why your fans love you?"

Rafe glared at her, hating how pretty she looked with her brown hair tumbled down around her shoulders, dressed in a GetRowdy shirt like a fan. The slightest remnants of the Montana sun remained on her freckled nose, in the shine of her beautiful eyes. Right then, all he could think of was her in his arms under the fireworks. And how he'd wanted to be the man she said she believed in.

A noble man.

"Your fans love you because you embody for us what we want to do."

"You want to ride bulls?" He reached again for his hat and wished she'd put up more of a fight when he grabbed it from her hand.

"No. I want to go after what I want with the kind of courage you have. I want to fight my fears and get on that bull and dig in my spurs and hold on to the dream."

Rafe swallowed, his throat thick and tight. He wanted to ask about her dream, but the words wouldn't emerge. In that moment he knew the answer he wanted and couldn't bear for it to be wrong.

But like she always did, Kitty knew him and how to read his mind to apply the balm he needed. She knelt beside him and ran her hand over his face. "I want *you*, Rafe Noble. I've been falling for you since the day you asked me if I wanted your autograph. I never should have said yes to Bradley, and I'm sorry for that. You make me feel like the woman I'm supposed to be. The woman who shows you that God loves you."

He wasn't sure what to say, how to speak the words piled in his chest. The ones that told her that she'd somehow freed him to be the man he wanted to be. The man who lived up to said name. So he gave it his best try. "I'm . . . falling in love with you too, Katherine. I should have said it, should have followed you to New York."

She looked away.

Rafe turned her face toward him and lifted her chin. "Please forgive me for the way I treated you. I'll do anything to help you raise money for those kids."

Kitty smiled and framed his face with her hands. "Yeah, I know." Then, while he sat there, broken in every way, she kissed him.

He curled his gloved hand around her neck and kissed her back. Like before, he lost himself in her touch, in her love. In the magic that was Kitty Russell Breckenridge.

Rafe leaned back, touching her forehead to his. "Wow, you're so beautiful; words don't seem enough."

She shook her head. "You're in delirious pain."

"That's true, but it doesn't affect my eyesight." He blew out a breath as a fresh wave of pain washed over him.

Kitty sat back, looked at his leg. "It's bad, isn't it?"

He nodded as she unbuckled his chaps and then the brace, easing it off his leg. He managed not to cry out, but when she ran her thumb down his face, he knew it showed.

"You're seeing the doc." Kitty came around behind him, shoving her hands under his arms, pulling him, with his help, from the floor. She looped his arm over her shoulder. "Then we're going to figure out how to get you through that last ride." It sounded more like a command than a pep talk.

"What? I don't—"

"I know you want this, Rafe. And I believe in you. You're the toughest bull rider I know, and you can figure out how to stay on that bull for eight seconds."

If he hadn't seen her forced smile, he might not have known what it cost her to say that. But she didn't understand the situation.

"I drew PeeWee for my next bull."

The name registered nothing on her face.

"The bull that killed my friend." He winced as she moved him toward the door.

She didn't pause or glance at him. "Mmm-hmm."

"Kitty!" He slammed his hand on the door before she could open it.

She looked at him. "What? So you have to ride the same bull. So you might need God a little more than usual for this ride. God never said bull riding would be easy."

He blinked at her.

"I'd think a big tough guy like you should know that bad things happen out there. It's nobody's fault. They just do. But God has asked you to do this big thing, and you have the opportunity to show the world that there's more to Rafe Noble than a bad attitude and a poster-boy smile. That you have the stuff inside that makes you a real hero. The kind of hero Manny needs." Her voice dropped. "The kind of hero I need." She ran her hand down his vest. "The thing is, I need to know that you're sold out for this and trusting God to help you if I'm going to sit in the stands and not go crazy with worry."

A tear formed in the corner of her eye, and she wiped it away. "I believe in you, Rafe. And I'm . . . I'm impressed. So don't let me down, cowboy."

Rafe didn't deserve her; he knew that much. But he wasn't so stupid as to tell her that. Or to let her down. In that moment, the cold streak of fear turned hot inside him. "Okay, cowgirl," he said as he opened the door. "Let's do this."

Kitty was right there, helping him down to the sports doctor; persuading the doc to tape him up, snap his brace back on, and sign off on his next ride; getting Rafe back down to the chutes; and kissing him hard before he climbed onto PeeWee, the killer bull.

She gave him a thumbs-up as he lowered himself onto the animal and smiled as he let the fear flush out, replacing it with a useful determination. He saw her fight face as he centered himself, wound the bull rope around PeeWee's chest, tightened it, smacked his grip and his vest, then gripped the rail.

Rafe didn't look at her then, but he knew she stood there, believing in him as he nodded to the gate men for the bull to take him on his ride.

Mary sat a long time in the pool of moonlight at Charlie's grave, smelling the prairie grasses, listening to the breeze, feeling it cool on her skin. Finally she rose and headed back to the house. Her house.

She let herself in the back door, and in the silence, just before she closed it, she heard footsteps on the back porch.

Mary jumped and grabbed the .22 she kept by the door. "Who's out there?" She stuck the gun out, muzzle first. "I'm not afraid to use this!"

"Don't shoot!" The voice came from the darkness.

"Show yourself." She flicked on the outside back light, but the trespasser moved away. "I don't want to shoot you."

"I don't want to be shot."

"Then leave now."

The man stepped into the light. "I'm not leaving."

Time and probably life had thinned him, scraped the youthful edge off his handsome face, drained the dreams from his eyes.

But the compassion remained. That same compassion she'd seen the day Matthias brought her home. He wore a pair of wool pants and clutched his cap in his hand as he took a step forward. "Hello, Mary."

Mary separated her disbelief from the other emotions that stole her breath. "Jonas?"

"I know I have no right to come back like this. I didn't mean to disturb you." He looked over his shoulder, toward the path she'd taken from Charlie's grave. "I was just making sure you made it home."

She opened her mouth, trying to comprehend his words. "You . . . saw me?"

"I . . . I've been around for a while. Just making sure you were all right." He gestured to the gun. "I guess you were."

She glanced at the gun and put it down. "You've been around *for a while*?"

He lifted a shoulder. "Since you married—or almost married—Erland."

"That was years ago! Why didn't you—?"

"You never wrote." He tried a smile but failed. "I assumed . . ."

"That I didn't want you." She stared at his work-worn boots, the way he crunched his hat. "I should have written."

He shifted his weight, saying nothing. Then, finally, he put his hat on. "I'll be on my way. I'm just glad to see you."

He turned to leave, and in that moment, Mary felt the last remnants of the woman she'd been—the one who'd let life have its way with her, who'd been a victim—die.

"Jonas . . . wait."

He stopped.

She walked off the porch. "I still believe, Jonas. I will always believe."

He turned, and she saw him smile. "I'm sorry it took me so long to come back."

"You're right on time," she said, reaching out for him.

He stared at her outstretched hand and gently took it. "I'm not leaving," he said. "I promise."

Jonas pulled her to himself and put his arm around her waist, and just as she'd always imagined it, he tenderly, sweetly, kissed her.

For all you're worth, I'll stand here for a lifetime,
For all you're worth, I'll sacrifice it all,
You can know that you're my treasure,
I'll show you how to measure,
You can look into my eyes for all you're worth.

Lolly heard the soft singing and struggled to open her eyes. Something seemed . . . She wasn't in her hotel room. She heard machines, and she ached so much that she groaned.

"Shh, Lolly, you're okay. You're going to be okay."

She blinked to clear her vision, and then she saw him. Reddened eyes, hair a mess, as if he hadn't slept in three days.

John.

He tried a smile, but his face, his voice broke. "Oh, Lolly, you really scared me." He set down the book he'd been reading aloud to her.

"What happened? I remember a man—oh!" The images came back, and Lolly moaned.

John put her hand to his mouth, kissed the back of it. "You're safe, honey. You have a couple of broken ribs, but you're going to be okay." He reached out to touch her, then pulled back. "I can't believe I left you. I should have taken you with me–"

"I should have told you. I'm so sorry." Her voice came out parched, barely above a whisper. "I know everything now. I know."

He leaned over, pressing his lips to her forehead. "I love you, Lolly. I have for years and years."

Lolly saw it then, everything that Mary had seen. The love that had healed her. Freed her.

The love that she had waited for.

"I know, John. And I loved you back."

He smiled. "I know that too."

She closed her eyes, feeling so very tired. "Will you be here when I wake up?"

John kissed her sweetly on her cheek. She felt the brush of his whiskers, and a quietness swept through her. "I'm not leaving. I promise."

CHAPTER 22

Rafe felt like a million bucks. Or at least five hundred thousand. As he sat on the platform and received the largest check of his life—four feet by eight feet—he knew the fear that had embedded his life no longer ruled the kind of man he chose to be.

He raised a giant silver buckle trophy—the gold would come later, maybe at the championships—above his head and dangled the keys to his brand-new black F-150 pickup. He scanned the audience for Kitty, knowing she should be up on the platform with him. But in the commotion after his ride—netting him the combined points that put him on top of the scoreboard—he'd been hustled away by the GetRowdy crew for an interview and the closing ceremony.

She had probably rejoined his family.

His family. Who had been here to watch him *win*. He turned, waving to them somewhere in the massive crowd, unable to see because of the fireworks. *This is for you, Mom.*

The music continued as he finished waving and left the stage. Every step he took was a little explosion of pain. But he grinned through it, even when he got backstage. Then he let himself lean on a bull rider from Oklahoma and hopped toward the sports doctor.

Doc Wilson wasn't happy as he unwrapped Rafe's knee. Rafe leaned back on the table, accepting the shot of painkiller, breathing through the residual pain as the doc wrapped his knee in a padded brace. "I think you need to take a trip to the hospital," he said, motioning to the EMTs.

Rafe sat up, woozy suddenly from the head rush of the medicine. "Right after I see my . . ." What? Fans? Maybe a long time ago. ". . . girlfriend," he said, trying on the label for size.

The doc patted his leg. "Don't wait too long."

An EMT handed Rafe a pair of crutches.

Rafe hopped down from the table, grabbed the crutches, and moseyed out into the hall.

Nick, Stefanie, Manny, and Lucia burst into a round of cheers.

"Uncle Rafe, you were so cool!" Manny said.

Lucia came up and kissed him gently on the cheek. "Manuel would be proud of you." She wiped her lipstick off his cheek, then a tear from her chin.

Nick smiled at Rafe and nodded.

"Where's Kitty?" Rafe asked as Stefanie hugged him.

She let him go, gave him a blank look.

"She didn't come to sit with you?"

"We haven't seen her since she left to . . . uh, check on you." Nick raised an eyebrow in silent question.

"She found me. And I expected to see her after my ride."

Nick's expression darkened just as his cell phone rang. He flipped it open. "Hello?" He glanced at Rafe. "It's Piper," he mouthed.

Stefanie rubbed her arms, looking pensive.

"What aren't you guys telling me?" Rafe hobbled closer.

"What? You're kidding." Nick's tone didn't sound at all amused. "We'll be right there. Do they know who–? . . . I know what *you* think, honey, but do they have proof? . . . At least John is there, but . . . You did? What did she say?"

Nick looked at Rafe again. "Really? . . . All right, we'll be there as soon as we can. Call me if something changes."

"What's wrong?" Stefanie asked before he even closed the phone.

Nick's eyes found Rafe's. "Lolly's in the hospital. She's been beaten up. And according to Kat's housekeeper, Kat left . . . on vacation with Bradley."

Rafe's jaw tightened. "I don't think so."

"Maybe–"

"Stef, Kitty loves me and I love her. Believe me when I tell you wild horses couldn't make her run off with . . . Slick."

A hesitation from Nick said that he thought Rafe might be a little on the desperate side.

Yep, because even if she *had* left with Bradley–which he didn't believe for a second–this time Rafe wasn't going to let her go without a fight. "She doesn't love him," he said. "She loves *me*."

Stefanie turned to Nick. "Rafe's right. She loves him. Something's not right here."

Nick tossed Stefanie the keys. "Take Lucia and Manny back to the hotel; see if anyone has seen Kat. Rafe and I will ask around here. Someone had to see something. Let's see what security comes up with."

Rafe followed him, half running, half hopping, absorbing the pain in a one-eyed wince.

Nick found a door marked Security and began to bang on it.

"What if Bradley *did* something to her?" Rafe could barely make himself say it, but nothing else made sense. He turned and added his own fist to Nick's pounding.

The door opened to an angry security guard. "Can I help you?"

Nick explained the situation, but it wasn't until Rafe stepped up and reminded him that he'd just stayed on a killer bull and he'd be willing to go round two that the guard let them in. Or the guard simply saw the panic in his eyes.

Rafe could barely stand still as they rolled back the tapes of the last hour, then hit Play. People moved in lightning speed, black-and-white figures that seemed somehow ghostly.

"There. That's her." Rafe spotted Kat standing in the corridor, hands clasped as she watched him ride. Yeah, that was her, jumping up and down, cheering, fists pumping.

Then she stopped and turned as a figure came toward her. He looked like a regular cowboy, with a wide-brimmed hat, boots, but something . . . Rafe saw him grab her hand, yank her through the crowd and out of view.

"Did that look like she wanted to go with him?" Nick asked.

"I'm going to kill him, whoever he is."

"Look at the time stamp. Do you have access to any other entrance tapes?"

The security guard brought up images of the four lower entrances on the closest side of the building.

Rafe peered over Nick's shoulder, his anger alive inside him.

Fifteen minutes passed on the screen.

"She vanished," the guard said.

"What did he do to her—there, see him?" Rafe pointed to the cowboy, who turned as he opened the back exit door and looked straight at the camera he obviously didn't realize was there.

Everything inside Rafe seized up as he watched Kat stumble out with Bradley. Her gait, her acquiescence looked odd. Bradley stopped in front of a limousine and shoved her inside. The driver shut their door and climbed in the front. The limo drove away into Manhattan's bright lights.

"Where are they going?" Rafe's voice sounded just on the edge of fraying.

It didn't help when Nick gave him a matching expression. "Piper had this . . . theory that Bradley was trying to—" he put a hand on Rafe's shoulder—"kill her."

"What?" Rafe pushed his hand away. "No one told me. Why?"

"Piper thinks he killed his first wife for her money. And Kat's next."

Rafe stood there a second, frozen. "Where would he take her?"

"Maybe the Breckenridge Hotel?" Nick was already turning toward the door. "I did a little online surfing about it back when you took out the lobby. You picked a real five star to destroy. It has a helipad."

Rafe followed Nick as he jogged toward the side exit doors. "Wait—stop! We'll never catch them in a taxi."

Nick stopped. "And?"

Rafe grinned. It felt reckless and desperate and exactly what he needed to chase after the woman he loved. "I just won a truck."

Nick smiled. "Yeah, you did, didn't you?"

Rafe threw the keys to his brother. "Pick me up. And try not to scratch it."

Nick took the truck right off the platform, laying on the horn as he drove across the stadium floor toward the giant gate where they'd unloaded the animals. Rafe watched as one of his buddies opened the gate for him. As soon as Nick braked, Rafe climbed in. "Don't let traffic get in your way," Rafe said as they peeled out onto Eighth Avenue.

"Go down to Fifty-seventh and hang a right." Rafe planted his good leg against the floorboard, his hand on the ceiling as Nick wove in and out of traffic to blaring horns and irate taxi drivers.

When Nick turned on Fifty-seventh, Rafe spotted Trump Tower. "It's only a couple more blocks; turn left on Fifth."

"Rafe, this is a one-way!" Nick said, already caught in the turn. He pulled out and scooted across the intersection toward Madison. "We're going to get killed."

"What are you doing—you missed the turn!"

"It was a one-way, for crying out loud. Calm down. We'll get there."

"It's not the woman you . . . really—just drive!"

Nick took a left on Madison and slammed the brakes. Taxis edged into his path, and they slowed to a crawl.

"I told you driving in Manhattan isn't that easy. These roads get confusing," Rafe said, wishing he could get out and run. "Turn left at the next road. It'll bring us right to the Breckenridge."

Rafe glanced up at the one-way sign over the light and grimaced.

They turned on Sixtieth and finally back on Fifth into a snarl of traffic.

Rafe had his hand on the door. "It'll take three years to get there at this speed."

"We're stuck." Nick leaned back and wrapped his hands around the steering wheel.

"Take the sidewalk."

Nick shot him a look.

"Take the sidewalk." Rafe pointed to an opening. "It's clear. And we're almost there."

"It's this kind of thinking that gets you into trouble, you know."

Rafe already had his hat off, had nearly broken the dashboard when he slammed his fist into it. He just about lost it when he saw a limo turn into the Breckenridge drive. "There's the limo. Take the *sidewalk*!"

"I'm not taking the sidewalk! People will get hurt."

"They'll move. This is life and death, Nick, *please*!"

Nick glanced at Rafe, then cranked the wheel, driving onto the sidewalk. "Please, God, don't let anyone get hurt."

Rafe leaned over and hit the horn.

Horns answered him.

"Punch it, Nick. They're moving."

"You don't even know that's the right limo!"

"I can . . . sense it. They're cutting around, pulling up to the entrance of the hotel." He dived for the steering wheel, pulling it to the right.

Nick elbowed him back. "I'm driving here!"

"You drive like a granny! Put some gas into it!"

Nick stepped it up, muttering as the limo pulled up to the front. The truck bumped across the plaza, scattering pigeons. Nick laid on the horn as they neared the limo.

The limo kept moving.

"Where's he going?"

"Calm down, little brother." Nick hit the gas and the truck jumped forward, then slammed into the back bumper of the limo.

The limo ricocheted and flew into the hotel lobby. Glass shattered; scaffolding rained down on Rafe's truck.

"He's not going anywhere," Nick said as the truck rocked back.

Rafe stared at him. "I think I learned everything I know from you."

Screams and the sound of sirens cut through the roar of Rafe's heartbeat.

"What is wrong with you?" The driver of the limo got out, a huge man who looked like he could do serious damage to both of them.

The bellboys crowded Nick's side of the vehicle while Nick opened his door and slid out.

Rafe climbed out of the pickup, then hopped around the back of the limo. "Kitty!"

The limo door opened. Out stepped an elderly man dressed in black-tie elegance from his gray ascot to his sterling-silver-tipped cane. "I am not Kitty, young man."

Rafe froze. But in that moment, as steam hissed out of the crumpled radiator of his new truck, as he heard sirens in the distance, he heard a scream. Despite the myriad of other screams, somehow this one found him and rattled him.

Both he and the elderly man turned toward the hotel.

Rafe grabbed a crutch, slid across the crumpled mess of the limousine hood, and landed on the other side.

Confusion reigned in the lobby as guests clogged the construction zone. Bellboys attempted to push the crowd away from the shattered glass and back into the foyer.

Rafe bullied his way through the crowd toward the elevators. The penthouse didn't have a button. He stood there, breathing hard, his frustration hot in his chest.

The roof. He must have heard her from the roof. He jammed his thumb into the top button. "C'mon!" *Please, God, don't let him hurt Kitty. Please, please.*

The elevator opened onto the fifteenth floor. Rafe fumbled to the end of the hall, opening the stairwell. The upper door to the roof was just whooshing closed.

He could hear the whirr of the blades as he climbed the stairs. He heaved the door open.

Bradley had clearly done something to Kitty; she wasn't walking well. She must have fought back at least a little because her mouth was bleeding. Bradley was trying to wrestle her into the chopper.

"Kitty!"

Bradley turned at Rafe's voice, and a snarl came over his face.

Kat wrenched away but fell precariously close to the edge of the building.

Please, God, don't let her go over!

Bradley grabbed her by the neck and pulled her to her feet. "Don't come any closer, Noble. Or she goes over."

It looked like Kitty hadn't the strength to stand, because she kept crumpling, falling over to one side, moving a little farther away from Bradley each time, only to have him yank her back up. What had Bradley done to her?

Rafe breathed hard through his desire to take the man apart slowly, make him hurt. "Okay, listen. I just want Kitty. You can go. Do whatever you want."

"You never should have interfered. Never come into her life.

The fact is, you did this. You wrecked everything. And now . . . you made her so distraught that she'll have to jump. But psychosis runs in her family." He smirked. "Sort of."

"Leave her alone," Rafe said, watching how Kat clawed at Bradley's grip. She didn't seem to be able to look at him but kept edging along the side of the building.

"You want her, you come and get her." Bradley pushed her, and she disappeared over the edge.

Rafe issued a cry that came from so deep within him that he thought he might lose himself with the breadth of it. He lunged toward the place where she'd been.

Bradley kicked him, dead center on his damaged knee.

The white-hot pain should have stopped Rafe, but it didn't. He scrambled to the edge, his heart already through his chest, moaning with an agony he'd never felt before. "Kitty!" He couldn't look.

Bradley kicked him again, and Rafe's head spun. Through the haze of pain, he saw Kitty.

She'd fallen. But not fifteen floors, thank God in heaven. She lay crumpled on her penthouse balcony, moaning but alive.

Rafe turned just as Bradley raised his leg to kick him in the gut. He caught Bradley's pant leg and pulled.

Bradley went down with Rafe landing on top of him. Bradley twisted under him, but this time, Rafe didn't hold anything back. "This is going to really hurt," he said as he sailed a punch into Bradley's nose.

Blood spurted as Bradley hollered.

Before Rafe could land the next blow, strong arms clamped around him. They pulled him off Bradley, dragging him toward the door as security swarmed the roof.

CHAPTER 23

"YOU REALLY MADE the papers this time." Cari came into Kat's bedroom without knocking, holding a stack of newspapers. She tossed them on the bed. "They all want to know how Bradley Lymon could have been such a creep."

"That seems to be the universal question." Kat pushed herself up onto the pillows. "I'm still having a hard time believing that everything you said about him turned out to be true. I knew that something wasn't right ever since I returned from Montana, but even long before that, I had all those strange migraines. But I never dreamed that he was poisoning me."

"I doubt many people would immediately assume the person they are going to marry wants to kill them." Cari sat down next to Kat.

"I should have listened to my friends sooner." Kat's arm still ached where she'd smacked it on the balcony. She'd spent at least one night in the hospital, where the doctors had flushed from her system the extra potassium chloride as well as the drug Bradley had shot into her arm at the arena. Thankfully, it hadn't taken full effect until after she'd fallen off the roof. However, by the time she awoke, Rafe had already been transferred to the Hospital for Special Surgery for his knee. Although she'd called and even pulled some strings, Rafe refused to take her call.

She tried not to let that dig a hole into her heart. But who was she kidding? Obviously Rafe agreed with the papers when they called her "naive."

"How bad is it?" Kat picked up a paper and saw a photo of herself exiting the hospital. She made a face.

"You look better than Bradley." Cari pointed to a color picture of Kat's former fiancé in his broken-nose glory.

Kat cringed. "Yeah, that's pretty."

"So, are you feeling better? Back to your normal self?"

Kat leaned back in her pillows. "I don't think I'll ever be myself. Actually I'm not sure who I really am. Am I Kitty, a cowgirl who rides horses? Or am I Katherine, my grandfather's princess?"

"Why can't you be both?" Cari leaned forward. "Or maybe it's Kat Noble, philanthropist and lovely wife to New York hero Rafe Noble?" She motioned to a picture of the shattered entrance to the hotel, with Rafe's picture next to it.

Kat smiled. "Those Nobles sure know how to make an entrance. How angry is Grandfather?"

Cari shrugged. "Not too angry, considering they saved your life—or tried to save your life. He's even thinking of dropping the first set of charges on the condition that Rafe pays the hotel reconstruction costs."

"He'll go broke."

"Not hardly. He's got sponsorship offers up to his ears, according to his sister. Like I said, it's all about spin."

"But he has to use that money for Manny's treatment."

"Rafe donated his entire purse to the Breckenridge Foundation, and I took the liberty of faxing Manny's medical information and grant application to Mercy Doctors. Hopefully, he'll be at St. Jude's by the end of the month."

"Really? Wow, Cari, thank you so much."

"And by the way—" she crossed her leg and pulled up her jeans, revealing cactus stiletto boots—"I'm seeing your fascination with bull riders."

Kat felt a sweet smile building from within. "Speaking of . . . He hasn't, I mean . . ."

Cari's smile faded. "No, he hasn't called. Piper did, though. He was going to start some physical therapy yesterday."

Kat rubbed the edge of her sheet. Why hadn't he at least called? "You don't think he thought that I really wanted to, you know, run away with Bradley?"

"Oh, please. I did arrange to install padding on the sidewalks around the hotel, just in case you decide to take another header off the roof."

"Funny. I think I remember being pushed."

"Yeah, well, sources say you were going to jump. Did you know the balcony was below you?"

"I saw it, yeah."

"Well, even with drugs in your system, your aim was pretty good."

"How's Lolly this morning?" Kat had moved her mother into the penthouse after her discharge so she could care for her, but honestly, John did most of the caring. He'd rarely left her bedside. And Angelina had mothered them all.

"She's better. Had pancakes for breakfast. Oh, and she identified Bradley as her attacker, which made the judge deny him bail. Flight risk."

"Is she still headed out west to work for Lincoln?"

Cari let out a burst of laughter. "They're engaged."

"Lincoln and Lolly? No way, she loves John."

"You're absolutely right. John gave her a ring this morning. It's gorgeous too. The funny thing is that he hasn't left here once, so he must have had it with him."

"Gotta like a man who is prepared. Only, I have this feeling he's been prepared for quite some time." Unlike someone else she knew. Kat blew out her disappointment and moved the papers off her lap and onto the bed, where she'd scattered her iPod, remote control, and recently finished B. J. King novel.

Cari reached across her and picked up *Unshackled*. "Can I read this? I heard it's good."

"It is. I love the romance–Jonas is such a great guy." Patient. Willing to stand by the woman he loves, unlike *some* people. Okay, she was clearly still reeling, because Rafe had stood by her–had chased after her.

Apparently, however, he'd changed his mind between then and now. His fingers hadn't been broken, had they? He could still use a telephone, right?

"Lolly liked the book–and Jonas too." Cari flipped open the front cover. "Why didn't you get John to sign it?"

"John? Why would he sign my book?"

"Because he's the author." Cari closed the cover. "Didn't you know that?"

"No. No, I did *not* know that." Kat suddenly understood Lolly's outburst of fury and frustration about being tired of waiting for her happy ending. "Did Lolly?"

"Not until recently. I heard them having *that* heated conversation yesterday all the way from my office. Before the ring."

"I can't believe John didn't tell her—"

"Would you? Think about it—a cowboy writing love stories?"

"Cowboys sing love songs."

"To their cows!" Cari lowered her voice. "But as I was coming in this morning, I heard him singing to her, so maybe you're right."

Kat smiled, thinking of the song Jonas had sung over and over, and guessed which song John had sung to the woman he loved. "Still, that's a big secret to keep." She might have decked him.

The thought made her sigh. No, she wasn't Katherine Breckenridge, because *she* would have never considered *decking* someone. But apparently she wasn't Kitty either.

"Not as big as embezzling money from your rich fiancée." Cari dropped the book into her bag.

"I can't believe that Bradley fooled me—all of us—so badly."

"He didn't fool Piper. Or me. I knew there was something about him I didn't like. I think the moral of this story is that all that glitters isn't gold."

"I should have seen through him too," said a voice behind her.

Kat found a smile for her grandfather as Cari got up and stepped aside. "I wanted to check on you before I left for London." He looked more tired than usual, lines on his handsome face, his white hair thinner. He still carried the regal Breckenridge air, however, in a three-piece suit, carrying his sterling-silver-tipped cane. He sat on the side of her bed and took her hand. "I wanted to tell you how sorry I am."

Kat looked at her hand in his, his thumb running over the top. "You were just looking out for me."

He tried a smile, but it came off as a twitch, and she saw his eyes glisten. "Yes, Katherine, I was."

"But you're not taking away the Breckenridge Foundation."

He pulled his hand away and shook his head.

"We don't need you to underwrite us anymore, okay?" Kat said. "But that doesn't mean I don't need you." She touched his arm.

He looked at her. Then took off his glasses and wiped his eyes.

Kat glanced at Cari, who leaned against the door.

"You were always so much more than I could have ever hoped for," he said softly.

Kat's eyes clouded.

"I'll call you from London." He leaned over to press a kiss to her forehead, then patted her leg through the covers before he left.

"As usual, I'm completely in the dark," Cari said. "Are you talking about Bradley . . . or something else?"

Kat touched the place where her grandfather had sat. "I'm going for a walk in the park." She pushed back the covers, slid out of bed.

"Are you okay? You want me to come with you?"

She shook her head as she started for her dressing room.

"Kat?"

She turned.

Cari stood in the door. "He'll call."

Kat sighed. "I don't know. Maybe he decided that he simply didn't fit in my world. That knowing me, loving me, was too much trouble."

"Please. The guy just about jumped off a roof for you."

"I nearly got him killed." Kat went to her dressing room. Why *hadn't* he called? She'd practically thrown herself at him. And hadn't he said he was falling for her too? She tugged on her jeans and an old sweatshirt and stared at her footwear choices. Right, like there was any question. She reached for the red boots.

The September air smelled of autumn leaves and fading flowers as she crossed the street and fell into the solace of the park. Two Canada geese paddled in the pond. A jogger ran by. Kat strode over the bridge toward the Chess and Checkers House, then meandered down past the ball fields, where a couple of kids were tossing baseballs. She finally turned up the path toward the carousel.

Another Karen Carpenter song hung in the air from the loudspeakers of the carousel, something about birds and all the girls in town following a blue-eyed hero. Rafe didn't have blue eyes, but those sweet-as-chocolate brown eyes worked just fine to attract the populace of Manhattan and beyond.

Kat bought a ticket at the booth, waited in line with four other people, then walked around the carousel until she found her favorite horse, Hornet. She climbed aboard, shaking her head. She'd never outgrow this part of her, the cowgirl inside. But she didn't want to either.

"All that glitters isn't gold." Maybe she hadn't found her storybook ending. But she *had* found herself and the grace and peace to stop striving to be someone she didn't have to be. Wasn't supposed to be.

In the end, perhaps that was the happy ending she'd really been looking for.

As the ride started, Kat closed her eyes, letting herself go back to Montana, the fresh breezes, the movement of her horse as she rode, laughter and strong arms, and two-stepping and bull riding, and . . .

She opened her eyes. The carousel was still moving, the song not quite over when she saw him standing in the shadows. He was leaning against a tree, his arms folded, watching her.

She closed her eyes again. She was just dreaming. When the music died, she opened her eyes.

Rafe smiled. He didn't move toward her as the horse stopped, but he simply uncrossed his arms. Then she saw why. Behind him stood a wheelchair.

She climbed down from Hornet.

"I'm looking for somebody." He pushed the wheelchair with one hand, leaning on it as he took a hop toward her.

"Yeah, who?" she answered, not moving.

He nodded toward the carousel. "Someone who can teach me to ride."

She touched Hornet's smooth wooden frame. "I got a great horse here."

Rafe took another hop toward her. "Bet his name is Shadow or Beauty."

"Hornet. Fastest stallion in the West."

"Is that so? Think I can stay on him?" He hopped until he was just a foot away.

"I dunno. Are you tough?"

"I think so."

"Can you handle pain?"

"Tryin' to."

"Are you afraid of a challenge?"

He grinned. "I'm here, aren't I?"

Kat made a face. "He's pretty wild. I'm not sure you can tame him."

Rafe shook his head, real slow. "Not sure I want to. How about I just go easy with him, let him learn to trust me. I promise not to break his spirit." He took a final step toward her, lowered his voice. "In fact, you can teach me how."

How was she supposed to stay angry at him when he looked at her like that, all his emotions in his incredible eyes? She stepped off the carousel, closed the distance between them, and curled her hands into his shirt. "Think I'm a pro, do you?"

"Oh, I know it." He pulled her toward him. "But don't tell anyone. It's our secret."

Kat grinned, running her fingertip down his handsome, unbarbered face. "Took you long enough. I was getting worried. How'd you find me?"

"Cari. And I figured out the carousel."

"You were paying attention, then."

"It was hard not to." Rafe cleared his throat, his expression sobering. "Sorry I didn't call, Kitty, but you gotta give a man some credit for wanting to be upright when he tells his lady that he hopes she'll give him a second chance. That, if she'll have him, he'll try to be everything she wants—a bull rider or a gentleman. If he has to, he'll even live in New York."

She ran her thumb over his chin, trying to find words but failing.

"So?" He smelled devastatingly good, freshly showered, if not shaved.

She wiped a tear that had escaped. "What if she belongs in both worlds, New York *and* Montana?"

Rafe let one side of his mouth turn up. "Then both worlds it will be." His face grew solemn again, and the scoundrel in his eyes vanished, and all she saw was the Rafe she'd known existed, the noble man inside who made her proud to know him. "You're everything I never knew I was looking for, Kitty. You believed in me when no one else would. And because of that, for the first time I was able to believe in myself, in the man God made."

Kat let those words sink in, find the empty places, and fill them nearly full. "That guy's all right, even if he does have a tendency to drive into things." Her eyes roamed his face, lingering on the scar over his eye that made him seem just a little wild. Those lips that curled into a smile that could turn her to liquid. Those eyes that could see the cowgirl inside her that had longed to be set free.

"Yeah, well, what do you expect? Perfection?"

She laughed. "From you, champ, yes." Then she wove her fingers into his hair and kissed him. Sweet and long and full of promises.

He pulled her close and kissed her back, the way a cowboy should.

Finally the carousel operator came out and asked them if they wanted another ride.

So the cowboy climbed up behind his cowgirl, on their black stallion, Hornet, put his arms around her to hold her tight, and Kat Russell Breckenridge rode off with her hero into the New York sunset.

An ending that even B. J. King would appreciate.

⚞ A NOTE FROM THE AUTHOR ⚟

I'm the first to declare that I am incredibly blessed to be allowed to write books. I love to write, to see the story unfold, to get to know my characters and see how God works out His plan for their lives. For me, writing a story is so much about a journey and seeing God provide each step of the way. Every book tests my faith, because when I sit down and stare at a blank screen, I have to trust that even when I don't have words, God does. Every book also brings me deep joy, because at the end I see how God has worked it out beyond what I can ask or imagine. It is a humbling thing to see God at work in your life, in the process, and in the end product and know that He has done this for His good pleasure and for my joy. To paraphrase Kat, it is no small thing to have the Creator of the universe working *in* you and *through* you to touch others. It takes my breath away.

This was an ambitious book for me—the different story lines, the book-within-a-book idea that I always wanted to try. I even had a song in the back of my mind that I wanted to write.

I started this story with an idea—that often we don't see the effect we have on others, and yet, as Christians, if we surrender to God and His plan, He uses everything we say and do for His purposes. More than that, everything we do—whether it's raising money for charity, riding bulls, or even just making our family dinner—can be used by Him for good. This thought has given me great peace over the years, regardless of where I find myself—in Russia, living in a high-rise and planting churches, or in Minnesota, tucked in the north woods, writing books. I wanted Kat to see that God had made her uniquely Kat and that she only had to be true to herself and let God work through that person to touch the world around her.

Of course, I didn't have to look too far to find Kat. I was a lot like her growing up—had a horse on springs in my basement, a turquoise cowgirl suit, and bright red boots. I ate up shows like *Bonanza* and *Gunsmoke* and dreamed of having my own horse named SunDancer or Hornet. But I grew up in the suburbs (no horse in sight) and loved letting out my "inner Kitty" for this story!

I was also fascinated with the world of bull riding. I was channel surfing one day and landed on a Professional Bull Riders event. It sucked me in with the danger, the bravado, the thrills, and the wrecks, and I wondered about the kind of man who rode bulls and what God could do with him if he gave his talents to Him. Many of the bull riders I researched are Christians, and for them, riding is a way to praise the Lord, just like writing is for me.

My favorite part of the book, however, was John and Lolly's story. I loved weaving their backstory throughout the book *Unshackled* and showing the different sides of love, including the biggest part, in my opinion: commitment. I loved setting Lolly free from her shackles and helping her see how John had been her hero all along.

Thank you for journeying back to Phillips with me, for reading Rafe's story. I hope you'll join me for *Finding Stefanie*, book three in the Noble Legacy. Meanwhile, I pray that you see God working in your life and through your life to touch people around you. And I pray that it takes your breath away.

In His grace,
Susan May Warren

~ABOUT THE AUTHOR

 SUSAN MAY WARREN recently returned home after serving eight years with her husband and four children as missionaries in Khabarovsk, Far East Russia. Now writing full-time as her husband runs a lodge on Lake Superior in northern Minnesota, she and her family enjoy hiking and canoeing and being involved in their local church.

Susan holds a BA in mass communications from the University of Minnesota and is a multipublished author of novellas and novels with Tyndale, including *Happily Ever After*, the American Christian Romance Writers' 2003 Book of the Year and a 2003 Christy Award finalist. Other books in the series include *Tying the Knot* and *The Perfect Match*, the 2004 American Christian Fiction Writers' Book of the Year. *Flee the Night, Escape to Morning*, and *Expect the Sunrise* comprise her romantic-adventure, search-and-rescue series.

Taming Rafe is the sequel to *Reclaiming Nick* and the second book in Susan's new romantic series.

Susan invites you to visit her Web site at
www.susanmaywarren.com.
She also welcomes letters by e-mail at
susan@susanmaywarren.com.

☙ FINDING STEFANIE

If she could, Stefanie Noble would get on her bay quarter horse, Sunny, ride over the chapped, frozen hills of the Silver Buckle Ranch, and disappear into the horizon. Just keep riding. Because it was only on Sunny that the loneliness, the stress, would slough off, and she'd hear the wind, the voice of freedom, singing in her ears.

After all, with her brother Nick running the Silver Buckle, she couldn't help but wonder if maybe the ranch didn't need her anymore.

Okay, *sometimes* she wondered. But perhaps not at 5 a.m., smack in the middle of calving season.

Singing—that's what she needed. Something other than the sound of a cow in distress. Her ears ached with the noise as the exhaustion of being up all night pressed down against her, into her bones, her cells.

"C'mon, old cow, push," she groaned, bracing her feet against the haunches of a weary Black Angus as she pulled on the chains attached to the hooves of a not-yet-born calf.

"She ain't gonna give."

Stefanie glanced behind her. Dutch looked as tired as Stefanie felt, his face droopy with skin and white whiskers.

"She's hip-locked. We're gonna have to C-section her." He already wore a pair of blue surgical coveralls.

"I can do this, Dutch." Stefanie's arms shook. "Just give me the puller."

"Stef—"

"It's almost out!" Even as she said it, Stefanie could feel the little calf slide toward her farther out of the birth canal. "I don't want to lose another cow!"

She refused to let herself feel those words, to remember watching the cow she'd so laboriously raised slip out of life as it bled to death. Stefanie could only blame a month of night calving for her unsteady hands, the way she had perforated the uterus and left a baby without a mother.

"I'm gettin' Nick."

"No!" Stef twisted, looking at him. "I don't need Nick. I need the puller. Come over here and lift her leg up, please."

Dutch said nothing, just handed her a long bar that looked much like the handle of a rake. Then he grabbed the cow's back leg and lifted it with his tree-limb arms.

Meanwhile, Stefanie affixed the bar across the cow's haunches, hooked on the chains that connected the calf's hooves to the puller, and started to turn the crank, applying pressure.

Slowly, the calf began to emerge. The cow let out a long moan as her baby slipped out into the straw. The little black calf didn't move. Afterbirth glistened in its curly black coat.

"C'mon, baby," Stef said, cleaning its face, its mouth. "Breathe."

Please breathe. She cut the cord and put iodine on it. The calf began to gasp. "Yes, breathe." She put her hand on his body, began to rub. In a moment, the calf had started to take in air.

Stefanie looked up at Dutch. In the shadows of the barn he looked much older than his fifty-seven years. But that's what all-night doctoring did. She probably looked about eighty-two instead of what some might call a young twenty-four. Most of the time she sure felt eighty-two.

Dutch gave her a half smile. "I'm going to check the other cows, see if they've dropped their calves yet."

Stefanie sat back in the straw, everything inside her shaking.

How she longed for, needed, *thirsted* for freedom. Just one day without *everything*—the weather, the calving, the bills . . . All of it gnawed at her, rubbing her raw with the weight of the shackles.

But this was her life, like it or not.

Although recently, for the first time in her life she'd begun to wonder . . . maybe not.

Detaching the hip bar from the cow and the calf, Stefanie watched as the mother turned and slathered her baby with her tongue.

"Good mama," Stefanie said, standing. Grime, sweat, and even blood had long ago seeped into her pores. She reeked of manure and straw, and her hair hung in strings, having escaped her long dark braids. Stretching, she got up and walked past the other stalls, checking the recent mothers and the two heifers who still had yet to give birth. Then, finally, she opened the barn door and slipped outside, letting the wind shear the exhaustion from her face, her limbs.

Behind her, Clancy, their half-shepherd, half-retriever, came up and nudged his wet nose into her palm. She smiled at him and rubbed behind his floppy brown ears.

The thaw had tiptoed in this year, haunting the land, giving the faint taste of spring, then shirking back, hiding under a blast of north wind and sleet. The pallor of today's sky, stalwart against the encroaching sun, told her that she'd find no hope in the forecast.

No, hope had long ago forsaken this land. Or perhaps it had only forsaken her.

It had returned for her brother Nick and his wife, Piper, now expecting their first child. And for Maggy and Cole, co-owners of the Silver Buckle, now that Cole had regained his health. And it had certainly found Rafe, recent GetRowdy Bull Riding National Champion. He had never looked as happy as he had at his celebration party when he asked Kat Breckenridge to marry him. They'd probably live happily ever after in her New York penthouse while helping raise money for Kat's charity.

Meanwhile, Stefanie would sleep in the barn and help birth baby cows.

Stefanie, the ranch hand. For some reason, it wasn't at all who she'd expected to be.

As the wind found her, her own smell made her wrinkle her nose. The ranch at this time of day seemed most forlorn, most eerie, old ghosts alive in the creak of the barn doors, the low of laboring cows. Sometimes she nearly expected her father's voice to emerge from a hidden stall, calling her to fetch clean water or help him with a calf. For a long time—*too* long—it had only been herself, Dutch, and Bishop, her father, running the Silver Buckle. Somehow even those years hadn't seemed as lonely as having Nick and Rafe return, to see their lives hook onto their dreams, to watch them turn into the men their father had always hoped they'd be, leaving her sorely behind.

It made a girl wonder: who had Daddy hoped *she'd* be? She'd never even asked. She always figured she belonged to the land. To the ranch. But with Nick and Piper having their first child, they'd need to move into the house instead of living in the hunting cabin on the hill. And then where exactly would she belong?

She stared out into the horizon, where the outline of the Bighorns just barely etched the gunmetal sky.

The horses nickered from the corral across the yard. In the quarantine pen, she noticed that the new quarter horses had huddled up, their noses together as they fought the wind. She'd put them in the shelter last night, but perhaps the draw of hay had lured them out. She should check on Sunny. He'd had a runny nose, a symptom that in other horses wouldn't register a great deal of concern, but in a horse nearly thirty years old, it made her worry.

The smell of the horse barn greeted her with a hospitality she craved as she opened the door. Call her strange, but she loved everything about horses, from their expressive eyes to the smell of their manure—so different from that of cows, pigs, or any other ranch animal.

The Buckle's horses stirred little as she entered. The ranch had a small handful of stock horses—lately Nick preferred to take his truck out into the field. Stefanie, however, couldn't surrender the nostalgia of working the ranch by hand, just her and Sunny, compatriots.

Perhaps that was where she belonged—with Sunny.

The quarter horse had been the first horse she'd rescued, right about the time her mother lay dying of breast cancer. Stefanie had bought him with a year's worth of chore money after seeing him waste away in the backyard of a house just outside Phillips. She'd ached with his neglect, how his ribs sawed through his tan hide, the razor bones of his spinelike spears in his back. He could barely walk when she'd led him to the trailer, and it took a full year before he recovered enough for her to start training him. She probably would have lost hope if it hadn't been for his eyes. They all but begged her to notice him. Begged her to care.

That year she'd brought Sunny back to the beautiful gelding he was born to be and discovered that she had a talent. A way of understanding an animal that ministered to both their broken places.

Nick's horse, Pecos, raised his head to stare at her as she walked to the end of the row of stalls. A beautiful black-and-white Overo paint, Pecos had a wild streak that at one time had seemed exactly fitting for her oldest brother. But Nick had worked his wild streak out of his system. As had Rafe.

She always thought she'd been born without the Noble propensity to rebel and wander. So why did she suddenly feel so restless, so unfit for the life she'd always known?

She flicked on a bulb midway through the barn, and light pooled on the dirt floor. Funny, she didn't see Sunny standing in his stall. Coming up to the paddock door, she spotted him lying down fully on his side. As if in distress.

"Sunny." She opened the door and crept in. "What's wrong, pal?" She knelt at his side, her hand splaying across his body.

He didn't raise his head, just opened his eye and looked at her a long moment before closing it. Under her hand, his breath labored.

Oh, Lord, please . . .

MEET NICK.

DON'T MISS BOOK 1 IN THE NOBLE LEGACY SERIES.

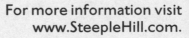